FAIR WEATHER

A GOTHIC TALE

BARBARA GASKELL DENVIL

FAIR WEATHER
By
BARBARA GASKELL DENVIL

Copyright © 2016 by Barbara Gaskell Denvil
All Rights Reserved, no part of this book may be
Reproduced without prior permission of the author
except in the case of brief quotations and reviews

Cover design by
Grady Earls

ALSO BY

BARBARA GASKELL DENVIL

HISTORICAL MYSTERIES COLLECTION

Blessop's Wife

Satin Cinnabar

The Flame Eater

Sumerford's Autumn

The Deception of Consequences

THE STARS AND A WIND TRILOGY

A White Horizon

The Wind from the North

The Singing Star

Box Set

CRIME MYSTERIES

Between (It can be murder in Heaven)

THE GAMES PEOPLE PLAY (A SERIAL KILLER TRILOGY)

If When

Ashes From Ashes

Daisy Chains

TIME TRAVEL MYSTERIES

Fair Weather

Future Tense

CORNUCOPIA

The Corn

The Mill (Available for pre-order soon)

The Dunes (Coming in early 2021)

CHILDREN'S BANNISTER'S MUSTER TIME TRAVEL SERIES

Snap

Snakes & Ladders

Blind Man's Buff

Dominoes

Leapfrog

Hide & Seek

Hopscotch

For
Sylvia

CHAPTER ONE

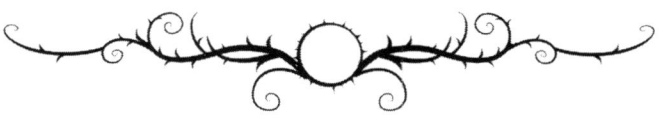

Like the Marquis de Sade, Winnie the Pooh and many others, I had my own secret place to go to.

But escapism is not always so easy. The mind does not always create an escape into joy or sunshine. Mine wasn't a happy place, no shining pool for lotus dreaming nor garden of perfumes. Yet I slid often into its shadows, asleep or awake, when life's expected attractions failed all their promises. Then my secret world sucked me in. I had not invented it for pleasure or meditative snooze. It had invented itself. Ever since I was born it had been there, whispering at me from the back of my head. Secrets, and my secret place, were in the background of all my daily routines. Sometimes, cuddled alone in my small bed, I heard voices. I smelled, when least expecting it, the stench of mould, of dirt, blood, sweat, and putrefaction. Believing them dreams, sometimes I even feared my bed. Of course, they weren't dreams at all, but I didn't realise that at the time.

The haunting of my imagination turned me, once I grew old enough to choose, into a writer of sorts. But it took me a long time before I understood.

Every reader, in some small sense, writes the book he is reading. Now I, the author, found I was being written by the book I was writing. Perhaps I had been unwise to set my new novel in medieval London's dark alleys. I soon recognised my own nightmares. Perhaps I had always known there were greater threats to come.

It wasn't always ugly. Now when I slept, I wandered the forest paths that looked down from their clearings onto the sprawl of ancient London and its shining ribbon river. The girl I saw there was very young, with huge grey eyes like bruises in a small narrow face and she was a lot more scared of me than I was of her. The woods around her were sun spangled. No conifers darkened the leaf flutter. Oaks, hazels and beeches entwined arms over gentle rises of moss, flower sprigged and mulched in old tangles of root and briar, raggy fern and many autumn's rotted leaf fall. The scuffle of small animals crept deep as I passed. It was not a peaceful place, but it was beautiful. How could I know then, that this distant past would one day be my home and that I would love it as I had never loved another?

The girl was just a child that first time I saw her, a bedraggled waif, wretchedly thin. She was sitting on a stone amongst the bracken. Her feet were bleeding. I thought she had probably walked a long way and I knew she was hungry.

That night I stood in the shadows and smelled the cool pungency of damp bark. Because I was asleep, I did not expect her to see me. Then she looked up and stared straight into my face for a moment. She gasped, her eyes widened, and her hands twisted into the threadbare wool of her cloak. I smiled, to reassure her. She thought I was a ghost. I left her still running through the forest and I woke to a winter's midnight and the sudden call of an owl outside my bedroom window. I was sweating but my nose above the quilt's feather embrace felt like ice.

For the next two weeks I took my laptop into the kitchen where it was warmer. I even baked bread, not to eat but to breathe in the scent of security and modern affluence. I shoved the instant powder onto a back shelf and unearthed the espresso machine from its bubble wrap, surrounding myself with reminders of success, machinery, and the conveniences of twenty-first century life. So, I banished insecurities and continued writing. As proof of confidence, I forwarded the first pages to my agent. He sent me back an optimistic deadline. Then everything started to go wrong.

My divorce was finalised as I began chapter five. I expected a further relaxation of the night terrors and at first daytimes seemed less stressful. Even the weather improved and lurking soft sunbeams hurried out from their late January clouds, burning the shadows sharp edged. The snow drops along the roadsides nodded and I nodded back. The first few early lambs in the fields, black nosed fluff dots across the Cotswolds, nuzzled complacent mothers, discovering after all that life had been worth the agonies of birth.

But instead of dissipating, my night time hauntings darkened. Children crept from the shadows, begging help, whispering of starvation, and of worse. Someone else made his own shadow. He was very tall and very dark, so that I could not tell which was shadow and which was man. When he spoke, his voice was cold and so soft, I understood no words.

Now frightened by the nightmare intensity, I abandoned my book, thinking instead to write a romantic comedy, a Victorian frivolity, a modern adventure. Of course, it was too late. My characters were already writing me. Medieval London had drawn me in and I had finally discovered that my secret place, so familiar after nearly thirty years of lurking in its unnamed alleyways, had always been perfectly real.

A few nights later I saw the girl again, though she was a little older now with the pinched face of growing maturity trapped in still fragile youth. She was crying. Someone was bending over her, but I still did not see him clearly as once again his shadow preceded him. He was dressed in deepest red and dust-hung black. His hair was shoulder length and very dark, straggled and probably unwashed. I couldn't see his face. He was talking to the girl and she seemed comforted by what he said. To me, he seemed a threat.

I knew she sat hunched over the kitchen table. There was no food and the barn-like room was cold. The frost swept under the door, the wind rattling and squealing into the dirty straw within. She rested her face on her crossed wrists and I felt her little cold bones beneath my own cheek. I felt the soft dampness of her tears on my own fingers. She sat on a rough wooden stool and I felt it wobble beneath me. I also felt her hunger, a pain so violent that I shuddered. When she looked up at the man who spoke, I knew her hope and her trust.

As it was with me, so it was with them. Winter, and the bitter wind that blew through their draughty windows seemed to be the same gale that blew down my valley with the same angry whine and glowering cloud. There was no fuel for their fire. But the man was untouched by weather and his hunger was just a passing inconvenience to him. As I woke, the faded pink roses on my bedroom walls transposed over the dream's bleak grey, and for the first time I heard his words.

"There is nothing," I heard him say. "Perhaps tomorrow I will find something. Patience, child. I shall do my best." His voice was as soft as the leaves on the wind, but quite clear. It haunted me for the rest of the day.

I was barely out of my pyjamas when Bertie turned up. Divorcing him hadn't really got rid of him at all. What he said had rarely ever made much sense, and it made none to me now. I was still lost in dream fragments.

"She won't let me stay," he was saying. "Well, honestly, that's gratitude for you. But when it comes down to it, better over and done with. So, what about it then, sweetie? Molly, are you listening? You wouldn't mind, would you?"

Behind Bertie's rambling clichés the other man's voice echoed, soft and insistent. He said he'd do his best but there was something wrong, some inherent danger in his words. I said, "But you never really do your best. Or your best isn't enough."

Bertie stared at me. "What the devil are you talking about now, Mol? Going off your head, I daresay. Always thought you would. Writers are all part balmy to start off with."

He brought modern reality bumping into garish focus. "Sorry." I wished he'd go away. "I was thinking of something else. I'm busy. Can't all this wait until another day?"

"No, it damned well can't. Want me to sleep on the street? It might even snow tonight." He glared at me.

I suddenly realised what he'd been saying. "You want the spare room? But we only got our decree absolute ten days ago. We're officially divorced. Honestly Bertie, I thought you were staying with the skinny one with red hair."

"Juliette. No, she was last month. This one's blonde. Buxom Paula. But she chucked me out last night. Says I snore. Well, O.K., a bit more than that. We had sort of an argument. I suppose you could say we more or less split up."

"Well, you can't stay here. I couldn't bear it. Bertie dear, I divorced you for a reason."

"Just a couple of nights on the sofa, then? Until I find a rental."

"I'm a spinster again, Bertie. It wouldn't be proper. And spinster is such a beautiful word. I've fallen in love with it."

Bertie moved his suitcases into the hall after lunch and I disappeared into the kitchen with the laptop. I sat there over the blank screen and the man's voice from my dream repeated over and over in my brain. "There is nothing. Perhaps tomorrow. Patience, child. I shall do my best." I had no idea what it meant but I couldn't get it out of my head. The voice was deep and low and very soft. I thought he had meant to be kind. But he wasn't a man to whom kindness came naturally.

CHAPTER TWO

Bertie was on the sofa with his big stubby toes sticking out from the end of the blanket. I was upstairs, snuggled in my feather bed with two hot water bottles and my nose under the quilt so I could warm my face with my own breath.

But I was also somewhere else. I was someone else too. Sometimes I forgot which one was the dream. Even before I slept, I could feel her. The girl was alive inside me, or perhaps I was alive inside her. She was many years younger and lived hundreds of years in the past, and yet we were merging. Fantasy or lunacy, whatever it was, it was far more vivid than any imagination and whether she dreamed me, or I dreamed her, I was becoming more than myself. And I found I was loving the girl. She was far sweeter than me. So sometimes I stopped struggling and without thought to madness and danger, slipped entirely into her mind. I knew her story.

It was my story now. Asleep or awake, I could remember her memories and tell the tale of her life as if it was my life. But there was no 'once upon a time' and I did not expect any happy ending. And the story began on the day when this other me first came into her world. My world!

The devil spat fire when I was born, and my father was fried there in the field where he stood, like they burn heretics in the north. After the lightning that struck him and the thunder that threw him down, the rain came, and his blackened body was soaked, and all the terrible charring was washed away, so that when my poor mother came out to look for him and saw him curled there peacefully between the tall wheaten fronds, she thought he had fallen asleep, poor soul, and could not believe at first that he was dead.

Then shock sent her gasping onto her knees and I was born there amongst the half gathered harvest, all wet and mud spattered beside my father's corpse.

She died of the belly worm when I was ten but she was worn out long before then, poor dear. Our Lord Rulfston took back our quarter virgate after he'd arranged for her burial in the churchyard, so then I set off walking for London. I doubt if the Master bothered looking for me, or even proclaimed me a runaway serf, for I could never have tilled those two strips of land on my own. He would have taken me into the big house, just another scullery brat and another useless mouth to feed.

It was a fine long walk and took me about a month. Late spring was bright in the hedgerows when I arrived. I'd never seen such a host of people. London was as impressive as I had expected. The river was grand and busy with boats and the markets bustled with good smells and colour and noise. Then I met Vespasian. It is nearly six years now that he has looked after me.

To run away and to head to the great city is a thing that seems to answer its own questions. If you have no life, then you go to where there is the most life of all, and that's what I did. Arriving was no disappointment, but I had neither plan nor friend and no idea what to do and where to go. The great London Bridge seemed a marvellous creation. Lined with shops and houses and gates, it was a walkway built like a castle with slabs of solid stone replacing the old wooden platforms which had washed away. It was here I found my first bed on the bank with a stone pillar at my back. It was mighty damp and reeking of shit, the bloated corpses of animals and stagnant slime around the bases of the bridge's arches – no meaty market smells here – and the effluent came sodden and thick down the drain runnels into the river just a few feet downstream. But I had my mother's cloak to wrap around me and my own little hemp mantle for a pillow. I could curl my bare toes up under my tunic and sleep like a swan with its head tucked under its wing.

I had loved the woods, walking from the West Country to London. The king's woodland was not all trees but also copses and clearings, open pasture and soft meadowland, heath, scrub and stream. I had kept away from the main thoroughfares with oxcarts making huge ruts in the mud, filled with spring rain and heaps of ox droppings steaming in the sun's reflections. Instead I'd kept to the country lanes and the paths between orchards and fields of buttercups. Once I saw a ghost in the forest and I ran, but nothing followed me, and perhaps there was no ghost after all, just the shadows of the birds.

Then the city was exciting, and I knew great things would come to pass. I could make my fortune, or marry a baron, for it was in London that anything could happen.

I ate little for those first days. A few pear trees across the river had hard little fruits not yet ripe which gave me a belly cramp, but a flap of three nuns, heading for the convent of The Little Sisters of Angelica out on the northern rise, stopped when I went begging and gave me a whole silver penny, not even cut, and almost too beautiful to spend.

About a week after I arrived and while I was still living under the bridge, Plantagenet John was crowned as king and, following the crowds just as if I had been invited to the ceremony myself, I saw him walk to Westminster Abbey under his bright cloth of gold canopy, his barons behind and around him. His nose was long and his shoulders narrow but he walked with a confident swagger and stared down that long nose at the world around him. The people cheered him though I heard some mutter under their breath once he passed. It was in the confusion and push of the crowd that I met Vespasian. He was stealing the purse of one of the minor nobles at the end of the procession. He saw me watch him and smiled. He was the first person who had smiled at me in a long time and I thought it a lovely smile.

I have never seen the king again for he is mostly abroad, fighting to keep his French provinces, and failing constantly they say. Now they call him Soft sword and laugh behind his back. It was King Richard they called hero, though he saw even less of the country he was king of, and never even learned to speak our common language. It's the crusading blood they cheered him for, but now it's all spilled and his little brother John sits on a throne far too big for his skinny arse.

But now Vespasian is my life and kings and barons and great far off lands do not interest me in the least. Vespasian has taught me my living. I can cut a purse and disappear into the shadows as easily as the scruffy black rats that crawl out from the thatch at night to steal food if they can find any and will nibble at our toes if we are not careful. Vespasian says I am the best thief of all of us, though it is Isabel whom he takes into his corner bed to sleep with and caress. He does not know I am in love with him. He calls me a child, and that is how he sees me for I was just ten years old when he found me, all bones I suppose, like a scarecrow half stuffed. But now at sixteen I am at least three years past marriageable age and the king's wife was just fourteen when she became queen. Isabel is prettier than I and she is about nineteen, though she isn't sure because, like all of us, she has no parents, though at least I know my birth week and she does not. Because she is beautiful and because she is older, she looks like a real lady and wears her hair up with a chin band and toque. I still feel like a country brat, with my hair long and loose but it is golden brown and when I wash it at one of the bathhouses, it shines and has little curls down my back. All the boys are in love with Isabel, though Richard, named for the late king, God rest his soul, says it is me he wants. This is small compensation, for Richard is just fifteen years old and has red hair which is an evil sign even though the king's hair is almost red too. Kings are permitted what is quite shocking for the common folk, but secretly I think it is an evil sign for kings as well.

Vespasian looks after us all and we eat when we can. We steal for him and he is our lord and master. It's not a bad life and we watch each other's backs. He is a tall man, far taller than our little king, and I watch him from under my lashes, liking the way his muscles move in a slow dance beneath the thin moulded wool of his hose and the soft linen of his shirt. His hair and his eyes are quite black as if through some fault of his own the Good Lord had forbidden the passing of colour, and he is made up of night time. But when there is a candle flickering beside us, there are stars in his night time eyes and they flick suddenly aside, catching my gaze, so that I blush as if caught out in some sin. His lashes are as thick as Isabel's and thicker than my own and his eyelids are heavy, like a lazy man's might be. But this is misleading for Vespasian has the energy of a fox dashing from the brush, or a wolf in ambush with the leap ready at the points of his toes.

He has never beaten me, nor any of us I think, though he has threatened to do so. We are all a little frightened of him but in fact it is his silences that we fear and the suspense of a man who is so unpredictable and seems capable of anything. Sometimes he leaves us and is gone weeks, off to court or castles or to some distant war which I do not either understand or wish to, Angevin and Normandy, against the wicked French king who puts his thumb into our English business and wants John's nephew on the throne instead of our own chosen monarch. But when Vespasian returns and comes striding through the open door, flinging his mud stained cloak to the straw and his gloves to the coffer, he demands ale or wine if we have any, and laughs and tells us that war is for fools and fighting only for brutes and idiots. He empties his newly filled purse onto the table and puts his feet up on a stool and looks at us all from under half closed lids with a smile that just twitches at the corners of his mouth. He speaks so softly that it is a discipline of a sort, demanding total silence and attention, for otherwise we will not hear each precious word. Then he will tell us stories, of blood and valour, of comedy and chivalry, and of the absurd stupidity of man.

When Vespasian is gone, we are lost souls, all of us. Gerald loses his dimples and his flaxen hair hangs limp like a swineherd who has mislaid his piglets. Richard and little Stephen, who is our baby at just eleven years, no longer tumble down the stairs each morning to throw open the doors and chase the chickens out to the sunny street. Hugh, who is the eldest, grumbles and tells us we are all useless, for he feels he should become our substitute leader and likes to seem superior, while Osbert and Walter do all the work in a tight lipped silence. Isabel flounces. She tosses those fair curls and doesn't always bother to wash or comb them before pinning them up under her wimple. She likes to pinch my arm and tell me how Vespasian will come eagerly into the bedroom on his return and sweep her into his arms and then his bed. It is rather sad for Isabel that this does not ever actually happen, but it is the dream she carries with her, and I never bother to argue. After all, if I did she would just pinch me the harder and tell me I am jealous. I am of course, and she knows it. Vespasian may never have swept Isabel off her feet, but he climbs into bed with her and I watch from my pillow as his hand slides over her plump breast, and she gives a little smug sniff and lets me watch a minute before she pulls up the coverlet and turns her back.

Gerald snorts at Isabel when she preens and pretends stories of romantic love. "With Vespasian?" his snort becomes a rumble. This is very hard to do, which I know because I have tried to copy it. Only Gerald can dismiss Isabel's vanity with such contempt. "He would as soon practise chivalry with the blacksmith's dog," Gerald says. The poor creature had distemper and was likely to die within the month. "You are a quick and easy lay, Issy, let's face facts."

I considered this harsh and often took Isabel's part, but all the boys teased her and, in the end, after she had burst into convenient tears once her powers of vocabulary had run dry, everyone would forgive everyone else and return to work, to busyness and to dreaming.

The boys share their pallets of course, but I sleep alone and so there is no one to laugh when I put my thumb in my mouth and hug my knees. The heat of the evening's fire comes up through the floor boards, but I am in the furthest corner and the oiled parchment across the window lets in a draught which finds me first.

Walter and Osbert sleep together and Walter snores a little louder than anyone else. He has trouble with his nose, which is snubbed like a penny and maybe can't breathe in all the air he needs. Close to their heads wriggle the toes of the next pallet with Hugh who is the largest and Stephen, our baby. Gerald and faithful Richard have the bed next to Vespasian and Isabel. When Vespasian is away and Isabel has the whole pallet to herself, she keeps her clothes on as I do.

The country's harvest failed at the end of last year and we have gone hungry many times since then. We are not alone. Across the land there is a terrible starvation and we have heard tales of cannibalism. The babies are dying at their mother's breasts and the old have such shrunken bodies that they shrivel and die in the gutters. Vespasian, with more initiative than many, keeps us fed most days but sometimes even he cannot steal enough for us all. It makes me cry sometimes, when my belly shrinks and I know there will be nothing for a day at least and probably three. When Hugh stole two candles from the nearby church, instead of lighting them we tried to eat them. Walter once went across the city to the woods and collected chestnuts, acorns and herbs, but he brought back the roots of monkshood which Vespasian said was enough to kill us all and laughed and threw them on the ashes of the fire. But ingenuity brings surprises and though one day we chew on nothing but our hopes or manage a watery gruel of stale cabbage leaves, suddenly Vespasian will supply a feast and laugh at our excitement.

Now the East Cheap has a new stall with ready cooked pies, steaming hot crusts and fillings of stewed meat and gravy, so Vespasian stole us all a pastry wrapped in buttered linen, a purse with six bright pennies and a pair of white leather gloves for Isabel, which she tucked in her belt and twirled around the kitchen while everyone else did the work. Then Vespasian leaned back on his stool with his feet up on the trestle, with just a little twitch of amusement as he watched her and didn't even order her to stop dancing and help us, as she should.

I was playing with the yardstick, re-knotting the feet, curling the rope around my hand. I had licked every one of my fingers, allowing not one dark drop of gravy to escape. Richer folk did not eat the hard pastry cases, but we wasted nothing. Then I looked up and saw Vespasian smiling at me. It is a smile I cherish and relive in my dreams since no doubt I will wait a long time before receiving another. All his smiles are precious to me for a smile from him is mighty rare. But sometimes I have a little fancy, which I cuddle to myself in the silence of the nights, imagining that tight within Vespasian's dark frowns and relentless severity, is hidden a light hearted man of humour and sparkling laughter, and that one day the smiling man will escape and come to find me.

CHAPTER THREE

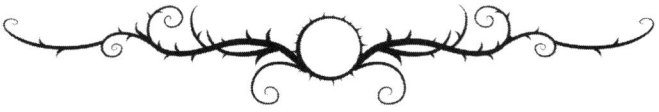

Bertie's cases clutter up the spare room. Actually they are my cases, but I lent them to him when I originally threw him out and I doubt if I'll ever get them back now. I just wish he would take them elsewhere. God only knows why I ever fell in love with Bertie all those years ago. Once love is over, how little of it we ever understand. It is many long years since my dreams included him. Now they shift like shrouded mists, spilling over into my waking hours so that sometimes, and especially when I am writing, I cannot be sure what reality is all about. Like love, it is only a relative experience after all.

I drift in apathy. My brain is all dust. I cannot be sure which world is worthy or where I belong. Bertie is at least an anchor but after two weeks of different women's voices on the phone, some angry, some pleading, all wanting him, I have asked for another telephone line. One day it will arrive. Out here in picturesque village obscurity, we are not supposed to expect efficiency. It is part of being picturesque. A reminder, while finally smiling to myself, of Plantagenet London.

I nod at Bertie when he asks my advice, but I am neither listening nor do I care. His affairs are irritating even though we are no longer married and I no longer want him. Ruby is the beloved, then Ruby flounces off and Evelyn takes her place. But Evelyn is short and plump and wears her hair in bubble curls and Bertie can stand it no longer and drifts off to Pam. Pam is prettier. Then Pam falls for our local butcher and Bertie stops eating meat for a week. Then there are twins. I was never sure which came first but Bertie dated both and both left him, possibly because of the other.

I was aware when Bertie started becoming seriously devoted to just one new lover and began an inexperienced period of faltering fidelity, but I was still abstracted, for my mind continued to delve into hauntings and soft velvet fantasies. My other world is hypnotically encroaching.

My girl is called Matilda, and usually Tilda. I have only to close my eyes and her face now absorbs my consciousness. As I slip more completely into a dream, night or day, so I become her. My secret place pulls me in. Its shadowed obscurity and intangible darkness then gradually clarify. Part of me lives there permanently. It is more than my dream state. It is the girl's world and I am the girl.

I have stopped writing. Now I sit and stare out the kitchen window over the black blank of the laptop screen, watching as the garden grass disappears under a spattering of white crystals. The sun dazzles across the frost and shoots its refracted rainbows along my stainless steel. It reminds me again that the magic of creation has nothing to do with solid reality, for reality is not solid and solidity is not real.

When I was a child, freely accepting that truth was only what you wished to believe in, I knew that I inhabited two separate worlds. In both I felt unloved but in one I sometimes escaped the misery and constant threat of home. I pretended happiness as I went to school and skipped along sunny streets. But the other was my secret place which took me in when I was frightened, and deepest sadness greyed my skies. It was secret because my parents dismissed me immediately if I talked of it. It was also secret because it smelled of secretiveness. It was dark and rustling, narrow, damp and confined. It neither attracted nor repelled me but I grew to dislike its hopeless grime.

Matilda's world contained threat, but the threat hurt less there than the threat I faced in my own modern home.

Tilda is very young and desperately thin. After the failed harvest she cried for hunger, but she is not unhappy. It is all she knows. Her thoughts now tug at me even during the day as I become gradually less myself. Bertie thinks I have become totally deranged. He is right. I am possessed. When I am Tilda and she is me, my consciousness of the bright and modern, the music and the comfort, the colour and all the fluff of gadgetry and bright entertainment, slips into a shuffling forgetfulness. I know these things exist. But I cannot shrug off the inertia which living between worlds brings, and I could not flick on the television, although I still see it here in my living room, for part of me says it is a fantasy and dangerous magic. Indeed, no such devilry has yet been invented. The electricity lightens my room in gaudy detail, but my eyes see only the spasmodic spluttering of lemon shadows from candle stubs. If Bertie lunges onto my horizons, hearty with noise and presence, I am spun into disorientation and feel nauseous as if rising too fast from diving the deep sea corals.

They live, these long lost people, in a world of accepted discomforts and dreariness. They have a house furnished in draughts and when the wind is strong, it rattles and bends and the thatch becomes threadbare, with gaps in the straw. One of the boys is sent up to tie it tighter and stuff the holes with hay. He clings to the beams and shouts to frighten off the rats.

Six boys and two girls live with the man who owns the house. Cradles of straw line the walls upstairs and the children curl warm amongst the fleas and cockroaches, clutching at each other when something disturbs them, and night terrors, hunger and pain interrupt the rhythmic snoring.

I love Tilda. I do not love the man. His smiles are rare unless he is a little drunk, when they tilt his lips but do not reach his eyes. He frightens me. I am not yet sure why, but his shadow swallows light and when I creep into his reality, his power over me seems menacing. Tall and very dark, hawk eyed and hard mouthed, he is Vespasian

Fairweather. I am sure I will not like him at all. I will despise his arrogance and the power he wields over these lost children.

He must have been named for the ancient Roman emperor, showing delusions of grandeur perhaps of medieval peasants, though educated peasants since they knew such names to call their child at all. But I find it strange and am intrigued. His surname comes from no trade, guild or town as those early surnames usually did, but is Fairweather, originally a nickname I suppose, and must be inherited from a father more genial than the son.

They are so alive to me. Yet it is eight hundred years since they are dead, buried and lost in decay.

Tilda, having arrived in the city when ten years old and now being, I think, about sixteen, knows old London well. It is her place of work. She is both ridiculously innocent, and painfully street-wise. She enjoys the taverns which crowd the Thames' damp banks between the wharves. The Bear's Head is the biggest with a colourful sign swinging and a heavy thatch jutting over the eaves. A few dark eyed whores gather in the alley at the side, business conducted where the chickens peck among the refuse and their customers rut quick to escape the smell of the sewerage running through the central gutters. No point trying to cut a purse here, however drunk the patrons, for they are all thieves themselves and won't be cheated by another.

The Fletcher's Arms is a small inn with a raised hearth and a warm fire in the winter with stables at the back and the landlord is said not to water his ale. But it is the Cock Tavern where Tilda makes her money most easily. The sacks of squirming cockerel ready for the fight hang along the outer wall and the courtyard is trampled hard and flat by a thousand feet. With the excitement of the wagers, no one notices a small girl with her hair in her eyes and a ready pen-knife. She can cut three purses and be gone before the cocks face off.

Next best are the markets, the smaller weekly gatherings where the farmers come into town to sell and barter and the big monthly Cheaps when traders come even from aboard and the purses are the fattest in the city. I follow Tilda and feel her rising excitement, the quick flick of the knife through the soft leather pouch, and then the squeeze through the crowds and away from notice before skipping home to show off her expertise. I go with her. I know all her movements now and travel her life beside her.

Sometimes I think her thoughts though I am also aware of my own. Then suddenly I am back with the vacuum cleaner in one hand and a glass of wine in the other, and I have no memory of how I even got here, let alone why I decided on housework when I've no interest anymore in dust or debris. I am disappointed when I find I am just myself again. So of course there was just one step further for me to go.

I was up on the lower hills beyond my own comfortable house when it happened. I was in wellies and plastic hood, following the downward trail amongst the stones, when my afternoon walk turned into sudden regret. The storm rolled over the crests like the smoke of a forest on fire, with clouds in billowing black and grimy yellow. There were still patches of snow on the hillsides, ice pockets, smears of white across the moss and fern. Then the slopes were mist ravaged and the clouds dipped down to touch the grass. Cotswold horizons are bleak during winter thunder.

Tilda had been born during such a storm. I knew. I'd seen her father fall, struck by lightning, eyes wide open in surprise. I'd seen her born amongst the sodden wheat. Now I stood, braced against the wind and lashing rain, and saw both my own skies ravaged by the bold white electrical strikes, and Tilda's lowering clouds split by the same intensity. I was trapped in two storms and had little hope of escaping either.

I'd left my car in the valley. I began to stumble back down the hillside, hood pulled low around my ears, rubber soles slipping in the mud. I fell twice into sheep droppings and thistles, up to my ankles in storm water. I tipped forward, twisting my wrist, my fingers squelching into a sluice of mud, knees on stones and jeans torn. I was still a long way up from the car. I fell a fourth time. I spun. As if I had fallen upwards instead of down, I was lifted. The sky cleared, and the stars whirled their million blues in a cream spangled arc around me. I thought I had died.

I was dizzy with light. I was part of light itself. The echo of my ears still thundered and the rain washed me cold and clean, but the fire of the stars dried me and flew me on. I passed through worlds. Time passed through me and moved beyond.

When I woke, I was curled small and warm amongst a thick prickle of straw with a thumb in my mouth and hunger in my belly.

CHAPTER FOUR

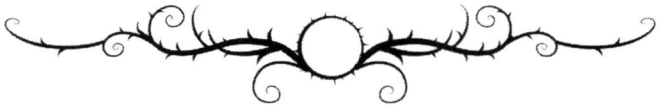

I share a body with Tilda and we are now, for the first time, totally and completely combined. For a little while, vaguely acknowledging me and glimpsing my thoughts and my influence over hers, she believed she was asleep and dreaming. I know that I am awake. I have never been more awake.

It is not a body like my own, but it seems strangely familiar and I am at home within it. We are smooth skinned, still flat chested and small boned, more angles than curves. There are no mirrors here, but I know my eyes are huge and beautiful and my hair is like a silk quilt which I can wrap around myself at night to help keep me warm. In fact, I am not cold for it is nearly spring. There is a fresh warmth to the air, a bright flutter of sunshine with a balmy touch. It is a much warmer world and a far quieter one. When I lived in the twenty first century I saw my secret place as dark and eternally shadowed, a place heavy with threat. Now that I am truly here, I love it. There are shadows but there is also dancing light. I am even getting used to the smells.

I have such little feet. My hands are rough and calloused with broken nails. When I first arrived, I saw my finger nails were permanently striped with dirt. Now I am trying to keep them clean. I take one of the hazel twigs we use as toothbrushes and sharpen its end into a point with my knife. The other children think this odd and imagine that I must have ulterior motives. Perhaps I have for I am waiting to meet Vespasian in person. Tilda thinks he is her whole world, but I have yet to see him for myself and I feel an absurd anticipation.

Upstairs one room under the rafters is the bedroom to us all and downstairs the only space is a living room, of sorts. When there are faggots to burn, we build a fire across the central stone slab. There is no chimney. The cooking fire smokes but we sit around it and watch the pictures it plays along the walls. There are benches either side of a trestle table, a flat earth floor, straw bundles like cushions, one special chair, two stools and a narrow day bed of knotted ropes strung between a wooden frame and sagging beneath woollen wraps. There is no other furniture. The little windows have no glass, but plank shutters close us in at night and when it is cold or wet. We think we are cosy. We think we are lucky.

Being Tilda is a growing delight to me. She is happy to be alive with a joy I myself have never known. We play with the other children, chasing and squealing, throw a ball made from tied pig skin, mark the street ahead with pebbles and hopscotch to market. Between such games, we steal. We are very good at it.

Richard, who thinks I am queen bee, was nearly caught this morning but the hue and cry missed him as he slipped down to the river and hid on a barge tied up to the bank. Little Stephen, who will surely be remarkably handsome when he grows up but for being slightly cross-eyed, stole hot bread and two pies from the street behind the Little Market. It is a dark narrow shop gorgeous with perfumes, medieval fast-food, and a luxury both to buy and to steal. I cannot believe how delicious all this food is and without sugar or additives somehow everything tastes wonderful. Walter, Osbert, Gerald and Hugh, the other four boys, are all older than me. Isabel is the oldest of us all and a little vain. I do not resent her good fortune in being Vespasian's chosen. It seems justly inevitable.

There had been word of his return, riding up from Dover

shepherding a troop of soldiers and a cart load of injured. "Vespasian will be back tonight," said Isabel. "It's such an age he's been gone. I'll sleep well again at last."

Tilda and I sigh into the long shadows. She said, "I know you've missed him."

"So have you," Isabel said. I noticed the smirk. Tilda didn't blame her. Nor do I, but I am becoming a little irritated.

"We all have," I said, which was true enough.

"I shall be covered in kisses tonight," said Isabel, with exaggerated smiles. "One for each day he's been gone." Tilda said nothing, though in fact we have never ever seen Vespasian kiss her, not even once. He was usually nice enough to Issy, but quick, practical copulation never included the chivalry of romantic kisses.

The boys crowded round. We were roasting apples over the fire, skewered on twigs. Richard's twig burned through quickly and his apple dropped into the ashes. I pulled it out for him, then licked my scorched fingers. He beamed at me. So easy to inspire adoration in the wrong person. Vespasian sometimes calls fire aqua nostra, which Tilda does not understand, but then, he says a lot of things which are totally obscure to everyone. I don't understand it either.

The fading winter is noticeably warmer than my own, but each evening ferocious draughts freeze my toes. I wear woollen gartered stockings to my knees beneath a coarse linen camise and then the long wool of my stolla, while my shoes are cracked leather, soles very worn with holes in the tops, but shoes none the less. Most disturbing to me was the absolutely lack of any underwear, but Tilda considers this normal and is perfectly comfortable without it.

There are other things that trouble Tilda not one jot but discomfort me enormously. There is neither bathroom nor toilet in our little house, and no means to find either nearby. We use chamber pots without much privacy and empty them into the street. There is no underground sewerage system although some properties access cess pits, but I am gradually becoming accustomed to all this, and to the smells too.

I don't mind the rats. Their intrusive faces, scratching and scampering, echo our lives. They are good mothers. I'd have fed them scraps if I had more food myself. There are also cockroaches and fleas, lice and bedbugs and I mind them a great deal more. Tilda does too, though they seem unavoidable. Itching is a daylong exercise and we all have little bloody spots and scabs on our bodies.

It is strange to experience real hunger. Often in my past life I have said I am hungry. Now I realise it was never the truth. I simply desired food in acknowledgment of approaching mealtimes, my body demanding to eat through habit. Hunger is something else altogether. Hunger hurts.

In this time when I am Tilda, I have gone twice up into the forest to find herbs to flavour the pottage and soups. Stealing pies cannot happen every day. Nor do we spend the money we steal if we can help it. Most of these cut snippets of silver pennies are kept until Vespasian returns.

They call it a forest, though much of it is lightly treed and some of it is pasture. It seems that since all forest automatically belongs to the Crown, the good King John can declare almost any free land to be forest, even if it is sparsely wooded. It then becomes forested in name only, immediately belongs to him and is strictly controlled by law. I walk under the huge open branched trees and watch the pale winter sunshine glitter in the spider's webs. Sometimes I forget to look for the food I have come to collect. Wonder is more important than efficiency.

Climbing the grassy rise to the edge of the woods where the freemen's cottages are surrounded by neat rows of beans and peas, staked and tied and growing in the sun, I could escape London's reek a little, though here the vegetable gardens were fertilised with fresh manure and not only from the animals. Tilda always spoke to the skinny swineherd who tended the local lord's pigs as they scrummaged for acorns under the first shadowed boughs of the forest. He was Mat, the pig boy, about seven years old though he didn't know exactly, and looked small for his age. I doubted he ever got closer than the smell to his master's roast pork on the spit. I had given him an apple I'd stolen, when the pigs began to fight. Scrawny little things like their guardian, they were all bones with angry pink eyes and tight dirty little tusks. Their sharp trotters scrabbled in the dry earth, heads down, butting, tails up, squealing and snorting. One caught the other with a side swipe and cut a bloody slice from its haunches, but I went running back down to the cover of the city while Mat strode between them with a high child's shout and a sharpened stick. I could hear Mat laughing behind me.

Running was now something I could do best of all, with the warm breeze in my long hair, narrow hipped and my toes all fleet and as light as leaves barely touching the ground. If I was caught stealing I could escape any hue and cry. Long skirts made no difference. I could feel the strength in my small calves and the spring of my thighs, a young body all fresh and rushing with energy. As Molly, it was an age since I had run under the sun. Molly was older and lived a walking life, full bodied with hips, breasts and a tired back. Tilda still knew the joy of self-made speed. With no intention of spending three days and nights in the stocks, her flight was her defence, but it was also her pleasure.

Each of Tilda's days is exciting to me and even the stink fascinates. The gentry walk the dung strewn streets with rose scented handkerchiefs held to their noses, but I am simply delighted not to smell petrol and diesel, the smoke and dirt of industry and the reeking claustrophobia of a thousand bodies crowding around.

I know that I am still me. I am Molly Susans who leads an affluent modern life, bathes each day and owns a DVD recorder. But I am Tilda as well, who has no surname and remembers no father. I live in London; it is the year of our Lord one thousand, two hundred and six and I am one of a band of thieves, all children, who risk our lives to live.

I have been here just a few days in Tilda's mind and heart and body. With Isabel's gloating in my ears, I snuggle into the straw, scratch absently, stick my grubby thumb in my mouth, and squeeze my eyes shut. When I wake, I will at last truly meet Vespasian, who is expected to return this night.

CHAPTER FIVE

But when I woke I was Molly again. Immediately I felt a grinding lurch of disappointment. It was then I realised someone was screaming in the distance. The distance came nearer. The scream was raw and guttural, and it expressed a terror even I had never known. I sat up, aware of a thundering headache, couldn't put my hand to my head – simply – it was the wrong head.

Becoming Tilda had seemed more right than strange. After years of glimpsing her world and then weeks of vivid merging, I had become her with a sense of absolute belonging. Now switching back to Molly, whom I still called myself, was far more alarming. I was in pain and confusion. Rocking sideways, I tried to attach to any sense of reality which might float past me, gripping even at the pain of the headache as a focus of who I now was. Feather pillows, sprung mattress, wallpaper, long curtains. The telephone beside my bed. It was ringing. I didn't answer it.

The screaming had stopped. I had no idea what I had heard or in which world it had occurred. I might have been screaming myself. I rolled over and winced, feeling my bad neck, bad head. Now I was able to recognise who I was. I could scratch my nose, rub my eyes, massage my forehead. They all belonged to me and Tilda had gone, taking her small body and her small consciousness with her.

I wouldn't have got out of bed for hours if Bertie hadn't come rummaging at the door. "I've made tea, sweetie." A pitiful request for attention. He'd always done this in the past after I'd found him out in some wretched wrongdoing. Not that a mug of tea was going to wipe away his infidelities, but for years I'd somehow accepted those sad and silently symbolic pleas for forgiveness. He always made tea like dishwater anyway. I asked him later if he had noticed any strange or disturbing noises earlier that morning. He hadn't. Self absorbed though he was, the terrified scream I had heard would surely have impinged even on him, had it come from this world. So it had been Tilda's world. Or no world at all. He said the storm which had blown me through time, had been just yesterday. That alarmed, then reassured me. For Tilda it had been four days back, the four days that I had been her.

Bertie had now made the spare room into his bachelor pad which I thought rather eccentric, though even more of me than of him. When he had girlfriend trouble, and they usually discovered his defects a lot quicker than I had, Bertie made tea, cooked me lunches and did more housework than he ever had while we were married. It was bribery. He paid for the opportunity to discuss his problems, to talk about himself and get the attention he yearned for so deeply, and which was probably the cause of his endless unfaithfulness to me in the first place.

"Bertie, you're boring." He looked as hurt as I had meant him to be and shuffled off. I knew I was going crazy but that somehow didn't matter much. I was a little curious as to how I had driven myself back from the deluged slopes of the hills and into my own home, presumably managed practical things such as eating and drinking, and then got myself into bed – all while I was busy being someone else in a world some eight hundred long years lost.

I'd adored my cottage forever, bought with book royalties well before marriage, my own little pride and security. Heritage listed, which bound me to restricted repairs – a good excuse to wallow in its cosy character with not too much housework. So pretty, so comfy, a little too worn and a little tatty, but sheltering accumulated conveniences. Yet now it was medieval discomfort I wanted, and a squalor that would have horrified me in my own home.

Each night I hoped to dream myself back into Tilda. At least I hoped to visit, to peep through and to discover whatever had happened. I worried, endlessly imaging obscure possibilities. One idea cemented, and I became convinced that the ragged and dreadful scream had something to do with Vespasian.

Dream snatches brought the man's threat into focus. One night in the half state of that foggy intangible where reality meets sleep, I saw his eyes searching and briefly I was Tilda again. Vespasian's eyes were heavy dipped and beneath the long curve of black lashes, his pupils were huge. I considered them eyes which have seen too much, both of life and within himself. He was furious.

Tilda knew the signs. She knew his every expression. Perhaps she knew why he was so angry, though I did not. He was honing the iron blade of the dagger he kept always in his belt, the whet stone between his knees. But he was watching Gerald. Gerald sighed and left the room. Vespasian remained tight lipped and did not speak. One candle was a guttering tallow glimmer in the far corner and the main light came from the low fire. It flashed suddenly on the thick gold of Vespasian's ring, the only ornament he ever wore. The brilliance caught his eyes, turning the black into sudden scarlet. I thought him devilish.

Tilda had waited, watching him for a moment before slipping outside, careful not to attract his attention. It was dark with no light in the street except the maze of milk white from the heavens, the spilled spangle of winter stars. Gerald was leaning against the water barrel, his arms crossed over his child's chest, his lower lip in a defiant pout. Isabel and Richard had followed him out to try and cheer him up. "No good sulking," said Richard. "He'll forget it eventually. You know he always does."

"Not until a day gone, at least," said Gerald. "And I shall feel wretched and ignored until then. It will ruin everything."

We were all miserable when Vespasian was angry. "Only Issy can get him back into a good mood," I said. Isabel was looking particularly pretty. She had washed her hair and without the wimple, it hung loose in shining curves.

"That's up to him," said Isabel, prim.

Richard and Gerald were staring purposefully away, declining to discuss such vulgar matters. "No it isn't," I said. "Go and climb on his lap. Best wait until he puts his dagger away perhaps, just in case, and then go and sit on his knee. Flounce, the way you do. Blink a lot and simper. Look provocative."

Isabel giggled. "What would you know about such things?"

Tilda tried to imitate Gerald's derisive snort. "Go and take your over-tunic off and undo the neck of your stolla," I said. "Cleavage is a wonderful medicine for the gripes."

I was asleep, Molly in Molly's bed, snuffling peacefully within my own private dreams when Vespasian's eyes interrupted me again. If they had been black in anger before, now the threat was cold controlled fury. I could not see his whole face, just the glitter of his eyes, with the soft menace of his voice. "If you ever," he said, each word distinct but quiet as a whisper, "do such a thing again, I will take my belt to you. Do you understand?" Tilda said nothing. She was in bed, as I was, and Vespasian was standing over her, looking down. "If you wish to emulate the habits of a pimp," he continued, "you can leave this house and I will find work for you on the streets. But it is not my libido you will service, nor my life you will ever interfere with again. Do you understand?"

Tilda nodded with a sniff. It was all she could do. She stifled the tears and nourished a determination to revenge herself on Isabel, who must have told. She did not blame Vespasian. She never blamed him for anything.

I woke the next morning with the knowledge that I was sane. No lunacy could have made me invent these people, especially a man I had begun to loathe.

It was Wattle who Bertie was having problems with now, the special someone he had been faithful to for several tottering weeks.

"What girl has to suffer with a name like that?" I asked him, though half absent. My thoughts remained always partially in the past.

"She chose it, it's her stage name," said Bertie. "She's an aroma therapist and juggler. I mean, that's got to be an interesting combination. And she's gorgeous, Mol. Even you'd like her."

I did like her. He brought her home to meet me twice, a bit like bringing the girlfriend back to meet your mother, only I was his ex-wife. Wattle should have been called Willow and she was sweet with green eyes and a rather firm chin. She believed in the power of oils and perfumes. I wondered what she would have made of the scent of medieval sewerage.

I think Bertie was actually in love. We sat together in my living room with the lights down low and the flames of the fire painting black and red pictures across my ceiling. It reminded me of Tilda's world, her cooking fire and the children's faces, avid and hungry, cuddling close. It had snowed again, spring clinging to late winter's bluster and the crunch of it outside was the only sound. Snow isolates worlds into an unnatural hush. I felt abstract shiftings. I was suddenly nervous of breathing too deeply. I'd only had two glasses of wine, but I stopped drinking. Wattle curled into the corner of the big couch, black hair against cushioned bronze. "But I'm not ready," she said. "I'm not ready for commitment. It didn't work for you two, did it?"

"Oh, I don't count," I said. "Perhaps we married too young. Bertie needed more than I could give him. Besides, I'm a ratty impatient bitch. But you're patient and kind. My head was always wandering off, planning books and following odd trails so Bertie felt neglected. You'd be nicer."

"I'd be as bad," said Wattle. "I don't want to belong to anyone else."

Bertie was in the chair beside the fire, his stretched legs blocking much of the warmth. "Look, I'm no macho pig, or whatever you're implying here. Come on, stick up for me, Mol. I never tried to tell you what to do, did I? Oh, well, maybe sometimes. But who made last night's dinner? Who made yesterday's lunch? Who made breakfast this morning? I even stacked the dishwasher."

"I like cooking," said Wattle. "So that's irrelevant."

We talked from first snow fall until star haloed moon. I went upstairs at two, leaving them both promising to make sure the fire was out before they went to bed. Bertie was still trying to convince Wattle to stay the night. It was so late and so cold, I was quite sure she'd agree.

When I finally got out of bed the next morning I found she hadn't, and Bertie had slept the night on the couch in deep depression. I made him breakfast for once, but he didn't eat it anyway. I went out and tramped the lane down to the stream that ran through the village. I could still see the tyre marks where Wattle had parked and then left. Bird feet, tiny splayed toe stripes, hardly impinging on the crust. A cat had jumped from path to wall, then disappeared into the big silver birch, leaving dainty symmetrical paw patterns. Nothing else spoiled the sparkle of snow under pale sunshine. I spoiled it myself, big boot indentations along the hidden pavement. I stood on the bridge and watched the brook carry fallen lumps of snow from north to south, creating more rainbow kaleidoscopes of refracted light.

For once I wasn't thinking of Tilda. I wished Wattle would go off and live with Bertie. For a start, it would get him out of the house. He was serious about her and that impressed me. It was so unlike him to yearn to settle down, to want just one girl, and to desire commitment. He would be good to her for a while. When they eventually split up, he could stay in her spare room. She would be good for him because she was nice. I wondered just how impossibly selfish of me it would be to encourage them.

I bought eggs and fresh bread. Aromatherapy. Fresh bread smelled so seductive. I pulled off the heel on the way home and ate the crust still warm. I was still dropping crumbs when I got back indoors and tried to ignore the phone. It was usually for Bertie these days, except when my agent or the publisher made polite murmurings. I crept past the phone as if it might see me if I stood up straight and went to sit in the kitchen. My computer was on the kitchen table between the bowl of lemons and the dirty coffee cups, but I hadn't turned it on in ages. Then I unpacked the shopping, but the phone kept ringing. Bertie must be out. I answered the phone.

It was the police. They had found Wattle. They had found her hanging by both ankles, her pretty black curls in the snow, her hands ripped and scratched as if by wild animals. Her face was marked by one violent welt, raised like a burn. She was fully dressed but had been brutally raped. Her throat was cut so deeply that she had been almost decapitated.

They had found her in the woods where she'd been suspended upside down from a chestnut tree just beyond the river. It had been a beautiful tree with mistletoe in the lower branches. Children, playing in the snow, had found her. Her car had been abandoned on the roadside a mile away. In it the police had found her purse and the radio playing softly to itself.

The children had been hustled away by their parents, mesmerised by a memory they would never ever forget, and which would influence the rest of their lives. Wattle had no more life to influence. She had been twenty three and beautiful and good and I had liked her very much. Bertie had wanted to marry her. A letter from him saying just that, had been found in her bag in the car. It had been the first thing that had led the police to us.

CHAPTER SIX

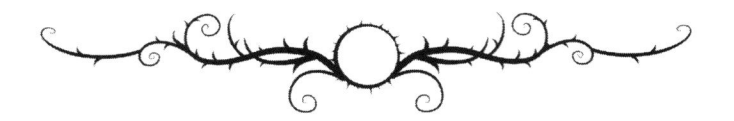

I didn't find out the details at first. Bertie and I spent most of the day at the police station, strictly separated, and it was later in the afternoon that the actual circumstances were gradually explained. I still had bread crumbs caught in the pink fuzz of my jumper, last night's mascara was smudged under my eyes, and I was sitting in a draughty police interview room hearing about horrors that couldn't possibly be true.

I kept crying. Eventually they got bored with me and drove me home, but they wouldn't let me speak to Bertie. He was still helping them, I suppose, with their enquiries. I hadn't given Bertie an alibi, but then, he surely didn't want one and couldn't possibly need it. I had gone to bed and left them together by the fire, though I had seen Bertie briefly in the morning when I served him cornflakes and packaged orange juice. He'd looked puffy eyed and had obviously slept badly, but that happens when one scrunches up on a couch half the night. But I kept telling the police, as they must have known themselves, that Bertie couldn't have done it. He was sweet and useless and gentle. The killer must have been someone brutally deranged. Wattle's throat had been sliced by a long, jagged nail. She had been strung up from the branch with great loops of ivy and mistletoe. Then she had been pinned to the trunk by a stake of sharpened wood right through her stomach.

When I went back indoors, I actually missed Bertie for the first time in eight years. There were echoes and the ashes in the grate smelled of misery and death.

I heard him come in later. The police had finally let him go at about ten thirty. I felt guilty about not rushing down to talk to him and try and cheer him up, but I couldn't move. I thought I'd vomit if I had to talk about what had happened. I slept as badly as was inevitable, in scraps interrupted by a heaving stomach, a bitter neuralgia and fits of sudden crying.

I prayed, literally prayed, that I might leave it all behind and dream myself back to Tilda and Vespasian's children and the sunshine of the mild medieval winter passing into sweet spring. I prayed for simplicity and the innocent company of my child thieves. It didn't happen. But then I remembered the scream which had woken me days before on returning from medieval shadows, and the conviction that there had been a link to Vespasian. Now I didn't know what to think so I tried not to think at all. Then I had to face Bertie.

I tried very hard to make him happier, but what absurd impossibility in the face of brutal murder. We wondered together about whatever would have made Wattle stop and open her car door to a maniacal stranger on a deserted road in the early hours of a dark winter morning. There were no signs of a struggle at the car. It had been left locked with the hazard lights flashing and the radio running. The battery was almost flat when it was found. Wattle still had the car keys in her jacket pocket.

"Her name was Doris. She hated it so much. Doris Davidson. So she changed it to Wattle. She was the nicest person I've ever met. Apart from you, I suppose. No, including you. She was just so caring. How can something like this happen to a good person?" They were the first coherent words Bertie said after lots of crying and bleak staring over my head and out of the window. It was starting to snow again, little soft flurries against a colourless sky. The birds were busy, finding hard pickings in midwinter. White horizontal stripes were collecting along the outside of the window frames and the trees were lacy tapestries among bare branches.

I hadn't faced housework, but I had collected last night's empty wine glasses and coffee cups. My hands were shaking and I'd dropped one. There had been Wattle's lipstick smears still on the rim.

Thinking about my books or escaping the limitations of a loveless marriage, I had often walked in those Gloucestershire woods over the years. The wide open freshness of the hills called me more often, immense views over the nestled villages with wind whistling over stone and scrub. But the woods in bluebell season were a fantasy of petal and frond. Fairy dreams. I must have walked a hundred times past the big chestnut tree where Wattle was found. I have picnicked there, close enough to the spot I think, solitary picnics with a thermos of wine, a cheese sandwich and something to read. I liked the loamy depths and the blue shadows. But I would never ever want to walk in that place again.

Bertie and I spent more time at the police station but then it was only Bertie they interviewed, and they knew I had nothing more to tell them. Poor Bertie had nothing more to tell them either, but they kept trying. After a couple of days and once he got legal permission, Bertie packed an overnight case and went up to Birmingham to visit Wattle's parents. Left alone again, I started pacing the house. I knew how many steps there were from front door to kitchen, how many treads up to my bedroom. I had never counted them before. Now I knew there were exactly eighteen. I trudged endlessly into the village, bought something silly, then went back in the afternoon for whatever it was I had forgotten in the morning. I sat in baths until they were cold, but I didn't use perfumed oils, even though I knew I was becoming increasingly depressed. The newspapers gradually found something else to write about and Wattle's pretty face disappeared from the front pages. The weather improved.

Bertie didn't come back for two weeks. The Davidson family found him a comfort and perhaps they were soothed by his simple adoration for their lost daughter. Perhaps they just found him a replacement to mother. They didn't seem to suspect him of any wickedness. When there is the embarrassment of death, people avoid the encroachment, and yet there is such a yearning to talk. With Bertie, the Davidsons could endlessly discuss Wattle and all her bright living memories. The police knew where he was, but they didn't bother us anymore. No one was finding answers to questions too hideous to unravel, so life just went on.

The first daffodils popped yellow heads into yellow sunshine, sweet jonquil perfume, pretty hedgerows and early puff balls of blossom soon blown by sudden winds. Gales rushed through the valleys like witches on broomsticks.

It was witches most of the village were talking about. Satanic cults seemed as good a theory as any. I didn't think the idea silly at all. I was sure that what had happened went beyond the capabilities of basic humanity, but I was thinking of more than that. My own strange experiences were magical too – or maniacal. Beneath the apathy, I was genuinely frightened.

Shops shut early as winter dark still slunk in by mid to late afternoon and everyone locked their doors, avoided the open roads and stayed in with the telly at night. This horror had happened in our own back yard and we continued to shiver even though the rest of the country moved onto the sensational attractions of other scandals. So when Bertie came back I wasn't sure if I was pleased or sorry. I wanted someone to talk to but his depression was deeper than my own and hard to live with. A couple of my London friends phoned, full of curiosity and invitations, but I couldn't talk. My lovely cousin Sammie phoned too often and I forbade her to visit me, though I recognised her sanity and caring. I didn't want to be pitied. A Sunday newspaper produced an article on Wattle and absurdly linked her interest in aromatherapy, and the fact that she'd recently taken a course in astrology, with the possibility of a black magic coven, blasphemies and deviations. The village muttered and Bertie cried in my arms. The local woman who'd taught the astrology course and who also drove the school bus threatened to sue the paper but also cancelled the course. Paranoia swept through our valley like the winter winds.

I dreamed about Wattle and the scream I'd heard before and then finally my dreams included Tilda. She came tripping back into my night wanderings like the warmth of the sun on my face.

She wasn't aware of me this time. She was taller, smoother, and just turned seventeen. More than a year had passed for her, though just a few weeks for me, and although nothing much seemed to have happened in her life, she was enjoying the new March sparkle on the river and the increased supply of food.

Vespasian had been again to France. He had followed the battle wagons, had bought himself a horse and had gone to help claim Normandy back for the king. He had returned with money and fine stockings and the crown's favour. The children had eaten well once more, but Vespasian had not altered his habits either for king or for country. He sold the horse and bought more chickens, a vat of strong French wine, (no prejudice there), hot pies, fresh rushes and two whole sides of bacon which were hung in the rising smoke under the rafters. Tilda's unquestioning acceptance gave me no clues as to any of Vespasian's decisions.

The scream had not been hers. Nothing terrible at all had happened after I had left the children and their cramped house three narrow streets back from the wharf. Although I was not her and she was separate from me in these short visits, I glimpsed her memories. I knew she had a blister on the side of her foot and I felt her discomfort. She had worn through her shoes but felt that going bare foot like Stephen and Osbert would be sadly shameful. Only Isabel had nice shoes without holes. I knew how Tilda still longed for shoes and I wished desperately that I could give them to her. In other matters, she was happier. I glimpsed her excitement when Vespasian had come home at midnight, clattering up on his tired horse which he'd ridden right into the house, slung its saddle and harness to the ground and left it nosing the pot on the hearth for the night. He had been slightly drunk and noisy with success. I could almost see him in her mind and feel her knee scrunched delight, curled in bed, listening to his laughter, peeping up to see if he would acknowledge her, the glee in accepting the gift he had brought her. Then he had stretched out on the straw pallet, too drunk to fuck with Isabel, and told stories of travel and heroism and exaggerated deeds. I decided again that I hated him.

Even then, when Vespasian had shoes made for Tilda, and for Osbert and Stephen too, I hated his smug generosity. He always seemed to have shoes himself.

CHAPTER SEVEN

Richard and Isabel had gone up to the market with Tilda when I became fully her again. Though seventeen now, she was no more a lady than when I had first met her as a child. With a rustle of shifting time, I slipped into her mind so easily that for a moment I forgot I had ever been anyone else. It was the sixteenth day of March and bright. Clouds danced across a faraway sky like children in petticoats playing tag or little sailboats in a flotilla. Tilda and I thought the market glorious.

I had left Molly and the rest of my consciousness in bed and presumably asleep, but I was not dreaming anymore, and I felt very much awake. I hoped I might stay longer this time.

The rats seemed larger out in the open. They scuttled past our feet, busy looking for the chicken heads, turnip tops and scraps of fruit dropped behind the stalls. I was suddenly startled by a rat almost as big as a kitten running over my toes and Isabel smirked when I tripped. She was pretty in long blue with a warm pelisse. I knew I was shabby in threadbare lilac like dying lavender, but I had new shoes, all soft red leather with a black ribbon, Vespasian's gift some months ago, so doubly highly prized. I loved Tilda's happiness, skipping over the old beaten earth with her, delighting in her delight and in each step of her new shoes. Sharing Tilda's joyful and undemanding consciousness again was an immediate pleasure.

We had silver pennies, worn thin and a little bent, snipped along their crosses into quarters. Fourthlings, said Tilda and I knew she meant farthings. We had come to the market to buy, as well as to steal.

The stalls wore bright striped awnings over tiny crowded counter tops. Itinerant sellers showed their pins, ribbons and wooden nails on trays hung around their necks. The salesmen carried leather sacks around their waists, jangling silver pieces. There was no other form of currency – just bright pennies, whole and etched with a cross or snipped into the pieces marked by the crosses. A whole unclipped penny was a rare excitement. Every sale rang like little bells as money disappeared into pouches. Butchers, bakers and fishmongers had their own corner, then the market opened into the brilliance and confusion of fruit, grains, herbs and vegetables. The variety of these foods seemed limited to me, my favourites were missing and much of it was smaller than I was used to, but the colours were brighter, and the smells sprang fresh and deliciously vibrant. There were little apples like rubies, hard topaz pears and small onions all moist and sweet scented, caterpillar pocked cabbages as green as limes and peas curled in their nests. Several stalls sold eggs, white and crusted in feathers and straw, still warm. Live hens strutted, free to peck. Others, plucked or still twitching, were strung up by their scrawny feet. I turned away. That had brought reminders I had no intention of remembering now. I moved quickly away from the butcher's quarter where the warm blood ran into the gutters, suet and lard sweated in bowls, skinless flesh oozed with intestines knotted into bows. It stank of murder.

Honey was rich golden in sealed earthenware jars or open tubs, sausages hung in neat coils, hams and cured bacon with their dark muskiness, cheeses and creamy thick milk, butter in urns and wooden kegs of wine and ale. Someone was selling rosy faced scarecrows; there were barrows of neatly cut and scrolled peat smelling loamy and moist, faggots of kindling rolled in leaves, quills and parchments, horns of inks from oak gall, tanned leather hides, huge rolls of cloth in many colours, candles both tallow and beeswax and readymade pies and pastries from a stall right in the middle of Cheap market.

There was noise. Everyone shouted and called to buy. Geese, ducks, chickens and pigeons clucked and squawked and bickered. The tooth-puller sat smug in his blood spattered apron, his own grin gaping empty-jawed, the queue in front of him waiting patiently and slump shouldered – resigned to the new pain that would replace the old pain. All around the chatter and laughter were loud. I liked the noise. It was small-town-bustling and very friendly. There were no engines, no mechanical buzz, no motor whine and no roar of traffic. The level of sound seemed charmingly personal as if exactly designed for the ear.

Richard chased Tilda through wool, hemp and fine linens and down into wooden toys. Isabel followed, complaining. She didn't want to run, it was undignified, but I noticed that she managed to steal a purse on the way. I thought the toys ingenious and I wished I could buy one of the little jointed oxen with its wide horns lowered and its big painted eyes smiling. But Tilda would never have done such a thing, even had she been able to afford it. It would have been a waste of precious money and shockingly childish.

Past horseshoes and the blacksmith hammering hot and smelling of damp horse and smoke from the forge, Isabel disappeared into the narrow alleys where the market led from the open street and back into the regular shops within the walled city. She had a fat purse to hide and needed to keep away from anyone who might remember she was close by when the corpulent country esquire lost his money. A disadvantage of being pretty, men remembered your face. Isabel slipped away and Richard and I, understanding the traditions, skipped in the opposite direction.

There were sacks of flour for sale and readymade bread too, small dark loaves hot from the oven. Tilda was hungry, and I said on her behalf, "Wait for me by the corner. I'm going to steal a loaf."

Richard looked at me in some surprise. "But not from him. You know better than that. Ned the Miller puts more grit than barley in his flour."

Tilda knew though I hadn't, one should only steal the best.

Isabel had already taken a purse and now I wanted to prove my skills. I was small and dexterous and could gaze earnestly with innocent eyes. I had the little knife up my sleeve ready to cut leather straps. A pen-knife, named for its bright blade designed to sharpen quills for pens, it had a thin bone handle and fitted neatly inside the cuff of my cotte. With just a twist of the thumb and wrist, it slipped into my palm. I could cut a man's purse from his belt in seconds and hide it in the folds of my skirts. I preferred to steal from men. Women were quicker and more suspicious. Three times I had very nearly been caught when stealing from women, but I was quick too, and if a hue and cry was sounded, I could outrun the mob. Usually I just disappeared into the alleys before anyone knew they'd been robbed.

I saw a young man lounging against the side of a stall. He was watching two women arguing the price for a pair of quails. He was well dressed and wore a full purse. I thought he looked bored and restless, perhaps a brother or son sent to market as chaperone to watch over them, but impatient to be off hunting, hawking or tilting with friends. He was too young to be easy prey, but his lack of concentration was a temptation in my favour. I moved to the side of the stall and into his long shadow. I was behind him, my knife already in my hand, when I felt someone's fingers grip my wrist.

"I don't think so." An elderly voice spilled sour breath against my cheek.

The younger man swung around, glaring at me. "What's going on?"

"Fool. You were about to lose your purse. Must I always protect you like a child?" The older man still had my wrist, and now my shoulder too. He was far, far stronger than he looked and his hold on me hurt like hell. I stood still and waited, trying to pivot on the balls of my feet, ready to run like mad as soon as I could twist away. The younger man looked down his nose at me. "A slum brat. Call the Watch."

"I didn't do anything," I said quickly, which was true. "And I wasn't going to do anything," which was a lie.

The older man squeezed down against my knuckles, forcing my

fingers open. The little blade had already cut into my palm, which was bleeding. I dropped the knife. The two women had bought their brace of quail and came bustling over, a flurry of brown feathers. A crowd of people had now encircled us, eager for any drama which might add interest to a morning's shopping. I could see Richard's little red head and worried face peeping between someone's legs. There were shouts of take her to the sheriff, get the bailiff, or call the constable. But the older woman stood between me and the mob. She was elegant and pleasant faced. "Who was the child stealing from?" I liked her pale blue eyes and the dimple at her mouth.

"Me," said the youth, sullen. "And I've seen this slut before."

The younger woman was little more than my own age, pretty with long fair plaits coiled tight to her face. "Poor foolish Malcolm. Then run and get the guard." I blushed. She was the sort of person I would have liked for a friend. They weren't married, for her hair was uncovered, so I wondered if the sullen young man was her brother even though they looked nothing alike. This Malcolm was dark and thick browed. She was dainty and blonde. I was absurdly ashamed and sorry that I was who I was and had done what was, in fact, something I did almost every day, and had never been ashamed of before.

"No, don't," said the older woman at once. "We really don't want to draw any more attention to ourselves. After all, the child didn't get away with anything. Let her go."

"It's too late. The crowd will lynch her," said the girl.

"They won't." I was red faced and squirming by now. "Just set me free and I'll run."

The older man did not loosen his grasp. "Where do you come from? Where do you live? Do you have a father?" His voice was intrusive and sharp. I hated his face so close to my own and I hated his breath. He held me in one clamped claw as the fingers of his other hand began to crawl around me, first along my jaw, rubbing against my cheek as if testing a plum to see if it is ripe, and then down my neck towards my breasts. I cringed and shuddered.

"My father's dead. I don't live anywhere." I hung my head, looking contrite and avoiding the man's eyes. "I have to steal to eat. But I won't do it again. I promise to be good. Just let me go."

He smiled but his lips disappeared into his tight black beard and it looked more like a snarl. "A waif with no family. This one could be useful to us."

The older woman grabbed my other shoulder, pulling me away from him. Her fingers dug into my collar bone. "No. Don't. Too many people have seen us with her. Do what I told you and set the little trollop free."

He released me so suddenly that I stumbled and nearly fell. Then I reeled into balance and ran like fury without looking back. Some of the crowd began to follow but they soon lost heart. Without the victim's compliance, there was little adventure to be had. Lifting my skirts, I ran until my ribs hurt and my stockings rolled down to my ankles. I was half blinded with my hair in my eyes, but I could smell the river, rancid with sewerage where it was trapped under London's wide stone bridge. Filth caught in the eddies between the pillars and their wide bases. Then I heard the great balloon of noise from the nearby tavern and knew a cock fight would give good cover. I could disappear entirely amongst the crowd. So I slipped around the back and edged into the squash. Respectable women would never be seen at a cock fight, but no one would ever have accused Tilda of respectability.

The betting was furious. The cockers held their birds to the ground in the centre of the arena, two lithe fowl vivid in crimson, bronze and golden feathers, pimply necks part plucked and straining, eyes wickedly bright. At a call, the men released their birds and the cockerels sprang, flying at each other's heads. I looked away, pushing to the back, my small body lost in the shoving excitement. The darker cockerel was the larger, beating his huge wing spread. It sprang and slashed. Its spurs caught the other's breast but fell in a pointless fluff of loose black quills. Both strutted, darting and gnawing, beaks like polished metal, crests catching the low sunlight in gorgeous iridescence. Soon the blood was seeping into the beaten earth beneath their claws, each lunge a wound. I had my head turned away when the larger was impaled by the smaller's talons and fell squirming in pools of pumping scarlet. The crowd was hooting, the victor's owner beaming as he lifted his proud, quivering bird, chest to loving chest, while the dying fowl was carried off by its feet, ready for the boiling pot. Tilda cared nothing for the birds, but I felt sick and turned away.

Though cautious, she was looking around for another purse to steal when she saw again the sour man with the tight black beard who had caught me in the market. He was collecting his dues, having bet on the winner. The thin sagging lines between nose and jaw wrinkled up into a sallow smile and black uneven teeth, an old man aroused by blood and pain and the death he had witnessed and profited by. He was alone, no wife or friend to hold him back. He had not expected to see me anymore than I to see him, but when he noticed me his glee was pronounced. He strode forward and grabbed my wrist. His breath was on me again, black breath that made me sick, hot and dark and full of a strange harsh power. I felt a panic I had not experienced since a child. Then the man was called to take the purse he'd won and had to let me go. I pushed between the throng and ran.

I sat on the river bank, catching my breath and feeling the sun soothe the back of my neck. I rubbed at my wrist. The marks of the man's fingers still imprinted my skin like thin red tattoos. I felt nauseous. It wasn't fear or all the running or even anger. It was as if I had swallowed the man's exhalation as he had bent down over me, peering into my eyes. There had been something wrong with his breath. I spat, as if I could spit out smoke. I was still bleeding a little from where my own knife had cut my hand as he'd grabbed me in the market. I wiped it on the stubby grass. Then I noticed that where I spat, tiny green globules glistened. I got up and walked the way the river ran, towards the bridge's shade where it would be cool and dark.

It was upriver from the busiest wharves. Here the buildings stood back a little from the sloping banks, for in winter flooding was common. I kept walking. It was the way home.

I walked slowly because I was still out of breath and because I still tasted bile and disgust. Then I realised that there was a bundled black shadow at the point where the bridge's first arch met the waters. I went down a little towards it. Often dogs were tied in sacks and thrown to drown. Sometimes babies. A child born without arms or wits would be quickly hidden and killed. Someone said a two headed baby had been found floating in the river just a month back. I didn't want to find something like that but I was prepared to save any creature left to die if I could. Once I had felt abandoned myself. I had slept under this bridge for many chilly nights before Vespasian found me.

I would have liked Vespasian to find me now, but Vespasian wasn't at home. We didn't know when he'd be back. He had gone away again, this time to one of the northern castles where the king was staying. The king had summoned him to a hunting party. No one disobeyed the king.

The fish were jumping and the Thames ran blue. London's sewerage had not entirely slimed its muddy currents, and though it stank, it was a great place for fish, fresh water crabs, eels and wading birds. Tilda didn't mind the smell. She had sometimes washed herself upstream in the river, though the city's bath houses were not too far away, and if it was cold she didn't wash at all.

As I approached the bundle under the bridge, the sky suddenly darkened. A black cloud rolled up from the west and the sun went out. A wind blew down my back and I shivered. Then the sun eased back, pushing out from the cloud cover, and all the world seemed sweet again. I went under the bridge.

It was a body, stretched out in the mud. Her hand reached into the water, limp fingers dappling in the eddies. She lay on her stomach and I couldn't see her face, but it was a woman all wet and weighed down by the weight of sodden skirts and a mud soaked pelisse. I was fairly sure she wasn't breathing. I bent down beside her, wondering what to do, tempted to run. I was choking on my own breath. Then I realised that the little stained pelisse was familiar, its soft blue edges trimmed with rabbit fur, still visible beyond the ragtaggle clots of sludge and black water stains. My hand was shaking as I touched the body and tried to turn the face. She was stuck, too heavy to lift. I tried again, calling softly that I would help her, even though truly I knew she was dead. Squatting, my precious shoes oozing mud, I grabbed the body around the waist. My fingers seemed to become lost in her flesh, as if some part of her was missing. I shrank back, wondering if the fishes had eaten her stomach away. But the rest of her was too fresh, her little hand was smooth, and I was sure she had only just recently drowned.

Then I managed to turn her. She rolled over in the mud as I tugged, and her poor face spun around to stare at me, open eye sockets empty. It proved what I had already begun to suspect, for this was Isabel.

But this was not the Isabel I knew. All her beauty had been ravaged. Before or after death I had no idea, but they had put out her eyes and they had cut off her nose. They had ripped open her throat and they had slit her sternum. Most horrible of all to me, crunched over there in the dirt beside the body, I saw that one hand and one foot had been flayed. All the skin and flesh had been rolled back like fleece from a lamb, and the tiny blood flecked bones revealed up to the wrist and the ankle.

I rocked backwards and forwards, trying to distance myself from this horror, gagging and panting. I was barely hanging onto consciousness. Then I knew I was fainting. I couldn't stay. A huge dizziness and a black force swamped me like iced rain and I tipped forwards.

I saw lights and a whirling fire. I was lifted. For a moment I thought I flew. Weightless, I was cradled.

Someone had taken me from the tumbled mud and the sad side of my friend's small mutilated corpse and was nursing my head against his shoulder. I felt the soft black wool of his cotte and the long row of tight wooden hooks against my cheek. He smelled of muscle and sweat and male protection. His hands were long and hard and held me very tight. On one finger he wore a heavy gold ring, carved with a six pointed star and studded with a large ruby. It was a ring I recognised. Even in our greatest poverty and close to starvation, he had never sold his ring, so I knew he must have considered it important.

My weight seemed insignificant to him and he held me easily.

With a sigh of complete relief muffled by confusion, I curled in towards his chest and raised my face to his. I gazed up at him, and at last, he looked down on me. He was very dark, and his eyes were quite black. "Hush, my quicksilver child," he murmured. "This is a place you must not be." He was Vespasian.

CHAPTER EIGHT

When I awoke I was still crying but I was Molly again and in my sprung bed with the quilt around my chin and all the tears gathering in the damp tangles of my hair.

I heard Tilda's voice gasping at me from somewhere far, far away. "It can't be Isabel. It can't be her." But I was back with the pink flowered wallpaper and the crushing disgust and the nightmare that was now only in my head.

Bertie's worried frown focused over me. He shouldn't have been in my bedroom, but he told me I'd been yelling. Bertie was furrows and loose skin. Since Wattle had died, he'd gone grey and gravity bound. "What the hell is going on?"

I sat up, clogged by surreality. "Bertie, I'm going mad."

"We both are." He only muttered these days, as if he didn't have the heart to talk out loud.

"I'm living in two worlds," I raved at him. "My dreams take me back in time. I'm someone else. I'm Matilda and I live in London and my friend has been murdered. I'm truly, honestly going mad." He patted my hand and tried to smile a sort of half hearted reassurance. To him, poor dear, bad dreams must have seemed a logical consequence of what we were going through. His own dreams must have been frightful.

"I'll make tea," he said. "I'll make us some breakfast."

I grabbed his arm. "Bertie, there's more than that. There's things I never told you about when we were married."

"That doesn't matter now, dear. Don't worry about the past."

"You don't understand." I insisted. "I've had strange daydreams since I was a kid. Sort of visions, really. I used to float off to another place every time I was frightened, or life got too upsetting or even just plain dull."

"Children do that." Bertie sighed, and his eyes clouded over. "Wattle said she had a dream place to escape into. Do you mind me talking about her? It was a magic waterfall. It always calmed her down. She said it was healing too."

"Wattle was lovely, Bertie, I know that. But, like you told me once, I'm not such a nice person as she was. My magic place wasn't all peaceful and beautiful. Mine was dark and damp and it came and took me in whether I wanted it or not. I mean, it wasn't some place I imagined for peaceful dreams. It was rat infested, for heaven's sake, and smelly. I went there for years and years, often when I least expected it."

"Lots of children have night terrors. You had a bloody hard childhood. I've often wondered what it must have been like for you. Awful, with a mother like yours. Poor kid, I expect you always had nightmares."

I nearly gave up. Whether Bertie understood me or not really didn't change anything. It was me just trying to offload more problems on a man who already had his back broken. But I continued a little longer. I hoped that talking aloud might help me make more sense of it myself. "Not always at night and not always when I was asleep. In fact, usually I was awake. But I just sort of accepted all that as part of my life when I was little and so I grew up with it. It seemed normal. But now, Bertie, it worries the fucking hell out of me, because I've started really going there. Now it's alive and I'm alive in it. I go between that life and this one."

"I think," said Bertie reluctantly, "you just need to calm down a bit, Mol dear. Perhaps you need counselling."

"You mean a psychiatrist."

"Maybe. I mean, couldn't this be a case of split consciousness? What do they call it? Multiple personalities? Sorry to say it Mol, but you fit the criteria. Abused childhood, deprived of love, all that stuff. Now it would be aggravated, wouldn't it, with what's happened?"

I actually suddenly believed him. In that moment, it made sense. I gasped and leaned back against the propped pillows and a black wave washed me with such disgust that I thought I would be sick again. "My God. That's true. I could really be mentally deranged, couldn't I?" But what I didn't say aloud, because I couldn't possibly say it, and what was making me stutter and lurch, was that Wattle's murder had been committed by a mad person, and if that was what I was, then I could have done it myself.

"Mol, slow down," groaned Bertie. "I'm not qualified to give any diagnosis, you know that. It's just an idea. I'm an insurance broker, not a psychologist. I don't think I can cope with this now."

"Yes, I know," I said. "Mad daughter of a mad mother. I'm sorry, truly sorry Bertie dear." Abject sincerity. "I'll get up. You make the tea and I'll be down in a minute. Don't take me seriously, Bertie dear. I'm not myself."

Not myself? No, I wasn't. I was half me and half Tilda and what Bertie had suggested was making me reel. Bertie smiled and nodded and tottered off, glad to get away from the crazy woman in the attic.

The central heating had switched on its automatic timer, but I was cold and shivering. I huddled into my dressing gown and trailed downstairs. Bertie was bustling, trying to keep his head off whatever chaotic nonsense his ex-wife was trying to confuse him with. He pushed a T-bag into the teapot and poured lukewarm water over it. His tea was always piss foul, but I drank it and thanked him. My laptop glared at me from the kitchen table and I hunched over it, as if it might talk to me or offer me some more tangible escape. Bertie scurried off, leaving me to whatever neurosis he suspected I had. My feet were freezing. I pulled the corners of my dressing gown down over them and held it wrapped by curling my toes. I clutched the mug of tea and peered into its sad little wisp of insignificant steam. It made my nose damp. Isabel didn't have a nose anymore. Someone had cut it off.

Although I knew many experts denied that multiple personality disorder existed as a genuine medical condition, if it did, that was what I had. Except that there were problems with that as well, for the two personalities weren't totally separate. As Molly, I remembered everything that had happened when I was Tilda. When I was Tilda, although her innocence took precedence and she seemed to have no knowledge of any other presence within her being, I myself was still aware. I could be her and live her life and accept all the restrictions of her simplicity, but I knew also my own background. I remembered electricity and mechanics and television and computers and being Molly. Being Tilda I could speak and understand as others spoke the ancient English of the early thirteenth century, but I thought and heard in the modern words I knew as myself. So as I believed, terrified, the possibility that I was mad, I also knew that I was not. Believing something and knowing it are different.

I couldn't face writing, so I made a decent hot pot of tea and took it back to bed. Then I decided something else. Tilda could not ever comprehend the electrical advantages I took for granted and she could not possibly imagine all the amazing changes that had been discovered or invented in the time between her world and mine. Anything she might glimpse would frighten her and seem like madness and magic. Now, in my own fear, I was as blind as she. What was happening to me with time shifts and split consciousness was beyond my understanding. There was no explanation in modern science but that didn't mean I was insane. This didn't have to be magic. Such processes just hadn't yet been discovered. What Tilda didn't know, had still existed, misunderstood but unaffected by the world's ignorance. She knew only the inconsistencies of guttering candle light, but she had been born at the same time as her father had been killed by electricity. I knew nothing of the mysteries of time or the budding quantum science that fascinated others, but sometimes I occupied the mind and body of a girl, far younger than myself, who had lived eight hundred years ago. Simply because I didn't know how – didn't stop it being real. I wasn't mad, but I was haunted. Now murder touched me in both dimensions and I had no escape from terror.

I apologised properly to Bertie that evening. "Dreams," I explained. "I'd woken suddenly from a nightmare. I don't need a psychiatrist. Don't worry."

With bleary, blood mazed eyes, Bertie looked like the madman, and his nightmares were haunting him too, though presumably they weren't as complicated. "I know. It's not you I'm worried about."

"We'll both get through it. And I'll help you more. If you need anything, just ask." With my own pseudo knowledge of psychiatry, I thought Bertie had always been insecure. He had a lot of rather inconsequential charm and had been deliciously handsome when I married him, but he'd started his infidelities after just a few months, though because of my own insecurities I'd refused to believe it for the first couple of years. Neither of us had been exactly lucky in love, if such a cliché ever needed saying. Bertie had married a neurotic harridan, got divorced, finally fallen in love and then lost the love of his life to a hideous slaughter before the affair had even tumbled into stability. He needed the hugs and cuddles I now tried sometimes to give him – but heavens, he was my ex-husband. You don't cuddle ex-husbands. So I felt desperately sorry for him, but I was in need of a lot more than just cuddles myself.

Once, long ago, I'd had such pleasurable expectations. For days, I mourned them. Then, three days later, I woke with the sunshine and sat up suddenly. "Snow," I said to an empty room. "There must have been footprints."

When Wattle had left my house it had stopped snowing and it had not snowed again that night for I had found Wattle's tyre marks when I went out. I had gone walking in the morning and loved the traceries of footprint and stories trodden into the white crust. Later it had snowed again but not for some hours. Wattle and her murderer must have left footprints in the woods. The police had not told me about that, but they must have found something. Even spoiled by the playing children who had found Wattle's body, footsteps must still have been visible.

I didn't discuss it with Bertie. In fact, we hadn't seen much of each other for the past three days which had suited both of us, but we'd watched some television together and pretended to be cosy the evening before. There had been a repeat of an old sitcom and Bertie had actually laughed a little.

For another two days I kept thinking about footsteps in the snow and eventually I phoned the police. I didn't really expect them to tell me their secrets but I needed to ask. After hanging on for what seemed like an hour, a woman's voice asked me if I'd like to come down to the station and talk to their detective inspector. I said yes at once.

He was tall and solid and practical. "I'll be honest," he said, sitting across the desk from me. I'd been brought coffee. He lit a cigarette and coughed. "We don't have any real leads. The whole case is very worrying. If you have any information at all, it's extremely important that you tell us. We'll keep it anonymous of course, unless we need you as a witness at the trial."

Trial? God – that was optimistic. I shook my head. He had misunderstood. "I'm sorry, no, that's not what I came for. It's just that I've been worrying about the idea of footprints. I mean, it had snowed really heavily. Wattle had walked a mile from her car into the woods. Whoever killed her had probably gone with her or followed her. What about footprints?"

The inspector leaned back in his chair and put the tips of his fingers together, peering at me over them. He looked disappointed. "I'm afraid we don't want any more detailed information getting out to the press at this time. We just need to get on with the investigation."

In other words, I should mind my own business. They were onto it, but that didn't need to include me. "I know. I wouldn't pass on anything. I want the newspapers to forget all about us, even more than you do. It's just that I've been haunted about the footprints thing. It took me some time to think of it, and now I just can't forget."

He was kind. He knew what a revoltingly awful situation I was in and he had all the experience in the world to know that I wasn't sleeping and that my questions and confusion were driving me mad. "I can't make a habit of this, Miss Susans." I smiled. It meant that this time at least, he was going to answer me. "I shan't be explaining police procedure in the future or going into any further details unless I believe it will help the investigation. I would also appreciate it if you would keep this quite private." I nodded, encouragingly. He went on. "The fact is, Miss Davidson's footsteps were clearly visible walking from her car, through the trees and on to the place where she was found. It wasn't a direct route. She seemed to be walking slowly and wandering a little. At one point it appeared that she walked in a circle. There appeared to be no haste. But then under the tree where she was discovered, there was a certain confusion and finally some signs of a struggle. But there was absolutely no sign of another person. No other actual footprints except her own were visible. We were able to exclude the small prints of the young children who found her body and the only other thing we discovered were some regular, deep holes, most unusual marks, like the claws of an animal poked into the snow."

Animals didn't hang their victims up in trees, raped, staked and tortured. "You mean a lion or something? Something escaped from a zoo?"

"No, I don't mean that, Miss Susans," said the inspector, exhaling smoke with a dissatisfied wheeze. "These belonged to no known species either wild or domesticated. In fact, more like a gigantic toad, according to our experts."

CHAPTER NINE

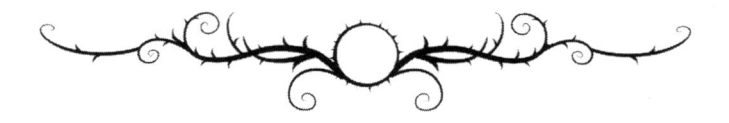

It was a week later when I caught up with Tilda again. Meanwhile it was still bitterly cold and sharp winds blasted past my chimneys and rattled my cottage windows. Winter's end might have brought a degree or two less frost, but it carried none of Tilda's balmy warmth and pale sunshine. The whole of March in my world rained like fury. On my birthday, I thought of building an arc. The wisteria which scrambled along the front of my cottage and sometimes caught its leaves in the front door's squeaky hinges was coming into bud but would need more sunny encouragement to peep into blue flower. Lying in bed at night I could hear the patter and scurry of mice in the roof. They used the wisteria as a ladder and sometimes they ate the buds when other food was scarce. Mice nesting above my ceiling had never bothered me. They rarely sneaked into the house and I hardly ever saw them though I wished they'd leave my pretty blossoms alone. At least these weren't the big brown rats that Tilda took for granted. I worried about Tilda. I worried about how she was coping. I wanted to cuddle her up and wrap my arms around her and make her safe. Which was utterly stupid, because she was me.

On the morning of the twenty third of March I woke with a headache. I could hear the insistent thrum of the rain again and a strong draught made me shiver. I tried to turn, to reach for the paracetamol on my bedside table, something I'd been needing a lot lately. I touched only straw. The prickle of wool was up around my neck and the itch of straw around my body. I was fully dressed and my skirts were entwined between my knees, restricting movement. It was dark. A voice said, "You must get up now, ma petit. There's a great deal to discuss. You're the last to wake. Richard is making porridge."

I couldn't see anyone and footsteps soft-echoed down creaking wooden stairs. I sat up, groaning, wishing I'd brought headache pills with me, then realised how absurd that was. I rolled to the wooden floor. I was barefoot and wondered where my beautiful new shoes had gone. With an effort, I reassembled my thoughts and memories, transfusing myself into the right personality, grasping where and what.

Downstairs it was warm with the fire spitting on the big stone hearth. A large black pot swung from its iron bracket over the flames, bubbling oats and goat's milk. The children sat cross legged, faces turning to me as I sat down next to Osbert. Eight fat chickens were clucking in one corner, keeping their distance from the fire. The baked earthen floor was soaking up heat. I saw my little shoes nearby, left to dry off their mud and river water. I couldn't see Vespasian.

Richard spooned thick pale porridge onto rough wooden bowls. It wasn't the sweet taste I was used to and I didn't like it much but Tilda was hungry and enjoyed it. We all ate fast and no one was smiling.

I heard Vespasian's voice behind me and I twisted around to see him. As usual his tone was low and soft and demanded absolute silence in order to hear each word. "I have to decide our next move," he said. "Every one of you is free either to come with me, or to go his own way." He had not shared our breakfast oats but now I was sitting at his feet, watching him. His ankle bones, snug in the faded black wool of his hose, were right next to me and I found myself gazing at the muscles of his calves. His legs were long, elegant and powerful but their slim grace did not hide the ferocity of his strength. I found myself looking too long, and blinked, embarrassed. But he didn't notice. Although he was talking to us, he was staring into the fire. It was the first time I could watch him properly. The sinuous muscles of his upper arms were pronounced and taut through the thin white linen, and the outlines of his nipples showed dark. Below the long belted shirt, he wore only hose and boots. I already knew him to be a strong man. I wondered then whether he might once have been a knight for he looked nothing like the peasant I had earlier imagined he must be. Then he suddenly became aware of my scrutiny and looked down on me. I must have blushed. I had never looked directly into such eyes before.

He raised one eyebrow. "Sorry," I whispered, and because I took it as a question, "I didn't mean to stare. But I think we'll all want to come with you."

The boys were nodding furiously. "What else would we do?" demanded Gerald.

"It means the forest," said Vespasian. "You know that."

"It'll be an adventure," said Stephen.

Vespasian squatted down next to me and took my hand in his, which surprised me. His hands were very dry and hard, ridged from sword and reins. His fingers seemed unusually long, and the rich crimson of the ruby set into his ring caught the firelight, turning to blood, and making me shiver. "There is no adventure," he said. "It'll be cold, it'll be damp. You often go hungry now. In the forest, that could happen more often. I can no longer return to king or court for revenue. We shall be exiles."

Hugh was the oldest of us all now Isabel had gone. He was frowning and shaking his big square head. He wasn't the most intelligent. "Maybe – I'm not sure – perhaps I won't come. And anyway, I don't understand. Why do we have to run away? None of us did this foul thing. We ought to be safe staying here and I don't see why not. None of this is my fault. It's not fair. I don't want to live in trees."

"None of us do," said Walter. He rubbed his button nose with the back of his fist and I wondered if he was trying not to cry. "But we don't have any choice. When the sheriff finds out who Isabel was, he'll come here. We're thieves so we'll all be dragged off to the gallows.

Who'll care that we didn't do it? They'll say – thieves are all murderers. Hang them."

"I don't mind living in the forest," repeated Stephen. "It's exciting. I'll build a hut up in the branches."

"And be caught and castrated for poaching the king's deer," I found Tilda saying.

"None of you are listening," said Vespasian very slowly, reaching through our ignorance, explaining the depths of the danger. "Isabel wasn't killed for profit, this was far beyond the brutality of simple rape, and she wasn't murdered in revenge for the purse she had stolen, which was still on her belt. She was mutilated and butchered and tortured for the pleasure of the killer. We are talking about darkest magic. Yes, we are an odd assortment, a gang of thieves, and for involvement in theft and sorcery, we would hang. I do not intend to hang. But there is also danger from the magic itself. The forest will not protect us from that, but it will conceal our whereabouts for the moment. I am going into exile and any of you who have the sense to come, I promise to protect with whatever ability remains to me. It is up to you."

"There's hundreds of outlaws in the forests," said Gerald. "Does that make it more dangerous? But if they can live there, so can we."

"And we have Vespasian, which no one else has," said Tilda.

I heard Vespasian laugh. "Yes, you have me. Whatever consolation that gives you, has ever given you, it continues. But remember, I shall be the hunted now, not the hunter. And I will be deemed more guilty than any of you." He stood again, letting go of my hand, but he was still looking at me. "You, Tilda, I could find you work in some castle or country estate. You'd be safe enough. You of all of us, need not come into the forest."

"I don't want to be a laundry maid," said Tilda, affronted. "I was born a serf but now I'm free. Since I've known you, I've always been free. I want to come into the forest with all of you and stay free."

Vespasian nodded. "Exile isn't freedom, but it's better than serfdom or slavery and it's better than gaol and hanging. Then it's all of you, except perhaps Hugh? We leave in a few hours. Pack whatever you want. Bring the hens."

"If everyone's going, then I am too." Hugh chewed his lip.

I saw there was already a sack, heavy cloth and tied with cord, waiting by the door, Vespasian's belongings, and little enough at that. "What about the beds? What about the pots?"

"Forget the beds and pots," he said briefly, turning on his heel. "Bring the blankets and pillows. I've sold everything else to Jack Saddler. There's very little time so never mind talking. Do whatever you have to."

I wanted Tilda to say that all of us leaving immediately and suddenly like this was going to look terribly guilty. Modern concepts still influenced me. I wanted her to say that we should stay, act innocent, help any official inquiries and cooperate with the investigation. Luckily Tilda wouldn't say it for me. Instead she said, "I'm ready now. I don't own anything so I haven't got anything to pack."

"Then help the others," said Vespasian.

It was raining more heavily when we left and I pulled my hood over my head. In minutes I was soaked and my little red shoes were splashing mud again. I carried a stiff sack with a fat chicken bundled up in my woollen bedcover, and a lump of brown bread. The chicken, tucked into the dark, had gone to sleep. It would wake soon when the rain soaked through to its feathers. Then it would wriggle and be heavy. The bread would go mouldy, but we'd eat it anyway. I wondered what it would be like in the forest in weather like this.

It was early afternoon, and the clouded sun was directly above our heads as we walked. We walked fast, keeping up as good a pace as was possible under the slosh and pelt. We didn't leave all together. Vespasian had gone ahead with Hugh and Stephen. I walked with Richard and Walter. Osbert and Gerald would be the last to leave and padlock the house. Jack Saddler already had the key.

We lived not far from the river and it took no more than a few minutes to dodge through the back streets, avoiding scavenging dogs and the piss pots emptied from upstairs windows, keeping tight to the walls and away from the central gullies and their dirt and slime splashed into sloppy puddles by the rain.

We crossed the Bridge above where Isabel had been slain. Wide, solid and proud, now it held a menace I'd never felt before. Straddling the surging river in pale stone, London's only bridge sat on twenty squat supporting pillars disappearing down into the surging water, with two wide gates above, a chapel, a central tower and poles for the heads of those recently executed for treason. This day no stinking, grinning faces watched our passing from empty eye sockets, and the gibbet beyond the far end also hung empty, jangling in the rain. I pattered behind the boys, head bent, my cloak drenched, clutching my sack of baggage over my shoulder, avoiding the push and shove coming from the opposite direction. There was always a crush during the day, the main thoroughfare leading into the city from the squash of Southwark and the countryside beyond. A group of tinkers was dancing and singing in the rain, quickly elbowed aside by three soldiers slouching past, knotted fists to their sword hilts, swearing into their beards, glaring at all of us. I stood back quickly to let them through. Behind was a flurry of sheep and the farmer with his crook hurrying them on, waggle tailed and bedraggled, wool as sodden as that of my cloak.

Narrow shops leaned both sides and hid the river from view; shop keepers sat in their doorways, shouting for business; the clank of hammers and the smell of leather and wax filled the air. Then before passing the great chapel, the wind whistled through and the dark water was visible. Richard didn't look down but I did. The Thames was turgid, high tide and churning. The place where I had found the body was now under water. It had been horribly close to the place where I had slept in London. I shook my head and hurried after Richard and Walter.

The far bank led first past the stink and steam of the blacksmiths and the taverns on either side, then through darker streets, sudden angles and turns, and finally straggled up into neat open gardens with their little rows of peas, parsley and turnips. Far beyond the gentle meadows, the forest crept in to shadow the muddy roadway and suddenly we were under the trees. At first there were cottages, goats and oxen grazing and chimney-holes in roofs puffing wood smoke. But soon the trees closed us into sunless damp with the steady rain intermittent and stifled by branch, needles and leaf. It smelled sweet to me after the sour sweat of London's rank tumble, but I was getting cold and the thick squelch of loamy leaf mould underfoot was leaking up into my stockings.

Walter knew where to go though I did not. I only recognised the first few green paths into the wood. We passed a moss crowned stone where Tilda had sat many times, to think, to be on her own and to watch the river sparkle below. It was where she had been sitting to ease bleeding feet as she first arrived, ten years old and following great Watling Street to the city from her mother's serfdom and West Country croft. It was when she had seen me in a sudden ghostly vision and been afraid.

It was many hours that we walked, hurrying now, until twilight slunk into first dark. A slivered slice of moon was behind the bare tree branches. I heard Vespasian's soft call.

We had arrived. It had stopped raining.

They had built a fire and though it spluttered and sparked with wet wood, it was wonderfully welcome and the smoke puffed out like little greenish grey waves on a blustery day, deliciously hot and bright in the dark closure of the night. All Hugh's nerves and resentment had passed and he was chuckling and prancing like a child, throwing dead wood he'd collected into the flames. Stephen and Vespasian were chopping the bigger logs and stacking them under a leaning shelter.

But what I had least expected, and what I now gazed at with delight, stretched behind the clearing and its dancing bonfire, was the long, low house with its wide thatched roof and its little row of shuttered windows. I had not expected a house.

CHAPTER TEN

Tilda stood in wonder. "It's Vespasian's own house," said Stephen proudly. "None of us knew. Isn't it beautiful?" The rain had stopped though a silver drizzle hung like a halo in the dusk washed air and I felt damp spangles on my face. The narrow moon was peering from the rich navy blue above us.

"Reckon there's lots of old houses in these woods," said Hugh, leaving the fire and coming over to us, arms crossed, puffing out his stomach and beaming like the lord of the manor. "Built before the king declared all this land royal forest of course. But Vespasian never told us about this, did he? What a secret! Look, it's a whole load bigger than the London house, and what a great, grand place it must have been with candles and fires and people. The park all around has grown over, just weed and bracken now, not even a vegetable patch. But you can see how it was once."

I could. Tended by servants and gardeners, bustle and service, glowing and gorgeous. Although neither castle nor huge country estate, this was once a large family home and still promised comfort. The walls stood strong though their wattle and daub was now all naked and the plaster crumbled away, moss threatened as everything leaned inwards. I stared through the dancing flames across to where

Vespasian, shirt sleeves rolled up over those strong tanned arms, continued to chop and stack wood. I wondered why this man had left a house so beautiful and gone to live in a slum with a hoard of orphaned brats. Even once the king had claimed the area, the original owner would surely have had recourse to some compensation. I wondered what the hell had happened to this man in those years I knew nothing about.

"What's it like inside?" I asked Hugh.

It was Stephen who answered, hopping on one foot, eyes bright with excitement, reflecting fire and moon. "Big and empty," he said. "Full of mice and lots of squeaky bats and massive spiders with hundreds of legs. The back door's all broken down, there's trees growing through the stable roof, and bits of walls have collapsed. But we can fix it all up. Vespasian says so."

"Oh yes," I breathed. "We certainly can. It's a palace." I knew Tilda would never dare ask Vespasian what had happened here nor what had happened to him. It would remain a mystery. His destiny was not mine and touched me only by coincidence. My curiosity would have to smoulder until it tarnished and faded. But I had the joys of the present.

"Stephen and I went through it all when we got here," said Hugh. "But Vespasian stayed outside and sort of stared. I reckon he doesn't want to go inside."

"Memories," muttered Stephen, eyes shining.

Hugh said, "Go on. Explore. He never stopped us." Richard was already scampering up the high doorstep. I followed him in a rush, as if afraid someone would disapprove. Walter grabbed at my arm and came behind.

We stood on the threshold like the band of scared kids we were and as if we had never seen any house before in our lives. Directly inside the hall was high beamed. A huge heavy legged table still stood central, scarred and covered in straw and leaves. The fire place, no central slab but a grand brick hearth built into the wall, was to the left, its ashes scattered across the years. Two rooms led off from a corridor either side but behind the hall, this once charming house was in ruins.

I dug under the accumulation of the encroaching forest and the damp cobwebbed corners. I found no secrets, but I was fascinated. Tilda had lived with Vespasian and the children in London for the past seven years. Others had been with him before her. Someone must know something. I turned to Walter. "Did you know he had a real house only a walk away? Did Vespasian ever mention to anyone why he came to live in London in the first place? What do you know about him?"

Walter stared. "What a pillicoot you are, Tilda. When did Vespasian ever explain himself to anybody? Certainly not to any of us."

We pushed each other out of the way and scurried through the other doors. One led beyond a corridor and into what was obviously the kitchen block. The remains of the cooking fires were blackened brick alcoves along one wall, still set with pot hangers and fire irons, a great roasting spit and the cauldrons dumped amongst the cold sooty charcoal. Leading off was a pantry lined with shelves, what might have been a dairy, churns and vats now rusted and broken, and beyond that smaller rooms now in ruins. "This would have been big enough to cook for real gentry," muttered Richard, awed. "Even royal hunting parties." He was imagining feasts. Those used to permanent hunger pangs could dream of little better.

"Maybe Gerald knows something," Walter said to me, shaking his head. "He was the first one Vespasian ever took in. As a baby I think. So Gerald has to know more than the rest of us. More than me anyway. Who'd have the courage to ask?"

I couldn't imagine Vespasian looking after a baby. I certainly couldn't imagine him changing nappies. Did medieval kids wear nappies? Well, they had to wear something, and they had to drink milk and that meant milking goats and filling bottles and burping the child afterwards and rocking it and staying up nights. For a moment I was lost in absolute amazement. But there was too much to explore, too much scurrying, giggling and excitement, with no time for thinking. Tilda ran through the tumbledown rooms, imagining grand balls, fiddlers and troubadours, dancing, whispering and romantic liaisons. Her adoration for Vespasian banished suspicion. She had no need to know all his past. "I'll sweep up the kitchen and shoo out the bats," said Tilda. "Richard, get me switches for a broom."

The house was low and one storied but right at the back three broken steps and the wobbling end of a balustrade meant there had been an upstairs originally, not over the hall perhaps since there the ceiling was high and the rafters were carved, but perhaps bedchambers had made a second storey at the rear. There were still sheds and outbuildings and big windows tucked under the thatch, now gazing out only to the trees. Where the roof had once been thick, now it hung in tatters and I could see bird's nests by the rough chimney opening. A tree had fallen across the eastern wall, revealing its pretty chequered layer of straw stuffing and daub. From there, the back had all tumbled and now only a few heaped stones remained. Most of the window shutters at the front were lying loose, but I knew we could make it beautiful again. Even without renewing plaster, without replacing polished timbers or rebuilding walls, I could already breathe in the magic, the smell of fresh growth, of clean running water, the promise of an open sky and birdsong and delicious, sun-spun mystery.

Vespasian kept the bonfire sparking hot outside for we had no way to lock or even close off our sleeping quarters and there might be wild boar in the forest, even wolves. The wolves were all long dead, they said, but the fear of their memory remained. If nothing else, they made good stories to frighten naughty children.

We ate a quick supper of barley pottage and collected dry leaves for our pallet beds. It was the huge kitchen, first roughly swept and cleaned, that became our bedroom. But Vespasian did not come to sleep with us that night. I do not know where he went, though I saw him take a torch and go out into the forest. I did not hear him come back.

I dreamed of myself. It was one of the strangest dreams I have ever had. I was Tilda but I dreamed of Molly and she looked back at me from her wisteria hammock, sorry that she was trapped there and could not come with me into the past and the sun dappled sweetness.

She was frightened of the woods and of what had happened there, but this was a different forest and her distant nightmares did not affect me. When I awoke, the dawn slanted its first shadows and light striped the flurried dust. Vespasian was sitting on the cold ground beside my makeshift bed. He looked down thoughtfully into my face. As always, the black depths of his eyes frightened me. I quickly wedged myself up on my elbow. "I'm sorry," I whispered, blinking back sleep. "Have I done something wrong?" I knew I must be late in rising and felt guilty at once.

He frowned. "I've spoken very little to you since finding Isabel."

I peered at him through the half light, scrabbling to sit up properly, scattering leaves around me. "Haven't I thanked you for finding me?" In effect, he had rescued me. I had collapsed. Seeing Isabel lying butchered had been more than Tilda could stomach, and after the horrors of Wattle, it was more than I could bear too. I had no reason to think anything but kindness of him, but a lurch of doubt made me shiver. I had no idea why he had been there, exactly where Isabel's body lay curled in its agony. He should not have been anywhere near.

So I avoided his gaze and looked meekly into my lap until he snapped me back. Vespasian always demanded focus. "That's entirely unnecessary," he said. "Don't be so timid with me." He kept looking into my eyes, as if he might read what I thought and knew that whatever I thought, I would not be likely to say it.

"You said it was dark magic."

"And so it was." He was still frowning but his voice was more gentle than I expected. "It must have been very hard for you, piccina, to find her like that."

Suddenly, shoving aside the suspicions and plunging upwards from Tilda's childlike self absorption, I remembered how horrible it must be for Vespasian. He had lain with Isabel night after night. He had seen the breasts he had caressed a hundred times now bared and thick with blood, her body split between them. He had seen the woman he knew most intimately turned into an awesome obscenity. I gulped with sudden sympathy. "Did you – love her?" I asked.

He paused. "Love? Good heavens, no." I had amazed him.

"Did you ever bring her to this house?" Tilda's jealousy. My own curiosity.

Vespasian stood, still frowning. He said, "Why would you think that?" He turned away and walked to the half shuttered window.

I really had no idea. "I just wondered. It's beautiful here."

"I haven't been back to this house in nearly twelve years." The subdued sunlight seemed to halo the black sheen of his hair. "Legally it doesn't belong to me anymore. It belongs to the crown. I have no right to bring anyone here, but since the house has been abandoned for so long, I don't believe anyone will trouble us. At least, not yet." He pulled down the remaining shutters, opening the room to the quick rustling breeze and the bright shimmering light. "No, I never brought Isabel here. It would never have occurred to me. I have brought no one here. Not since my wife died."

I don't know why he told me that. I don't think he knew himself and perhaps immediately he regretted it. He turned sharply and left the room. Whatever words of comfort he was originally going to give me, were left unsaid and I was sorry. I crawled from the bed and stretched. The floor was worn flag stones and colder than I was used to. In London the upstairs floor boards had sucked up warmth from the cooking fire below, and the gaps between the timbers had acted as heating vents. Now all that lay below me was stone cut and set over the damp forest ground.

All the others were already outside, building up the fire, cooking breakfast, exploring the forest with tentative steps. The birds were darting tree to tree, disturbed by intruders into their private paradise, and the sky was all drifting clouds. New green was gathering along the branches and sprigs of yellow flowers caught the sun. I wasn't hungry. My mind danced with the words that Vespasian had left unsaid, as well as those he had spoken. I ignored the calls to come to the fire and eat and I wandered off into the first tall shadows.

Isabel's echo remained with me. I wondered if her spirit roamed by my side, whether perhaps she had come into the forest with us after all. I knew nothing about her or where she had come from. I knew nothing about any of these people though now I was one of them. I thought about Wattle and how her death in another forest far from here had somehow mirrored Isabel's murder. The surreal split of my existence, whether I could explain it or not, could not be unrelated. Magic had entered my life and some of it was deep and dark.

It was this life I chose. I feared to open my eyes once I had closed them, in case I might see the worried grey furrows of Bertie's hesitancy, his pink nose and fluttering lower lip gazing down at me. I didn't want the comfort of my own bed. I didn't want electric heat or kettles, mundane modernity and winter barricading my frigid doorstep. I desperately wanted to stay with the springing sunbeams of old England.

Now March brought budding delight. There were herbs growing wild under the trees. I recognised many. Vespasian had taught us all a little herb lore, which he seemed to think significant. Winter's remaining mushrooms still sat fat and brown, embedded in the woody earth. There was a scattering of acorns to be discovered, left over in their autumn leaf nests, now to roast. There were bundles of fresh nettles to boil into soup. Our hens, though waking up damp feathered in such new surroundings, seemed quite unconcerned and busily laid their little white eggs in the dust piled corners of the house. We didn't dare let them outside yet in case we lost them. Richard and Gerald had slings for pebbles and they killed two black crows and a thrush. This gave little enough meat for all of us but in a soup with wild thyme and nettles, they made a good hot broth. Vespasian sat on the wide smooth stone of the high front step with his back against the open doorway, and watched us, legs stretched, half closed eyes, as if he was dreaming of things far away. Perhaps he was. He must have drifted back into the wealth of memory resting within this house. A wife. Perhaps children. I wanted to creep into his dreams.

Over the next few days he cut himself a bow and arrows, each straight as the wind and black fletched with three crow's feathers for the flights. Gerald helped him. With no yew for the perfect bow, Vespasian used unseasoned wych-hazel and made a Welsh style nearly five foot long, then strung it from the horns with strands of hemp. He said it wouldn't last well and would distort after use, but at first it had a perfect cast, though its resistance was too great for any but Vespasian to bend. He made another, just a little smaller, for Gerald. They sat together, Vespasian on a tree stump and Gerald at his feet, while Vespasian measured the correct distance for the centre of the string to the bow with his clenched fist. He spliced arrows, but could only point them in well sharpened wood, hardened in fire.

Day after day they went off together and came back with hare, little red squirrels, quails and a pheasant. I sat beside him one day and plucked the pheasant. Its tail feathers were vivid and glossy in the pale sunshine. Molly would have been clumsy and squeamish, but Tilda knew exactly what to do. I watched my tough sun-browned fingers dance like little needles across the bird's scaly back and the pile of coloured fluff rose in the breeze. I felt Vespasian' eyes on me but I was too nervous to meet his gaze.

Then the weather closed in and it rained for a week. We had begun repairs on the house, working hard each day until sundown. There were solid doors we rehung that now we could shut. We wedged them to keep out foxes. Now beside the broken walls there were spindly twig fences, tall enough for safety if not for warmth. We continued to live close together in the kitchen but it was a wide room and clean now, a warm hearth with a big fire and pots hanging over the flames all bubbling with wonderful smells.

We met no one else under the greenwood. Whatever exiles wandered these great forests, we saw none of them. If they saw us, they kept away. We were too far into the depths for farmers grazing their animals or coming in to collect kindling or chop wood. The king never came to hunt here for it was too near the city to which he had licensed partial self rule under law. He preferred the north. We were left alone. Gradually, stick by stick like the walls, we built our lives. We piled stone, packed with mud and wood, and so stretched our living into other rooms. Now we had a new shared bedchamber, the boys two to a bed and a straw pallet for me to cuddle into on my own. We still ate in the kitchen but used the great draughty hall for hanging meat, storing food and stacking wood to dry. The hens stayed with us in the kitchen but now we let them wander free outside during daylight. We had no cockerel, so no chickens were hatched but our hens were young and fat and in a week, gave us enough eggs to scramble.

Vespasian slept apart. He took a small space which had once been little more than a cupboard or pantry, but now he made it his bed. It was a mattress found already in the house and Gerald helped him pull it into the place of his choice. On a knotted rope slung between heavy wooden sides, it was stuffed with goose feathers, which Richard helped me shake once a week. Once well filled, the feathers had become damp over the years and now collected into lumps which could not have been much more comfortable than my straw and leaves. On fine days, I dragged it outside to air in the sunshine. Tilda seemed determined that Vespasian would sleep well, even if it was alone. Indeed, the bed seemed big enough for four.

She had hoped, though undoubtedly timid and a little scared, that he might take her into his bed since Isabel could no longer share his nights. Tilda retained a surprising ignorance which I found endearing. Though a country child and surely experienced in the mating of animals, there were nervously ashamed confusions within her timorous imagination. With the medieval lack of privacy which so troubled me, Tilda had watched Vespasian take Isabel to bed. She had watched surreptitiously as he had slipped his hands under Isabel's camise, long fingers lifting the skirts, his eyes focused unblinking on her body. Tilda had gazed across the deep gloom at the contrast between his sun darkened hands, the sudden flash of the gold and ruby ring, and the startling white of Isabel's breasts, slim back and buttocks. Even when drunk, Vespasian had always remained fully clothed and utterly silent. Isabel, soon undressed, had sighed and moaned a little into his shoulder. Tilda had sighed too while curling deep into her straw pallet. But Vespasian clearly did not intend Tilda to take Isabel's place and he made no move towards her. Tilda was sorry but I was not. I doubt I could have coped but I admit I was surprised at his reticence. I supposed his easy coupling with Isabel was bred from a different past and perhaps he rescued her from a life of child whoring, just as he had rescued us all from the risks of homelessness. He had certainly made careless use of Isabel, yet intended no such repetition with Tilda. I wondered, momentarily uncomfortable, if he found us unattractive. I wasn't sure if this man was capable of respecting Tilda's innocence, but when she blushed and reached out, shyly touching his hand or brushing carefully against him, he smiled and moved silently aside. Tilda wore dull faded lavender and the round neckline was high and modest. There were no laces to leave loose or belt to tighten. When she tugged the neck a little lower and tried to push out her breasts, fluttered her eyelashes or wiggled her hips, Vespasian looked away, the dimples twitching at the corners of his mouth. Whatever the reason, he now slept alone.

Then, when the weather cleared again and the sun came out and sparkled diamond glitter all around us, Vespasian told us he was going away for a few days. Because of the times we lived in and the way he had trained us, we were an independent band and not one of us complained. Stephen said he hoped wolves would come so that he could prove his own courage in Vespasian's absence but Tilda secretly knew she would sleep badly until he returned. I was roused to curiosity. Tilda would not allow me to ask him where he was going but I managed to say, "Will you discover whether they're searching for us, while you're gone?"

He looked at me strangely, as he often did these days. His fine black hose were threadbare and dust streaked and his glossy black hair was growing wild and long but the pride and arrogant confidence had not changed one jot. I thought he'd ignore my question, but he said, "That is precisely what I want to discover, amongst other things." Then he frowned, which made him look dark and angry, but his next words were mild and unexpected. "Do you have nightmares about finding her?" he asked abruptly.

He often surprised me as much as I now seemed to surprise him. "Yes," I said. "I do. About finding her and how she was and what she must have felt before she died."

Always within the recurring nightmare was Vespasian's appearance at that same terrible minute, but I couldn't tell him that.

Instead, he told me. "And you're troubled, because I was there at just that instant. A strange coincidence perhaps, to catch you as you fell? But clearly not soon enough to save Isabel." I was absurdly nervous. Tilda nodded and looked down without the courage to speak. "Do not quake before me," ordered Vespasian. "I have never beaten you, and it's highly unlikely that I ever shall, in spite of frequent temptation. Stand straight, face me and I shall answer the questions you haven't the courage to ask. This time I choose to explain something to you. There's no reason for you to have more black dreams because of me." Then he surprised me even more. "You see, I believe I know who killed her. These are people I had dealings with long ago. I was aware that Isabel had been manipulated into a particular – call it circumstance. I was following her to find those who were using her. But since I had chosen to follow in the shadows and remain surreptitious, I was far too slow and far too late. This was my fault. But I did not expect what I found."

I gulped. "Shouldn't you tell the sheriff."

"That's neither the way of life nor of the law," said Vespasian with a faint smile. "You are irrepressibly naive. But I intend doing something else considerably more interesting."

I looked straight at him, summoning courage. "I could help," I said.

He stood up at once. His frown deepened into quick irritation. "Under no circumstances. And don't consider meddling. It would be exceptionally dangerous for all of us. I have waited until you are all settled. You will therefore stay here and wait for me." He walked away abruptly, and I felt foolish and rejected, a seventeen year old with the thoughts of a child, who imagined herself thirty one and wise.

CHAPTER ELEVEN

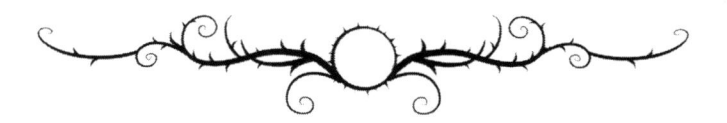

There was a hedgehog in the bottom of my bed and he snuffled from his winter hibernation as I awoke to rain leaking through the thatch onto my nose.

Gerald was rummaging above my head. "It's been dripping all night. How do you sleep through thunder and gales and rain streaming through the roof?" He peered down at me from the rafters where he hung upside down like a tousled marmoset. He was retying the thatch from inside. A hand came through. It was wide, short fingered, extremely grubby, and I recognised it as Walter's. He was presumably on top of the roof.

"I never heard a thing," I said. I'd slept sound and deep, and back in the twenty-first century.

"You'd be no good if wolves broke in. You'd be eaten before you could squeak."

"Winter's gone. We won't get wolves now. If there are any at all, they'll be after the spring lambs and the baby deer."

"Just as well for you."

"Leave her alone," my champion, Richard, bouncing in from outside. He always stuck up for me. "She's as brave as you. Maybe more."

"I wasn't questioning her courage," said Gerald, looking haughty. "Only her ears. When she's asleep, she's as deaf as the blacksmith's wife."

I had dreamed of Molly again. She was struggling with dreams of me, as I was with dreams of her. Our identities were now so tangled, I had forgotten which life had more grip on my belief in myself.

The hedgehog was no comfortable sleeping partner and probably flea ridden. I had fleas myself. The forest hosted a brilliance of insect life, parasites and crawling things. Molly would have been disgusted. Tilda cared very little. There were no rats and the mice were tiny, pink eyed and pretty. Birds still nested in the ragtaggle thatch and a large owl was protecting her egg in a big hole in the oak tree which shaded the kitchen window.

Richard was trying to shave, using the propped surface of an axe as his mirror, his own small penknife as blade. There was not much soap and it was a little slimy. The knife needed sharpening. He only had one shirt and it was now so blotched, it looked as though it had been embroidered.

"You should get Vespasian to teach you first," muttered Gerald, uncomfortably eyeing the third graze seep blood down Richard's stubby chin.

"I did," admitted Richard. "He said I was too young and he wouldn't waste soap."

"Then at least hone your knife," scowled Gerald. "And then I'll show you myself."

"But you always cut yourself too," Richard pointed out.

"Then ask Hugh," said Gerald. "He loves showing how to do things, and anyway, he's the only one with a steady hand."

"Oh, Hugh," Richard, dabbing at the fourth cut, callously dismissed our solid eldest. "It's just that he's too stubborn to admit it hurts him as much as anyone else. But he did mutter about growing a beard the other day."

There was no vellum left in any of the windows and we were back to shuttered draughts as we had been in London, but Tilda loved to sit and look out at the forest and its green shadowed tangle. For hours she sat alone by the kitchen window and waited for Vespasian to return. She wanted him back so desperately, and I tried to comfort her. Life was far more peaceful without him, yet, somehow, there was a dullness, as if everything was a little blurred and muddied. Nothing glowed with the same vibrancy, nothing dazzled. The sun had lost its balm. The routine slunk heavy and there were no moments of sudden delight.

The weather did not improve. There were sunny moments but heavy rains and wind continued and Vespasian did not come back. We kept up the fires, since collecting fallen wood was easy now, but since it was mostly wet, the fires smoked and the house started to stink of it. Gerald and Walter fixed the thatches and I put another family of hedgehogs out into the wet forest patter where they rolled into scruffy balls of timid belligerence. Hugh caught a heron with Richard's sling and we had stew for three days, mixed with wild roots, herbs and weeds. The next day was little more than broth but it was hot and perfumed and we drank it all the same. Without Vespasian's expertise with bow and arrows, food was still scarce but Tilda was accustomed to the nudge of hunger, and now I was too. She pushed up her sleeves, country style, and the skin of her arms was golden tanned and most unfashionable. The chickens now laid every day and we had an egg apiece on every second, counting out our share but keeping some in the pantry in hope of Vespasian's return.

The well overflowed. Its blackened reek was clogged with the rubble of its broken stone rim, the rotten boards of its pail which had long since fallen in, and clambering weed and bracken. No one drank the water from the well. London's water was never entirely safe to drink, the cause of biliousness, rashes and diarrhoea rather than quenching thirst. Ale was preferable. Even sweet mead or light wine was healthier. But this water was truly rank and putrid and no one even tried to lift it. Nearby was a forest stream that silvered over shale and darting minnows. It was the best water we had ever tasted. We collected it in two buckets a day and no one got sick. We took turns, since the buckets were heavy, but Richard always took my turn and I let him, or he would have been cross. He was awfully ashamed of his red hair, but he was proud of his courage, and he copied the chivalry Vespasian had told us about.

I washed, sometimes, in that stream. It was cold with a shock of ice so bitter that it burned but I adored it. There was a pool where the water lay deeper and swirled into little green currents before drifting back into a shallow pebbled meander. Here I stripped under the sun's warmth, the only time I dared be naked, held my breath as a man drowning, and plunged. The water reached my breast and as my lungs shrank, adjusted, and expanded, I sank to my knees and let the water rinse though my hair. We could not afford the hard Spanish soap that once we had stolen from the market but we used a soft soap of tallow grease, potash and soda. I mixed wild mint with mine and scrubbed the grime and wood smoke from my body.

Tilda missed stealing. It had been her daily work and she had been good at it. She felt she had been made redundant. She was not as good at housework as she had been at petty pilfering. I slipped into her memories. As a child she had been taught to sew and to embroider. She could grow rhubarb and make a pink marbled suet pudding that could feed a whole family for three days. Anyone could sweep a floor and truss a bed, but they each kicked their own pallets into shape and helped with the cooking. Tilda did not want to do housework and nobody told her to, though Hugh sniffed sometimes and considered giving orders. But he knew she would argue or ignore him, so he said nothing after all. The other children, except in Richard's secret fantasies, accepted her as just another boy. But Tilda thought of herself as a woman, and in love with Vespasian. I believed him capable of cruelty but her thrill in him influenced me and troubled my nights. Just what Vespasian thought of Tilda, I was no longer sure.

Gerald was practising with the smaller bow Vespasian had made him. The arrows could kill at a greater distance than the pebbles from his sling and he brought down a young male roe deer still in velvet. Tilda wouldn't let me feel sentimental for the big brown eyes and soft wide muzzle. We roasted the carcass on the spit over the kitchen fire, taking turns to slow turn for this meat was too precious to boil. Tilda wished Vespasian was there to share it. Probably, so did Gerald. He would have liked the praise and the glory. If he'd been son to aristocracy or the gentry, he would have been taught archery among many other skills long before now, but as a slum brat and one of a pack of thieves, he had learned only how to steal. The little stag was delicious and his flesh kept us well fed for many, many days. Still Vespasian did not return.

The boys had energy to spare, even Hugh who liked to play leader and was organising further repairs to the back walls. Osbert displayed some expertise with the mud plaster, but it rained too much and there was little time between storms for it to harden. Stephen had whittled himself a wooden handle which he attached to an old nail, making a good dagger and longer than his penknife. It was for skinning the wolves, he said, when he found some to kill. He planned a wolf pelt bedcover before next winter set in.

Osbert, Gerald and Stephen went out looking once. Being vermin, wolf carcasses could bring a payment of up to five shillings. A fortune. But we were exiles, I reminded Gerald. "Don't be a fool. Even if there are any wolves left, you couldn't ask the sheriff for a bounty. They'd put you in gaol instead."

"I'm not officially an exile." He pouted. "There's no warrant. I've never been to court. I'm not guilty of anything. Besides, it doesn't matter. I just want to see the wolves. I want to shoot one." But we didn't see either wolves or boars, nor even foxes. We saw none of the lepers that made their isolated villages in the woods, nor other outlaws, wild men, hunting nobility, or indeed anyone at all.

Tilda and I began to worry about Vespasian. The others thought he was invincible but it had been a very long time since he left us and I began to think he had been killed or taken by the law. One night I imagined him with his long, thin fingers flayed as Isabel's had been. I saw the sun bronzed skin peeled back, the hardened calluses of his palm all removed, the sinews and muscle uncovered before whitened bone protruded. I had seen one of Isabel's hands tortured and now I saw Vespasian's. I heard him scream, long and guttural, and it was the echo of the scream Molly had once heard as she wakened in her own bed.

I was not asleep and I sat up, horrified and doubled over with bilious cramps. Around me the shadows slunk low from the moonlight leaking through the slats of the shutters. I was partially dressed, still in my chemise, as I always slept. The boys were grunting in their shared pallets. The oldest slept in their braies but neither Richard nor Stephen had underpants and they slept naked. Stephen was quite unashamed as he jumped under his coverlet, all grubby knees and grimy feet but Richard was careful to climb into bed unseen by me. His adoration made him shy.

No one woke. I watched them turn, grasping at each other's arms as they moved and twisted, each pulling at the woollen blankets to snuggle more warmth than the other. I got up. I could hear a little eared owl calling shrill, a witch's warning. Peering through the shutters, I could see only the flutter of dark leaf. The creaking of the big door as I opened it did not wake anyone and I tiptoed barefoot from the house, closing the door behind me. I stood on the doorstep, stone polished smooth over the years, high enough to keep out mud and sudden flooding, and perhaps discourage insects. Before me the forest swept in endless marching black, flecked in moon gilded silver. Nothing moved, not even myself.

I could hear my breath heavy and felt it swell in my lungs. There was a great suspense in the stillness. It was a cold night and a faint frost hung like smoke around my nose and mouth and I shivered. Then I realised that I was afraid. My dream of torture and pain still whispered at the back of my eyes but I stayed where I was.

Then I heard the soft stepping of some large animal. Its pace was slow but deliberate and echoed slightly, a vibration that I felt through my toes rather than through my ears.

I expected slanting red eyes and curved teeth. I expected wolves or the pig eyes and slashing tusks of the boar. Most of all I expected some demon, the disguise of the devil, the call of magic and witchcraft, evil and murder. I didn't run back inside. I waited to face whatever it was. The steps came nearer and I recognised the four footed trudge of some weary thing along the path to our house. The creature that approached was high and black as the shadows and as determined as my own heartbeat. Then demons faded back into the undergrowth. Nightmares shrivelled.

Vespasian had come back with a horse and a terrible wound in his shoulder.

CHAPTER TWELVE

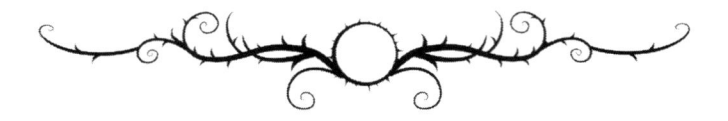

I thought he must fall but he rode up to where I stood and slowly dismounted. Even in the dark I could see the blood still black and wet across his chest. I could smell it. The cloak was thrown back and all the shoulder of the cotte was slashed. He leaned over, clutched the pommel of the horse's saddle, and slid to the ground. I caught him against me for a moment before his height and weight toppled me backwards. I propped both of us upright by the wall of the house. Within minutes the boys had rushed from their dreams and their beds and were helping us indoors.

Vespasian's blood was across my chemise. It was very thick and sticky. I lit the tallow lamp and caught the wicks of two candle stubs from its flame. Osbert and Gerald tried to help Vespasian to his bed but he pushed them away. He slumped into the big chair by the guttering ashes of the kitchen fire. It was the only chair of the house, tall and straight backed though hard, for the cushion had long since rotted away. He leaned back his head and stretched his legs. "Come here," he said. His voice was always low but this time I could hardly hear him.

"I must wash and bind that wound," I said.

"It can wait." I wondered how far he had ridden in that condition and how weak he must be from blood loss. The horse would not have known its way here and could not have guided him. I wondered where he got it. But I didn't ask anything. Vespasian rarely answered questions. "Where's Gerald?" His eyes, half closed, seemed hugely dilated. If we had been in modern times, I would have thought he was drugged.

"It was Gerald helped you in here. Now he's seeing to the horse."

"The horse can wait too." He lifted himself up and stared at me. "Call Gerald. He must stay beside me."

Tilda would have obeyed immediately but now she shared her mind with me and I made her query what she was told. "Why Gerald? Hugh's the stronger. He can protect you better."

"Fool." He slumped down again and looked away from me, as if deciding I wasn't worth attention. Instead he gazed into the scattered embers of the sinking fire. "It's not to protect me, but to protect him. But don't tell him that. He must share my bed. Now, call him. Hugh can tend to the horse."

I did as he told me. Hugh was already outside, struggling with an animal beyond his experience. None of us knew much about horses. Walter came running in and knelt at Vespasian's feet. "We've tethered your horse in the barn, and we've taken off the saddle, but we can't remove the bridle. It wants to bite us and the teeth are so big. I'm sorry. I've never liked horses."

"I do," said Richard, jumping up. He had been getting dressed in the bedroom since he'd never appear naked in front of me. "My dad had a horse for years, a poor sumpter he rescued when our lord whipped it until it bled. It dropped dead at the plough the day before my mother died. But I loved that horse. I can look after yours."

Stephen had been cross legged, sitting beside the kitchen hearth. He sprang up too, following Richard out into the night. Gerald had come back in and sat beside me, both of us at Vespasian's knee. "Now I'll look after you," I said. Vespasian looked at me, then relaxed a little and half smiled.

"If you must be my nurse, then very well. But I doubt the wound is so serious." He looked bitterly weary. I wished I could get him to bed.

Instead, I sent Osbert and Walter out to get water. I set a cauldron full to boil and stoked up the fire. Tilda had some knowledge and I had some too and together we might do well enough.

Vespasian released the clasp of his cloak and I began to undo the laces at his neck and the heavy leather of his belt. I struggled to get the cotte off the shoulder and I know I hurt him, but he continued to smile and looked as if he was bemused that I should go to so much trouble. Then he pushed me away gently and with his right hand, removed the sleeve from his left. "I am not yet so useless," he said. "And I shall be stronger in the morning. Bind the shoulder if you will and then I shall rest." Tilda would be busy repairing the shirt and cotte for the next two days. Vespasian had only one other and clothes were now even harder to get. But what he wore now was new to me and grander than he had worn before. The material was badly slashed, but it was still beautiful. The fine linen of his shirt was almost transparent and its sleeves were detachable. The left side was so heavily blood stained that I had to peel it back, then carefully unpick it from the shoulder. Finally the arm was naked. Vespasian slumped now, his head against the chair back and his eyes half closed, but still watching me and everything I did.

I used rags torn from an old threadbare sheet and began to wash the wound. It was extremely deep and long and unpleasantly wide, hacked into the flesh with a heavy bladed sword. The muscle within lay open. I was no doctor but I knew it should be stitched. "It'll go on bleeding," I said softly, "and become infected. You must have lost too much blood already. That'll make you dreadfully weak. It needs sewing." Tilda had sharp needles in three sizes and fine thread. They had never been designed for human flesh, but they would do.

He was watching my reaction. Vespasian had always been able to see through all of us, especially the women, and this time my expression must have been easily read. The sliced flesh was weeping, folded open like meat on a butcher's block. I felt a squeamish revulsion. I was also absurdly nervous of touching him, half naked in the flickering candle light.

"I am never dreadfully weak," he said with what I suspected to be mild amusement. "I imagine the wound should be cauterized. Unfortunately, it's too high on the shoulder for me to see. I doubt I could manage it myself as yet."

I gulped. "I'd sooner sew it than cauterize it," I said. "I think I can manage that."

"As you wish," said Vespasian. He still seemed faintly amused.

"I haven't any mead or wine," I mumbled, "or anything else to help take away the pain."

The corners of his mouth twitched. "There's not the slightest need for it," he said. "I imagine I'll survive the experience."

I washed the needle in boiling water and then held it, arm outstretched, into the little flickering flames of the fire to sterilize the point. Gerald leaned over behind me and held the injury's gaping edges together as I sewed. Osbert stood straight at Vespasian's back and held the candle high. I felt sick, but Tilda was efficient. Vespasian never moved. The shoulder continued to bleed and I had to stop stitching several times to wipe away the bubbles. Finally Tilda seemed satisfied and put her needle down. It was stiff with little globules of flesh and torn skin. It had not been so sharp after all. Vespasian watched me, unblinking.

I tied the bandage tight and, just as I had known about hygiene and sterilization, so Tilda knew which herbs to put in the binding to hurry the healing. She folded fresh periwinkle and wild mint within the bandage and used a washed dock leaf over the wound. "It's done," I said. He was still gazing at me, though he hardly moved.

"Then I shall go to my bed."

Gerald helped him up. "Tilda says you want me to share your palliasse. I'd be honoured."

I followed them from the kitchen to the tiny bedchamber Vespasian used, once an old pantry, his bed fresh tidied and ready for him and a brazier of hot cinders just out of reach of the bulky mattress. He stopped in the doorway, looking at Gerald. "Just don't roll over in the night across this damned shoulder," sighed Vespasian, "or Tilda will want to sew me up all over again. And I do not," he smiled back at me suddenly, "intend becoming a tapestry."

Walter snored heavily and I slept very little. I drifted from past to future and dream magnets whirled me into chaos. I saw Bertie, I heard knocking at the door, pulled the coverlets over my head and listened to an owl calling across the stars. I did not know which world it called from. Dawn had touched the top of the trees when I finally crawled from a bed that was no longer comfortable, with all its scratch and itch tumbled into dissemble. I slipped outside again, my shoes in my hand, and sat on the doorstep to put them on. My stockings were already in holes. Here I had to be careful of my clothes, as replacements could no longer be stolen.

I went first to the barn. The big grey horse rolled its eyes at me and showed me its teeth, lips raised and wide nostrils flared. I laughed. "You don't frighten me. In fact, you're telling lies about what a great, dangerous beast you are. You carried a sick man for many miles, when he had hardly the strength to guide you. You brought him safe on a long road and past all the mystery in the night. You must be a good horse, and I'll try and get to know you when you let me." As Molly, I knew little more about horses than Tilda did but there were plenty around the local farms and riders passed my cottage every day, plodded down the main street and stood patiently tethered outside the Post Office, the local shops and the hotel bar. At least I was used to them. But the horse saw me as Tilda and ignored me with contempt.

I went down to my pool in the forest. The sun was shining its first dragonfly glisten over the water's surface. It would be icy but I couldn't wait until the day was high when the other children would be around and my privacy would be lost. I took off my clothes and folded them carefully on the moss of the bank. I stepped down into the water, absorbed the shock of the cold, and began to swim.

Under the water's surface the algae danced in shimmering threads, weed entwined and river snail studded. It was dark, a fairy grotto, but the sun gleamed through in slanting gold, lighting the crystalline pebbled bed. I submerged and felt the eddies through my hair. My body warmed, accustomed now to the cold. I circled the pool underwater and opened my eyes like a mermaid, watching the little brown fish that tickled my legs. I had left the soap pot with my clothes. Ready to retrieve it, I came up for air.

Vespasian was sitting on the bank. He still wore the shirt with one sleeve detached, and that shoulder heavily bandaged. Blood had seeped though, a red smear spreading slowly. The one naked elbow rested on his knee, the skin paler up an arm long shielded from open sunshine, but the muscles sleek and pronounced. He smiled wide at me as I looked at him in surprise, then quickly splashed down into the modesty of dark water almost to my neck.

"Too late," he said mildly.

"That's not fair," I said, gulping water and spitting out weed. "You should have looked away."

"Knightly courtesy?" he smiled. "I don't think so. I do not believe in dishonest chivalry." He stayed where he was, comfortable on a jutting stone. "Besides, you're a child. I see you as a child."

"I'm seventeen," said Tilda, a little hurt.

"I'm nearly old enough to be your father," continued Vespasian, "if you stretch the facts of puberty a little. I think of you as my daughter."

(I'm thirty years old, you idiot, I shouted inside her head. I'm nearly as old as you must be.) Tilda sniffed. She often dreamed of Vespasian undressing her, but catching her unawares was different. "But I don't think of you as my father," she muttered. "So you watching me isn't fair."

Vespasian got up. "But life," he said, "is never fair." He turned and began to walk back into the shadows of the first trees. "However," he turned briefly and I ducked back down into the brackish water. "I did not come to spy on you. I came to make sure you were safe." He stood for a moment as if remembering something, then shrugged it off. "There is now an increased danger, which I do not yet intend explaining to you. It would be better if you stayed with the company."

"I can't bathe in company," I said. In spite of having to crouch underwater, I wanted him to come back and tell me more.

But he began to walk off. "Then this will be your last bath for some time," he said over his shoulder. "Hurry and finish. Come straight back to the house. I shall be waiting for you."

I grabbed the scrap of hard dried soap and scrubbed, dipping back into the stream to wash the slick of pale bubbles. The soap made few suds but I felt cleaner and fresher. Vespasian's blood had been sticky on my arms and across my chin. As I washed, I could see my reflection float at my knees. I was painfully thin and looked just like the child Vespasian had called me.

His blood was also on my chemise, but it was now too hard to budge. I let it be and ran back to the house, my body still damp and tingling in my clothes, my hair all trickling rats' tails down my back. He was waiting for me as he had said he would, sitting at ease on the doorstep and he laughed when he saw me. I knew exactly what he was thinking. Tilda blushed and hurried indoors. She curled on the cushion of rushes by the kitchen fire and began to mend Vespasian's cotte. First she had to clean the needle, then held it in the flames a second as she had the night before. Tilda had no idea about sterilization but I did. She was obedient, far more so than I would have liked, but in matters such as this she not only did what others told her, but more importantly, what I commanded too, and I was thankful. It had not occurred to me the night before, but now I wondered what Vespasian had thought, watching me attend to a hygiene unknown for the time. He would, I hoped, have been too feverish to notice.

Tilda stayed there for an hour stitching neatly. The warmth dried her body and her hair until it was all silky gleaming brown curls in the shimmer and shadow of the fire. When Vespasian came in I did not look at him and continued to concentrate on my work. I hated sewing but Tilda was wondrously practical.

It was some days that Vespasian could not use his left arm as he previously had, but he was right handed and so lived his life exactly as he had before, except for hunting with his bow. He was not a man to allow disability or discomfort to inconvenience him. The bandages twice became soaked in blood seeping from the badly stitched wound. I changed these while he sat patiently and watched me with a half smile. Such intimate contact thrilled Tilda but made her absurdly nervous. For me, it was faintly uncomfortable. I was equally discomforted by Vespasian's smile. It told me he fully understood Tilda's unsteady fingers and her hidden blushes as she touched his body. He never flinched, never moved away. He just smiled.

He gave us absolutely no explanation of where he had been or how he had been wounded but he kept Gerald, Stephen and myself especially close. I doubt he let us from his sight for more than a few moments each. I got no further chance to bathe in private and could wash only face and hands and feet. Since this was about all the others cared to do, I quickly accepted becoming the medieval slattern that I surely was.

Vespasian initiated further improvements to the house and he went hunting with Gerald, Stephen and sometimes the others, leaving me always with one or more of the boys and strict orders to keep together and watch over each other. With Richard he had no need for orders, for Richard followed me like a new hatched gosling. Osbert and Hugh were less enthusiastic about playing big brother. "But there has to be a special reason," Osbert scowled. "He never bothered with you before."

"Thanks." Well, it was true. "Anyway, of course there's a reason. Do you honestly think he was wounded running away from the sheriff or something? That wouldn't be like Vespasian, would it now?"

"So, he got into a fight. It happens," said Hugh.

"Especially if he was drunk," Richard pointed out. "He often used to get drunk. And the man has a bloody bad temper at the best of times. When he's drunk, he's worse."

"And he used to follow the king sometimes, and go to war across the sea," said Osbert. "I never knew what he was up to, I mean, he never told us, did he? I thought he might be keen to go on the crusades, but he never did. In fact, he was always rather rude about the crusaders."

Richard grinned. "He's always rude about everything."

"You still aren't getting the point," I insisted. "Vespasian said he'd be away a few days and he was gone more than a month. Then he came back half dead. So who attacked him?"

"Robbers," said Richard.

"Robbers and outlaws," said Hugh.

"We're robbers and outlaws ourselves," I said.

"Not strictly speaking," insisted Gerald. "We've never been tried and we've never been exiled. That was Vespasian's point, wasn't it? To disappear before we could be arrested and judged. So in fact, no one's looking for us at all."

"Oh, I bet they are," I said. "Don't doubt it. The law has linked us with Isabel by now. But there's more than that. There's whoever killed her."

"I don't want to talk about that," said Hugh, hands behind his back and sticking his belly out. "I expect Vespasian was robbed. That's all. It happens. We ought to know."

"I certainly can't imagine anyone getting the better of Vespasian that easily."

"A big gang of ruffians, and he'd be outnumbered ten to one. Even Vespasian can't fight ten men at once."

"Then he'd be dead," I said. "Besides, he's still wearing his ring."

"And he came back with a horse. So perhaps he robbed someone else who tried to fight back."

So we shifted again into a sort of routine and the weather warmed, the birds nested and in spite of Vespasian's caution, no one came looking for us at all. He ripped off the remainder of the bandage one evening. The scar across his shoulder was red and raised with a puckered edge. Tilda's sewing had been sadly erratic but the wound was closed and healing. "Does it still hurt?" I asked him once.

"Hurt?" He raised both eyebrows. "I hadn't thought about it. I imagine it does. But I do not consider pain a priority."

"Well, it's healing." I looked at him carefully, wondering if he'd be angry if I pushed my advantage. No one asked questions of Vespasian, but he had been gentle with me lately. Unlikely as it seemed, I even suspected him of gratitude. So I sniffed, increasingly embarrassed, and said, "Who did it? I mean, who was it? Who tried to cut your arm off?"

He stared at me for several minutes before answering. Then he said, "Nobody."

It was a pointless answer and I was disappointed. "Someone did. You didn't fall on your own sword."

"No one tried to cut my arm off." He didn't seem cross. I saw he was amused again. He was suppressing a smile.

"Then what? Who?"

"He is nobody now, because he is dead. I killed him," said Vespasian. "And that is enough of your curiosity."

CHAPTER THIRTEEN

With no access to either markets or shops, so nothing to steal and no one to steal from, we lived an oddly adapted and makeshift life in our grand house. We could not buy candles. They had always been expensive and considered a luxury, so always better stolen than bought, although I wasn't sorry when the last stunted end of smelly mutton grease spluttered away and its dirty smoke burned up into the rafters. Vespasian's tinder box was the only one we had, so we made torches of rushes bound in thread from the nettles and lit from the fire. They had to be kept far from the beds and low enough so the flames would not catch in the thatches, but they gave a good light and a clean smell though the smoke was thick and made us cough. We still had two tallow lamps with reed pith wicks which we had to keep renewing, but we started to conserve these, and kept them for special needs. We no longer had oats to make porridge and ate just one meal a day in the late morning. In the evening's firelight we sat amongst the dried threshes and told stories. Osbert was a great story teller. He made up tales of the crusades and King Richard, the mighty Coeur de Leon, who killed all the Saracens and was now in Paradise with the saints, escaping purgatory because of his exceptional virtue and valour. Osbert's own father, he said, had ridden away on the crusades, but had never returned. Osbert had heard he'd been drowned at sea before reaching the Holy Land, and if this was true then no doubt he now languished in purgatory, waiting until his sins were finally forgiven before joining his beloved king. We argued over this detail for an hour. If crusading automatically extinguished sin and sent the crusader to an immediate paradise as our holy father the Pope had announced, then did death on the road still count? Or not?

"Purgatory," said Vespasian softly from his high chair in the shadows, "is a dubious invention of the church."

"Well, that means God has to have it now," said Stephen, "if the church says so. The Pope makes the rules."

"I shall come back and inform you, one way or the other, when the time comes," murmured Vespasian.

"Hush," begged Tilda. "Don't talk of ghosts."

Stephen loved ghost stories. He told tales of the little church yard where his sister had been buried before he ran away from his home in Lincoln. "On Hallowe'en," whispered Stephen, "they crawl up from their graves, all misty and dark, hands reaching out of the damp earth, with red eyes like bats."

Vespasian had almost said something after one Hallowe'en story, sitting forward as if about to speak. But then he had sighed, and leaned back again, closing his eyes as if tired. Then, mindful of the dark magic and Isabel's death, Tilda would not let Stephen tell stories of Hallowe'en either.

Richard told the stories she had liked once, of chivalry and tournament, of Havelock the Dane and knights who rescued the poor and oppressed. Even Hugh told a story once, of a hare winning a race, then ending up in the cooking pot.

But Vespasian told the best stories of all. He told us about King Richard taken hostage and rescued by his troubadour and about King John's vicious ineptitude, of war in France, cruelty in Constantinople, of intrigue, jealousy and revolution. He described strange lands in Italy where the houses were built on water and the people sodden with corruption, though he called them beautiful and their blasphemies all glittering like jewels in the distant sun. He spoke of the dangers of being sold into slavery in the east and the dark skinned Arab traders. We knew markets, he said, where we sold vegetables and fish and horseshoes and earthenware piss pots. In the east, the markets sold shimmering silk and naked slaves. He explained libraries of ancient books as if they were more precious than gold, and teachers of mathematics and science more important than any king. He also described palaces and castles and the habits of princelings, barons and their adulterous wives, and sometimes his tales were vulgar and bordered on sardonic obscenity. But then he would glance towards my rapt, upturned expression and he would smile and shake his head and moderate his language, changing the story altogether.

As if in shame, he would switch to the only Christian tale I ever heard him tell, Perlesvaus and the grail, a story he had sometimes told us, with prevarications, by the fireside in London. "Of course," he would interrupt himself, "the symbolism of the grail is misappropriated by the church from a tradition far older and closer to the purity of the spirit." None of us understood this at all, but we adored his every soft hypnotic word and would nod as if we fervently agreed.

If the boys talked bright eyed of the crusades, then Vespasian would frown and say that they fostered only fanaticism where great cruelty on both sides had annihilated all previous beauty and progress. He called the crusades a glut of barbarity, simply in order to gain some holy advantage for oneself through causing suffering to others, an abomination in the name of someone who preached loving one's neighbour as oneself. Since I suspected that Vespasian was clearly as capable of cruelty as any crusader, I would lower my head and stare at my shoes. Then, suddenly changing the mood, he would make everyone laugh with absurd tales of comic embarrassment, nobility humiliated and pride ruined, and so to bed with dreams all fired and delicious, to keep us warm and the night terrors away.

I wondered how he knew such things or if it was all invention. But he had come back to us the last time not only wounded, but in rich new clothes of expensive cloth and fur, with a heavy cloak lined in sable which now he used as a bedcover. His new belt buckle was gold and studded with pearls. I had wanted to examine it but he had put it away in the chest by his bed. His cotte, now heavily mended, was black velvet and embroidered in two panels. The hose had been fine silk. He no longer wore those clothes and I had packed them away in bay leaves and dry parchment. He wore the threadbare suit of before and he was our Vespasian again. But I wondered.

One thing he kept with him. Vespasian had rarely worn his sword unless riding to war, carrying only two daggers, one beaten iron and bone handled, the other fine steel with a heavy silver cross on the hilt. Now always ready, he kept the long two handed sword close within its carved scabbard and he rarely let it from his sight. Seeing it often, I was fascinated by the hilt and haft, carved with two crowned serpents entwined around a central pillar.

But the difference which Tilda found most wondrous, and which interested me also, was another. Vespasian still demanded absolute obedience but his general attitude had softened almost into friendship. Where he had previously been an utterly autocratic master, now he laughed occasionally, his orders often resembled guidance, his demands became advice.

Encouraged by the mellowed change, Hugh asked three times if he could practise with Vespasian's sword. With the rural life, carrying water and tree chopping, Hugh had developed what had always been thick set strength. Although not as tall, his muscles were now as pronounced as Vespasian's and his chest was barrelled. "Teach me the skills, and I can protect us all," he said.

Vespasian's slow smile was still rarely benign. "I am not yet in need of your protection, child," he said. He would not lend Hugh his sword. "I want it neither notched nor broken. When you've mastered your own dagger, I'll consider some more meticulous education." He turned his back, but his voice remained mocking. "Hopefully it will be some time before my dotage precludes me from defending myself. Should I need you to stand guard over my infirmity at any time, I shall let you know."

I had rarely seen Hugh blush, but he did then, right to the roots of his tousled brown curls.

It was some days later, wildly encouraged by Stephen, that Hugh decided to try for himself. Vespasian was asleep. We thought he was drunk. For the first time since the shoulder wound, he had gone to walk alone under the trees and when he had returned several hours later, had sat in the drowsy sunshine under the oak by the barn, drinking in silence. Tilda knew when he had drunk too much. She recognised all his expressions and knew what it meant when the black eyes glazed and the usual intensity of his focus blunted.

He lounged under the dancing shade of the tree, his head back against its trunk and all his long length stretched out on the ground, his hands limp crossed on his chest. None of us dared approach him then and we waited quiet as mice until he shut his eyes and his breathing became very deep and steady.

"Go on, do it now," whispered Stephen, peering out from the kitchen window. "He'll never know."

"You are horribly irresponsible," Tilda told him. "It's all very well being adventurous but poor Hugh will end up getting his hand chopped off for his pains."

"Oh well, if he's scared –" said Stephen, which left Hugh no choice at all.

In total silence, Hugh tiptoed barefoot over to Vespasian's sleeping body. He leaned out and touched the tip of the sword hilt where it lay unbuckled. Immediately he was lying squirming on the ground, squealing, his face puce, and his arm bent over in an impossible grip. Vespasian's reaction had been instantaneous. No drunken sleep ever held him sufficiently to dull his senses and Hugh was lucky not to have his wrist broken. Vespasian did not release him, but looked down at him in mild irritation, his dagger blade raised in one hand, Hugh's twisted arm in the other. "Now that," said Vespasian, "was a very bad idea."

"I apologise, forgive me," gulped Hugh, which was difficult since the pain was obviously considerable. "But please sir, will you let me go?"

Vespasian gazed at him for a moment longer and then released him abruptly. "You have interrupted my sleep," he said.

We all made sure not to do so again.

Hugh's wrist was an interesting purple for some days and badly swollen but Vespasian took him out hunting several times after that and began some basic lessons in archery. His own wound seemed not to trouble him anymore and he could cast an arrow again.

With daily hunting, we ate more meat than we had ever done but I missed the roots and occasional fruit. I wondered if we could somehow find seed and roots and start a kitchen garden. I asked Vespasian. I'm not sure why Tilda let me ask because she didn't actually expect any positive response, but Vespasian thought for a moment and then nodded. "I'll think of something."

A few days later he told Walter and Osbert they could go into market. Spring was easing into early summer and the showers needed for sowing were mostly passed. Strong winds blustered through our thatches still and blew the nestlings from their trees, but Vespasian said there was still time to plant for a late crop. "Go to the East Cheap and buy exactly what I tell you," he said. "No stealing. That cannot be risked anymore."

We were excited, as if we had been offered some amazing treat. "I'm the oldest," said Hugh. "You should send me. I want to go."

"And I'm next oldest," said Gerald. "Why send Walter and Osbert?"

"You will do exactly as I tell you," said Vespasian, with the quiet menace we recognised. His voice was as soft as always, but I saw the glint in his eye that no one would challenge.

Tilda and I knew why he had chosen Walter and Osbert. Hugh was too stupid and might say or do something to risk our secrets. Gerald he would not allow anywhere far from him. Stephen would insist on adventure and try to steal. Richard might too, and anyway was conspicuous with his bright red hair. Me he kept always close. I missed London's bustle but Tilda would never have dared argue with Vespasian.

Then after that, there were several visits to the market and soon we had more chickens and a cockerel with gorgeous feathers and a vile temper, which crowed all day from a perch on the stable door. The horse hated it and would neigh in fury and kick at his straw.

We had barley and meal flour and Tilda baked bread which tasted good though fell flat and tended to end up burned at the crust and soggy in the middle because the oven wasn't right. We grew cabbages, turnips, peas, leeks and beans. I planted apple seeds and hoped for a sapling to mother, watering my seedling twig with water stolen from the kitchen bucket when Hugh wasn't looking. Being the strongest he collected the water from the stream more often than the rest of us. He hated to see his work wasted. Sometimes we had a little ale or wine. Ale was for breakfast, wine for the evening but we drank more water than anything else now for the dangers of dysentery did not affect us here and the stream water was wonderfully pure and fresh. I tried a mug of English wine which Vespasian unexpectedly offered me, but it was sweet and fruity and I didn't like it.

When Osbert walked a young goat and her kid all the way up from London, we were wildly enthusiastic. There was a butter churn and a cheese press in the kitchen and Tilda knew how to use them. Stephen milked the goat each morning and we drank milk thick with creamy bubbles and still warm. It was the best breakfast I have ever had and Stephen grew very fond of the goat and called her Cecily.

I wondered when the money would run out, but somehow Vespasian always seemed to have more. This puzzled me, but no one questioned it. Osbert and Walter went to market like the rich did, with fat purses they knew well how to protect from any thieves.

We were not permitted too many visits to the great East Cheap, therefore alternating with the West Cheap, or some of the smaller weeklies or the regular market in Bishopsgate. The West Cheap was the richest market in England and welcomed not only London's goldsmiths but workers in fine metals from other lands and grand merchants from Italy, Flanders and France. I yearned to explore there again, but Vespasian would not let me leave the forest. I didn't complain. We lived increasingly well. I had a new stola of very white linen and an over tunic of deep cherry pink. It had not been made to fit me properly since I could not go for measuring but it gave form to Tilda's burgeoning slimness and brightened her brown eyes.

It was Richard chose the cloth and had it made, for his sister, he told the seamstress. Vespasian now let him go to market once a month because he had begged so consistently, and finally had asked permission to buy something for me. Tilda was gloriously honoured. She had never owned a new gown before.

"Are we rich?" Tilda asked Richard.

"Don't ask me. Ask Vespasian."

"A lot of good that would do."

"Well, he just keeps giving us money."

"I suppose that counts as rich."

I wondered whether this new wealth was directly connected to Vespasian's injury. He was, after all, only a thief. His wound could easily have come while robbing some travelling baron, and if so, the attack must have been successful in spite of his injury. I wondered whether his absence had never had anything to do with Isabel after all, and nothing to do with black magic either. We were all thieves. Vespasian had, for once, come back with a fatter purse than we had ever been able to steal before. I thought of this until it filled my thoughts and made my beautiful new clothes seem a little dirtier and less exciting. I packed them away with Vespasian's velvet and jewelled belt and went on wearing my faded lavender.

Money was heavy and took up an inordinate amount of space. A pound value was a pound in weight and all made of silver pennies. There was no sack of it in the chest with the clothes. I did not know where Vespasian kept his new wealth. I did not know anything. I began to feel a strange lassitude, a dissatisfaction creeping in like fog from the hills on a sunny day. My days sullened into doubts.

Then one day in late June, Richard did not return from market.

CHAPTER FOURTEEN

I had been away so long that coming back to Molly was grindingly hard. For the first floundering moments I was lost in cloud. I heard voices like ships passing in fog over a flat sea. I was breathing heavily, trying to centre my consciousness. Then I heard it, the scream, rising from the calm between the opening mist like a beaching whale. It was thin and shrill and echoed in an agony I had never experienced myself.

I blinked, terrified, still unsure as to my world and time. Bertie was sitting on my bed, holding my hand.

"Thank God, old girl, you're back."

"Have I been away?" I knew I had, but how could he have known? I was surprised to find my voice so quickly.

"You've been ill. So ill." He had lost weight and I wondered if he'd been ill himself.

"But this isn't hospital. Bless you Bertie, but I feel fine. Honestly I do."

"You've been strange," he muttered. "The doctor's been a hundred times, but he couldn't understand what it was. In the end he said it was stress and I suppose it was. You've slept for days. Then you'd wake up and act crazy and then you'd sleep again. Sometimes it seemed like more of a coma."

"I was dreaming."

"At least now you sound like your old self. I've been so worried. We all have."

Oh Hell. "All? You mean you called other people. Don't tell me you called Sammie?" He stared back at me, silent and a little pink. I squeaked, "Don't tell me she's here?"

"I'll make some tea," said Bertie.

I leaned back against my own familiar pink pillows and closed my eyes. I could hear the rustle of distant voices again, distant voices from a distant world. They were worried about Richard. "I shall go." Vespasian's voice seemed only a whisper in the dark. "Don't leave us, please." It was Tilda. Me. I had begged him not to go. I wasn't there, but I spoke the words that now I heard echoed back to me. "Send me," said Gerald. "No," said Vespasian. "I will not." We would all obey him of course. He would ride out and we would be left with memories of Isabel and fears for Richard. "At night," continued Vespasian into the space behind my eyes, "you will bar the doors and open them for none but Richard or myself." "If it's so dangerous, you may never come back," I mumbled. "If I do not," said Vespasian, "you will be well rid of me."

I doubled over, stomach churning, shaking my head to bring me into focus with Tilda's world. Then a bright voice said loudly, "Well, well, so you're awake at last. And how are you feeling today?" Sammie was wearing a miniscule orange mini skirt and wedges of her hips overlapped the waistband. I presumed it had to be summer.

She held the tea cup as if I might be feeble and spill it. "Put the damned cup down, idiot," I said. "Tell me, what's the date?"

"Oh dear," she wavered. "So you're still not entirely yourself love? Well, it's June the twenty eighth. The sun's shining, and hopefully, all's right with the world."

"It isn't," I said. "Not with you here to crow over me. I'm fine anyway. I suppose you think I ought to thank you for being concerned and coming all the way up from London to pat my fevered forehead."

"You could try being nice for once," she nodded. "Though I suppose that would worry us all even more. Then we'd really know you weren't acting normally."

She leaned over and hugged me and I kissed her plump pretty cheek. I hoped my breath didn't smell of puke.

My lovely cousin had already moved in. She had taken the spare bedroom and Bertie had moved onto the sofa again which meant that there was no nice private place anymore to stretch out and watch the telly. Instead I went outside and sat on the hammock in the gentle sun. Sammie joined me there, bringing wine, an improvement on Bertie's piss awful tea. Even though I just wanted to be left alone, I was actually extremely fond of Sammie.

She said, "I'm not leaving until I'm sure you're OK. What you've been through, well, it must have been hell." It was an expensive Burgundy and glittered like rubies turning amber with the faint gleam of sunshine through the goblet. "I've never known you to crack up before. This must really have got to you."

"It's poor Bertie who deserves the nervous breakdown," I said. "Not me. I hardly knew the girl." Tilda didn't like the light, sweet medieval wine. I hadn't either. This was a whole lot better. "Thanks for the booze and the care, pet. Don't let me moan at you. You're a darling and unbelievably patient. How long have I been off my head, anyway?"

"Ages. Bertie phoned me ten days ago. He left it to the last minute because he knew you'd winge if I came bustling down to look after you."

"Poor Bertie."

"You keep saying that. Actually, it's been good for him having you fall to pieces. Mothering you stopped him thinking about himself. It's made him stronger. He even lost his appetite and he looks a lot better for it."

The late summer evening was soft on my face and I closed my eyes as the rays slanted down behind the hills, the sky suddenly more vivid in contrast to the long shadows. My chestnut tree, supporting my hammock, blackened into Rackham silhouette.

"Sammie, you're sweet. I love you really. You're my favourite cousin."

"Your only cousin."

"There's frigid Fred."

"He doesn't count. Listen love, you've got to start talking to people. Tell us what's wrong with you. Stop bundling up all those feelings inside and let people help you."

I wondered just what she might say if I did unburden all those stifled fears of mine and tell her exactly what was troubling me. I nearly laughed.

"That sounds better," she said.

I drank her wine and lay back in the hammock until the last glimmering twilight sheen slunk behind the roof tops. There were thatched roofs in this village too, although not on my cottage. In this life my pitched roof over its snuggled eaves was all curly terracotta tiles. I had bought something easier and cheaper to maintain than thatch since I'd heard thatch was hard work. Now I knew how true that was.

Nearly ten o'clock and a polished moon peeped through the trees. I went back indoors and Sammie followed me. The small rooms and their big windows retained the day's warmth and the place seemed still golden lit, echoes of sunshine. I curled on my sofa which was now Bertie's bed. Bertie had escaped to the pub.

"I could tell you stories of the crusades and eastern slave markets that would make your toenails curl." I watched her wonder if I had gone mad again. "I could tell you stories of ancient chivalry. Tristan and Isolde. Havelock the Dane. Arthur and Camelot. Perlesvaus and Parzival."

"Molly darling," sighed Sammie, "do remember that eccentricity is over-rated."

"Can't I tell stories around the camp fire? I'm a writer, after all."

"Wait until we have a camp fire."

The police had made no noticeable development into solving Wattle's murder. The threat of witchcraft, the blackest of magicks and the insanity of sadism still swathed our little village, but it had not deterred the tourists. This year there were more of them. The big inn on the edge of the stream by the bridge was booked up for six months ahead. Bertie stopped going there for his evening pint, aware that whispers and hurried glances pointed him out as a prime suspect.

Bertie was telling me about the discomfort of it when I shifted into a different consciousness. He said he'd been sitting at one of the small umbrellaed tables in the garden outside the hotel. "Cold beer in the sunshine," he said. "Nothing better. Best summer weather for weeks. Well, then this beady old dear sidled up. Brummy accent. Kept muttering, 'Is that the one? He's the one that did it.' Honestly Mol, I had to leave my pint on the table and go."

I was in the middle of sympathising when the other voice came through on the wind, low and soft. I had to strain to hear the words but I had to listen. It was hypnotic and I was tugged into its orbit.

"When I am gone, you must put mugwort, dill and betony around the door and the window sills. Cover the doorstep in vervain and the hearth beneath the open chimney too. You will not need to light fires except for cooking, but if you do, cut no living wood. Remember, at night you answer the door to none except myself."

"Or Richard." It was Stephen, whose voice was shaking.

"Indeed, or Richard. But I no longer believe that Richard will return on his own."

The voices began to fade and I was desperate to hang onto the echoes. I knew there was something else I had to hear.

Vespasian continued, "Hang henbane and chervil from the window shutters. Do not forget what I tell you. It is important as few matters have been important before." I knew he had turned to me. "Tilda, listen." At first I couldn't answer. I wasn't there. Only the very edges of my consciousness caught the rustle of his words.

"Yes, go on. I'm listening," I whispered.

"You must not return to the pool," Vespasian said. "Do you understand? You must not go back to the water where you bathe."

"I'll do whatever you say," I nodded. "You know I'm obedient. But you have to come back to us."

"This time, I may not," said Vespasian.

The shadows flew and I was back with Bertie who was plainly unhappy. "What the devil is it now Mol? You'll do whatever I say? That'll be the day! You don't know the meaning of the word obedient."

"Sorry." Indeed, I was sorry. Vespasian had much more to tell me and I could no longer hear him. I had a terrible headache and my temples thudded. "I think I'll go to bed."

But the visions did not return, and I dreamed of nonsense and the irrelevance of a modern life.

The morning's sunshine seemed incongruous. I walked down to the library and found a book on herbs and another on shamanism. Neither helped me in the least. The Anglo-Saxon dark ages were long over by the time of Tilda's birth and the Druidic practises my book fumbled over, were quickly forbidden by Christian conversion. Vespasian's Plantagenet society within the reign of the despised King John was truly Catholic with the zeal of the crusades and the tightly controlled ordinances of a fervently intelligent pope.

Sammie was amused by my choice of reading though Bertie was used to my odd interests, usually research for my own varied writings. They went off to the pub together while I sat by the window in the kitchen, read about the magic of trees and stirred the minestrone. I could hear pigeons cooing restlessly from the church spire and I thought about religion and witches and wondered what had happened to Richard. My Richard, the lost child who had admired me and brought me presents and been my troubadour and might have been buying something for me at the market when he was taken. Vespasian knew he had been taken. Vespasian did not believe it was the sheriff, though Tilda thought it might be. I wished I could go back to them.

I had put dandelion flowers and fennel in the minestrone and great handfuls of parsley. I was still thinking about the magic of herbs when the liquid splashed up and burned my hand. I jumped back, dropping the wooden spoon into the pot. I swore and went to put my palm under the cold water tap. It was then that the next vision flashed through, so blindingly that I fell against the sink, my head whirling, my eyes seeing fire. Someone else had been killed. I could see her, wrapped to a stone column, her head half way up, her feet even higher, her hands dragging on the mosaic tiled floor. She was held all around by barbed wire, a forest of spurs that cut and tore at her, across her face and her blinded eyes, ripping at her clothes, holding her tight to the pillar of her prison. She was quite dead. The shadows around her were cool and gentle but her death had not been that. Now her back was to the alter and her face to the font. She had been killed and gutted in the local church.

I was on the floor now, with the water running over the edge of the sink and flooding my kitchen floor. My hair was wet and I let it trickle down my neck, trying to wake me back into coherence. At least I knew which world I was in. I had no idea what had happened to Richard, but this woman had been killed in my own time and I was terrified that it was Sammie.

I was hysterical by the time I was interrupted, sobbing and hanging onto the cupboard door handle under the sink. My soup was boiling dry and there was water everywhere. Then I felt strong hands lifting me and I gasped, "Vespasian," lost for a moment in the dark gap between worlds.

"Molly, darling, what in God's name?"

Sammie's voice. I was, at first, sufficiently incoherent to think it came from beyond the grave. Stephen had told stories of the churchyard and hands groping up into the air from their crumbled burial pits. Six foot down to protect the decaying body from flood and seepage, and where no wolves could come and dig up the ravaged flesh.

Then I clamped my mind back into Molly's life, the smell of burning soup and the sound of Sammie's voice. I grabbed her legs and clung on. "So it isn't true," I kept blubbing. "It isn't true they killed you. You're not dead. It isn't true."

She reached over my head and turned off the taps. "Dear God. What is happening to you? What is going on?" She helped me stagger upright and then upstairs to the bathroom where I sat on the loo. She held a wet sponge to my forehead and kept repeating, "Hang on to logic, Molly. No one's been killed, no one at all. Stop driving yourself crazy. Everything's alright. No one is dead. I'm here."

So if Sammie was going to be murdered, it wasn't yet. I lived half my life in the past, so it was reasonable to think I could also have visions of the future.

"You and Bertie are right," I told her. "I'm going mad. It was bound to happen, wasn't it! Great family genes after all. One day I'll join my wretched mother in the straight jacket and the loony bin." Since I was crying all the time, the words must have seemed even more demented. I hoped she'd noticed the burning pot and turned the gas off. "But I saw something, Sammie. I thought I saw something, in the little church, another murder, like Wattle."

"You never go to church," Sammie pointed out.

"I mean in my head. I was making lunch and stirring the soup and it just came flooding in. The vision I mean."

Then Bertie came rushing up the stairs two at a time, shouting and stamping, appearing pale faced and out of breath at the open bathroom door, gasping out the latest news.

It wasn't Sammie that had been killed, it was the poor little woman who drove the school bus and had given astrology classes to some of the locals.

She had been discovered by the vicar, tied to a central pillar in his nave, bound upside down with bloody barbed wire, her throat cut and her hands flayed down to the bone.

CHAPTER FIFTEEN

I had struggled though less than a week of Molly before waking back in the forest with the boys.

Sammie was trying to drag me back to London with her, away from murder, rampaging fear and cold stark horror. Bertie said he would stay and look after the house. I refused vehemently and pushed them both away. Bertie wasn't feeling strong either and it wouldn't have been fair to leave him so alone. But my motives were also selfish. The foxgloves were up to the lower branches of the chestnut and the delphiniums were vibrant gentian against a gentian sky. I would stay with the beauty that nourished me, my home, and the troubled interweaving of the two lives I lived. I was pinned tight to the blackness of each and I was sure that trying to break away might break me.

Sammie told neither Bertie nor anyone else that I had foreseen the murder in the church, so the police did not interview me. They spoke briefly to Bertie and then they left us alone. Sammie stayed. She was a comfort, but I was terrified of causing her harm. Then finally it was me who went. I went back to Tilda.

Without echoes of screaming or nauseous discomfort, without storm or dream, I slipped back and became Tilda again. So easily, as if

I had become better practised, I underwent no trauma and was not even asleep. Late afternoon, alone for once, I was lounging in the faded old armchair, thinking about Tilda. And then I was her.

The light still danced in brilliance as the hot day seeped into warm evening. Tilda sat at the kitchen window watching the sun beams disappear one by one into evening shadows. A tall man was riding through those shadows, emerging from the forest density like a hunched crow from its nest. She thought it was Vespasian.

"He's back," shouted Tilda, grabbing Osbert and Gerald who were standing behind her, staring suspiciously into the gloom. "Has he brought Richard?"

"There's someone slumped over the saddle in front of him," said Gerald. "So yes, maybe. Perhaps he found Richard after all."

"But look, I don't know if he's dead or alive. It's just a sack, something just hanging there." I was peering, waiting one second longer before rushing to open the door.

"It's not Vespasian," I said.

It wasn't. The shape was not as tall, not as straight. It was a different horse, all pale moon silver with a long mane. There was great pride in the horse which carried the man. It wasn't Vespasian and it wasn't Vespasian's horse.

"Remember what he said," Gerald grabbed me as I turned to go into the hall and approach the door. "Not to answer to anyone except him."

"And Richard," said Osbert. "And that's Richard."

"But it isn't Richard," I said, hesitating, frightened. "It's just Richard's body."

Stephen pushed in between us. He'd heard horse's hooves and came, all excited, to tell us Vespasian had come back to us. "How do you know it's not him?" he demanded. "You can't see anything in the dark. Wait until the rider's a bit closer to be sure. I think it's Vespasian and he's carrying Richard home."

There was a silence, everyone peering out, no one sure what to do. "I know it's not Vespasian," I said flat voiced, breaking the silence, "because I know who the man is. I know because I know." I couldn't explain it but I knew, so completely, remembering a tight black beard and breath like hot bile.

We stood in a little group and stared at each other, hovering in indecision, scared rabbits. Hugh came running in then, and Walter immediately behind him. "Is it Vespasian, or isn't it? It's not the same horse as last time."

"Tilda says it's someone else and Richard is dead."

"Tilda's right," said Gerald. "Look, now you can see clearly. That's an older man and the body lying over the saddle pummel is just a lump."

"Then we don't open the door," said Osbert. "We've put all the herbs around the threshold and windows like Vespasian told us to. The door step's two fingers thick with vervain. If we don't open up, no one can get in."

"I don't believe in those silly old herbal myths," said Hugh. "I was surprised when Vespasian told us to do it. It's pagan. How about we make a cross out of twigs. That works against evil, doesn't it? Herbs are just old witch's tales."

"Go on, make a cross then," said Tilda. "But we keep the herbs too."

She was cold and there was ice down her back. She hadn't thought about the bearded man for a long time. She had forgotten him almost entirely. Yet now the disgust of his presence crept back in such detail and I knew there was no mistake. I didn't even know his name, but it was the same man.

We all moved back from the window. Now unable to see, we heard the shuffle of someone dismounting slowly and coming towards us. The knock on the door was slow and deliberate and the door frame shook. We were standing in the hall now, scared to breathe, staring at each other.

A harsh voice, muffled within the invisibility of the forest outside, said, "Where is the boy, child of de Vrais? Which one of you is his son?" I recognised the voice. We remained silent, mouths open, frightened and confused. "I bring you back one of your own," said the voice. "I will give this one to you and in exchange you will give me de Vrais' child, the son of Vespasian."

Stephen looked around, wild eyed. "If we can get Richard back –"

"Hush," I whispered. "It's a trick. Poor Richard's dead."

"Vespasian hasn't got a son," mumbled Gerald. "It's a mistake."

"Come out and face me," said the voice from beyond the door – a sour, sombre voice, slow and unpleasant. "See what I have brought you."

Still we didn't answer. There was another echoing thud on the door, so that it shook but it did not open. The figure remained outside but another noise sounded like the dropping of a weight on the doorstep.

The night sounds began to rustle into the growing gloom. The owl shifted from her hole in the oak tree and hooted softly before flying off into the darkness. The wind shuffled low in the leaves. The scamper of small animals was reassuringly familiar. The bats, squeaking like tiny birds, began to leave the rafters of our main outbuilding where once we had kept the horse. Our ducks and chickens slept under their wings and behind doors locked against weasel and fox. We also stood behind locked doors, but it wasn't the locks that kept our troubling visitor out, it was the herbs woven and spell bound.

I understood nothing of the magic that now poured black around me. My books had not prepared me for this and Tilda knew only superstition and fear. We stood in the hall and listened as the footsteps faded, retreating from our door step. Then we heard the horse ride away. "So quickly? So easily?"

We ran into the kitchen again, a flurry of pushing children, rushing to the window. We watched the horse become part of the distant gloom under the trees.

"Why would someone come all this way, and then go off with nothing? Why wouldn't he try harder? He could break the door down, couldn't he?"

"It's a trick," I said. "He hasn't gone far. He can't break through the door, it's protected by the magic and herbs Vespasian told us about. But the old man will stay out there, waiting until we go outside."

"We have to open the door," said Walter. "We have to see if it's

Richard's body on the door step."

"Not until the morning," I said. "Poor sweet Richard can't be helped now. We can bury him then."

Hugh glared at me and shook his head angrily. "What if Richard's still alive? Maybe just barely alive? But we leave him there in the cold all night to die and get eaten by wolves? We can't do that."

"Tilda's right. Richard's dead," whispered Stephen.

But we couldn't be sure. I wasn't ready yet to cry over Richard and I knew we could no longer help him. I was haunted by the rider's words. He had spoken of Vespasian's son. None of us believed Vespasian had a child, and if he did, it wasn't one of us. But the dark rider had been so sure. We knew the danger must be terrible but none of us understood what it might be and that made it more dangerous.

"I'm going out to get the body," said Gerald. "At least see if it's Richard and if he's dead. If he's still breathing – it would be like killing him myself –"

"You're the last one should go," I said at once. "Vespasian was so adamant at the end about you. You had to share his bed. You couldn't go to the market. It was you he kept protecting."

"All the more reason for me to do something to help now," insisted Gerald. "I was sick of being treated like a baby. Perhaps it was because I was the first child Vespasian took in, you know. I was just little then, before any of the rest of you. Perhaps he had this secret affection, well – I don't know. But I'm not a child anymore."

Something clicked in my head, but not in Tilda's. "Alright. Perhaps. So he protected you the most because you're the favourite. Me because I'm a girl. And maybe Stephen because he's the youngest. Not that he ever seemed the sort of man to be sentimental like that, and when he was angry he got just as angry with Gerald."

But Tilda was naive. I knew something terrible had to happen. In a way it didn't matter. After all, it was already so far gone into the past. Tragedies from a thousand years ago. How do you care about people already dead a thousand years? Even when you are one of them?

So Gerald went slowly back into the big hall and opened the door. The hand took him at once.

CHAPTER SIXTEEN

I set out the next day. Walter and Osbert came with me. Hugh lent me his heavy fox trimmed cloak since mine was threadbare, but it was high summer and the sun steamed in a golden mist across that night's scattered dew.

Hugh stayed to look after Stephen and the house – the oldest to look after the youngest, though Stephen would have come if we had let him. And if Vespasian came back, well – someone would be there to explain. Hugh did not want to come but he gave up his cloak which was the thing he was most proud of in all his small world. They would bury Richard after we had gone. His sad little body lay on the kitchen table. I kissed his cheek before we left.

He had been decapitated but we laid the head in its rightful place on the dark stump of his child's neck, closed his frightened eyes and wiped the dried blood from his brow and chin. Hugh went out early and brought back fresh water and we washed him and put Hugh's little twig cross on his breast.

I had cried so much, I had been sick in the small hours. Mostly I had cried for Richard, but there was Gerald to cry for too, and then the tears for myself. Tilda was so frightened. Her heart churned and her eyes were burning and red as torn poppy petals. But her determination was stronger still. We had a long way to go.

"The tracks are easy to follow," Hugh told us when he came back with the water from the stream. "That horse was heavy laden with two bodies to carry. You can see its hoof prints clearly in the mud. And look there, in the wet undergrowth. But they'll stop later on. The sun will dry them up."

"So we leave quickly," said Osbert.

"The prints don't go back down to London," nodded Hugh. "I've looked. I followed them a bit. They go the other way."

I said, "I expected that."

"We'll bury Richard this afternoon," said Stephen. "But it won't be consecrated ground."

"That doesn't matter," I said. "The church never saved him. It was magic kept out the creature last night and magic took Gerald. Bury Richard by the little silver pool, under the big ash tree. There's magic there too. It feels more holy than any dreary churchyard."

Hugh frowned at me but Stephen was crying, sniffing and wiping his nose onto his sleeve. I had to leave quickly before Tilda broke down again.

I walked bare foot with my shoes in my pack, saved to put on dry once we reached a safe roadway. Each of us carried as much as we could and Walter was laden so his back was bent but he wouldn't give up any of the load. "Food and blankets," he said, "and especially fresh water from the stream. When we leave the forest, there won't be any clean water for who knows how long and we can't afford ale."

We hadn't found Vespasian's never ending supply of money. Once we knew what we had to do we stopped worrying about anything else, so we searched Vespasian's mattress, under the wooden frame of his bed, in every chest we could force open, even in the old copper cooking pots we'd never used, still stored on the high kitchen shelves. We found nothing but dust and dead flies.

I loved the forest. Richard's face all bloodless chalk and glazed staring eyes remained constantly in my mind but I also saw the flutter of leaf under sun and the dash of a bird's flight through the upper branches. There was the sudden curiosity of a squirrel, small red and bushy over my head. Beneath my feet was the march of ants and huge shining beetles in the undergrowth. A golden spider hung in unmoving ambush from its dew sparkled tapestry. Walter led. Osbert followed behind me. They kept me in the middle.

The indentations of the horse's hooves were so distinct that I felt it unnatural. I believed they were markers, purposefully left, like Hansel and Gretel's breadcrumbs leading to the candy house and the waiting witch with her hungry oven. Although she knew nothing of Grimm's fairy tales, Tilda felt so too. She expected the candy house and she expected the witch though she had different names for her fears. She expected a sorcerer too, for the conviction that she knew who had taken Richard and Gerald grew steadily stronger. When Vespasian had been wounded, she had suspected him, finally and sadly, of simple roadside robbery. She had felt a bitter disillusion. But she knew now it had not been that. He had attacked the creatures who had now slaughtered Richard, and they had waited patiently for their revenge. So if the night rider knew where we were all hiding and about the house in the forest and who Richard and Gerald were, then Vespasian had also been taken. Gerald was now in danger for his life, and impossible though it seemed, so was Vespasian. They might both already be dead.

As I walked, my shoes protected in my pack and bare toes curled into the tangled wet bracken and moss, I wondered how Gerald could be Vespasian's son. Gerald was all blonde thatch and eyes like sapphire crystals, pale lashed like wheat in the sun. He was a little short for his age, but wide shouldered, stocky and strong. He was also good and kind and surprisingly innocent. And so very noisy. Clearly Gerald was of Saxon lineage. There could be little more contrast to Vespasian's taut muscled height and glossy black hair, black onyx, black pitch, all shadows, hooded eyes and light olive skin. He was menacing elegant arrogance. So Norman heritage, or even further east. Yet Vespasian had told me there had been a wife. Could a golden wife have given him a golden son?

We stopped to eat under a hazel tree. The goat's milk Osbert carried was still warm from the udder. Stephen had milked Cecily soon after dawn and the leather flask was sweating already. It made a good lunch. We picked tiny sweet red apples and there was a wedge each of cold chicken wrapped in oak leaves in my pack, the last of the market pullets we'd broiled several days ago. We wouldn't need to eat again that day.

That night we slept under an oak tree. Its spread was nearly as great as the thatch of our house and I knew the tree must be ancient. The cooling shade of its whispered memories was a song for sleep, but we didn't need a lullaby. We were exhausted. Having planned to stop once the dark hid the footprints we were following, we then discovered a moon as bright as the sun. Everything had turned to luminescence and alchemy. So it was deep into the night when we finally rested, and only then because the moon's halo slunk into mist and confusion.

I dreamed of strange things. A body hung in ragged, writhing agony from the pillar of a little church, but the woman's dead face turned into Richard's lost childishness and I leaned over to touch him and kiss him and tell him I was sorry. Then I heard someone behind me. Vespasian stood there, all dark shadow and his face stern. "You must come no closer," he said, though I could hardly catch his words, his voice was so low and threatening. Then I saw Bertie leaning over me and Sammie clutching at my hand but I shook them off. I refused to be dragged back to Molly yet. I had to help Tilda. She couldn't do this without me.

Then there was someone else. I couldn't see him but I knew he was there. I could smell his breath all rancid as if it had already decayed within him. "No," I shouted. "Give him back. Gerald doesn't belong to either of you."

I sat up and found myself clutching desperately at Hugh's cloak which I was using as a cover. The dawn was a pink shimmer through the leaves. "Time to get up," said Walter, "before we lose sight of the last tracks through the forest."

Osbert was already on his knees. "We'll have to go slower today, so as not to make mistakes. Look, the signs are already indistinct."

"We'll find them," I said, sitting up. "We won't make mistakes. We're meant to find the right way. We're being led to the candy house."

"What's candy?" said Walter in surprise.

But Tilda didn't know. She had no idea why she had said it.

I combed my hair with the only comb Tilda had ever owned, lacking in teeth now, but it scraped through the tangles like a rake through ivy. I winced. We used green hazel twigs for toothbrushes and washed our hands in the dew wet shrubs at our feet. I folded Hugh's cloak back into its bundle. The sun was still gentle but promised golden fire. This time Osbert led and I followed close with Walter at my side. The path was open and wide beneath a flurry of beeches and willows. A young roe deer darted between the tree trunks. I felt a churning excitement and optimism. My dark dreams had somehow made me strong. Both Molly and Tilda knew we had to go this way. I would avenge Richard and Wattle, Isabel and little Muriel Bunting. I would find Gerald. I would do everything that I owed to them for having brought magic through the gap between the worlds. Then Vespasian would find me. What he would do with me when he found me, I wasn't sure. He might kill me. He might love me. He might be dead already, lying slack and cold in Gerald's arms. I swallowed back the panic and walked on.

Three nights I dreamed the same dream and three times Vespasian came threat-voiced into the shadows of my moonlit confusion. "Come no closer," he ordered me. "Stop now. Return the way you have come." Then, "It is forbidden to follow me." Each time I woke shivering and stiff, cramped on the damp hard ground, though it was summer and the air mild and softly balmy.

I had always obeyed Vespasian in the past, yet not once did I consider obeying these dreamtime commands. Nor did I repeat them to the boys. Something stopped me. Sometimes, walking in the safety of sunshine and watching the beauty around me, I tried to make logic of my decision. Vespasian's dream-shade warned me away. The hoof prints led us on. So this was not a situation where logic ruled. Magic was the only law that mattered anymore. And if Vespasian was in danger, then I didn't care if he wanted me or not. I'd try to save him anyway, like he'd saved me more than once. Besides, it might not be Vespasian speaking at all. It could be the sorcerer's trick.

It was six days before we came to the end of the forest. For six days we followed tracks that never faded. Even though it had not rained for a week, fresh mud still held the marks of a horse's passing.

Only once had we met people. There was a leper colony, a hospice beyond a wide stream. Two men were collecting water, holding the cauldron between them. It must have been heavy and the men were barely able to stand. They backed away when they saw us. They wore long black gowns, patched with white to mark their contagion. One turned his head, ashamed. His nose had been completely eaten away. I smiled at them and one of them, lips deeply scarred, smiled back. We didn't have anything to give them so we kept walking. All our food was gone by now, but we had refilled our water sacks from streams almost every day and often found unripe fruit or hard little berries in the forest. I kept herbs in my purse.

Then the forest began to change. From the yellow-green of summer leaf we scurried along a narrow pathway between dark whispering spruce into a glade, a nemeton of watching trees. I imagined wolf eyes between the trunks but we saw none. The glade troubled me and the feeling of being watched troubled me. I started to run and escaped into thicker cover. But soon the trees thinned again, sparse across a slope leading steeply downwards. The grass was striped in buttercups and wild thyme. Pockets of perfume rose into the sunshine as we walked. The heat rushed in as the cooling shade retreated behind us. We had come to the end of the forest. Way below, a narrow river coiled black curves into the depths of valley shadow, and beside the river was a house.

More a small castle than a house, three narrow towers in mossy yellowed stone, tall and turreted, stretched upwards while leaving their reflections pooled in the river water. Osbert and Walter and I stood tight together on the hillside and looked down and sighed. "That's where they are," I said.

I sat down on a stone to buckle my shoes back on. The boys sat down beside me, tired and a little sweaty, pushing hair back from shining foreheads. The horse prints we had followed for a week were still clear on the ground, etched into the springing grass as if they had been burned there with a blacksmith's iron.

"What do we do now?" said Osbert, voice tentative on the breeze.

"I don't know." But I did know. I owed it to all of them and especially to Gerald who might still be alive. I had come to save them because I believed I had let the demons in. I owed them salvation, both the dead and the living.

Walter said, "Then we go on down. We knock on the door. We've come all this way. There's no sense being afraid now."

It didn't seem dangerous. A gilded beetle was scuttling in the thyme flowers. A tawny butterfly was drinking sunbeams. But I said, "Something's not right."

Walter looked at me. "Nothing's right. That's why we're here. For God's sake, Tilda, Richard is dead. Isabel was murdered too. Some sorcery has taken Gerald. Vespasian has disappeared. Of course something isn't right."

"But that's it, isn't it?" whispered Osbert. "What you said – sorcery. It's not that I'm sorry we came. Without Vespasian, we had to try and get Gerald back. Someone had to anyway."

"It's just that you're frightened," Walter nodded, not unkindly.

"Well, we ought to be," I said. I smelt evil. "But we've found the place. Now we can take our time."

"No we can't," said Walter. "There might only be minutes before they kill Gerald. They might be torturing him. We can't risk going slow. Let's get it over with." He was so sensible and brave and determined. He had my arm, tugging me up.

I knew the boys dreamed of chivalry. Knights rescued maidens and children from magical dungeons. They challenged sorcerers to tilt at the lists, and claimed victory in God's name. We had told these tales around the evening fires, giggling and nudging, innuendo too, but shining with purity and personal crusade. So many stories over the years, so that magic seemed almost ordinary. Believable at least. Then I stopped thinking about the stories because it had been Richard most of all who loved the tales of romance and tournament. He had always wanted to rescue Tilda from some threatening danger. He had not been able to rescue himself. He had been just a little boy and someone had cut his head from his neck.

My shoes slipped on the dew damp slope. I sneered at myself for having tried to keep them safe through the forest when the pretty red leather had worn away already, leaving long holes beside my instep. The bows were gone, the buckles were loose and the flaps hung open. I looked down at my feet as if they represented my own ruin. But they kept my feet steady and for a few bright moments the slope seemed to carry us forward. Then the air thickened and we slowed. Something intangible began to block us. Invisible hands pushed us away.

Each step down that hill carried the weight of resistance. I became as weak as breath against stone. Plodding, gasping, forcing my shoulders against the unseen barrier, I kept on going. Walter was just in front, nearly doubled over with the effort. Osbert was solid beside me, hair in his eyes as usual, pink in the face and puffed cheeks, all obstinate courage and determined persistence.

I tried to gulp the breath back into my lungs, muttering, "If they don't want us to go any further, why did they lead us here, every step of the way?" Then quite suddenly within the invisible prohibition, I saw his eyes, black focus, intent upon me, no heavy lids but wide, bright and utterly furious. "Go back," Vespasian ordered into my mind. "Come no closer. Return the way you have come." Then the vision was gone, dissipating into mist.

The boys took my pause as their excuse and they stopped beside me. "It's going to rain," panted Osbert.

"No," said Walter. "That black cloud is only over the castle."

Across the sweet azure of the summer sky a globulous density shaped one fat dirty cloud, concentrating into a violent threat of storm but leaving all the heavens around us in their untouched sunlight. Then directly between us and the castle, light shut down. A grey depression quickly filled the space, the clouds bled and shadow shapes swirled into the cracks. The castle was folded into a tidal fog. As it faded and lost coherence, a hundred turrets loomed up into the most surreal of fantastic space, toppled, and flew into shredded billows. Spits of lightning sprang from the wavering walls. We stood and watched the castle disappear and become a hurricane. As time had deserted us, I do not know how long it took but I saw things that raged like dragons across my terrified consciousness, huge shapes and colours and mountains of grotesque luminescence.

I was only aware that I had fallen when I felt myself slipping downwards. I was on my back on the hillside, alone and staring up into the deformation around me. I was sliding fast. The slopes of gravel crushed against my back as I gained speed. Walter and Osbert were no longer with me and I screamed.

I was flying. Then I was back in two worlds, standing on the hills beyond Molly's cottage, all wet in their sheep droppings and chilly cloud. I could see my own village down below, perhaps even my own little roof with its silly rusted weather vane and the chimneys in a row. Then through the mist the magic castle's highest tower rose like a black finger pointing from one world into the other. At once I was back in Tilda's time and thunder roared and exploded around me. Tilda knew, where Molly did not, that lightning and thunder always marked the entrance into the Underworld and she knew that the slope streaming faster and faster beneath her was the road to Hell.

I twisted around, reaching out for something to slow the descent. I was flung face downwards and continued to slide. My hands were ripped and filled with stone. I felt my flesh tear in shreds and instinctively moved my face to the side.

Tilda shut her eyes as I did, but I felt them fill with blood as she hurtled into a tunnel of ice. I opened my eyes when I hit the bottom. It made no difference for I could still see nothing at all.

CHAPTER SEVENTEEN

With my eyes shut I could see, but with them open, I could not. My clothes were tattered remnants of dirty blood-stained lilac. I could feel blood striping me like lashes from a whip. I guessed I must be in the castle, and I knew I was in a dungeon. Tilda had little concept of what a dungeon meant but she felt the damp cold stone and knew she was closed off from the warm air of the world above. It was underground, where dark things crawl. The Underworld.

I lay curled, spinning between conscious awareness and the deception of sleep. Then gradually I solidified into myself and was able to struggle up without nausea. It was indeed a dungeon, and utterly inescapable. I stumbled the limits of its confines and quickly found the only door. I could trace it with my fingertips, high and heavy with huge hinges and no handle at all. It was impossible to open and made no echo when I rammed my fists against it. So I sat on the ground in one corner and tried very hard to think. My fall down the hillside had left me scraped and bleeding. The jagged gravel must have cut me down and across, but I suffered from more than scratches, however many, however deep. The black dread I felt was not rational, but the creeping hopeless inertia was. Trying to think was like stumbling through fog. Vespasian had commanded me away. Yet he, or something else, had willed me on. Finally, the impulse was so strong, I had been slammed by storm and dragged into imprisonment. It made no sense. I clung momentarily to consciousness but then let it go. I am not sure if I fainted, or if I slept.

When I woke I stared into dazzling scarlet flame. I thought I was indeed in hell. Then I saw Vespasian. He had his back to me and was bending over the fire where a pot swung on its chains. I heard bubbling water and smelled wild mint. I was in altogether a different place. I struggled to sit.

"Stay still," ordered Vespasian, though he did not turn around or even look at me

I lay as ordered, staring at the tall back of him. The fire threw wild crimson shadow wings against the high curved stone above us. It was a small room but it was not the same room as my dungeon. Three arrow slits, just narrow openings, gazed out at a sky glistening with stars and the night's deep sea blue. I lay on a wooden slatted bed and a narrow feather mattress with no coverlets. In spite of the narrow openings, it was quite warm and the fire kept out the draughts from the stars. I felt the sizzle and hiss, and the stone walls and arched ceiling shone in the firelight. Then all I saw was Vespasian's face as he leaned over me.

The ebb and tide of the huge firelight etched beneath his cheekbones and against the squared sweep of his jaw. His eyes glittered as fiery as the flames they reflected. He had cut his hair shorter but it still swept across the high forehead, as black as the shadows. He was angry. For a moment he just gazed down at me. He said nothing, and I did not dare speak. Then he put both his hands on the collar of my blaud and the stola beneath it and ripped downwards. The already frayed materials opened at once to just above my hips. I felt the sudden scorch of air across my body. Vespasian was still looking at me. Then he reached behind him, took a cloth from the hot water and began to wash my breasts.

The sleeves of my clothes still clung to my shoulders, but

otherwise I was quite naked to below my waist and lost in blushes, shame and surprise. The water was scalding. Gradually, even though it relaxed me, the pain became more intense. Vespasian said, "No doubt this troubles you. But there is no one else to do it and you have been badly injured."

His voice was, as always, so soft that I heard him almost as a vibration and the sound merged into the crackle of the fire and the busy water.

"It's too hot," I whispered.

"It is not," he said without expression. "You must suffer it. I have no mandragora to smother the hurt and though I believe there are opiates somewhere here, I will not give them to you. Nor do I have albumen or wine to cleanse and disinfect. I have only water and so it must be as hot as you can bear."

I closed my eyes and felt the humanity of his hands against my skin. I knew I was shaking.

"Be still," he said.

"I can't," I muttered.

"I'm not interested in your embarrassment," he said. "You must be still, or the cloth will open the cuts even further."

"I was gentler," I mumbled, trying to strengthen my voice, "when I treated your wound."

I saw the flicker of a smile, but he was concentrating on what he was doing and did not look at my face. I realised he was still furious. "If you think your stitching was gentle, then you are mistaken." His voice remained soft and even, still without emotion, and he continued to bathe me. Then as he worked I realised how gentle his touch was after all. He was intensely careful, the brush of his fingertips gossamer soft, and though the skin of his hands was hard and calloused, he was attentive so that both his hands and the steady handling of the wet cloth were more soothing than brusque. Across my breasts, I felt the brief tingle as his palms crossed my nipples, then easing down over my ribs and belly. Yet his face remained hard and he did not disguise his fury. "I told you not to come," he said, words disappearing again into the whispered haze. "I warned you. Repeatedly I warned you. You have made every detail and every challenge a great deal more difficult. You should not have come."

I still did not understand how his warnings had come into my mind. No man could purposefully enter another's dreams. So I lay half naked with his hands across my body and the warmth of his fingers on my skin. "I had to," I whispered. "They killed Richard and brought back his poor body. Did you know?"

He looked up momentarily and caught my gaze. "I knew," he said.

"And they took Gerald. Did you know about that too?"

He nodded. "Of course. That is why I'm here. Gerald is downstairs. He is with his grandmother."

My mouth must have hung open as I gasped. "Gerald hasn't got a grandmother," I said stupidly.

"Indeed?" Vespasian threw the blood stained cloth back into the pot and glared down at me. "Gerald has both a grandmother and a step-grandfather." He rinsed and squeezed out the cloth and continued to wash me, easing back the edges of the torn camise from the places where it had stuck with gravel and mud and blood. "And he has a step-father," he said.

"He can't have," I said, trying to hang onto cohesion. "Who is he?"

"Me," said Vespasian.

My thoughts were interrupted by the sudden wind whining through the arrow slits. The fire shivered, shrank to its coals, and burst anew. I closed my eyes and mumbled, "Yes, I think I knew."

"You know nothing," said Vespasian, "except how to be a damned nuisance. I might have expected the boys to act the chivalrous knight and come meddling and bounding into my business. But not you, when I had warned you so many times. You are, without doubt, both the least useful and the most dangerous to have come. By what arrogance did you think you could help me?"

My eyes were full of tears. The pain was enough to make me cry, but that wasn't the reason. "Please stop being angry," I whispered. "Walter and Osbert did come with me, but I don't know what happened to them. We didn't know where you were. We came to help

Gerald. We were all together on the hill and then the storm came and I fell and found myself alone. Then somehow I was here."

Vespasian looked up at me sharply. "It was not a storm," he said. "You know it was not. We will not yet discuss what it was but you have a very good idea. It took only you, and the boys are safe outside. They do not and will not understand, which is better. Now, it is time to be quiet and let me work." He was silent for some time, his hands busy and efficient on my body, the steaming water removing the blood and torn flesh. He washed me from my neck, firm across my breasts and down my ribs to the flat plain of my belly. Then he began using the points of small scissors, picking out the shrapnel and tiny stones from the wounds where the fall, or something else more malicious, had imbedded them. It was extremely painful and I clenched my teeth.

The cuts across my breasts were the most painful where the rocks had ripped deep into the flesh. Now, opening each injury to remove the splinters and then to carefully close the wounds again, so once again his fingers were against my nipples. I felt them tighten. Vespasian's face softened momentarily into slight amusement. For once he misread me. "I repeat, embarrassment is pointless," he said. "You need hardly be concerned that I find you attractive like this. You are covered in blood and your flesh is striped like a piglet. I do not happen to find blood-letting or the results of torture appealing."

The pain was becoming excessive and my head rolled, while dizziness and nausea swelled over me. I wanted to slap him but instead I felt myself falling. This wasn't like the fall down the hillside where I had been remorselessly dragged and dashed against stone. This time the fall was gentle, like floating. Then suddenly I realised Vespasian's thumb was pressing against my neck. His eyes locked mine and I disappeared into his frown. His last words thumped in my brain. He said I'd been tortured. Not a fall, not an accident after all. It made such absurd sense. But now my temples were simmering, my eyes blind with tumbling lights, and I turned and retched. Vespasian was holding my head, my hair lifted carefully away from my face, his hand cool on my brow and the cloth against my cheeks. I tried to pull away; I knew I would vomit, but he held me tight. I coughed and then heaved. I vomited almost into his hand, but he never budged.

When I could bring back nothing more than acid bile, he leaned me backwards again, calmly washed his hands and the cloth in the pot of simmering water and began at once to wash my face. His own face was so close to mine now that his breath was in my eyes, warm as the water he cleansed me with. His voice seemed magical, like a chant or a spell. "Sleep," he ordered, very softly. "Sleep now, little one."

The warmth and the comfort and the shifting breath swam into my nostrils. I tumbled into the pupils of his endless eyes. He was utterly in command of my mind and I did as he commanded and slept.

It must have been a long time before I woke.

When I did, I was alone. The room was day lit and empty. I lay on the same bed but the fire in its small central hearth was little more than smouldering ashes, lifting a little in the breeze from the windows. But I felt drowsy and warm and I was covered up to my chin with a clean linen sheet. Beneath this, all across my breasts and ribs, down over my belly and hips, stopping just above the hair at my groin, I was neatly and heavily bandaged.

My chemise, ripped down the middle, had been drawn together again, barely covering me, but my blaud, although still attached to me at the shoulders, was ripped beyond repair. I shut my eyes again and set my knowledge into its new lists, organised between Tilda and myself, sharing the difficulty of comprehension. I wondered if I had been drugged and remembered that Vespasian had mentioned opiates.

But strangely it was not my own condition that now interested me so much as his. I was sure of nothing, but I remembered Vespasian speaking of torture. Then although he was clearly furious, he had nursed me and tended me. I had spewed all over him and he had patiently held me, wiped it up and cleaned me afterwards. He had bandaged me so efficiently and so completely that I was immovably encased. I wondered just how much practise he must have at healing the tortured.

I was not sure if his anger was simply because I had disobeyed his dream warnings. He had told me to go back, but I had come forwards.

I had come to help him, and to help Gerald. He had shown me the absurdity of both intentions and he had given me no credit for the attempt. Of course I hadn't spoken to him about wanting revenge for the dead, or the fact that I felt myself to blame. I blundered between two time frames, and something foul had followed me. I couldn't tell him about that, but perhaps I was now being punished for it.

Vespasian explained nothing. Now I could not do so either.

It was an hour before I tried my legs and tottered from the bed to the door. It was locked. So, clutching the remnants of my clothes around me, I leaned against the wall and dragged my feet to the first arrow slit. Looking down initially gave me vertigo. My room was at the top of a tower amongst the clouds. Beyond the dark spread of the river below, the hill rose up to the first skirts of the forest. There remained no visible marks of my terrible slide. The slope was gentle, and the grass was peacefully lush. I could see no jutting rocks, nor anything that might have wounded me so badly. There was no Walter, no Osbert. The sun shone. A rural England smiled back at me, pretending life was normal.

The sun was high when someone brought me food. I recognised her at once. She opened the door with a key that clanged like a smith's hammers and she puffed in, all out of breath from the stairs to this attic in one of the castle turrets. Uta must have climbed a thousand steps. She told me her name, but I already knew who she was.

"We met once, at the East Cheap," she said. "I was with my uncle and aunt and my cousin. You tried to steal my cousin's purse." I nodded. Her hair was no longer plaited but hung loose in golden curls. She was prettier than Isabel had ever been. "Of course, we didn't know who you were then. I'm sorry you have to be here. But I've brought you food." It was far better food and more plentiful than I had been used to. No umble pie, but a pottage of venison and peas with fruit and foreign wine.

"I want to know about Vespasian," I said.

She stared at me, as if believing me simple or befuddled. "What a ridiculous name. I've no idea who you mean."

"Vespasian." I had liked her before but now the woman was my gaoler and I had no need to be polite. I was impatient. "I'm not stupid. Don't look at me as if I was. Vespasian's the man who cleaned my wounds after I was abducted. Perhaps he did the abducting, I don't know. Anyway, he was in this room last night. He helped me and he bandaged me." The bandages were clearly visible, seeping scarlet where the blood was oozing through.

"No such person lives in this house," said the girl, tossing her curls, contempt in her eyes. "It must have been my aunt who tied your bandages. She can be kind sometimes. It must have been her. I don't know anyone called Vespasian."

"You're lying," I said.

"Think what you like." She shrugged. "But I've never heard of anyone with such a name. You should not have come."

"That's what he keeps saying."

"Eat," said Uta. "You'll need your strength. Stop making silly stories about people who don't exist." She left the room and locked the door behind her. I took the trencher she had given me to the small table under one window, settled on the high stool and spooned the stew from the bowl to the bread. I thought the food delicious and I could only hope it was neither poisoned nor drugged.

I imagined it would take more than food to make me feel better but in fact, I regained some strength quite quickly. Perhaps it was the wine which was considerably more alcoholic and of a far greater quality than anything Tilda was used to. The improvement however, only increased the frustration and my awareness of each grinding, jabbing pain. Across both my chest and my back my body ached and throbbed, burning until I cried. I marched the small room, kicked at the cold coals in the grate and peered endlessly from each high arrow slit. There was absolutely nothing else to do.

Apart from the small bed, the table and the stool, there was a huge carved chest which was locked and a tall wooden dresser with empty shelves except for an assortment of misshapen bowls in baked earth and pottery. Each contained ashes and the seeds of some dried plant. There were no tapestries on the walls, no shutters or parchment on the narrow windows and no other thing to take my interest. I watched the sun sink below the curved hilltop horizon and the silhouetted twilight. The stars came out slowly in their tiny bright pairs and there was no moon. I had been watching for some time, still leaning by the window and eased by the calming beauty of the night sky, when Vespasian came back.

CHAPTER EIGHTEEN

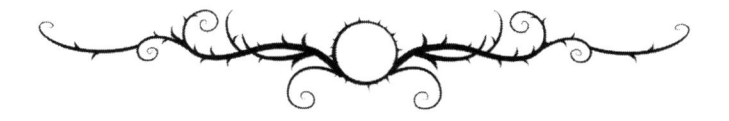

The glitter of cold fury had faded from his eyes but his expression was masked and I had no idea what he might be thinking. He came in quickly and closed the door behind him though I noticed he did not lock it. I still leaned on the open ledge of the arrow slit. After a moment he sat on the edge of my bed and looked across at me. He said, "Come here."

Tilda obeyed him at once though I would not have done so. My legs were very weak but I walked slowly across and sat beside him on the bed.

I was careful not to touch him or sit too close, but he took my hand and turned it over, studying my palm. I was still excessively uncomfortable with each unexpected intimacy. Absurd perhaps, since he had recently put his hands all over the most intimate parts of my naked body, but he still made me nervous and shy. Yet in spite of the hard callouses from use of sword and bow, his clasp was now gentle.

Then he said, "Who are you?" which was the last thing I expected him to say. His words made me sit upright with a sudden lurch.

I just looked at him. Neither Tilda nor I could find an answer. There was no fire left and the chill had begun to creep in. Over the top of his head I could see the stars' cold blue sparkle in the deepening sky. I looked back into his eyes, but his focus was too demanding and searched too deep.

"You know who I am," I whispered at last into the expectant silence. "It would be more to the point, it's more of a mystery isn't it – to ask who you are?"

He relaxed a little, releasing my hand as he shook his head. "No. Too many stories, too long to tell, and of no benefit to me to tell you. But there is something – something about you Tilda, which has long troubled me. For the last few months in particular, I've felt – the Other. You do things you should not know. You have matured in ways you cannot realise. You prove experience you cannot have. So piccina, are you just the same skinny brat I found on the streets seven years ago, or are you something else altogether?"

So he remembered how long I had lived with him. Tilda was absurdly pleased, but she was also confused. "I don't understand. I truly don't understand you at all."

"So innocent, and yet there is –" he stopped. Then his gaze hardened. "You know, do you not, little one, that if you deny what I believe to be the truth if it is in fact the truth, you endanger not only both of us – but perhaps a thousand others. Perhaps an eternity of others. So is the innocence of one child worth the degradation of so many?"

Now I really didn't know what he meant. I was suddenly frightened. Tilda stammered, "So many others? What others? You speak of things I cannot see. Please, what are you doing here?"

He began to smile. Vespasian was a man who smiled so rarely and this time, as usual, I found his smile vaguely malicious. "I am here to talk to you, and to check on your condition."

"That's not what I mean," I muttered, feeling ridiculed. "You know what I mean."

"I am here in this house," said Vespasian, unblinking, "because it belongs to me."

I stared. "Someone called Uta came with food." I pointed to the bowl which still sat, empty now, on the table under the window. "She said she'd never heard of you."

"She was telling you the truth," said Vespasian. "Now, you have been bleeding again and have ruined all my nice bandaging." He was still smiling faintly but somehow it seemed more genuine and ironic amusement had replaced the menace.

"I'm all right," I said quickly, mightily uncomfortable with the idea of being stripped naked a second time. "They don't need changing. They'll only get spoiled again. I'm sorry, I don't want to sound ungrateful, but it hurts. It would be easier not to go through all that again just yet."

He kept looking at me as if expecting me to reveal some secret, or to turn suddenly into someone else. I swallowed back the uneasy realisation that he knew something about Molly. "Very well. They can wait until tomorrow," he nodded at last. I thought he was going to get up and leave me, but he sat back down again and spoke even lower, as though someone might hear him. I looked into his eyes. They were so black they showed no difference between iris or pupil. He said, "I want you to remember something, Tilda. Sometimes pain doesn't matter. It has its place in the scheme of destinies. You can ignore pain if you go inside and find other places in your mind."

I stared back at him. "I know," I whispered. "But I've never been able to control it."

"There are places in your head where pain cannot touch you," he murmured. "Everyone can find them when they need to. You, perhaps, more than some others. Control is not always demanded. The necessity of the moment opens the doorways."

"I have places," I admitted, "places to go to. I've always had that. But sometimes they're more painful than the place I started in."

He looked less confused than I felt and nodded. "Then change those places," he said.

"What's going to happen?" I asked quietly. "What are you warning me about?"

He stared at me. Again his gaze was so close and so vibrant that I could not look away. "You should never have come," he said and stood up. "But it is too late, and you are here now. I will help if I can. But there are some things I must now do myself, which I will do, but do not choose to do. Not like this. And not yet. But now I must put necessity before choice. And after me – it will be them." He paused, looking away. After a moment, he sighed. He said, "Though that, perhaps, I can stop." The soft murmur of his voice was as contained as always, but I thought he was speaking more to himself. Without looking at me again, he left the room.

I watched him go, concentrating on the mystery, dismissing the impossibility of escape, ignoring the growing threat of his words. He had said this was his home. He looked at home. He was never out of breath when he came to me, up those hundred stairs while carrying water and bandages. He wore just a simple white linen bliaud with no cotte, as he was used to do at home in London, though this time its detachable sleeves were embroidered at the cuffs with tiny black mussel pearls and the belt was heavy Spanish leather, gold buckled, the tongue hanging long and loose by his legs. His hose were dark green silk and his shoes were such soft leather they seemed more like polished cloth. I took particular notice of his clothes for I had never seen him dressed so finely, even when he had returned with the wound in his shoulder. So perhaps he was, indeed, at home.

I was, therefore, his prisoner. I remembered all the things I wished I had asked him while he was there, but most of all I hated him all over again. I also wished, very much, he would come back.

But he did not return, and eventually I slept. It was while I was sleeping I repeated Vespasian's words to myself. "Then change places," he'd said. For a moment I wondered if he knew, somehow, the places I had. Then I realised that it was exactly what I could do. I could go back to Molly. Was he telling me that? Tilda was surely in more danger than I could manage. Vespasian spoke of pain. It was a promise of torture to come. Instead I could go back to Molly where Bertie would have the kettle on and Sammie would take me to lunch in the new Pink Panther Parlour where they served a help yourself and eat all you want buffet and that included puddings and cake smothered in chocolate, which the medieval world had never even heard of. If it was summer there still, the pansies would be out under the chestnut tree and the foxgloves would be all lined up by the fence. There would be bird song and ducks on the stream and all the tourists coming down to see where the grisly murders had taken place. I shivered with delicious temptation and I started to think myself back.

In my dream I traced the village street and came to the church with the hollyhocks in purple flower and the sun bright on the high rose window. It was my own world but I was Tilda who dreamed of Molly. I looked down at my long skirts, hems ragged and mud stained, black woollen stockings threadbare with the rips at the ankle bone and the garters unravelling, little torn shoes with the red leather flaking like shredded paper. But my tired feet trudged the bright modern paths where Molly lived, with the street lights, aluminium and electricity, television aerials and the little telephone box by the bridge. Mrs. Hackett was walking across the bridge towards me, struggling with her shopping bags, but she didn't see me. She walked right by me without a glance, for I wasn't there.

Then I heard the scream from the church. Tilda stopped. I stopped. Then I began to run towards the sound. A car whipped past me, its wheels tossing up dry dust from the road, and I felt the heat of its exhaust on my face. Tilda's face. She kept running.

At the arched doorway I stopped and stood still in the sudden shadow of the porch. Within the church there was candle light and all the pews stood silent in their rows, little hymn books placed neat along their wooden polish. The screaming had stopped. Then I heard a rattle, breath dying in a torn throat, open cavities filling with blood and slow choking death. Someone approached me from within and the light of the church candles silhouetted him from behind. He was tall and dressed in medieval black. His cotte was velvet and his belt was Spanish heather, its long tongue hanging loose from a heavy gold buckle. "You should not have come," said Vespasian.

CHAPTER NINETEEN

I turned and ran. I ran behind the old hotel with its creaking sign of rutting deer and across to the stables with their abandoned jumping fences. I held up my long skirts so that I could run faster. I ran beyond the dark square of the little cemetery and abruptly turned the corner into Molly's street. My house was last on the right, a corner block where the chestnut tree stood proudly extending its roots beyond my low dry-stone wall, pushing up through the pavement slabs. I stopped, panting, looking in at Molly's windows. They were open to welcome the summer warmth and the white linen curtains ruffled in the breeze. Vespasian's shirt was white linen, as fine as silk and through the transparency you could see the dark circles of his nipples and the line of black hair leading down like a signpost to the navel, and beyond.

I heaved and gripped at the gate. It swung open. Across the lawn and under the dappled shade and twining wisteria, Sammie was lying stretched in the hammock, her eyes wide. I shivered. I thought she could see me. Then she shook her head as if clearing me out of her thoughts, and she turned away.

I clung to the swinging slats of my own gate and desperately wished myself into one world or the other. I needed to escape the vertiginous nausea of two merging existences. I heard the gate's hinges squeak. Sammie looked up again. Then slowly she pulled herself up, sitting, moved her legs over the side, and slipped neatly to the ground. For a moment I smiled. I had never been as elegant in climbing from that hammock and often tumbled on the grass. Sammie was always better than me at the intricacies of physicality. Then she came across and shut the gate and her hand passed right through my waist.

I gasped and doubled over. She twisted around suddenly and looked directly into my face. She looked as terrified as I was. We stared at each other. Then Sammie shook her head again, turned and tramped back to the house. She pushed open the front door, went inside, and closed it behind her. The hammock continued to flap a lopsided rebound. The sunbeams sprang through their leaf cover and the shadows danced on my lawn. I watched for a few bleak moments and then retraced my steps the way I had come.

I sat down beside the stream. The sloping banks were thick with daisies. Tilda started to make a daisy chain as her mother had taught her when she was a small child, splitting the stems and pushing one through another, caught by each tiny yellow centre, careful of their soft white petals.

Tilda had never heard of gentle Muriel Bunting and her peaceful life. She had never heard of the terrible violence of its ending. But at the doorway of the church where Muriel Bunting hung butchered, she had seen Vespasian emerge from the sinister shadows. He had emerged in the wrong world at the wrong time.

Tilda sat curled and bent her head. I was as miserable as she. Then I saw the reflections that frightened me even more. Visible in the sparkling water of the stream beyond my feet, the sky burst and ruptured. Above me, the heavens were peaceful azure summer, but they reflected the massed black and red storm that had already thrown me into the castle dungeon in Tilda's world. Across the river water, clouds billowed like udders oozing black filth. The dark was struck by colour; luminescent gold became slime green. Jagged lightning split the stream. Thunder rolled around me, wrapping me in vibration. I felt the rain pound on my shoulders and was soaked.

I opened my eyes, waking back in my truckle bed. The fire had been lit again and flared against the dark stone walls. It was night and outside the arrow slit windows it was black. I could still hear the thunder. I sat up, cold and frightened, reaching out my hands to the warmth. I was locked in a stone tower with a high beamed ceiling solid over my head, but I was still clutching the little soggy daisy chain and I was drenched in freezing cold rain.

The room was empty but a bowl of food steamed on the floor beside the bed, a pewter mug of ale and a trencher of dark bread. I heaved my legs over the side of the bed and watched the mattress stain with the damp indentation I left behind me. I stared at the bedraggled daisies, picking at the petals.

I had no idea how long I had been wandering in Molly's world between dimensions but the bandages across my body were wet not only with rain but with blood. Clearly the wounds Vespasian had cleansed and treated were still unhealed. I looked for something to dry myself but there was nothing in the room except for the sheet on my bed, which was already wet. I huddled on the floor beside the fire and let its heat steam across my torn clothes and body. Fear raced back and forth through my head. I tried to eat but I could not swallow. I remembered the ripped throat of the woman in the church.

They came in behind me. I whirled around, expecting Vespasian again, but it wasn't him.

They came one by one, each looking at me with curiosity, peering down at me as though I was a specimen. The old man came first, then the woman. I knew them both. Uta and her cousin came behind them and then others I had never seen before. Vespasian was not one of them. I didn't count the faces but there were four women and at least twelve men crowding into my turret room. I became very small, shrinking into the space between the hearth and the bed, squeezing my knees beneath my chin, staring back, defiant, at their curiosity. The fire was burning lower. One of the younger men pushed forwards and threw a handful of small coals into its heart. An unexpected spit of orange brilliance raged up to the vaulted ceiling arches and I cringed further back.

"Who has treated it?" demanded the old man, pointing down at me. His fingers were dirty and gnarled and the nails were too thick and too long. He spat, "Someone has dared to nurse it." The firelight shadowed his face in virulent cinnabar highlights, emphasising the ridges from nostrils to mouth, the runnels down his cheeks and the hooked beak of his nose. His lower eyelids sagged in scarlet streaks like scratches and his eyes were small lashless pits. His face disgusted me and his breath smelled of decay and corruption. I crossed my arms over the torn front of my tunic and the seeping pink bandages and, defiance intimidated, stared into my lap.

A rustle of concern interrupted the concentrated attention of the crowd. All black clothed like craning ravens, the people stared at me, looked warily at the old man who spoke, then back at me. Uta, all pretty and fashionable with her pale face and rosy plump cheeks, yellow hair in sleek combed curls down her back, said, "My lord, the girl spoke of a man called Vespasian. She told me he had bandaged her. I thought it must have been my aunt."

The older woman glanced crossly at Uta and quickly shook her head, starched toque bobbing. "Not me, my lord. I've not yet spoken to the girl. I would never disobey your orders."

"So it was Jasper," said the old man. Each word spat saliva. His lower lip, though wizened, hung loose, revealing yellow horse's teeth in a jaw stubbled in sepia beyond the narrow trimmed beard. His black hair was lank and aged in silver smears. The fingers of his hand were so long they seemed grotesque. He reached out to me and poked at my breast beneath the bloodied white strips of linen. I felt the points of his nails press into me. I was forced to look up and met his gaze but his eyes went nowhere. He said, "De Vrais has done this. No one else would dare," and his breath in my mouth made me nauseous.

Uta flounced a little, pleased to know all the answers. She said, "Jasper's downstairs with the boy."

"But surely, there's no harm done," said the young man who was

Uta's cousin. He shrugged. "It's kept the trollop alive. If she'd lost too much blood, she might have died before we could make use of her."

The old man spat directly at the boy's feet. His phlegm was green slime. "The slut would not have died, I would not have allowed it," he said. "No one dies until I'm ready and I permit no one to interfere with my plans. I had her ready sliced, prepared for flaying. But now the breasts are closed again. I can smell his filthy magic on her. De Vrais will pay dear for this. I'll make sure he pays for everything."

"Then you'll continue with the girl today?" asked another, panting with impatience and polished in sweat. "Has de Vrais set up barriers, then? But my lord, his barriers are surely not strong enough, not against your power, my lord. Will you still prepare the sacrifice?"

"No," the old man said, turning with a sneer. "You all know what I'm waiting for. The Great Other will come when the time is right." He looked down at me. He looked hungry and dribbled saliva from the drooping lip. "But perhaps we'll play a little first," he smiled. "De Vrais' puny magic has no power over me." He leaned even closer. I could see the red veins in his tiny eye balls and the grey hairs curled in his nostrils. His mouth was wet. He grabbed one of my wrists, wrenching my arm away from its clutch across my chest. He spoke two words I could not understand and then his fingers closed so tight, I felt my bones snap. With three fingers he had broken my wrist. I screamed. Then the man forced my hand into the flames of the fire and held it there.

I fell into black heat and I fell a long, long way. It was a tunnel, stone, narrow, lightless and violent with heat. I heard someone scream over and over and it echoed around me in a wail of terrible hopelessness. I had heard that scream before, several times. Now I knew it came from Tilda, and from me.

Time stretched interminable. But the pain disappeared into the distant unreality outside the safety of my tunnel. I floated in cool and peaceful light, feeling only gentleness. I expected a blistering return to the turret room and the fire, night visible through the arrow slits and the feather mattress soft beneath me, yet I saw nothing. The voices I heard came from very far away. A man and a woman were whispering somewhere above my head. Vespasian always whispered. His voice was always so low that the words barely brushed the air. Vespasian was speaking now.

It was a long time before I risked opening my eyes. But when I did, I saw Molly's bedroom and it was Bertie and Sammie talking softly, and a small bald doctor whose name I could not remember. I looked at them and began to cry.

"Dear Mrs. Walding," said the doctor, "please don't be so distressed. The morphine will kick in soon."

"I'm not Mrs Walding," I sobbed, though managed to stop myself claiming Tilda. "I'm divorced," I prevaricated faintly. "I'm Miss Susans."

I watched Bertie look increasingly uncomfortable. "I apologise," said the doctor with a bedside smile. "Molly Susans, of course, the name you write under. And don't worry, we'll have you out of bed and back at the typewriter in no time."

I was floundering in misery and anger and I wondered if he was senile. "What's a – typewriter?" I mumbled. Then I remembered again where I was. I forced myself back into the present and prevaricated once more. "It's all done on – computer – these days." I knew I sounded silly but claiming medieval ignorance would have been a damn sight sillier.

Sammie interrupted before I made a complete idiot of myself. "Mol dearest, calm down. You're probably a little light headed. I mean with the accident and then the pain killers. Just lay back and think of England."

"What accident?" I demanded.

"It's what we'd like to know," muttered Bertie somewhere over everyone's heads. "What the hell were you up to anyway? Playing with fire as usual, I suppose."

I looked down to the concentrated source of the pain. My wrist and hand lay heavily bandaged on the blanket. I stared at it as if it didn't belong to me at all. Which it didn't, because it had to belong to Tilda. "I've broken my arm?"

"Darling," said Sammie, sitting down on the edge beside me, "you must have fallen over the gas stove or something. You have been very vague lately you know, really distant some days. But Bertie says you get that way when you're into a book. Anyway, we found you unconscious on the kitchen floor with your hand all twisted and the palm so badly burned, well the doctor has called for an ambulance. I'll come with you to the hospital. You need X-rays of course. He says you've probably fractured your wrist. Third degree burns too, but he doesn't think you'll have to stay in overnight. You'll be an outpatient at the Burns Unit."

"Oh fucking hell," I said wearily. "Fuck. Shit. Pissing bloody hell."

"Yes, well," said the doctor with a disapproving blink, "I suppose it must be an unpleasant surprise."

"You're damned right it is," I said.

They bundled me into the ambulance even though I insisted on walking to my own front gate. I stopped there a moment, remembering. Visions of the hammock, the church, and Vespasian, once again, where he should not have been. I almost expected to see a wet daisy chain lying on the doorstep.

Sammie came with me and sat patiently as I was wheeled through one white tiled corridor into another. The X-rays on my wrist proved what I knew already for I had heard the little bones break. I was repulsed when I saw what the old man had done to my hand. It was burned beyond blistering, with seeping red muscle and gristle exposed. Serious, said the burns unit. Well, I could see that. They assumed I'd fainted over a gas flame, continuing to burn until Sammie found me.

And yet the old man had held my hand steady into the fire and his grip had never wavered. His own hand had not even scorched. He had smiled, staring at me, blank eyes glittering with the first glimpse of emotion. A hungry smile that made me shudder.

I let Sammie chatter on. Then I interrupted. "Has anything odd happened lately?" I asked.

"You mean apart from this?" she said, pulling a face.

"Like seeing ghosts," I said.

"Oh God, Mol," she said. "Sometimes you scare the living daylights out of me. How did you know about that? I never mentioned it. Not to anyone."

"I saw it too," I said which wasn't an explanation and wasn't true either really, but she accepted it. "How long ago was it?"

She thought a moment. "Two days."

"And no more murders in the village?"

"You remember ghosts and you don't remember murders?" She shook her head at me, telling me I was a lost case. "No Molly dear, no more. Just poor Wattle and little Miss Bunting. I hope to goodness you haven't seen any more visions of future horrors. I never told anyone about that either you know."

"Just as well. And no, I haven't. But all the same – I think there will be." I leaned over to her suddenly, in a sudden terrified panic. "Sammie, promise me you'll be careful. No talking to strangers and don't go walking on your own. Please, please, be totally and ridiculously careful all the time."

"I could say the same to you," said Sammie, taken aback. "You're always wandering off into the hills. Or sticking your hand into fires."

"Nothing I do can actually make any difference," I said, looking out of the long window at the sun over the trees. "Or at least, maybe it will. But then it will get worse. I don't know how to make it better."

"Oh dear," said Sammie. "I don't suppose you'd agree to come back to London with me? Away from all these nightmares? Away from – you know."

"Well, London's hardly risk free," I managed to smile. "Anyway, no, not on your life. I have to stay put. At least, I think I do."

"I shan't try to understand," sighed Sammie.

"And the police haven't arrested anyone? Or made any headway at all? Any announcements? People helping with their inquiries sort of thing?"

Sammie shook her head. "Not a thing. Everyone says black magic, but no one says who. There just aren't any logical clues by the sound of things. Poor Bertie is getting a bit stronger though. Fancy him getting a new girlfriend."

I had no idea, but I wasn't going to admit to that. "Well, he's always needed his sexual status injections and a good dose of reassurance. Wattle wouldn't blame him, I'm sure. Me – I'm delighted."

"I wish you'd get a boyfriend, Mol," she said, turning to me with a cousinly glint. "Now that would really do you good. It would be exactly the tonic you need."

I shivered. Something wet and cold moved into my head, like the coils of a snake behind my eyes. I forced myself to smile. "No thanks. You couldn't drag me – not even kicking and screaming – well, not unless you can introduce me to Johnny Depp."

Sammie's smile seemed reluctant too. "Sorry. I think he's busy elsewhere. But I know this gorgeous man in London, Mol. Honestly, he's an architect and just your type."

"Sammie stop it. I'm really, truly not interested and don't you go fixing something up behind my back because I'll shoot you and him too."

We were waiting for the doctor to come back. My wrist and hand were now in a neat white cast, and the cast in a sling. The pain came in small dizzy waves, but I expected to be allowed home once the doctor had lectured me on being more careful in future. Sammie had already written her name with heaps of kisses on the side of the plaster. I sat and stared at the little black crosses. I felt sick. I wanted very much to go back and look after Tilda. I even wondered if she was dead.

CHAPTER TWENTY

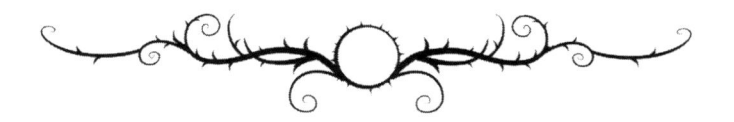

With my wrist in plaster, I was more handicapped than I had expected, and it was not until the first proper bath I felt strong enough to take, two days later in fact, that I realised something else about my condition. From mid belly to shoulder, my body was marked by scars. Like faint silver threads, they striped up from my stomach, over the navel, around my chest and thickly across the swell of my breasts. I peered at this alien tattoo on my skin. I was deeply thankful that the hospital had been given no reason to strip me off completely or demand an X-ray on anything other than my wrist, for they would have been amazed at these indications of torture. No doubt I would have been back for questioning by the police, black magic as the subject.

The bath water seemed troubled, ebbing into turbulence, the seas of a huge swell instead of the small soap scummed waters of a bath tub. I sat still, waiting for my mind to calm and my heartbeat to steady. As I drifted into acceptance and relaxation, so the water became my own bath again. I pulled out the plug.

I was becoming so entirely confused between two identities that Tilda's scars marked my body, her injuries appeared in my life, and now I could no longer rely on any part of my own sanity. But at least there was one thing that pleased me. My merging with Tilda did not stop Molly from functioning. In some way, even if vague enough to worry her relatives, Molly could carry on without me. I smiled. Showed how dispensable I was. Hardly anything to smile about. But it brought up another and most uneasy thought. If Molly could continue her life without me and if Tilda was not me either, then who the bloody hell was I?

I slouched around with a broken wrist for a couple of weeks and panicked privately over Tilda. I was sure I would know if she was dead. She was sort of me for God's sake. If she died, then I might too. But it was absurd, because she had in fact been dead for nearly a thousand years, and I was surely tumbling into insanity.

If I was, Sammie didn't seem to notice. She told me I'd always been eccentric even as a kid and after all, I'd had an extremely eccentric childhood. I knew she'd always felt sorry for me, but I'd admired her and never resented her pity. She hadn't ever patronised me for the tragedy of my mother. Now we walked together up on the hills under the sun. Sometimes Bertie tagged along but he had a new interest now to absorb him and sped over to Oxford at weekends to wine and dine the lady while I stayed with my cousin. We had picnics with wine from a battered thermos and cold chicken in foil, and I remembered Tilda's walk through the forest with Hugh's cloak in her bundle and wedges of chicken wrapped in its folds.

I believed Tilda was being systematically tortured. I had no wish to share her suffering, but I felt I'd deserted her when instead I might have helped. My dreams continued to be disturbing echoes of another world but I remained staunchly Molly. I even returned to writing, one finger to the keyboard. The palm of my left hand, though healing, remained so scarred that the flesh was withered and puckered into weeping furrows. I had been treated by a modern burns unit in a modern hospital and I wondered what pain and deformity Tilda endured, or if – since her injuries marked me – my healing helped heal her.

Then one slow morning as late summer drifted into its downward plunge and I was sitting alone by the village stream making daisy chains, a cold trickle of wind blew so sharply down my back that I knew something had happened. I got up and started walking. My instinct had been to go home but soon I realised I was actually walking in the opposite direction, taking neither the path back into the village nor my usual track up into the hills. Instead I followed a little used lane behind the old cemetery to the first trees of the bluebell woods. I had not meant to come here but then, I had not meant to come at all. I continued, and knew I was led.

The trees grew closer. There were openings where the wild roses still blossomed pale tawny under the filtered sun, but soon I was clambering over knots of root and bracken, snagging my skirt on thorns, lost deep in shade. I walked due east and far away from the older groves where, some miles off, Wattle had been butchered. I was still nervous of being alone among the trees. I wondered at my own stupidity in coming here, and yet I still walked on as if I had no choice at all.

The natural pathway was winding, then began to slope steeply and I started to slip. I was wearing sandals and their rubber soles weren't sensible in thick undergrowth. Then below me I saw the great yew tree. I had no idea I had come so far, though I had often been here before, visiting the rare and ancient beauty. The ravaged trunk twisted into strange shapes within the pitted bark. Its branches created its own massive canopy, as if it was a forest within itself. It must have been home to many birds and other creatures, yet it was entirely hollow. It was dying from its own aged weight.

I walked around it and sat at its roots on the far side. Below me were the silver shallows of a small pool and the yew tree was reflected there. On the banks among the thickening ivy, stretched Vespasian. His hands were clasped behind his head and he looked up at the wisping summer clouds. I looked down at him and he smiled.

I sat beside him. He didn't move or seem surprised. I watched his smile gently lift the corners of his mouth and deepen into his eyes. It was such a defenceless smile, far more benign that I had ever seen from him in his own time.

I looked down at my own reflection in the water at his feet, my face partially obscured by floating weed and summery green algae. It was deliciously balmy. I tugged off the old pink cardigan I wore and wriggled out of the rubber sandals. I was wearing an old flowered skirt and a pink T-shirt. Beside me, still watching me, Vespasian wore the white linen shirt, narrow belt and deep green hose that I had seen him wear before. His cotte was crumpled as a cushion, his hands clasped beneath his head. He cast no reflection in the pool at all.

"Do you know me?" he asked.

The right voice in the wrong place. "Yes, I know you," I said. "At least, I know your name and I've met you before. I don't really know you at all. Does anybody?"

He continued to smile. "Perhaps not."

"Sometimes I've visited you in your world," I said. "This time you've come into mine."

"I sent someone here, and then followed her," he said. "But I've come into many worlds, many times. I travel, when I will and when I must. Which name of mine do you know me by?"

That surprised me. "I know you as Vespasian."

"Ah." It was a breath, or a sigh. "Then certainly, you do not know me at all."

"Then tell me now," I said, leaning forwards. "There might not be time for fencing and puzzles. You could disappear any minute. So tell me who you really are. And then tell me about Tilda."

"My Tilda? Yes, I knew there was something –" he paused, watching me intently. "Can I expect any answer so explicit? Perhaps I can. So tell me first who you are."

Well, it wasn't going to help him at all, but I answered anyway. "I'm Molly Susans and this is the forest we call the Bluebell Woods, in England's West Country. It's the year two thousand and fourteen so you've been dead for a long, long time. Interesting, isn't it?"

His smile deepened into a grin. I had never seen him smile with such genuine amusement. "It would seem so, though I am not conscious of having died. Well, Madam Susans, I am Jasper, Baron de Vrais and that is who I am, whether I choose to use that name or not. I am Vespasian Fairweather because I invented a mask when my birth name became – let us say – inconvenient. If you are who I believe you are, you know about that already. I have no intention of explaining myself further – even in dreams. Come back into my own world if you dare, open the gates once more at my command, and find out for yourself."

"I shall," I said, "though not at your command. But if you won't tell me anymore about yourself, then tell me about Tilda?"

He sat up so suddenly, unwinding from the ground like a spring, it startled me. There was twenty first century ivy stuck to his medieval sleeve. "Why?" he said. "What have you done? What will you do? And why Tilda?"

I lowered my gaze, knowing his eyes could read me. "Because you may be torturing her and I need to know why."

He stared a moment at my still bandaged wrist. "What I do, or do not do," he said at last, "is for me. My decisions are my own." His voice slid back into its soft menace. All the bright ingenuous smile had quite gone. I was uncomfortably aware that my skirt was bunched around my knees and my arms were bare, and to a medieval man I must have appeared almost naked. But then, he had seen Tilda more naked than I, and touched her without arousal. He did not look at me now, and there was no sign that he cared what I wore. But he said, very softly, "The power is mine now. You may believe you can ignore my commands, but you will find you cannot. I have leeched your control and will now stand at the portal when I wish."

Cross and frustrated by his answers, I pointed to the water. "Look," I said. "Like the devil, you cast no reflection." But when I looked up for his reaction, he had gone. There was no one there. A dent in the ivy was all he had left behind him

I stumbled home, repeating endless questions in my head.

A thumping headache was zooming up from the back of my neck, circling my forehead and swirling around my eyes. The sun through the trees rebounded like flashing Christmas lights, blinding and reverberating. Before I reached home, I began to heave and felt feverish. I truly expected to enter Tilda's time. I believed I was losing grasp on dimension and expected to roll immediately from my world to hers. I nearly sat down to wait, but I did not for I felt sick and drugged and drunk and beyond all else, I desired the secure comfort of my own home.

But I was surprised to get as far as my gate and the faded hammock and the big chestnut tree giving blissful shade. I pushed at the front door which was swinging half open and called Sammie. I called a few times because it seemed strange that there was no answer, neither from Sammie nor from Bertie, though the door had been left ajar. Since the murders, no one left their doors unlocked.

I made tea. The kettle steam quickly became condensation as I buried my nose in the heat of the tea cup. I slumped at the table until the tea was tepid enough to drink. Then I took my cup upstairs with me into the bathroom, kicking off my rubber sandals half way up the steps, hurrying to the vitality of a cool shower and the desperate need to clear my head.

The house was serenely quiet and only my own pattering centred my thoughts in the correct time zone. I kicked the bathroom door open, first right at the top of the stairs.

Sammie was in the bath. The water was cold and it curdled around her like pink milk. Her face was sunken pale beneath the coagulating surface and her two little feet protruded at the other end, toes neatly varnished bright scarlet, like the stripes of blood from her ankles up to shins. Her hands were crossed across her groin, shimmering underwater. She had not been flayed as Isabel and school bus Muriel had. Instead her body had been dissected from neck to navel, all opened like a biological book, its pages wide and the contents carefully detailed.

I reached into the water and took her hand. It wasn't cold, though the blood formed black ridges between the fingers. Her palm was soft with long submersion. I told her, a hundred times, as I cried and heaved and squeezed her hand, how desperately sorry I was. I knew it was my fault. In my dance between worlds I had opened a gate and Vespasian had found the way through. He had just told me so himself. He had admitted it though I had not understood at the time. I swore to Sammie that I would kill him though it meant me dying too, and

Tilda with me. I sat in the pools of bloody water on the tiled bathroom floor and kept crying until all my words became incoherent even to myself.

Fresh blood, old blood, pain and death, they all had their own special stench and together they reeked, and I added to it by being sick in my own lap. Then I walked downstairs and phoned the police. I was sitting on my doorstep when they squealed their brakes to a stop under the chestnut tree and came stomping in past me. A young policewoman whose mother lived in the street behind and her garden backed onto mine, kneeled beside me and put her arm around my shoulders. It was sweet of her because I was covered in blood and vomit. Within half an hour I was back in hospital and Sammie was in the morgue.

They gave me a heavy dose of tranquilizers. "I need to talk to the police," I muttered. "I don't suppose I can help much, but they'll want to ask questions, won't they?"

"There's time for all that, my dear," said the nurse, injection poised. "You have to sleep first. A good rest will give you strength to cope with what follows."

"I doubt it," I said. "Nothing can give anyone that sort of strength." They had cleaned me up and I smelled of lanolin. The nurse stuck the needle in the flesh of my upper thigh, rolled me back and covered me up. I felt like a small, swaddled puppy. I closed my eyes.

Then the shapes kicked in and I didn't sleep at all.

CHAPTER TWENTY-ONE

At first the mists of unconscious stupor moved into symbolic shape and darkness. I saw Sammie's face sunk under the bloody bathwater but then she rose, holding out her arms. Congealed blood and pus had collected around the huge wounds of her upper body, but she smiled. I knew what she meant. She was telling me it wasn't my fault, but she was wrong and I knew better. Though my involvement had never been malicious, the fault still stayed with me and my wanton travelling. I travelled now, floating in billows of scarlet cloud. I clung to intergalactic consciousness and waited to spin down into Tilda's pain.

"Open the gates at my command," Vespasian had said. Now I understood. "I sent someone here and then followed her." He had come for Sammie and I had somehow let him in.

When I landed, Tilda was lying on cold stone. The pain I had expected hit me like thunder. It covered my body with a series of burning and overwhelming horrors. I had never, could never, have imagined anything like this. I lay and shivered helplessly and wondered how I could get out of a body that could no longer bear me. I was stretched unnaturally and could feel the chains looped around my wrists and ankles. I tried to move and could not. Then I heard noises, whispering voices and the scuffle of movement, and knew I was not alone. My eyes were blind with tears of utter hopeless wretchedness and terrified agony, I could see nothing although my hearing, though faint, seemed clear.

Practical but doubting, the first voice said, "If you continue now she'll die. You said you wanted to wait for Her."

"I have control," said the harsh voice I knew. "The slut won't die until I give my permission. Not until She is here to see."

"My lord," said the woman, "would you have me nurse her back then, ready for the second invasion?"

"No," said the old man. "The hand's already healing. This one may have her own secrets. I feel some form of undisciplined power in her that interests me. The broken bone is so quickly mended and see, the burns fade quickly. It's unusual and even I did not expect –. But the left hand passed through fire. The fire must be preserved but whatever protects her must be stripped of energy. De Vrais may have interfered more than I realised. I'll see how these latest injuries mark her and how soon they heal. Feed her but give no other assistance."

"And Jasper?"

"He won't dare interfere this time," said the man. "Since his damned inconvenient escape, I can't deny him right of precedence for having brought her here. He's claimed first penetration. The rules must be kept sacred. But I'll only allow him to play after seeing the initial effects of my experiment. The sacrifice is mine alone and my power is far greater than his. Do you doubt it now?"

A worried hesitancy, and the woman whispered, "But if – just suppose, my lord – if this is – one of them. The opener's servant, perhaps. Could it be so? These signs of magic are – surely unexpected. And if Jasper is so interested, there must be a reason beyond simple –"

He was cross and interrupted her. "Fool. Would I not recognise the power of the gatekeeper herself? This is just a pauper's brat, a slut from London's gutters. Don't you remember where we first saw her?"

The woman's murmur, "I do."

"Then," snapped the old man, underlying fury guttural in his throat, "Do you dare suggest I would not recognise the truth? Do you dare suggest Jasper would know when I do not? Do you even dare suggest his power is greater than mine?"

"Never. My lord, forgive me."

I heard them leave. Then from deep beneath me I heard chanting. It was musical and rhythmic, and I thought it beautiful. It gathered up my awareness so entirely that I was no longer conscious of my own body. I felt I changed dimensions. I passed through time as though time itself was symbolic of something far more beautiful.

Great realms of reassurance rolled over me, and years passed, or I passed them. I was rocked, nestled, protected. Removed from sequence. A strange inconsequential happiness cocooned me. Then I tried to lift my hand and at once the pain came back. I was strapped down and could not move and the bed which had once been sweetly comfortable was now hard and cold. The slabs were wet with my own blood and urine. I was spread eagled and chained. A brazier close beside me was hot. It scorched me to one side and I heard the little busy crackle of its flames. I was caught between extremes with heat to my left and seeping cold beneath me. Through the centre where heat met ice, a ridge of splitting pain cut the centre of my groin. I had no idea what they had done to me. I had no idea why. I lay still and tried desperately to lose consciousness once more. But time had imprisoned me again.

Then I was aware of water. I could hear it singing. It became merged with the chanting. Then I felt water surge above me and thought I drowned. But it was Sammie they had murdered under water, it wasn't Tilda, and I was Tilda, I couldn't be Sammie too. Other waters tumbled around my ears until everything I heard was an amalgam of waves. I saw the silver pool where Tilda had bathed and where she had told them to bury Richard. I saw the algae pool in the bluebell woods where Vespasian had slipped unasked into my world. I saw the little stream that trickled through my Cotswold village beneath the tiny bridge. I saw white waterfalls and wide brown rivers and last of all I saw the ocean, birth of creation and symbol of spirit.

The sea parted in fountains, and bubbles of dancing golden water began to gather speed around me. I felt strong hands all across my body, exploring, adjusting, bringing together what had been somehow ripped or defiled, as if they could remake a body once desecrated and destroyed. The hands were kind and efficient. They neither trembled nor hesitated. I knew I lay in my own blood, my own vomit and my own urine, but the hands avoided nothing. They were strong palmed, long fingered, and hard ridged. Although I knew they held me and touched me everywhere, even within where decency forbade such intimacy, I felt a surge of utter trust.

A soft voice said, "In the power of water, the fetch of the soul is preserved and inviolate. As it is above, so it is below and I demand the right of birth restored. I summon the sacred purity of merit. With ash, mistletoe and betony, the crossroads shall be shut. The way shall not again be opened by other than myself, and I claim that power now, to make the vessel whole, and to heal her." It was the magic of the chanting again, but just one steady passage of words and just one voice.

I tried to open my eyes.

"Hush," said the soft voice, strangely gentle and barely rising above a breath. "I have nearly finished, little one. You will fly soon."

"So I'm dying?" I whispered. "You mean heaven? Will I fly to paradise?" Then I realised these were just thoughts and I had no strength to speak aloud.

The voice in the water answered my thoughts and said into my mind, "Your escape is not into death but into life."

"Please," I thought, since I knew he could hear my thoughts, "please don't hurt me again."

"No," he said, though the words floated away on the rushing tide. "The pain is over now. I will not hurt you anymore."

There was a light, very bright, growing in my consciousness. It took force from the words I had heard, and though my little world was silent now, the light expanded. It seemed to come at the end of a long tunnel and the tunnel was all water, a parting of the seas into a great passageway of dark blue, muralled with the crawling tendons of reaching things. There, at its vibrant ending, the light continued to beckon. Someone seemed to take my hand and lead me safely through.

Then all the tunnel broke apart, the tentacles wound around me and the light exploded. I heard a spluttering screech of fury and I opened my eyes. Uta was pulling at me, her hands gripping my shoulders and her mouth distorted. Her spit was in my eyes. "You won't," she kept screaming at me. "We won't let you. You can't get away."

"I want the light," I whispered. The light was receding. It had almost faded into silver glow.

I had always thought of her as so pretty and I had wanted to be like her. I had admired her and now she had turned into a maniac, grabbing at me and shouting. Her spit was on my lips. "You're not going anywhere. You haven't the power. You've been through the fire and the blood."

"She's been through the water," said the voice which had guided me before, though I barely recognised it. Where it had always been so soft that I had hardly caught its words, now the sound was strangely harsh.

Uta twisted around. "You. But you put her through the fire too. You claimed the first rights. I was your witness. You're one of us." She grabbed him by the collar, reaching up with her plump little fists and her face heaving in sweat. I could smell all the musky violence of her. "You're mine."

"I have never been yours," said Vespasian and the threat in his voice was cold fury. "Now let her go."

I don't know what happened. I was blasted into the white light with an impetus that was suddenly brutal and totally unexpected. I must have lost consciousness at last because I remember only vague flames, the rush of water, an amalgam of blurred faces, and then darkness.

It was only a narrow point of light that penetrated through the darkness. The great white brilliance that had seemed so wondrously healing had left me alone and night had come back. Within the blackness, one solitary star wavered. Once again there were faceless voices in the gloom and I struggled to recognise them. I expected and feared the old man, Uta and her cousin, Vespasian and the room in the tower. I hoped, lurchingly, that it might be Sammie and Bertie – then realised it could not, of all people, be my own cousin. There were several people, whispering around me. Then I knew that my eyes were already open and what I saw was real. The wavering cold star in the night was a little candle flame and it was held unsteadily by a child's hand.

"She's coming back," said Stephen, "I think she can hear us." The candle moved closer to my face and its spluttering tallow smoked under my nose, making me cough.

"Thank our merciful God," sighed Hugh.

"Thank Walter," said Stephen.

It was Vespasian's house in the forest and it was night and I was lying on Vespasian's bed with the feather mattress and the woollen coverlets and the duck down quilt, and around me knelt Hugh and Stephen and Osbert, small worried faces in the candle light. I tried hard to say something but my throat hurt too badly and I spluttered and then just looked up at them all, trying to change the grimace of pain into a smile of gratitude. I didn't have the energy for anything else. Then Walter's snub nose and dark eyebrows shoved through the other faces, and a smell of something hot and aromatic.

"I expect you just want to sleep, but you have to eat first," he said, all gruff with worry. "I've heated up the pottage Hugh made earlier. It's really fine with lots of leeks and onions and you have to try."

When shaking my head didn't work and my neck wouldn't obey my brain, I managed a word. "Can't," I said.

Walter grinned. "You have to. After carrying you all the way back here through that interminable forest, I won't have you die now. Come on, try."

Hugh put his big flat troll's hands behind me and lifted me up on the cushions. I flopped like a baby but he supported me. Walter spooned the soup. Because he was right, and the heat and substance immediately gave me strength, I managed to eat a great deal more than I had expected. Finally Walter put down the spoon and gave the bowl to Stephen to take away. "Now," he said. "Is there any chance, even just a few words, to explain what on earth happened to you?"

Didn't he know? How had they rescued me if they didn't know? The heat of the soft food in my throat had given me back some of my voice. "Vespasian," I said. "The castle was his. I was his prisoner. They tortured me. I don't know what they've done to Gerald. But I suppose he's dead."

They were all staring at me. "But you were only gone an hour," said Walter. "You can't know all that in such a little time. And you weren't Vespasian's prisoner. How can you think such things about him? He was the one who carried you up the hill and told us to take you home."

I didn't understand and stared back at them in total confusion. "You're all crazy. I was gone weeks. I don't know, it was hard to tell, but it must have been weeks."

"It was an hour," said Osbert, "or maybe less."

"Oh my God," I said. "Tell me."

"We were hoping you'd tell us," said Water. "All we know is, once we arrived at the river and saw the big house, there was that terrible storm that just came down from nowhere. We got flung down the hillside and we hung onto some thorn bushes and then we saw you'd disappeared. We were all scratched and bleeding, but we managed to sort ourselves out and we started searching for you. Everything was wet and muddy, but the sun came out just like the storm had never happened. There was this enormous rainbow, with the colours all shining, like an arc right over the house."

"Anyway," interrupted Osbert, "we couldn't find you. We went right down by the river and walked around the house, but it seemed to be empty. The big doors were locked but there was no sound and the stables were abandoned. We shouted for you but there was just the wind in the trees. And that odd rainbow. The most amazing rainbow I've ever seen."

"Then we looked back up the hillside and saw someone standing at the top, looking down at us," Walter hurried on. "So we went scrambling up and there was Vespasian, looking all grand with pearls and rubies on his cotte but so exhausted and sort of grey. I'd never seen him look so haggard."

"He looked really ill," said Osbert with reverence. "More ill than when he was half starving in London, or when he got that wound in his shoulder. Anyway, he was carrying you in his arms. And you looked even sicker than he did. We thought you must be dying. You were all bloody and unconscious."

"He put you straight into my arms," said Walter. "And he told me to carry you home. She's injured, he said. Be careful of her. Just take her home."

Osbert sighed. "Then he said he'd come soon and he'd be bringing Gerald with him. He went back down the hill without looking back. When we couldn't see him anymore, we started walking through the forest, taking turns to carry you. You might be just a little thing, but you were heavy, I can tell you. We got you to drink a bit every day, but you couldn't eat and you kept fainting again."

"You haven't eaten since Vespasian found you and told us to bring you back here," said Walter, "and that's days ago. So that's why you have to eat now. If you die after all this, well, goodness knows what Vespasian would say to us."

I smiled. I was amazed at myself for managing it. "And I was only gone about an hour before you saw Vespasian carrying me?" They nodded. "For me, it was weeks," I told them. "Time is playing tricks and Vespasian's part of it."

Hugh grimaced. "Vespasian's clever, but he's not a magician."

"Oh yes he is," I said. "That's absolutely exactly what he is."

What none of them realised of course, and what I wondered at but did not mention, was the fact that I had come home in new clothes. Plain, serviceable, but totally new to me. I hated them and I did not know who they belonged to. I scrunched them away in a chest and changed into the pretty clothes Richard had once brought me from market.

It was some days before I felt strong enough to let the summer warmth slip me back into the lazy slumber of routine. I asked no more explanations of the boys and they asked no more of me. They assumed I had hit my head in the tumble and had fainted into a nightmare. I knew I could understand no more of the truth until Vespasian came back. I knew now that he would, and I wondered whether he would bring Gerald back alive or dead.

I remained convalescing in Vespasian's bed. Hugh hung a little cross on the bedpost above my pillow. I told him I was sorry I had lost his beloved cloak. He said he didn't mind and Osbert said he could go into market and get me material to make another. Stephen repeated that one day he'd kill a wolf and make a cloak from the skin. I just smiled and said, let's wait for Vespasian. That's what we were all doing anyway.

Slowly, having no mirror and wanting none, I discovered some of the injuries that had been inflicted on me. I had been marked in strange ways. The broken wrist and burned hand which had been mended in Molly's hospital, now hurt very little though the palm remained scarred and puckered and I had limited feeling in two finger tips. Other burns seemed more recent and were distinctly more painful. The stripes of wounds across my chest which Vespasian had bandaged were now just thin silver memories, but they were newly crossed and hatched by deeper, newer marks. I recognised the unmistakable signs of lash and whip and knife across my breasts and shoulders.

Healing was already advanced, and I was no longer bandaged. I traced the scars over my chest and ribs, down across the belly to the groin and on to my thighs. I saw the evidence of clear sadism and perversion but had no memory of their infliction. I remembered finding myself on the filthy stone, chained and exposed like a slave. But my other memories were of dazzling light, cool water and chanting and I had felt nothing of the hideous things that had obviously been done to me. Even stranger, there was a tiny pattern of black lines resembling a dragon, tattooed onto the inner curve of my left breast. It was drawn very exactly, its wings unfurled and its mouth open; dark furrows were imbedded into my most sensitive flesh. It was both repulsive and beautiful and it frightened me. It also throbbed with pain, a piercing stab often waking me in the night.

Around the curves of the wings were puckered and minute blisters, as if the thing had been painted with fire, but I also discovered a soft greasy patina across my breast, as if it had afterwards been treated with ointment.

It was well past the Festival of Lugh when Vespasian finally came back, riding that thin brown horse of his. Gerald sat on the pummel in front of him.

CHAPTER TWENTY-TWO

Gerald jumped from the saddle and ran over to us, all smiles and excited dimples. He was dressed in pale blue velvet like a young prince and his cloak was fur lined. Vespasian dismounted behind him and stood looking directly at me. I looked back without blinking. He looked magnificent.

I said, "So you let them have me in exchange for saving Gerald."

He paused a moment and finally he said, "Yes." Then he walked past me into the house and called for wine. The boys ran to obey him, just like old times, while Gerald swirled off his grand cloak and called Walter to help him look after the horse.

I followed Vespasian and stood in front of him while he stretched himself into his big chair in the main hall and began to pull off his boots. "Gerald's your step-son. So you gave me to them for torture, because I don't matter, and you made a pact to get him back."

He frowned, just a twitch between the brows. "Yes," he said again. "So it was." He tossed his boots across the room. I was looming over him and he looked up at me. I thought that somewhere deep in the backs of his eyes there was the gentleness of pity, and a hint of smile.

"I'm amazed that I was worth such an exchange," I persisted. "Just a half starved country brat to swap for a baron's step-son."

"You misjudge your own value," he said softly. But now he was looking at me with less sympathy, as if suddenly aware of something. He said, even more softly, "You see, you were a virgin."

"Were?" I would dearly have loved to slap him. Tilda wouldn't let me. "Was? Not anymore?"

The smile had gone cold and contained more malice than pity. "Tell me, Tilda," and his voice was hard as ice. "How is it you know I'm a baron?"

I paused for a moment. I shouldn't have known. He'd told Molly, not Tilda. It was a dangerous game and Tilda was uncomfortable and confused. I looked back at Vespasian. "Molly told me," I said. I swear I heard him smile as I turned sharply around and marched from the room.

It was impossible with the boys around to be private again with Vespasian. They were too excited, so I hardly spoke to him for days. The boys bounced about him like delighted puppies so proud to have their master back. Even the nightmare loss of dear Richard had drowned beneath new life and new excitement. Gerald had a lot to tell us and it was in the long evenings of late summer that we sat around the cooking hearth in the kitchen and told stories just as we had before. The smoke wisped up to the hole in the thatch and bustled around the high beams where we hung the bacon joints for drying and the bunches of herbs and nettles and the twigs of laurel for cooking and hazel to season for arrows. Vespasian lounged in his chair and the rest of us curled on cushions or stretched out on the matted straw.

Vespasian's face was always in the shadow, as if he carried his own shadows with him. As Gerald and the others talked I doubted that Vespasian listened. He drifted in dream. But if there was any sudden noise, he was the first to snap alert.

Although I knew some of it, Gerald's story amazed us all. "You'll never believe it," he said, which was true at first. "Well, of course, I didn't know myself. All these years and Vespasian never told me."

The old man who had grabbed Gerald from our doorstep and carried him off into the forest, turned out to be a man of some importance. "I don't know why he stole me away like that," puzzled Gerald. "If he'd just come and explained himself, why, we'd have let him in, wouldn't we?'

But Gerald remembered nothing of the journey to the strange house on the river. He had woken as if from a very deep dream and found himself already wrapped in blankets in a soft narrow bed with a charcoal brazier beside him and a beautiful woman looking down at him.

"I wasn't scared," he lied. "I just wondered where I was. It was just so weird. Anyway, this woman bent down and kissed me on the forehead and she smelled of roses and lavender. That was just the beginning. It was the most exciting time of my whole life."

"I don't know why you came back," said Hugh, rather sour, "if it was so amazing and good."

"I came back to be with Vespasian," said Gerald. "He's my step-father and guardian. I don't know why he never told me before. Why didn't you, Vespasian?"

It took a moment before Vespasian looked down on him and acknowledged the query. "It was safer," he said, soft voiced. "Safety in ignorance and to keep you with me and away from them. Now, go on with your chatter. I am not in the mood for questions."

Gerald was slightly taken aback. "Safer? But they're wonderful people. No one harmed me." Vespasian ignored him, so he turned back to us. "I don't know all the story of course and maybe one day Vespasian'll explain it to me. but I know I was the child of his wife's first marriage."

"Wife?" squeaked all the voices, except mine.

Gerald nodded, huge with importance. "My mother was Lady Ingrid and my father was the Baron of Tennaton. When I was just a baby my father was killed on the crusades and then my mother met Vespasian and married him. Well, I don't think Vespasian really liked my mother's kinfolk, so he and my mother went away together and took me with them." He looked up for agreement and confirmation, but Vespasian was once more lost in the scarlet flame-dreams and far away. Gerald carried on. "So we were in this huge house down on the river at the other side of this forest, and it used to be Vespasian's house, but my mother's people live there now. I'm not sure why that is, but that's what's happened. I met my grandmother. She's the beautiful woman who kissed me when I woke up. She's married again too and he's Arthur and quite old. I admit I didn't like him much. He's the one who came to this house and took me away. He and Vespasian seem to hate each other. Anyway, everyone else was wonderful."

"So, where's your mother? Where's Vespasian's wife?" whispered Stephen in awed anticipation, peeping up at Vespasian's half closed lids. Mothers were every boy's secret fantasy.

"She's dead," I said suddenly. "Arthur killed her. He killed your father too."

"What a ridiculous thing to say. You can't know that," said Gerald, going pink and turning angrily to me. "My father died on crusade to the Holy Land. That's what they said. Arthur's a strange man, and I suppose I was a bit frightened of him to tell the truth, but he would never have killed my parents. Why would he? And why would my grandmother marry him if he did? And you couldn't know anyway, Tilda. You're just being mean. You don't know the first thing about it."

I suddenly felt all the intensity of Vespasian's eyes on the back of my neck, but when I looked up at him he was still staring into the fire as if his thoughts remained absent. I turned back to Gerald.

"He killed Richard too," I said. "Doesn't anybody remember anything about Richard?" Again I felt Vespasian's eyes piercing my mind, but he didn't say anything and I decided I had better not say anything more myself.

I often walked down to the silver pool in the forest where they had buried Richard. Vespasian had forbidden any of us to wander alone, so sometimes Stephen came with me and sometimes Walter. Once Hugh came, bringing a little wooden cross he'd carved. Gerald ignored me, still angry. Osbert avoided me too, as if scared of who I'd become and the things I said. I piled wild thyme and vervain on the grave's piled earth and watched as gradually the ivy and moss grew over it and absorbed it back into the soft green undergrowth.

No one returned to the market, either the East Cheap or the West

Cheap, but Gerald and Vespasian had brought two fat packed panniers back with them. They went, hidden beneath layered bay leaves, straight into the locked wooden chests, but sometimes Vespasian pulled something out and the gifts were always unexpected. He gave each of us long knives like short swords. They had handles carved and set with pearls or jet or crystals. Mine was all golden metal with a great lion's head carved on top and a shaft so sharp that I was frightened to carry it with me, even in its worn leather scabbard. It was heavy and made my wrist sore.

"It's not real gold is it?" I stammered. "That would be worth a fortune. I wouldn't dare carry it around."

"Never leave the house without it," Vespasian ordered me. "Especially when you go to the pool." He spoke to me rarely these days and never in private.

"How do you know I go to the pool?"

"You go to visit Richard," he said, "and I'll not stop you. But you must never go alone and must always take the sword with you." We were standing at the edges of the first trees that encroached upon the boundaries of the house. Vespasian was looking across my shoulder, as if he saw the pool and the grave mound, and not myself at all. "I've had reason to go there many times in the past," he said, in a manner that surprised me. "It is a beautiful place. But it is also dangerous."

He gave me more clothes too, which surprised me even more. The worn lilac tunic and white chemise which had once been my only garments, had been ruined by Vespasian himself when he had ripped them apart to bandage my wounds. I had no idea where those rags were now and now I loved to wear the cherry pink which Richard had given me, and which made me think of him. But Vespasian gave me other things. I had a camise so fine that it seemed like lace. I had a stola of turquoise, the colour of a bird's egg. There was an over-tunic of a summer day's blue with a hem all the way to the ground, like rich women wore. There were stockings of thin wool as soft as fur and little leather shoes with bows. To replace Hugh's cloak, not so warm but far more beautiful, there was a sea blue palla lined in silky black velvet, a rich lady's toy.

I loved my new finery but I didn't thank Vespasian. I had never thanked him for rescuing me either, for I had first been his prisoner and I still did not know how much of my torture had come from him. So I looked at everything and then I went and put them all on in the tiny cupboard room where his framed bed stood against the dark wall, and where I still slept. When I walked out to show him, he had gone. He was outside teaching Gerald and Hugh how to wrestle.

We all had lessons. Things he had hardly bothered teaching us before, now became daily rituals. Riding, archery, sword fighting and other matters even more practical.

"I will not bother teaching you French," said Vespasian one evening, to our general astonishment, "as even the king uses it less these days, both officially and in private. Nor will I teach you Latin," he looked around at us, eyes half hidden under the heavy lids and sweep of dark lashes, "unless any of you contemplates a career in the Church?"

There were some stifled sniggers in the candle flicker. Even Hugh, who had once contemplated such a future, chortled as if he knew it could never happen.

"Cum magna calamitate civitatis et periculo vester? No? I thought not. Then I will limit your education to the more useful skills of self defence and basic manners. You all behave like wild piglets, which of course, is entirely my own fault. Now that is about to change."

He made me a small bow and three arrows plumed in partridge feathers, gave me soft brown gloves to protect my fingers against the pluck of the string, and patiently taught me to cast straight and strong. Standing behind me with his body close to mine so that I felt the pull of his muscles against my shoulders, his arm around me and his hands on my hands, I learned to shoot nearly as far as his own huge bow could cast, a hundred arrows in every direction, each and every one then dutifully retrieved, until eventually I felt myself a master. I was an attentive student and I loved the soft thwang of the flight and the spring of the string against my right ear. I felt like a little soldier, a Joan of Arc, though it would be a long time before she was born. The practise also made my weak wrist strong again. "Nock and draw," Vespasian commanded from just above my head. "Now, loose." Only when I had shot a wood pigeon from the sky and saw it tumble sadly at my feet, was Vespasian satisfied.

The boys each learned to ride, much to the disdain of the horse. Aware that none of us could understand him, Vespasian, reminded of his Latin, muttered "Culus inadequate," as each of the boys fell off with lesser or greater bruising and a lot of bad language. However, since we had only one horse and I was at the end of the line, I did not learn to ride until much, much later and under very different circumstances.

The other lessons were less exciting. They began with table manners "– wash your hands immediately before and immediately after, do not grab all the choicest pieces or blow all over hot food in a shared bowl. Put a clean napkin over your right shoulder and use it to wipe your mouth and your fingers. Do not use the back of your hand or your sleeve or the edge of the tablecloth (there are plenty of linen napkins folded in the kitchen chest), don't slurp or drop half your food on the table or into the lap of your companion and do not pick your teeth with the point of your knife. Nor should you unearth wax from your ears, sneeze in anyone's face, or cough over the wine."

Tilda found these fascinating insights most interesting, but I found them hysterical. I must have snorted, almost as contemptuously as Gerald had once taught me. Vespasian lifted one eyebrow, turned away and ignored me.

"When invited to dine in company, remove your hat when spoken to and do not shuffle or avert your eyes when asked a question. You'll look either stupid or guilty, whether you are or not. If you are, it's even more important not to look it. As a guest in the home of a social superior, which with you means everyone, you first leave your weapons with the steward, and then bend your knee to your host." Stephen and Hugh had particular trouble with some of these orders, but it was the other more general etiquette that delighted me most.

"Spitting directly in front of your companions, picking your nose and pissing in public," said Vespasian, "are considered especially heinous. Shitting in public is the worst, whether or not you turn your back. Find a quiet place behind a wall or a tree if you have no access to a chamber pot. And if you do come across someone in the act of pissing, do not address them directly until they've finished.

Nor are you to search inside your clothes for fleas or lice, especially under your tunics and in your braies, and belching or farting in public is far better avoided. What you have indulged in all your lives, will stop completely and at once." His eyes, switching suddenly to me as I stood behind the others, danced with genuine and spontaneous humour. I had been trying not to laugh myself. "This is not necessary for Tilda, I think," he said, dismissing me with a grin. "Only for my disreputable boys."

In fact, I believe it was only meant for Gerald, but perhaps Vespasian decided not to single out his step son and so included everyone.

The increased skill in hunting benefited us all. Vespasian killed a wild boar, which was strictly illegal in the king's forest. I had not been with him, but Gerald, Stephen and Walter had, and they came rushing back full of glory to tell of the creature's fierce charges and red piggy eyes. Its tusks were long and curved, dirty white from an ugly wide mouth. Poor thing, defending its life, killed for meat, though little enough flesh for it was bony and tough. We boiled it for hours and made jelly from its trotters.

Vespasian had stopped wearing all his grand clothes and he seemed like the man Tilda had always known, the quiet, scruffy man with the hidden menace, hair a little too long, face a little unshaven, clothes too worn and too old. He did not remove me from his comfortable bed and instead he slept on my straw pallet amongst all the boys. Usually I avoided him. I wanted to ask him so much that I knew he would refuse to explain, so instead I kept away. Sometimes I felt him watching me. Most of the time it was as if nothing had ever happened between us, or in any other way. Gradually my body eased and the aching paled. Energetic youth made healing quick. Being Tilda, I began to accept everything without question. I could bring back Sammie's face only in my dreams. I remained Tilda while Molly's memories began to fade but her consciousness was still mine, and mine was hers. We shared our opinions, but when Tilda's wishes and mine contradicted, she won and my knowledge was quickly stifled beneath her innocence. It was her language I spoke and her thoughts that took precedence. Just sometimes, when I could slip through her naivety, I could order her actions. I still meant to kill Vespasian and I knew I could make her do it. I practised with bow, and sword, and knife. I imagined an attack in the quiet of night, but I also remembered how, even asleep and drunk, Vespasian had nearly broken Hugh's arm. Then I reminded myself of my own broken wrist and the evil done to me and that reinforced my determination.

But life became calm. There was no threat. No dark strangers came riding through the forest to our doors. No bands of highway robbers, no foresters on the king's business, no outlaws. Gerald had said the old man's name was Arthur and his wife, Gerald's grandmother, was Joanna. I knew them both. Arthur was the devil who had murdered my friends in two worlds. But Arthur had not acted alone. I needed to know how much Vespasian was involved and how deep his hands dabbled in blood.

Except for the dragon brand, I soon felt wonderfully healed and exercise gave Tilda new strength. As a teacher, Vespasian was strict and assured. He did not know he was training me to kill him.

CHAPTER TWENTY-THREE

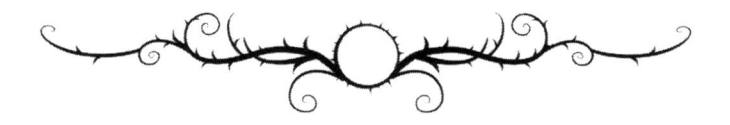

It was late summer and nearly autumn. The forest was a great fantasy of trees in burning colour. The winds blew cold, but the colours were hot and the sun kept shining. There were squirrels collecting for approaching winter, the weasels were growing their thicker coats and the deer were rutting. The boys and I wandered into the forest collecting herbs, apples and wild fennel. "Keep together," Vespasian repeated each time. "There is to be no moment when any one of you is alone."

I was with Walter and we had taken the path to the pool. I stopped there as always and put herbs on Richard's grave. "Was it really like you said," asked Walter suddenly, "or were you making it up? About Richard? About who killed him?"

I was kneeling on the mossy stone, my hands smelling of thyme, tiny white flowers on my palm where the old burn still looked angry and distorted. I stared up at Walter and nodded and he came and sat next to me on the ground.

"If it's true Gerald's grandfather killed Richard, what about Isabel?"

"Yes," I said. "Her too. But it's no good asking me anything else, because I don't know."

"But you were there," insisted Walter, his dark eyebrows furrowed.

"You said you met these people. You said it was like being there for weeks. I've seen what your hand looks like, all twisted up in the middle. I know what makes those marks, it's fire. You were burned very badly. It was never like that before we went to that house. So when you say you were tortured, you're telling the truth."

I stared back down at Richard's grave mound and remembered his small decapitated head with the eyes glazed and the gaping mouth full of dried blood. "I always tell the truth," I said, which was a lie, so I amended it. "At least, about things that matter I do."

"So why?" demanded Walter. "What were the killings for? Why in God's name would anyone want to do that?"

"Well, not in God's name," I said. "Perhaps in the devil's name. I don't know. But there's powerful dark magic. I don't know much about evil. Perhaps they worship Satan."

"That's silly. Vespasian would never have got mixed up with anything like that," decided Walter. "I don't believe it."

"Look," I said, "Vespasian saved me in the end. He brought me out of the house so you could bring me home. Maybe he even saved my life. But he was there, all through everything and nobody hurt him. He was free to leave, because he carried me out. But then he went back in."

"Vespasian saved every one of us," persisted Walter. "In London, he rescued us when we were beggars and orphans. We're only alive because of him."

I got up, wiping my tunic down, brushing the remains of the herbs from my hands into the pool's water, the scent of them remaining with me. "So," I said, with a deep breath, "it doesn't matter. Think what you like. But what about Gerald?"

Walter looked cross. "Gerald has nothing to do with it. He's my friend. He's your friend. It's not his fault if he was dragged into all this mess and mystery."

"But think," I said softly, "just think a bit, and you'll see none of it makes any sense at all. Gerald is heir to a long dead baron. His grandmother's still alive and she's rich with that huge house and land and jewels and a title. Gerald ought to be Baron Tennaton now, oughtn't he? So why is he back here with Vespasian living like an outlaw and a pauper in the forest?"

"Well, there's no shame in that," said Walter. "After all, Vespasian is his guardian and now we know Vespasian is a baron too."

"Who has always used an assumed name ever since we've known him and doesn't claim his title? Think, Walter, he was a thief when he first took us in. Just a thief and he taught us how to steal too."

"So you don't believe anything he says?" Walter wasn't prepared to give up that easily.

"Oh, I think what he says is probably perfectly true," I told him. "It's what he doesn't say that worries me. There's just a whole world of terrible secrets he never tells us about at all."

"Why should he?" demanded Walter. We had started walking again, back down the track into the forest under the wild profusion of autumn coloured leaf. "We don't belong to him and he doesn't really have any responsibility for us, even though he's looked after us for years. He doesn't have to explain himself to us. Who he is, is his own business."

"Didn't Gerald have a right to know?" I said. "And now he has to tell me. He owes it to me, if not to you. He's done too much to tell me nothing now."

Above us the sun spangled through the trees' canopy. Walter reached out and took my hand. He turned it over and looked at the ugly red deformity. Then, quite unexpectedly, he leaned down and gently kissed it. "I'll marry you, if you want, Tilda," he said suddenly. "If Vespasian lets us, I'll marry you and look after you."

I stared at him, but I didn't pull my hand away. I tried to smile. His little snub nose was all wrinkled up with worry and the frown was so deep that it clasped his eyebrows across its bridge. He didn't look as though his offer was causing him any optimistic delight. Tilda was uncomfortable and looked at her feet as she continued to walk through the shadows. Personally I wondered if Walter was just about young enough to be my son. But of course it wasn't me he had asked to marry, it was Tilda.

"Thank you," I muttered. "I don't know. Do you really want to? And why should we have to get Vespasian's permission?"

"Because we live in his house and he looks after us," said Walter. "He's our sort of father, isn't he! And yes, I do want to. I've wanted to for ages."

We walked back very slowly to the house, still holding hands. Osbert gave us a strange look when we arrived, but no one said very much. Vespasian was in the stables, scrubbing down the horse. Stephen was sitting on the doorstep, skinning a hare. There was blood all over his lap and the fur came off in wet tufts.

"You're spoiling that," said Walter. "That pelt could have lined winter shoes, or a hood."

"Why are you holding hands with Tilda?" demanded Stephen, looking up with a challenge. Then I was aware that Vespasian was standing behind us. I could smell him. He was musky with sweat. Walter had not heard him come.

"Because I've asked for Tilda in marriage," said Walter.

I turned around. I knew what Vespasian would say before he said it. The pause made me angry. "Yes, I thought you might," he smiled. "But you see, I'm afraid that I cannot give my permission."

Walter blushed and hung his head. "We're old enough to decide," he said. "She's eighteen already. I'm eighteen too and I'll be nineteen soon I think. I'm strong enough to look after her."

I glared at Vespasian. He said, "It is out of the question. I am not interested in arguments."

Stephen scurried indoors with the half skinned hare. Walter stared at his boots. "I'm sorry," he said after a moment. "I'll wait then. I'll ask her again another time, after all this difficulty is sorted. I mean, when we can go back to London. Then I'll find work or set up a shop. I've done some cobbling. Old Wat can teach me more and put me up for the guild."

I had thought Vespasian was angry but suddenly he smiled, a wide genuine grin that crinkled up his eyes. "Then Tilda is lucky," he said without looking at me. "I wish you both happiness. But you must wait. You will make no promise or contract until all risk has passed."

"Risk of what?" I said.

Still he didn't look at me. "Risk of death," he said.

For the rest of the day I avoided Walter as well as Vespasian. Tilda had never intended to accept his proposal. She had no wish to marry him at all. I curled in bed at night and Walter's young, crumpled face never entered my thoughts at all. Nothing sweet ever entered my thoughts, only flame and blood and pain.

But Walter continued to stay close to me, found me the warmest cushion next to the fire each evening, ladled out the best portion of meat onto my trencher and held my hand crossing the yard when I let him. If I carried a basket of apples, he would take it from me. "Don't worry," he whispered to me one morning. "The contract is made, whether the others know it or not. We'll be married in the spring. We'll marry at a church, if you like."

"There isn't any contract," I answered at once. "Don't say there is and don't think there is. I never answered you when you asked me. Vespasian told you no, but I never got to tell you anything at all."

"It wouldn't be such a bad match," said Walter, with a sniff.

I weakened. "Perhaps. But sudden death, that's what Vespasian said, isn't it? Please, Walter, don't let's talk about this again at least until we understand what's going on."

We were in the kitchen. The largest cauldron was hanging over the low fire, the pottage thick and highly scented, simmering in little creamy bubbles. To avoid him, I went over to stir it but Walter pulled me back. He pushed me against the far wall and held me by the shoulders. He was only slightly taller than me. His eyes were narrow and always seemed a little startled under those strong brows. He leaned down and kissed me hard. His mouth was shut tight and very dry. When he came up for air and let me go, I could see Vespasian's cold eyes watching us from the doorway.

I stared back at Walter and when I looked up again, Vespasian had gone. "Don't," I told Walter. "I'm not ready."

"That was the first time I ever kissed anyone," said Walter. "That ought to mean something."

"It was the first time for me too," said Tilda. "But I don't want to do it again."

It had meant very little to me. Such an inexperienced child's kiss. I felt guilty, but Tilda remained unimpressed. Walter, like all the boys and like me too, was grimy and unwashed. He smelled of the horse and manure, the wild garlic and the thick dark earth in the vegetable garden. He smelled like a boy who worked very hard and hadn't had a bath in months. His kiss had been rough and he hadn't known how to do anything except press hard. I could feel the desperation of his desire and Tilda didn't like it. But Walter expected girls to be difficult. "I can wait," he said, walking off.

The next time I went down to Richard's grave at the silver pool, I went alone.

CHAPTER TWENTY-FOUR

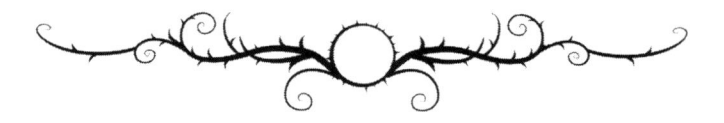

I slipped out of the house at first dawn. There was no breeze and it was a mild night of soft air and a full moon without aura. Pure silver, the moon's only blemishes were a tracery of valleys on a thoughtful face. I took my short sword, leather sheathed. The baldric came to my waist and joined my belt, but the sword hung heavy. I wrapped it in my skirts to stifle any noise. No one woke. The boys cuddled tight, a foot or an elbow thrust from the straw, noses wheezing beneath the coverlets. In my old bed, Vespasian slept on his back, eyes closed and dark lashes long against the golden tanned planes of his face. His hands were clasped behind his head and he breathed so silently that he seemed not to breathe at all. No one moved as I crept past into the big hall and its still smouldering fire and unlocked the front door. I stepped over the long dried herbs still scattered across the step and hurried across to the first trees.

I felt the night chill like a sudden warning, but scurried on into the blackthorn cover, pulling my hood over my hair to disappear completely into the shadows. It was only a few minutes, ten perhaps if I ran, to the cold pool I loved. I sat beside Richard's grave mound and played my fingers in the wild dew trapped violets clambering up its shallow sides. I wondered if he would have been jealous had Walter asked for me in marriage while he was still alive. But Tilda would have taken neither of them. It had been more comfortable when they had treated me like one of the boys. It was only Vespasian that had ever peopled Tilda's muddled dreams of making love and chivalrous adventure. Now she had pledged to kill Vespasian, whether she still loved him or not.

The sun tipped the moonlight from its pinnacles and drenched the dewy grass with gold. Quickly I pulled my clothes over my head, tumbled them into a heap on the bank with my sword on top, and walked into the water. Sudden cold made me gasp but I sank to my knees and flung my head down until all my long hair floated like water weed on the surface. It was warm then. I began to swim.

Tilda had never known how to swim but I did and I took her underwater, breaking up through sun kissed bubbles, and beneath again past the little darting fishes and the surprise of the water snails. I had brought soap. A sluggish froth caught the first long rays of refraction and splintered into rainbows.

Shaking the water from me, I clambered back up the banks and stretched on the springing green, rolling onto my stomach and closing my eyes against the march of the ants and the wild mint tickling my nose. The rising sun slanted through the clearing and glazed my back in warmth. I felt the energy of it up my spine. It was a long time since being free of grease and sweat and grime, with my body trapped in the same outworn clothes and my hair bedraggled. Cleanliness and naked freedom now felt deliciously exciting. I rested my head on Tilda's crossed wrists, stretched my toes, flexed the muscles of my thighs and buttocks, laid my cheek on violets and smelled loam.

"Did you expect that I would come, or did you hope that I would not?" said Vespasian.

Panicked, I wriggled around, worm like, trying to hook one toe under my tunic lying nearby. I tried to manoeuvre it up over my back but it didn't budge. So I gave up, stuck my chin up, folded my arms beneath me and gazed up at him with dislike. I felt more naked than ever before. I said, "You were asleep."

"I am apt to wake when my orders are disobeyed," he said. "Have you any idea how dangerous it could be going alone into the forest? You cannot have forgotten what might happen. Is a simple bath worth risking your life?'

"It seems dangerous everywhere," I said. "I felt – I had to be alone."

"You sleep alone," he pointed out. "I have given you my bed. And in truth, we are all of us always alone, whether we appreciate it or not."

"It never feels like it," I muttered. Peering up while lying flat, made it extremely difficult to talk.

"I told you once," he said, "that you should cultivate the secret places in your mind. In those places you can be eternally solitary. You can dream all the dreams of your unenviable youth. You can escape pain."

"But I didn't escape pain," I said, wishing I could sit up, wishing I could accuse him, retain my small dignity in defiance and demand all the explanations I longed for. "You tortured me anyway. You and the others."

He kept staring down at me and now he frowned. "Then you should have learned the lesson well," he said, "from now on never to wander unwatched."

I tried to glare, but it was difficult with my chin stuck in the mud and my blushes vivid. "Please," I said at last, "would you let me dress? And leave me, just for a moment?"

"No," he said softly. "I will do neither."

"I don't understand," I said. "You've told me off. I apologise for going off alone. I've finished my bath so if you go home now, I'll get dressed and hurry straight back to the house."

"Not yet," he said very softly. "You see, I had another reason for following you, for which I also need privacy." Then he came and knelt beside me, one leg bent on the grassy bank. His gaze was intrusive and intense.

I squirmed away. I was horribly conscious of my naked back and my chin stuck incongruously in the grass. "You shouldn't look at me like that," I mumbled. "Once you told me you thought of me as a daughter but I'm not."

"I know," he said. "And it's no longer the way I think of you."

However, there is something that must be dealt with, whether you are embarrassed and I am discomforted, is of no matter. This has to be done."

"I don't owe you anything," I muttered into the grass. "I'm not interested in doing anything you want me to."

He smiled, though it was not a particularly pleasant smile. The taint of malice was, as usual, playing at the corners of his eyes. "You misunderstand."

I waited, since I had no choice. But for a long time he looked across my shoulders down at the pool and its still waters now reflecting the rising sun. Finally I said, "Please. If you'd just let me put my cloak around me."

"No," he said, looking back suddenly at me as if he had just remembered I was still there. "Be quiet and listen to me. This is – important. You must answer my questions carefully and truthfully."

"I don't want to marry Walter," I said into the pause.

He laughed, which offended me. "I know," he said, "and that has nothing to do with the questions I need to ask." He knew he had me trapped. I was far too timid to get up naked and run. So I tried to look brave but then he surprised me. He said, "Tilda, tell me, your monthly courses, your woman's bleeding, is this still regular? Have you noticed any delay or interruption?"

I was shocked, humiliated and angry. He had no right to ask such things. But Tilda was less squeamish and more practical. She demanded, "Why?"

"In the weeks since you returned from my castle, have you felt different in any way?" Vespasian asked, ignoring both my blushes and Tilda's question. "Do you suffer attacks of nausea? Have you felt physically changed? Have you experienced any bodily sensation that you do not understand, internally or externally?"

"Yes," said Tilda bluntly. "I'm covered in scars and blisters. My hand's deformed. I've been beaten and burned and whipped and cut. Most of the pain's finally faded, but not all of it. How could I feel the same? How could I not feel different?"

It was the first time she'd been so direct with him. It sounded accusatory as she meant it to. Yet he was quite unashamed, and persisted with his questions, staring at me under hooded lids.

"In any other way? More intimate ways?" he demanded. "And concerning your woman's bleeding? Be precise."

Tilda had started shivering. "No," I said. "I won't say anything – intimate – not to you." She was increasingly angry, and I encouraged her.

Vespasian smiled. "Then," he said, "you must sit up."

"Certainly not," I said.

"But I must insist," said Vespasian and the malice was back. "If you do not do so willingly, then I warn you, I shall force you."

I really didn't understand and I was furious. "You want to torture me all over again?"

"No," he said, very, very softly. Yet his voice seemed unwilling, as if he now said what he had not intended to tell me. "This is not an arbitrary demand," he murmured. "I need to know if you have conceived a child. Tilda, I must know if you are pregnant."

I sighed. It began to make sense. I could have simply said I wasn't, but Tilda was hopelessly ignorant. "It's not possible," she said, hanging her head.

"Then sit up," said Vespasian, "and afterwards I will let you dress."

Very slowly, Tilda brought her knees up beneath her, legs tight together, damp from the swim and the dewy grass. She let her hair fall over her shoulders and folded her arms across her breasts. Then she sat up straight. I glared back at Vespasian as he gazed at me.

"Lower your arms," he said.

Reluctantly, I uncrossed my arms and clasped my hands in my lap. I knew I shivered and my nipples were taut with cold. His stare was momentarily intrusive. Then he smiled and reaching down, caught up the bundle of my clothes and tossed them to me. "Now you may dress," he said. His voice had lightened.

He continued to watch me as I dressed. I struggled with the ties, aware of his eyes on me until the final buckling of my belt. "Now explain," I said as forcefully as I could. "You owe me an explanation. You have to tell me everything."

"I will not tell you everything," he said. "But I will tell you some of it, if you wish."

Fully dressed again, I hoped my face would begin to fade back to its normal colour. "So I wasn't just tortured in that house. I was raped?"

He sat where he was on the damp ground, still relaxed, one arm resting casually on his raised knee. He looked straight back at me. "Yes," he said. "You were."

"It was your house. You tricked me into going there. It's your responsibility."

He nodded. "Yes. It is my responsibility," he said.

"You kept coming into my head, telling me not to follow you. But you kept the horse's hoof marks clear all through the forest. You made sure I'd come."

"It was not my horse," he pointed out mildly. "I did not steal Gerald away."

I sat directly opposite him on the grass and glared hard into his black eyes. I was trying not to tremble. I said, "Before the storm that took me down the hill, there was a force pushing back against me. That was them. They didn't want me there at all. But you did. You led me on. You wanted me there so you could swap me for Gerald."

"Let us say that is accurate," he said so softly that I could hardly hear him, though the silence all around us was broken only by blackbird song. "Let us say, for the sake of it, that you understand correctly."

"And then," I went on, "you knew I'd be tortured. You bandaged me up for them once. You thought I'd lost too much blood and you thought I might die. You kept me alive – for them to torture again. I heard them talk about it. You even warned me about the pain. You knew what they'd done to me and what they'd keep doing. So I expect you knew they'd rape me too. Which one was it? The foul grandfather? Arthur?"

I was shuddering. The thought disgusted me. Vespasian stared back, and I could see no emotion in his eyes at all. The birdsong faded into silence.

"No," he said after a pause. "It was me."

I stared. My astonishment was complete. I hated him and distrusted him, but I had not expected that. Almost, I disbelieved him. "You?"

He nodded. Once Tilda would have given herself to him willingly. I believe at the time he knew it well. What he was saying made no sense. Now he said nothing. He continued to look unblinkingly into my eyes.

"Why?" I whispered in a sort of gasp.

"Yes, I am sure I owe you an explanation," he said, and it was the first time that he seemed to sigh. "But I do not intend to give it to you. Now I wished merely to be sure you are not carrying my child. That would have been – how can I say – most inconvenient. You are not. At the time, I ensured that you would not conceive, but even I can sometimes make mistakes."

I sat open mouthed and mumbled, "I don't understand."

"I know," he said. "I am sorry."

If it was an apology, it was the first ever. And nowhere near sufficient. "Did you," I said, struggling with thoughts tumbling from their established patterns into incoherence, "stop one of the others? Who would have been – less gentle?" I was trying to make sense out of something that seemed hopelessly and embarrassingly senseless.

Vespasian didn't smile. "But I was not gentle," he said. "I'm afraid I was not gentle at all."

He got up abruptly. I was still staring at him like an idiot with my mouth hanging open and my head spinning. He pointed to my sword which was still on the ground at his feet. I picked it up. For a moment I thought of trying to attack him with it but I knew his skill. He was too quick and would have struck me. Instead I buckled it to the belt around my hips. Then Vespasian turned away. He walked quickly back through the forest and I followed him at some distance. When we neared the house, he stopped briefly and looked back at me. "You're free to marry Walter if you wish," he said.

Tilda was still furious and I felt patronised. I was even angrier than she was. I took a deep breath and said, "Because you've had me.

You've finished with me. And you accept I'm not – with child. Your child."

He seemed momentarily surprised, but he only said, "In part."

"I've no desire to marry Walter. Or anyone else," she said.

"Very well," he replied, walking on. "It is better that way."

CHAPTER TWENTY-FIVE

Tilda was desperately miserable. In no part of the house could I escape or feel as I had once felt. Returning injured and in pain with Walter and Osbert, I had been precious cargo and immediately protected, cared for and central to the life that continued among us. Now it had changed. I could not bear to look at Vespasian. When he recommenced the lessons in archery and sword fighting I could not accept him touching me, looking at me or holding me, steadying my position or guiding my arm. I refused lessons. I avoided Gerald. I avoided Walter.

Stephen avoided me. He felt betrayed. I saw his discomfort. Walter's spoken intention to marry me had broken up the intimate boyishness we shared, shattered the lack of self consciousness and the easy speech which even Richard's death apparently hadn't altered. Only big Hugh and Osbert seemed unaffected.

"If you don't fancy marrying Walter," Osbert said to me one quiet afternoon in the vegetable plot, "just tell him so. It won't kill him you know. He just wants to be gallant. He doesn't really understand love so what you say won't hurt him that much."

"Can you tell him for me?" Tilda asked. She was snipping off turnip greens for the pottage.

Osbert laughed. "What a child you are after all. No, I won't tell him. You have to tell him yourself."

"Well," I said. "Actually, I have. But he just thinks I'm shy or I'm not ready. He doesn't believe me."

"Well," said Osbert, with a fleeting blush, "girls always say no when they mean yes. But there's one way to make it clear to him. If you really decide not to marry Walter, you can always marry me."

I stared. I thought he would try and kiss me and when he put out his arm, I ducked beneath it, grabbed the vegetables I had collected, and dashed inside.

That night when I was curled small in the big soft bed and all the others were out in the main sleeping room snuffling into their straw, Tilda and I cried ourselves to sleep. What had been sunshine on sweet meadows had turned into grey rain clouds and the threat of thunder. Tilda felt she had become suddenly very ugly.

Instead I, equally suddenly, knew she had grown very beautiful. She was attracting interest that had previously quite passed her by and now the boys saw her as a woman instead of a friend. But what Vespasian thought of her, I had no idea.

Tilda's dreams wandered lost, and the innocence of her imagination became distorted. She pictured what had been done to her. It repulsed and terrified her. She knew little or nothing in detail, for she had been tortured and reviled when she herself had not even been present in her own head. So I had no memory of the rape, and little of the beatings and burnings. But I knew I had been the victim of great cruelty indulged in by a group of inhumans with Vespasian among them.

Vespasian had long since repudiated Tilda's timid adoration. The offer of a loving young girl in his arms had evidently not attracted him. He'd chosen brutality and force. Then she remembered being shackled to a stone table. Having no concept of rape, she imagined it. She imagined Vespasian staring at her nakedness and holding her down. Now she was torturing herself.

She decided to run away.

It was more than a week before I felt confident enough and could give sufficient confidence to Tilda. It was another week before we could even decide where to go. In truth, there was nowhere to go but Tilda had been homeless before and she was less scared of that than of staying. She didn't mourn the loss of her virginity, which seemed to mean comparatively little to her. But she mourned the loss of her adoration for Vespasian and the last passing of her respect for him.

"You've been avoiding my tutoring with the short sword," he said to her. "You must learn whatever measures of self protection you can."

"Protection? Against who? You?" she said, because they were alone.

"If you want to see it that way, yes," he said. "I'm sure you'd like to hurt me if you could. So learn how."

"Learn how to attack you?"

"Yes. How – and where."

I stared back at him with whatever expression of contempt I could summon. "I don't want you to teach me anything because I don't want you to touch me."

He smiled which I considered quite inappropriate. "I shall try hard not to do so," he said. "However, the skills I can teach you are essential. To protect yourself against me – and anyone else."

Reluctantly I followed him outside. Hugh and Gerald were practising a series of flying strokes that seemed more likely to behead the woodpigeons. It was the hottest day of autumn and I was still sweating from the cooking pot. The sun on the blades blinded me momentarily, reflecting daggers against my eyes. I lost coherence. In a sudden glitter of flashing images, I saw Molly rushing to the police station and the inspector's grey frown, past the tiny bridge and the stream in a high white flurry, storms, floods, terror. A wide arched darkness opened before me and a buzzard flew through, its wings spread, obscuring the light. I thought Molly's cottage was on fire and then I saw it was the setting sun's reflections. Trees swept up in a marching menace towards a flaming sky. Something huge and terrible sprang from their shadows. I heard a door swinging shut, the grind of its hinges and the grate of its key. I heard horses galloping and felt the ground trembling beneath me, vibrating through my toes. A great urgency made me topple and faint.

I had fallen, all my bright confidence melting away like oozing butter. As my eyes closed I felt sharp metal slice though me. Then blackness.

But it was only seconds. I was swept up so quickly that I swung through the air like a little bird. I rested my head against Vespasian's shoulder and could breathe again. "Piccina, what did you see on the other side?" he demanded, his voice unusually harsh and tight against my ear.

As usual, it was not what I had expected him to say. "Put me down. I'm alright. I can walk now."

"Don't be a fool," he said, and carried me indoors. It was cool in the great hall. He sat me in his high backed chair and knelt at my feet, his arms either side of me, holding to the chair arms and keeping me still. I stared back at him. "Now," he repeated, "what did you see?"

I had feared him touching me. I'd hated the thought of his hands on me. After what I knew had happened, I'd only wanted to kill him. But now nothing else mattered and I just wanted him to hold me against him. "The sword," I muttered. "It must have been a mistake. One of the boys?"

"Explain," he demanded.

Wasn't it obvious? "The blade went through me. I can't tell where. Can't you see? It must be bleeding."

"There's no sword and no wound," said Vespasian softly. "You've not been hurt. Not this time, little one."

"I felt it," I insisted. "Steel and fire."

"I believe you saw a vision, or a series of symbols," he said. He reached forwards, gently tucking strands of hair back from my forehead. I felt the sweat like wet trickles on my brow. His voice was normal again, each word low and clear. "It's important that I know exactly what you saw," he said. "Now, pequena, describe everything that happened."

So I told him. Already the memory was blurred and of course none of it made sense. I told him about the huge black bird and the floods, the fire, the trees, the horses and the sun. Then I told him about the great arch and the closing door, and it being another world, or perhaps the same world in a different time. I told him I had seen Molly, though I didn't mention the name at first. "It was all just nonsense," I said, looking away and breathing easily again. "Not visions, just silly dreams. I thought I was burning but I wasn't. I thought I felt a sword cut me almost in two, slicing me into separate pieces, but that was silly too. Perhaps I came out of the shade too quickly. The sun in my eyes made me faint. It doesn't matter, does it?"

"Yes, it matters," he replied. "Tell me about this other woman. You've seen her before, many times I think."

I looked him in the eyes and I said, "Yes, I see her. She sees me."

"And you know her name." His expression was unusually earnest, his eyes clear and free of either irony or malice. "Don't be frightened," he said, and he was entirely gentle. "Although you may not believe it, you can trust me in this. Besides," he seemed to sigh, "you've already told me so much more than you can possibly appreciate."

"She's Molly," I said, hanging my head. I already regretted having told him what I saw.

He frowned, waiting, but when I said nothing more, he sighed again. "She has another name," he said, which astonished me. "A more – dangerous name, and a more dangerous power. Do you know her other name? Does she speak to you of opening the doors between time? The worlds of future, and present, and past?"

I was suddenly freezing cold. I shivered. "No. I don't know what you mean." Then, rather pathetically, "In the dream there was an arch and a door and a key and a lock. But that's nothing to do with Molly. She's – nice."

"You have seen the symbols of transgression, degeneration and transmutation," Vespasian said, though he seemed to be speaking more to himself, and his voice was even less audible than normal. "And through the opening of the ways comes this woman from the future time whom I have met, though she only cloaks another who has not yet come. Tilda," he looked up sharply at me, "you're bound into the danger that surrounds all of us. More deeply than any other – except myself. I am sorry. It was not what I intended."

I was uncomfortable that he knelt at my feet, when in the past I had usually knelt at his. "But it was you who pulled me into it," I said rather plaintively. "You've admitted it. You exchanged me for Gerald, knowing I'd be tortured, almost to death. I could have died. You didn't care."

He smiled and for once it was a small, gentle smile though it barely tucked the corners of his mouth. "That is what I allowed you to believe for reasons of my own, but it is not, in fact, the truth." His eyes went very dark. "At least, not the whole truth. Perhaps you have a right to know – a little – of what happened. In the end, when there was so much already spoiled and lost, I exchanged your pain for Gerald's safety. At first I warned you repeatedly not to interfere. You should not have come to the castle. It was not intended, at least not by me. When you were younger, and just my Tilda – you were a more obedient child. I expected you to turn back and obey my warnings. But now you have complicated a situation which was already deeply complicated. Instead of helping me, as I suppose you wished, you became an additional responsibility. No, I did not intend you to come. I was furious when I found you."

Yes, I remembered how angry he had seemed in the turret room as he bandaged my breasts. "I don't understand." At last I was beginning to.

"I went to bring Richard back. I knew where they'd taken him. I thought it was possible he was still alive because I knew they wanted Gerald and might bargain an exchange. I would not have given Gerald, but I might have rescued Richard. But it was purely sentiment. A weakness. I should have sacrificed Richard and stayed to protect the rest of you. I misjudged the risk of leaving. You have suffered for that, little one. I do not normally permit myself misjudgements. I am therefore to blame."

He never usually talked like that and I valued it. "So who led us on and kept the hoof marks clear? And sent the storm that dragged me into the castle?"

"Arthur. You know who he is," said Vespasian. "You were a virgin child and as such, useful to him for sacrifice. He also has his own lusts to satisfy. More importantly, he believed he could use you as a lever against me. He almost succeeded. Then he began to suspect what I already knew, that there's a division within you Tilda, an inherent power, that I doubt you begin to understand yourself. I created the barrier when you arrived at the river. I tried to force you back. It was Arthur who brought the storm and dragged you in. His influence was stronger than mine, for it was multiplied by every other person in the castle. I was alone, and at that moment, held close."

"And it was you who found me in the dungeons and took me to the turret room?" Vespasian nodded, and I said, "It's real sorcery then. Real magic. Terrible magic."

"It is," Vespasian said, his voice just a breath. "Now, although undoubtedly it will seem remarkably unjust, this is more explanation than I have ever given anyone and is enough for now. You should rest."

"Please – just one more thing." I sat forward urgently as he stood, reaching out to him. "When you said, when you admitted it was you. I mean, what you did. That – particular – torture. You said you did it. Were you lying then as well? Was it – him too?"

He looked down at me, black eyes and no emotion. "That it was I who raped you? No. I was not lying, pequena. That was the truth."

That night I ran away.

CHAPTER TWENTY-SIX

Tilda chose to return to London. She had spent the few happy years of her life in London's back streets and there the memories of Vespasian were untroubled and remained innocent.

She had been born in the West Country but if she returned there she could be taken as a runaway serf and put back into bondage. That had been the first time she had escaped a life she refused to accept. Nor would she risk the direction of the castle. So she went back to London. It took only one day and though twice we were lost, nothing in the forest could frighten me anymore. She and I found our way again and kept the setting sun to our left. There were streams for drinking and I had packed a hunk of brown oat bread in my pack. I had baked it myself, but it was not very nice.

A cold wind blew low through the branches, and flurries of red and brown leaf deserted their trees and drifted below, all patterned like Turkey rugs. I picked blackberries from their thorns, pricking my fingers until blood collected under my nails and mixed with the sweet berry juice. I knew it would be late and the city gates locked against me as I arrived, so when I came to the edge of the wood and saw the distant huddle of London's wood and thatch, I walked no further but settled for the night, curling beneath the furred cloak Vespasian had given me and the woollen coverlet I had brought from his bed. When I woke it was already morning, the sun was warm and the dew was steaming damp around me.

I crossed London's Bridge over the wide brown Thames. Shoved by traffic, shoppers and travellers, pushing and squabbling, I mingled with the sweating crowds. A tight knot of brown skirted monks elbowed me back, thrusting their own way to the front. I was splattered with mud from cart wheels but avoided the pile of mule droppings and quickly lifted the hems of my cloak. I loved the cloak Vespasian had given me. Blue and velvet lined with a trimming of white miniver, the palla of a girl who should be riding her own palfrey and not shuffling through the dirt.

London was bustling. It wasn't market day but the bath houses were open down by the river and a welter of women and their bundles were arriving at the gates, the whores slipping in around the back. Outside the Crusader's Tavern two lounging knights flashed their chain mail in the sun, drinking ale and playing chess while their squires bickered over a game of dice. Up beyond was the Shambles, the butchers' quarter. Its alleys were open drains and the blood and chicken heads, feathers and bones too small for the pot, all streamed down to the river. Three barges were moored to the muddy banks, piled with fish, while a small crane cranked proud, unloading crates of best cloth from Flanders, the fat captain screaming his orders. Two small boats skimmed mid river. Experienced boatmen, they had shot the bridge as only experts dared, speeding beneath one of the nineteen wide arches and avoiding the surges and whirls of water around the fat stone pillars.

I stepped over the stream of urine and excrement that found its level down the middle of each lane, packed earthen streets dipping to a central valley. The pillory was empty but the gibbet had taken a new body and it swung in the breeze, spreading its stench. The three others in the row were old bones but the new corpse had been a fine young man and he still wore most of his clothes except his boots. The hangman always took the boots. I hurried into the back streets.

Our old house bent outwards, peering over to the smaller building opposite. The alleyway was so narrow that I could almost stretch out my arms and touch both sides. There were no shops here. This was a place of forgotten people. Our front door was shut and barred and that surprised me for Vespasian had sold to Jack, the saddle and leather merchant, a friend whose business we had never been allowed. Jack and his fat wife had always kept open house and she baked her own bread, finer than the miller's, which she had sometimes given me free. Now the house was locked fast. The wooden tub which stood beside our door collecting rainwater, was now broken as if someone had splintered it with an axe. Those barrels stood by law, ready to fight the hundred fires which caught so regularly in the smoking wooden chimneys and thatches. But no one had replaced it. The upper storey was lightless. No smoke, no smell of baking, no movement. Dogs were barking somewhere. I whirled around and ran back down the alley.

Jack Saddler's shop was tiny. In the back shadows a hundred flayed leathers hung to dry over the smell of tallow soap and candle and the rhythmic scrape of scrubbing hides. He brought them in from the tanneries out east, but sometimes finished off any rough work, and even sometimes cured his own. Now Jack sat in the doorway, working the thick hard leather into supple beauty. His face had become as tanned as his hides and his eyes seemed like dark studs in the sides of a saddle.

"How are you?" I asked him. "How's business? How's Agatha? And Wat and Emma and Mabel?"

He looked up at me. "That really you Tilda? How you've grown. I'd only have recognised you from your voice, if you hadn't reeled off all the names of my little ones like you always did. You look like a proper grand lady. Pretty as a picture. So Vespasian married you after all, then?"

I stared at him, momentarily distracted. "What on earth would make you think such a thing?"

Jack winked. "I saw the way you looked at him all those years. And the way he looked at you."

"Well, you got it wrong," I snorted. "It was Isabel he liked," and then I wished I hadn't mentioned Isabel at all.

"Well, that's just the point, isn't it now?" said Jack. "You was too young. Vespasian, well, reckon he had too much respect. He were saving you for later and a proper decent marriage."

"He hasn't been showing me much respect lately," I said, rather bleak. "Anyway, that's not what I came here for. I'm not married to anyone and I'm not going to be. Ever. I just passed by the old house and found it locked up so I wondered what happened. Was there – any trouble?"

"There certainly was," said the saddler, putting down his tools. "You mentioned poor Isabel. Well, all about her, it was. I suppose you heard. They found her all cut about and half drowned, poor lass. Quite dead she was, a nasty business. The sheriff come around looking for Vespasian. But I spoke up. Told him you'd all gone away some time before."

I thanked him and asked, "What happened?"

"I were sent to the mayor's office," said Jack, looking proud. "I told them what I knew but that weren't much. Well, I'd seen Isabel for some weeks before, flirting with that sour young knight what used to hang around. Well, we all knew what poor Isabel used to be way back, before Vespasian took her in, poor lost sinner she was. I warned Vespasian when I first saw her with that fancy man. But I didn't know no names and I didn't know where he come from."

"A knight?" I moved into the shadows of the shop doorway. "Dark and skinny? Short cut hair, loose jawed and eyes that slant?"

"Yes, I suppose so, though I hardly remember now. It were another man entirely what came to the house afterwards."

"What happened?" I had guessed already.

"This old gentleman come riding up. My Agatha was at the brick ovens across the square and the young'uns was playing in the street outside. A right foul looking gent he were, but him being elderly and maybe some lord, I were polite at first. Asked me impertinent questions and wanted to know all about Vespasian, though he called him by some other name first, until I put him right. Jasper, he said. No one o' that name, I said. Man owned the house and sold to me is called Vespasian Fairweather."

Small clues clicking into place like the wooden beads on a rosary. "What did you tell him?" I asked, holding my breath.

"Well, I didn't have no idea where you'd all gone so I couldn't tell him, could I? He got right nasty. Flashed his sword and well nigh cut my nose off. I threatened him with the law and he laughed. Well, the next day the bailiff turned up and chucked us all out the house. Locked and barred the doors, he did, and told us not to come back. Confiscated by the crown and we was forbidden to come near. Not a penny compensation and a few more threats thrown in. Well, we'd no choice and I wouldn't risk no trouble, not with Agatha expecting again."

"So you're back living in the room over the shop?"

"It don't bother us none," nodded Jack. "I don't want trouble. But you'd best warn Vespasian when you see him next. I don't want my money back nor nothing, seeing it weren't his fault. But warn him, will you?"

"Yes," I said. "I suppose I should." I thought of Vespasian's never ending supply of money and would have liked to give poor Jack his money back. But I didn't want to see Vespasian at all.

I slept under the eaves of the bath house that night, but it was cold, and the forest had seemed a sweeter bed. The dirty street was a bastard place, neither natural nor human. I had expected the great bathhouse tubs of water and hot fogs of steam would insulate the walls and keep me safe for the night, but I was wrong. It stank and the damp reek was colder than the fresh breeze in the leaves. I woke very early and shivered my way back into London rhythms.

If Jack Saddle had been living in our old house I would have had friends and a pallet with one of the children. I could have helped Agatha with the cleaning. I would have been safe and warm until I decided on a more permanent destination. It hadn't worked that way I expected, as life never does. Jack was back living in one room above the shop with no space for me. He thought I was well dressed, proof of affluence, and never guessed what I was hoping for. So I moved on.

London was full of beggars. They slept where they could. Once Tilda had been one of them and she had slept under the stone bridge until Vespasian found her. But I would not sleep under that bridge any more, not since Isabel's death. At least I could steal enough to eat, though not enough to buy me a lodging.

The Convent of the Little Sisters of Angelica stood behind high brick walls out beyond Cripplegate. Once I had begged from the nuns, and once I had stolen the pennies the fat prioress had collected for the poor. A sin of course, but I was one of the poor and considered myself entitled. Now I walked through the narrow back streets heading north towards Cripplegate, looking for the sloping roadway that I would eventually recognise. With the autumn sun sinking, I hurried through the gateway and into Grub Street.

It had already begun to drizzle and my pretty cloak lost its blue shimmer, now smelling slightly of mule shit and leaf litter, but its rich velvet lining still kept me snuggled warm. It was evening when I found what I was looking for. Tall trees peered over the top of the walls and the iron gate was locked. I rang the traveller's bell and it clanked through the echoes of the wind. The stars were peeping through a sullen darkness. I could hear the rustle of skirts and a whisper of impatience, but they opened the gate for me and I slipped inside.

Between the shadows was a long pathway wide enough for carts and horses. A small plump nun muffled in her rigid black habit, led me quickly towards the lights in the high windows beyond. An owl called shrill across the clouds. I put my head down and scurried behind. The convent door was open and welcoming, the warm flicker of beeswax candles and the smell of hot food. "Quick," said the little nun, "you took me from my dinner."

"I'm sorry," I replied beneath my breath.

The convent was the largest building Tilda had ever seen and even greater than the strange castle on the river. Inside, once the door clanged behind me, it was deliciously inviting. A hundred embroidered tapestries in brilliant colours lined the walls. A hundred candles lined the hall in iron sconces and the high beams collected flickering shadows. At the far end a huge wooden cross was embossed in gold. Below, five long tables and their benches stood in parallel rows. Hunched on the benches were the nuns, each a busy back, leaning over their bowls and trenchers. Few bothered to turn as I and my guide hustled in. At the head of one table the Abbot carved the roast venison and the perfume beckoned. I was reminded how little I had eaten for two days. The meat fell tender from its carcass, spilling juices across the long table. Not a convent of frugal self-sacrifice, I assumed, nor strict vows of poverty. The Abbot licked his fingers.

"An hour more, mistress, and you would not have been admitted," he told me, looking up briefly. "We lock our doors after compline. But now you're here, come in and share our meagre supper. Find a place. There's food enough and you're welcome to stay one night. All travellers are welcome to stay one night."

I had hoped to stay longer but I said nothing and bent my knee to him. There was space at the bench of the novices. My young neighbour helped me fill my trencher and passed me a spoon. I had no knife, so she cut a thick slice of meat for me. Tilda had rarely eaten so much or so well. I kept my breath for the food and not for talking. No one spoke to me. Passing travellers were common enough I expect, though surely young unaccompanied women must have been rare. Yet no one seemed curious about my arrival alone and at such a late hour. There was wine and ale and clean water and seemingly endless food. Finally there was too much and I put down my spoon and watched the faces around me. The Abbot could exhibit his bad manners at his own table, but I resisted licking my fingers, one of Vespasian's lessons, and wiped them instead on my napkin. I didn't want to look like the country child that I felt.

It was a rich convent and I already knew its reputation. A large splinter from the true cross and the whole of Saint Gregory's right leg bone were kept in the holy chapel. Once there had been a few well publicised cases of miraculous healing so this had become a place of pilgrimage, but when the new Italian Abbot had taken charge several years back, all that had changed. He had brought wealth from Europe and now the convent welcomed the younger daughters of the great barons, widows of princes and sisters of bishops.

The Little Sisters of Angelica were not so little and if all their evening suppers consisted of six courses, then I wasn't surprised. I already knew the prioress as a square woman and short sighted. It was the indulgent Abbot I liked the look of. He was simply dressed in rough hemp habit and although he had eaten his way through a mountain, his eyes were gentle brown and quick with humour. I felt his gaze on me but I kept my own eyes lowered.

Two small girls, eight or nine years old, crept into the big hall to clear away the plates. The nuns did not do their own housework it seemed. I'd heard that the convent took in orphans from time to time and once a rumour about some being the illegitimate children of the previous abbot. But there were always rumours.

The novitiate sitting next to me finished her meal. "I can take you to the visitor's rooms," she said, "but first you must see Abbot Bernardo. He likes to speak to everyone who passes through here. I expect he'll bless your journey."

I thought it might even help since I needed all the help I could get, so I bowed diplomatically and waited until the tables emptied. A bell was ringing, perhaps for prayers. I thought they might expect me to join them but no one did and I was relieved. I was far too tired for a mumble of Latin I would not understand.

"Now," said a sudden voice above me, "so this is our new guest?" He had an accent and spoke with rolling consonants, but his English was perfect. "We rise very early in the mornings and I shall not be able to see you again before you set off. But come with me now for a cup of wine in my rooms before you sleep. I'll give you a blessing and directions for your journey tomorrow." The Abbot had me up off my bench and scurrying after his bare heels. If the bell had indeed been a call to chapel, he clearly had no intention of obeying it.

His rooms were grand with a silk canopy over a high chair. As good as a throne, I thought, not that Tilda had ever seen a throne. The chair was soft cushioned. I sat on a stool by his skirted knees and tried to look attractively beseeching. "Father, is it ever permitted for a guest to stay longer than one night?"

I trusted his eyes and hoped I read kindness. "Perhaps," he said, scratching his chin. "You travel alone?" He looked a little deeper, smiling and nodding. "You're in some sort of trouble I expect? As a man of the cloth, perhaps I could help."

"Trouble of a sort," I said with a sigh of gratitude. Molly's bizarre imagination shoved poor Tilda aside. I said, "Can I tell you, then, Father? Please don't send me back. You see, my brother's the Baron d'Azur. He threw me out of the castle when he discovered I was, well it's embarrassing to admit it, but I was in love with the stable boy." Absurd of course, but I thought it would serve well enough. "I left with my maid but my horse went lame. Then my maid died of the dysentery. I've been walking for some days."

"Good gracious," murmured the Abbot. "What a series of dreadful calamities. Do you have no other family?"

"Yes," I said, thinking fast, "my sister but she lives on the Scottish boarders. That would be a terribly long way to walk. Besides, she might just send me back to my brother. Instead I was, well, perhaps, even thinking of joining a convent."

"Indiscretion with a stable boy," said the Abbot, "hardly seems a good preparation for a life in the cloisters."

"I can atone for my sins," I suggested.

"Baron D'Azur?" smiled the Abbot. "Perhaps I know him? Is he rather stocky and sandy haired with a short beard?"

I was confused. "No," I decided it was safer not to agree, since I thought I'd made him up. "He's slim and dark and has a terrible temper. But I'd need time to think about taking holy orders of course. If I could just stay for a few weeks, to meditate in peace and clear my mind?"

"Well now, I think that would be quite acceptable," said the Abbot, standing up and stretching his fingers like a concert pianist, though I was fairly sure even harpsichords hadn't been invented yet. "Our hospitality here is an important part of our Christian service and although most guests stay just the one night – and we usually encourage short stays – restricted premises you see – under special circumstances, well, that's quite another matter."

I was genuinely grateful. "Thank you Father," I said. "You're a man of charity. I appreciate it."

"Oh," he said, smiling down at me, all jovial chins and twinkling brown eyes. "These can be hard times for young women cast out alone. And don't worry." He leaned over and patted my hand. "I shan't send you back, my dear. Neither to your wicked brother the Baron D'Azur – nor to my wicked friend Vespasian Fairweather."

CHAPTER TWENTY-SEVEN

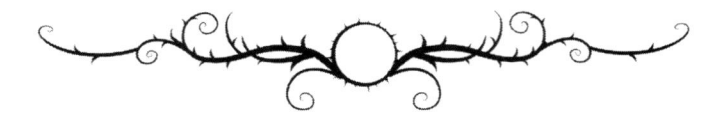

Autumn blew east and Molly shivered. I was sitting on the edge of my own doorstep, looking up to the hills. Their wavering peaks rose from a damp mist of low fog that seemed to sink into me as I was breathing, causing depression and had no idea what to do next. So I sat all alone and watched the Cotswold Hills blur into cloud and felt it symbolised my life. Vespasian often talked of symbols. But I was back into the twenty first century and Bertie was indoors making lunch. He had become a better cook during my last vaguely muddled half-absence as Tilda.

Sammie's loss still hung over the house as a constant reminder of terrifying evil and awful sadness. Wattle's death had hurt Bertie deeply, but Sammie's murder was an even greater horror. It had happened in my own home. Sammie was my cousin and I had loved her dearly all my life. She was the only person in all the world who had ever even remotely known me, had understood me and loved me for who I really was, instead of the way I pretended to be, as Bertie had. She had clutched my hand all during my short confused childhood. I had not been with her to hold hers when she needed me. I refused to talk to anyone.

The police shuffled between sympathy and suspicion. I talked very little even to them, but they seemed to believe I was traumatised and in many ways, I was. They suggested a counsellor and I visited a little William Morris woman with tiffany lampshades who tried to get me to talk to her. I just looked at her and admired her lampshades and her cushions. She had a beautiful ash tree in her big back garden and I admired that too. I sat staring at it over her shoulder through the smears on the window and decided it would be excellent wood for making well spliced bows and nice straight arrows. There was an ash tree bending over Richard's grave mound and I wished I was there instead of here.

I slept very badly. Sammie's face opened its eyes at me under the swirling blood coloured bath water. Tilda called, lost in the guttering candle light of her long past world. I saw Abbot Bernado sitting on the edge of his desk piled with rolled parchments, swinging his plump hairy legs, his uncut toenails peeping through his sandals. He was patting my hand. "I won't tell Vespasian what a bad girl you have been," he told me. "But how strange to love a grubby stable lad, when Vespasian is there to love instead." Then his face blurred into eagles' wings and flew away across the tree tops. Sometimes Richard came through the fog and stood by the side of the misted river. His eyes were hidden behind silver pennies. Behind him Isabel emerged ghostlike, reaching out her arms. Wattle stood between Richard and Isabel and put her hands on their shoulders, guiding their blind eyes. Sammie rose from the river waters, which had all turned red. She smiled at me before she turned and climbed the far bank. She took the arm of Muriel Bunting who was waiting for her there, and they walked back into the fog together.

I hated my dreams. I cried and cried, stayed awake half the night and couldn't get out of bed in the mornings.

The trees lost their leaves, a sad death for summer beauty. The sodden creased leaf colour turned to sludge in the gutters. It was the first of October and I had left all my courage behind with Tilda. She needed it more than I did.

Sammie's murder had left no clues and it was common knowledge that the police were totally bewildered. I spent many hours with them.

I went to the tiny station house behind the village, covered in ivy with spiders scrambling through the half open windows, but it wasn't the local constabulary who interviewed me. It was the top brass from London and they had taken rooms in the big hotel by the stream, sitting huddled in the station each gloomy grey day. They came to my house as well and I made them tea and Bertie handed around biscuits as if they were old friends, which was almost how they seemed. They had come to my hospital bed, sitting outside the isolated private ward, uncomfortable in the squashed passage and occasionally helping the nurses with their lunch duties. Detective Constable Peterson fed me soup for two days. I liked him best. They did not suspect me of butchery and madness and never mentioned my mother's history though they must have researched it, but they suspected I had secret friends. They thought I might have forgotten some dreadful past acquaintanceship, some awful dabbling in the black arts, some occult dalliance. They suspected Bertie sometimes, or some of them did sometimes. Bertie got fed up with it and fed up with me too and my wearisome lethargy, irascible moods and vague absences. He invited himself back to Wattle's parents and drove off in a hired car one dull morning, packed up with everything I had hoped he would take with him, leaving me with my spare room spare again. I had been longing for him to bugger off. I had thrown a plate at him (my cooking, not his) and all the shepherd's pie had slodged down his beige waistcoat like vomit on a rug. "That's the last damned straw," he had shouted at me. "I've been trying damn hard to help you, Mol. Have you no idea how damned stupid you're being?"

I knew. "I have to be alone, Bertie. You don't see it, do you? You're so terribly miserable you need company. I'm so terribly miserable, I desperately need to be left alone. Privacy, for God's sake. Doesn't anyone know how valuable privacy is?"

"For a month you act like a damned zombie hardly opening your mouth. Then you come back to life and turn into a harridan."

"I'm so sorry," which was true.

"Phone me some time," said Bertie and disappeared up the road in a puff of exhaust fumes and dust.

I did phone him and apologised properly and I even missed him once or twice too, which I could do more easily now I couldn't actually see him anymore.

He'd been such a shit as a husband, selfish, utterly self absorbed, and so regularly unfaithful that it seemed more of a career than a hobby. I had worked endlessly at understanding him and being the good wife. Then one day I'd realised how my idea of a good wife was boring to both of us. Not only was Bertie unfailingly unfaithful to me, but somehow I was being unfaithful to myself.

So I divorced him. I felt it was essential and overdue and would set us both free. I was excited at first, about getting myself back. It hadn't resulted in anything of the sort of course, because I hadn't appreciated how little conscious control any of us actually have over our own lives. And now Bertie was turning into the patient and tolerant housewife, while I was the self absorbed shit.

But privacy was my bliss and I cherished it. There had been so few really solitary corners to discover during my medieval meanderings. Now I spent all day by myself unless the police called. I even avoided the shops. If I had nothing to eat already mouldering on a shelf, then I missed meals. I had learned a lot from the past and hunger no longer bothered me in the least. I lost weight, my tummy went concave, and I looked far better than I felt. But I had to wear high necks, easier in the autumn chill, as Tilda's wounds and scars were etched across my body. With the modern inconvenience of mirrors everywhere, I could now see more clearly what had been done to her. In my dreams, I saw her face. I saw she had become beautiful and thought it bitter that all her pain and experience should have widened her eyes into smoky wistful innocence and filled her body into sensual curves with firm new rounded breasts. She had grown. Her legs were long and slim and strong muscled. I had run and walked and run again. Molly's sluggish disinclination to exercise had been honed by Tilda's hardships.

But I loved to walk too, trudging up onto the hills and through the country lanes. I was filling in time until Tilda would have me back. As Molly I was lost. Most of all I feared hearing of the next victim, for death now all seemed my fault. At least, a selfish thought, there was no one left who was close to me. There was Bertie of course, but the victims were all female, wretched, defenceless women. So the next killing would have to be a stranger. There would be a next killing but I did not know in which world it might come.

One afternoon when I walked on the hills, I saw a figure coming towards me through the mist. I was so easily spooked in those first weeks of returning to Molly, that I nearly turned to run. Then, even through the clouds of paranoia, I could see that it was neither Vespasian nor Arthur nor anyone from the past. This man wore rubber wellies and had tucked the bottoms of his baggy tweed trousers into his knitted socks. He was the clichéd country gentleman and waved his walking stick at me as we passed. I nodded back, no need to speak.

I scrambled up the scrubby hillside beyond the little pathway, aiming for a jutting rock where I often sat. It wasn't intelligent in the mist and drizzle but the weather no longer worried me, just as hunger, tiredness and confusion had become familiar friends. Then I slipped in the damp mud and loose shingle and landed heavily on both knees and the palms of my hands. I was certainly still susceptible to pain, perhaps more so. I grunted some sort of expletives and twisted round on my bottom to sit and rub my knees. Then the hand reached out to help me up. "Oh dear me," he said, "I do hope you didn't hurt yourself." He needed his walking stick to lean on himself and wasn't the ideal person to help a damsel in distress. I could see his own boots were about to slip in the mud and I didn't want to end up having to help him. "Not ideal weather is it?" he said as he managed to haul me onto my feet. "Perhaps you'd like to come down to the village with me for a hot toddy at the Smith and Joker? That's where I'm heading, if you'd care to join me. I don't think you should be up here on your own, you know."

I had never seen him before in my life, though I knew most of the village faces. He had a moustache and looked like a retired colonel. He must have been about seventy. He looked vaguely like a character in a film about a respectable country squire. I shook my head. "Thank you but really, I'm O.K."

"I hope I haven't offended you?" The moustache looked quite bedraggled in the steady damp. "I'd like the company. I assure you, I have no despicable ulterior motives. I'm much too old for that."

I didn't want to join anyone for anything and opened my mouth to say no. But my mouth was obeying someone else. "It's kind of you and I'd love a drink. Just what I need in this chill," I said. It was not what I had meant to say. The words drivelled out like they did when I was Tilda and she spoke against my will. Perhaps I was lonely without realising. "I'm Molly. I'm delighted to meet you." I wasn't at all, but he had a cosy smile.

"Thomas Cambio, and it's a great pleasure. It's a very long time, I can tell you, since I took a pretty young girl out for a drink."

He was all brown tweed and plastic mackintosh. He seemed very sweet, but it was a nuisance and a distraction. I wanted my confusion all to myself.

The Smith and Joker was a smaller pub in the little street behind the Post Office and I'd rarely been there. It had a fire in an open fireplace and a stuffed fox on the mantelshelf, reflecting the flames in its manic glass eyes. The old man seemed to think I needed to dry off and he sat me next to the fire on a wide cushioned bench where the fox could gaze at me and I could see the graffiti on the table through the base of my glass. The drink did me good and I let the spices clear my nose. Thomas Cambio sat opposite and raised his whisky glass in an age-spotted hand. "To better weather soon. What a dreary October it's been so far."

"It's only the beginning of the month."

"The fifth," said Thomas. "Five days of rain."

We talked about the weather and the new shop in the main street that had recently opened and sold terrible junk for tourists and the latest headlines in the local newspaper all about the council and what a mess they were making of clearing the verges and about the old elm tree outside the hotel which had been diagnosed terminal and was going to have to come down. We discussed the bikers mob that had driven through the village yesterday and frightened everyone by revving up at every corner, bursting the school lollypop lady's eardrums and frightening the sparrows. Then we chattered about the Newsagent's son who had been caught smoking reefers on the bridge and contaminating our stream by dropping his hallucinogenic ash into its pretty waters. We didn't talk about murder.

The whisky, cloves and hot water and the warmth of the fire made me drowsy. I felt slightly dizzy and cuddled back against the corner wall. "Time to go," I slurred. "I'm more tired than I thought."

"I'll see you home," said Thomas. His moustache had perked up in the heat. "No, please don't argue. I really would feel better if I knew I'd walked you to your door. And I promise, no ulterior motives. As I've said, I'm far too old."

So he walked me home which was only down the road but it was dark and wet, and it was nice of him but I didn't invite him in. I said goodnight on the doorstep and he didn't even come inside the gate. "It's been a pleasure." I nodded because it was almost true.

Then I forgot all about him for three days, until I met him again.

Miss Ruth Ableside was my counsellor and I called her Ruth though she was considerably older than me. I liked her taste in furnishings. She owned a small cottage not far from mine and its thatched roof reminded me of my other life. I was supposed to visit her every week but I kept cancelling. If only I'd turned up to each appointment, the commitment would have been over by now. Bertie had arranged it all as he'd used her services himself, trusted her and promised she could help. The police encouraged me too. Well, they would, under the circumstances. I knew no one could help but it was often easier just to let other people make the decisions.

Three days after meeting Thomas Cambio, I went to see Ruth because it was my final appointment and I wanted to get it over with. I had paid in advance and I took her a bottle of wine as a Thank you. I had nothing to thank her for, but it wasn't her fault that I was no better after meeting her than I had been before. After all, I never told her the truth. Tell anyone the truth, and I'd have quickly found myself in a straight jacket, probably sleeping in the bed next to my mother.

Ruth and I sat and drank the wine I'd brought. It was five thirty and the evenings had closed in to early darkness. Ruth had a sweet face, a baby face, although she was in her late fifties. She had lit the fire. I sat in the big wing chair where the firelight scorched one side of my head and played shadow games on the striped wallpaper. Ruth's cherubic mouth pursed though she wasn't drinking much. "This is very cosy. So pleasant. Perhaps, since we are so delightfully relaxed, you have something more to say to me today?"

I suddenly decided I liked her. I had never really bothered one way or the other previously, it hadn't mattered. Perhaps I had liked her anyway, without specifically noticing it, or I would not have taken her the wine. "I'm never talkative about myself," I said. "I write. I don't talk."

"I've read some of your books," she said, which was always a statement that warmed me to people. "Some of your heroines are extremely talkative. In your books, you seem to believe talking helps unblock emotions and releases inner demons. Shoos away the ghosts."

"Ghosts and demons," I muttered incoherently. It was my third glass of merlot.

"Tell me about them," said Ruth.

With an idiocy of intoxication and pent up stress that seemed almost like a delirious compulsion, I began to talk. "Well, I suppose it's the murders that set it off, but it all started before really. Even as a little girl."

"I must admit," smiled Ruth with a rather overpowering smile of reassurance, "that I do know something of your childhood problems. It can't have been easy for a little girl. Mr. Walding told me something of the situation when he came here for counselling. Your dear husband and I got on very well."

"He said so," I mumbled. "Actually Bertie recommended you." I finished the dregs in the bottom of my glass and Ruth leaned over and refilled it for me. It now smelled quite glorious which was surprising really, since it had been quite cheap.

"Go on. Tell me a little more. This is so cosy."

"Well, it's hard to explain," I explained. "I drift off into other worlds sometimes. No, that's not entirely true. I don't drift. And it's not other worlds, it's just one specific one. I stay there and I become another person. She's me or maybe I'm her. Do you believe in reincarnation?"

"I keep an open mind, dear," she said, professionally diplomatic.

"Tilda's much younger than I am," I went on, "and she's – well – this must all sound so hopelessly ridiculous – but she's in incredible danger. I don't understand everything that's going on. It's all to do with witchcraft. It links up to the murders. There have been awful murders there too. I suppose you think it's all subliminal subconscious auto-suggestion or something."

"Oh, what I think doesn't matter," smiled Ruth from her shadowed corner. She topped up my glass, which impressed me, since I had thought the bottle must have been finished ages ago. "But it's so exciting. So interesting," Ruth was saying. "You must go on and tell me more." She refilled her own glass and I thought perhaps the bottle had an endless capacity with more inside than outside, like a Tardis. I kept drinking and lost myself in verbal diarrhoea.

CHAPTER TWENTY-EIGHT

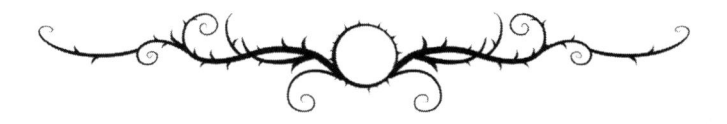

It was coming out from Ruth's house that I bumped into Thomas Cambio. I barely remembered who he was. Besides, I was in such an inebriated condition that I barely remembered who I was.

"What a pleasant surprise," he said, tapping his walking stick at me. Everyone was so damned charming these days.

"I have to get home," I said, less charming. "Sorry. Can't stop."

"I'll walk you home," he said. "No, please – no arguments. We know what troubles there have been lately, no point taking risks. And you don't live far from here if I remember rightly."

I let him. "Been to see Ruth whatshername," I muttered. "Talked too much."

He nodded, a bit like a tortoise from within the turned up collar of his mackintosh. "I know dear Ruth. She's a good friend of mine. But I suppose she does tend to chatter a little too much."

"Not her. Me."

"Oh well, no harm done," said Thomas. "Professional visit perhaps? She's a good counsellor. Not that she usually makes appointments for such a late hour."

"Half past five. What's it now?" It was deep night and no moon. "Seven? Eight?"

"It's midnight," said Thomas. "In fact, ten past."

"Good God," I said, stumbling over the doorstep to my own cottage. "Can't believe it. Must get to bed."

He had to help me with my key. "Perhaps I should come in and make you a coffee?" he suggested.

Ghastly idea. It was the very last thing I wanted. "Perhaps you could come in and help me make the coffee," I said, tongue not obeying brain.

We sat in my living room and he sat on the couch where Bertie used to sleep and I sat in my big leather chair with the foot stool and we drank coffee. Thomas made extremely good coffee and I began to wake up. "I don't want to seem ungrateful," I said, less slurred now. "But this has to be brief. I'm desperately tired and I've already talked enough tonight. Thank you and everything, but five minutes, and I'm afraid you'll have to go."

"The choice is yours, of course," said Thomas, "but I believe I could help." I was in the middle of shaking my head when the coffee and the slow return to sobriety actually got through to me and I realised something. Thomas was unscrewing the top of his walking cane and something strange was coming from the open cup. The man sitting rather taut and upright on the couch in front of me, silver haired and neat, was not after all a polite but ineffectual old gentleman whose presence was pure coincidence. I stared. He was filling my little room with a kaleidoscope of rainbows.

The room had been cold for I'd been out, no time to light the fire and my central heating was on the blink. Now it was wondrously warm, like a summer balm dancing straight through ice and into sunshine. The colours were so beautiful that I had no time to be afraid. And anyway, magic had become such a normal part of my life these days. "Who are you?" I asked, as if he might just say, 'Joe Bloggs the refuse collector,' or 'Mr. Smith the accountant.'

"I'm afraid I can't answer that yet," he said, "but there are a lot of other things I can tell you. Of course, it is rather late but if you aren't too tired, perhaps we could discuss one or two matters." The strings of colour were enclosing the room.

So for the second time that night I did what I never did, and I talked about myself and the magic of my life. Thomas Cambio became Tom and the colours he spun kept glistening and turning the night into timeless fascination. "You know Vespasian, don't you?" I said, not a sudden guess but a sudden certainty.

He smiled. "Time travel," he said, "is more common than you think. I have been to many places in many times during our history and I've been to medieval England on several occasions. In my line of expertise, it would have been impossible to go there and not meet Vespasian. He's quite an interesting fellow."

I had never thought of Vespasian as a fellow. "He's a magician?"

"He has many talents," said Tom. "But I'd call him an alchemist rather than a magician. At least, that's certainly what he'd call himself."

"And Arthur and the others?"

"I have no idea," said Tom, shaking his head. "I've never met them, I'm afraid. Perhaps one day, but it's impossible to know everyone."

"But you have your own magic. You're a magician yourself."

"Am I?" Tom leaned back in the couch and the colours from his stick began to concentrate around his head in a swirl of opaque pinks like an aura. "In one sense, you could say that. But that isn't really what I am." He smiled. "Now, let me tell you what you need to know."

"Something special?" Were time travellers so incredibly common that I had just coincidentally happened to meet one in my own neighbourhood? And – of course – coincidentally someone who had met the increasingly suspicious Vespasian?

"How to control where you go, of course," said Tom. "How to switch from past to present whenever you wish. And, very importantly, how to leave the door ready and open behind you as you pass. Then you're never trapped, and can always return, in both directions."

I woke up feeling deliciously alive. I had a quick very hot shower (I didn't take baths anymore) and a quick breakfast, got dressed and settled back in the living room with a cup of tea. I sat in the leather chair that I had sat in for many hours the previous night, and looked at the empty couch where Tom had sat when he told me the things that had changed my future.

I could remember very little of what had happened with Ruth Ableside. Perhaps she had counselled me to the best of her ability, but it was getting me drunk that had helped the most. Not that she really got me drunk. I did it myself. It was what I had needed, loosening the attachment to the material, which allowed Tom to enter. He explained it later. Most of what he said I could remember very clearly indeed though some of it was a little blurred, after all, we had talked for almost five hours. He'd offered to stay the night in order to help with the transference, but my common sense had reasserted itself and I'd thought it an unnecessary suggestion, even from an elderly magician. I had refused quite firmly and he just smiled and left.

There was no discomfort about Tom. He was so essentially benign, so reassuring, like homemade bread and the smell of vanilla custard. And I thought the excitement, after he left, would make me restless but it had not. I got to bed eventually, slept dreamlessly, and was awake six hours later with no headache and no confusion.

So there was more magic in the world than I had ever imagined and just because people didn't talk openly about it, didn't mean that they weren't having experiences just like my own. I didn't talk about it either. Now I hoped I was closer to controlling my little part of it.

I also knew a whole lot more about Vespasian. And now I trusted him even less.

I finished my tea and washed my cup. I dithered a little as if preparing for a long absence. I made my bed, tidied up, left the phone on answering machine and made sure the front door was locked from the inside. Then I went back into the living room and sat on the floor. Part of me was still nervous and some senseless paranoia stuck in my throat like fish bones. I wasn't having trouble believing things, I was just having difficulty deciding whether I should be frightened or excited. It seemed they tasted almost exactly the same.

I was going to have to do without the sulphur and mercury which Tom had recommended but I had the little pile of rosemary needles from my own back garden and the small glass bowl of dew that we had collected together that night, which had now been absorbed into the teaspoon of sea salt he had carefully measured for me. And I had the sealed pewter jar he had given me tucked into my pocket. I had slept with it. It contained the final ingredient, the one I could not produce myself.

I was lucky – not that there was any such thing as luck as I reminded myself – that there had been a new moon that night, deep blackness and a fresh feeling of potential beginnings. Everything else was ready.

I opened the pewter jar and took one tiny hard grain of the calcified substance from inside. It felt dry and hot between my fingers. I put it into the glass bowl and added the rosemary. I resealed the jar and put it back in my pocket. Then I took the bowl to the kitchen. It smelled sweet and had begun to smoke. I waited patiently until the kettle boiled, and added one tablespoon of hot water to the mixture.

I drank it immediately and closed my eyes.

"It's time to get up now," said the woman's voice. "Abbot Bernado wishes to speak to you urgently."

CHAPTER TWENTY-NINE

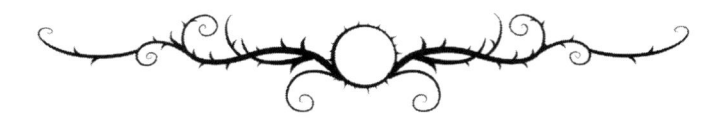

"You must understand that you've been living with a man capable of great evil," said the abbot. He sat behind his desk, a small cluttered slope of polished wood whose height dwarfed him.

Tilda stood in front of the desk and stared. "He's capable of great kindness too," she muttered, almost inaudible. "I thought you said he was your friend." She knew about the evil too. But I still felt some wavering loyalty.

"Originally, yes indeed. But he's a man who despises morality," said the abbot. "I should know. At one time, I was his pupil."

It made no sense. I wondered if engineering the switch myself had made the transition too abrupt. I was having trouble assimilating. The abbot stared at me as if he expected a reaction that Tilda wasn't giving. "I've known him for seven years," Tilda said. "Seven and a half now – that he's looked after me and most of the other children before me. He didn't have to care for us. He took us in when we had nowhere else to go and he had little enough just to keep himself alive. But he shared everything with us. That's kindness, isn't it?"

"Well, it rather depends on motive," said the abbot. "But I'm not saying he's devoid of human kindness. Just that it doesn't come first with him. His capacity for evil and terror is the greater."

"I'm sorry to sound curious," I said, "but you said you were his pupil." Personally, before the move to the forest house, I had only known Vespasian teach one thing, and that had been how to steal. It was hard to believe that the abbot had ever been one of his thieving brats. For one thing, the churchman seemed a great deal older and probably at least in his forties or fifties. Vespasian had also taught us self defence whilst living in the forest, but that seemed as unlikely a tutorship for this small plump Italian. "Was he once a teacher?" I asked. "I know he lived a very different life when he was younger."

"Indeed he did," said the abbot, "but I'm not here to tell you about another man when he's not even present. I only wish to warn you, and then set you on your way."

"But how did you know who I am," I insisted. I probably wasn't as polite as it should have been but I extremely puzzled and even a little alarmed.

"That's easy," said the abbot, unoffended. "I knew you when you lived in London. And of course, I knew Vespasian. I saw you several times. You stole our charity collection once from poor dear Sister Rosamund, and I went to Vespasian to complain. He asked me to overlook it, and I did. I've also seen him after he left London and took you all to the de Vrais estate in the forest, though it's some months now since I've seen him at all. The last time he came here asking about Gerald, his step son. So, you see, I guessed what you were doing here, cold and hungry and all alone. I shall protect you from him, if that's what you wish."

"I don't need protection," said Tilda, hanging her head. "He won't come after me."

"Then you may stay here for the time being," continued Abbot Bernado. "You'll be made welcome. But I think you should forget about joining our convent on a permanent basis. Holy orders are not your calling, I think."

"I made that part up," admitted Tilda.

"Just remember," said the abbot, standing up to show me to the door, though not much taller standing than he had been sitting, "should you fall under Vespasian's influence again, that his adopted name of Fairweather is hardly an apt description. He despises Holy Church, and is sunk in blasphemy, idolatry, and other wickedness, with some sins even worse which I will not utter in this sacred house."

The room they had given me looked out over the gardens. Tilda had never known a garden before, unless it joined the kitchen and was used for growing herbs, salad and vegetables. Here the convent was surrounded by sloping greenery, almost unnaturally peaceful. I wondered if spirituality had something to do with it. Already I found the medieval world deliciously quiet. In spite of the convent's obvious wealth, here it was silent. It was what both of us needed and the simple austerity was soothing. I had a lot to remember and Tilda had a lot she wanted to forget.

The bed was wooden framed, no curtains, straw stuffed mattress and a feather pillow on a linen sheet. The bedding was sparse but sufficient. The window was fine oiled sheepskin parchment with strong wooden shutters that I kept down. Mid autumn, the nights were chilly but I liked the glitter of star shine. There was a low box chest in the room, unlocked and empty, waiting for my belongings, should I have any. There was nothing else in the room except the wooden cross on the wall over the bed.

I left the room only for meals and for necessity. For two days I did little but sit on the bed and stare from the window. I watched the sun sink each evening into fleeting glory. Still within the dark of new moon, night magic was hidden but I watched the breeze take shape through the autumn mist and slink down the slope behind the trees. I thought a great deal about Vespasian.

Tilda had run away to escaped Vespasian but it was impossible to forget him, so we thought about what he had done and what had happened because of him and in spite of him. I knew considerably more about him and his strange past now but no one was speaking about Arthur. I had recently met two men, one in each world, both of them mightily unexpected, both of them ambiguous. Neither of them should have known anything about a man such as Vespasian, but both of them claimed to know him intimately. One claimed to like and admire Vespasian, but had told me many things about him which troubled and sometimes frightened me. The other evidently held Vespasian in contempt and distrust, but I suspected the abbot's attitude concealed envy. In any case, I trusted both Thomas and the abbot a great deal more than I now trusted Vespasian.

I had time to lie in my silent bed, follow monastic routine or wander the grassy slopes interrupted only by birdsong. My thoughts calmed. The convent bells divided time between peace and duty. The bell was actually a little discordant and almost unpleasant, leaving no echo. I suspected it was cracked. The bell rang for prime at dawn, the second of the day's calls to prayer. Still warm in dreams, I ignored their insistence until they rang again at mid morning for tierce sext and breakfast, which was when I first left my room. The third peal rang for midday and more prayers before dinner, which I rarely ate. Later the bells reminded us of evening vespers as Venus rose bright white from the diminishing horizon and then for the supper that followed. The final bells sent us to an early bed, if we had a mind to it. The abbot smiled at me sometimes as we wined and dined but he did not speak to me again. Nor, strangely, did anyone ever suggest I accompany them or follow the calls to chapel. I was pleased and the days floated by on warm breezes and good food.

It was a week before I saw the prioress. She had taken no notice of my presence in her convent during all that time which I found a little vacant of her, considering that most guests were allowed to stay only one night. I assumed that the abbot had suggested she leave me in peace. Then I bumped into her in the long hall leading to the cloisters. She glared then blushed and swept by with a flourish of fine black skirts. Her stiff white toque over its ample chin band flounced defiant as she lifted her head, clenched her jaw and pushed past.

I was shocked. Tilda paused mid bow, looking back over her shoulder in surprise. Then I hurried round and followed. "Blessed Mother. Excuse me." The prioress walked faster. Tilda no longer gave in so easily. My footsteps pattered like rain on the long tiles. "I'm sorry, Mother Rosamund, but can I speak with you?"

I wondered if, recognising me, my long ago theft of a few silver pennies could possibly have inspired such startling dislike. Tilda grabbed her arm. The prioress pulled her elbow away with force. Her eyes had dimpled into little round pebbles in the creases of her face. She was a lot shorter than I was and I looked down on the prominent bridge of her nose, the first of several chins and the furrows of her forehead. "You will never touch me again," she said. I thought she might spit at me. "You will keep to the visitor's quarters except at meal times. You will never address me in any way at any time. As far as I am concerned, you do not exist."

She turned again and marched away into the long blue shadows and I stood there behind her, shivering. I wondered if she thought I was the Abbot's whore.

CHAPTER THIRTY

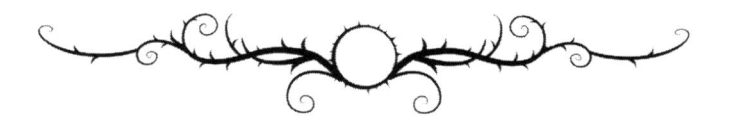

I walked often in the garden, enjoying the frosty autumn sunlight. We were not impatient, Tilda and I. We accepted the gift of peaceful convalescence and I loved being alone. I made no further attempt to talk with either the abbot or the prioress. Plentiful and regular food began to smooth out more of Tilda's angular immaturity. I had no mirror but I watched my legs curve and my breasts rise plump and firm. But I avoided peering down at the tiny dragon, so obscenely snuggling in my cleavage.

It was October the eighteenth, day of Luke the Evangelist. The bells reminded me of breakfast and my own burgeoning appetite. I stretched from my cocoon and dressed, splashing my face briefly with the water from the big jug beside my bed, too cold for twenty first century hygiene. I could smell food. The benches in the main hall were already bustling and the first course served. I shared the wide hard trencher with the novice I sat next to, bread which would be used to soak up meat juices and later thrown out to London's starving poor. The ale, sprinkled with cumin, sank a little scummy in the pewter cups. She was Katherine, my young friend and neighbour. We shared only meal times but it was a companionship of sorts. She would be given a new name once she took her final vows and I would never see her again but in the meantime she cut my meat and passed the salt when it came down to us, gossiped to me and made me welcome. "The Abbot? He's a grand man. Italian of course, and that was resented at first. So many Italians are sent by His Holiness, even to the villages and they take all the stipend and the revenues and don't even speak our language. But Abbot Bernado is quite different. He's much loved here now."

There were fresh eggs from the hens who shared the kitchens, and warm milk from the goats. The convent had its own bakery and the bread was warm too, unbleached brown and grainy, rye and barley. We started with turnip greens and onions in a sauce of milk. Then trout, mussels and oysters in broth, thick slabs of roast pork and poultry. Being what they called a simple breakfast, we then finished with pancakes and honey, curds and whey and oat cakes flavoured with crushed grape pulp. No stark winter rations here.

"And the prioress? I'm a guest in her convent but she doesn't speak to me."

"Oh," smiled Katherine, "Mother Rosamund. I'm afraid she's the one soul here who doesn't approve of our beloved Bernado. They say she was secretly in love with the previous abbot. He was a giant of a man and very knightly, but had a shocking reputation. I wasn't here then but he died of an infected sword wound and no one told us how it happened. A drunken brawl, according to gossip, or the revenge of a cuckolded husband, but I shouldn't be telling you that. I just know our abbot and our prioress don't speak to each other. We don't care. It's the richest convent in England. And the most powerful."

I walked back alone to my room, passed the alcove of privies where the late sunshine dappled the tiles and into the guest's quarters. The first open doorway led to another passage and a meeting room for travellers. Already a fire had been lit on the central hearth. I'd never chosen to sit there before but it was a frosty morning and I approached the fire. Stools and cushions surrounded it on three sides. I sat, hugging my knees, lost in dreams. I had eaten a little too much and perhaps the ale had been stronger than usual. The heat of the fire made me drift. I pulled three of the cushions together and curled, looking vaguely through veils of flame. One cushion was a rich tapestry of herbs and flowers and in its centre was the gnarled umbrella of a yew tree. As I drifted into a shifting sleep, the woven picture seemed suddenly alive beneath my cheek. The wind shuffled the leaves and the flowers bent in the breeze. I couldn't lift my eyes and as they closed, I saw a young man cross the passage outside the doorway. It seemed he came from my own little bedchamber, passing back into the courtyard and the cloisters. He was small and thin, dressed sombre and dark. I saw his face only briefly but I knew him.

My body was weighed down. I felt imprisoned as though trapped by the roots of the embroidered yew. I could not have risen, even had the man come flying at me. But he did not. It seemed he did not see me. It was Uta's cousin Malcolm.

When I woke and could see and move again, it was night. I had lost the whole day. I was a little numb, my head hurt and my back ached. The fire had shrunk into faint glowing ashes and through the thin window parchment I could see the curled shaving of crescent moon. I clambered up like some poor thing only able to crawl and scuttled back to my cell. Sitting on the bed, I stretched each muscle, forcing myself to think. After a good sleep the night before, I had been awake only for breakfast. Then I'd slept again, somehow remaining comatose for close to twelve hours. It was unnatural. Nothing in my room appeared to have been touched and the very few belongings I kept in the chest beside my bed were as I had always left them. I was sure that Malcolm had been in my room, and somehow he had drugged me. Then I saw something fixed to my wall.

I knew every detail of the room for I spent so much silent time there, staring at nothing. There was no furniture. There was no decoration except for a large cross above the bed. But now a small object, circular and neat, was attached to the wall at my left. I went over to examine it. It was a little wooden carving of a coiled snake which, wide mouthed, ate its own tail. I stretched one index finger and touched it. The craftsmanship was intricate and the wood dark grained and smooth. I went back and sat on the bed and looked at it. I knew Malcolm must have put it there.

It was a cool night and there was no more than a thin scrape of moon. A few stars hung low across the horizon, pale silver smudged behind cloud. I could hardly sleep again so I went back up the passage and out to the main hall. It stood in deep shadow, its empty benches scrubbed clean. The Little Sisters of Angelica went to bed early. The Abbot would be in his study. The main entrance was locked from the inside but the big key still hung in its place. I took it and unlocked the door, wincing as it creaked, echoing up into the rafters. I went out into the night.

I wondered if Malcolm was still somewhere within the convent and I wondered if the abbot knew he had come here. Knowing Vespasian, he must also know who Malcolm was. Perhaps my jovial cleric with the kind eyes and the hospitable attitude was, after all, what he had accused Vespasian of being – a man capable of evil. Clutched tight in one hand and hidden in the folds of my tunic, I held the little snake chewing its own tail. I did not know what it meant but if Malcolm had put it there, I did not want it.

Under the first trees and down the slope of lawn, the faint starlight lit the dew like silver dust. The mist hung creamy across the grass. My thin shoes were soaked and the hems of my skirts sodden and heavy though I lifted them. I pulled out the snake and held it up. Its blind eyes were open and looked back at me. I threw it as hard as I could. It spun like a toy and disappeared quickly down the hill. I trudged back to the building, slipped in through the door opening, and heaved it close behind me. I locked it and tiptoed back to my room. It was now so dark that I had to feel my way along each wall. Then I entered my room, almost fearing to find Malcolm waiting there for me in the deepening gloom. But my room welcomed only me. I sat on the bed and sighed.

I was not tired, could not sleep and my breathing was ragged, short and tense, but I lay back on the mattress with my hands clasped behind my head. I looked out of the window, though the sky was obscured not only by cloud but by the translucence of the parchment and I could see almost nothing. I wondered what I would do with the rest of the night. Then I looked to my left. On the wall hung the little circle of carved wood in the shape of a serpent eating its own tail.

I held my breath. I thought I might turn to see Malcolm standing there. I closed my eyes and opened them again and thought the thing might dissolve but it did not. It hung on its small peg and gazed back at me. So I got up from the bed and went over. The wood grain was exactly the same. It was the same object and not another. I went back and lay down again on the bed. I thought I might revert to Molly, but I did not. Nothing happened at all, except that the thing which I had flung into the night just minutes before, had reappeared in my room as if I had imagined everything.

I did something then which had not occurred to me for a long, long time and I prayed. All through the horrors of Wattle's death, the suspicion surrounding us all when little Muriel had been killed in the church and then the agony of Sammie's murder, it had not occurred to me to pray. Tilda had never done so either. She had not asked for help from a God which frightened and alienated her. Neither of us had asked for help though sometimes we had received it in ways we had not expected.

Now I was in a convent and a cross above my bed glared back at the small circle on the other wall, so I prayed. A little discomforted and creaky as if I needed practise, I asked any God to find me a way out from the threat surrounding me. I was terrified to be burned or flayed or whipped or raped again. I thought I might be murdered. And there was the terrible possibility not only that this might happen to me, but that it might happen twice, and in two worlds.

Then I unhooked the coiled snake from its perch a second time, tucked it again into the folds of my skirts and went out.

This time I took a different passage and found the way to the abbot's study. The door was partially open and the room flickered golden with candle light and the sweet smell of beeswax. Abbot Bernado's eyes were just visible over the rolled papers on his high desk and he looked straight at me and said, "Come in. I have been expecting you for some time."

CHAPTER THIRTY-ONE

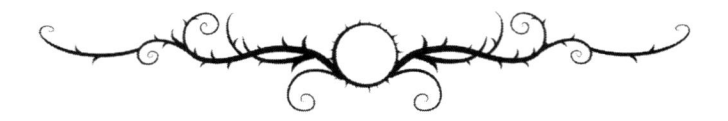

"The symbol of infinity," the abbot said, "a fundamental part of the study of alchemy. Though not usually an evil sign, and I have no idea how it came into your cell. This is a house of God and not of witchcraft or magic. I cannot approve."

"You said it wasn't evil," I said. I had placed the thing on the abbot's desk and he looked at it with dislike and did not touch it.

"Not of itself," he answered. "But just as you do, I would certainly mistrust its sudden appearance in your room. Besides, there are many things which are not evil, but which I cannot approve within my own house."

"But you said you were expecting me. If you didn't know about this, why did you expect me to come?"

"Because," said Abbot Bernado, "there has been a disturbance. I felt it. I am trained as I once told you and I can feel these things. Something passed through the veils."

"I don't understand you," I said. I was standing in front of his desk, wishing I could sit down. I felt weak. I felt ill. "And you never told me you were trained in such things. Do you mean magic?"

"Alchemy," he said. He pouted a little. "I told you I was once Vespasian's pupil, though that isn't something I'd willingly admit to others. Few people know and if you repeat these words to anyone else, I will deny them. But you didn't come here by coincidence. There are no coincidences in life, which is a fundamental teaching of alchemy. I thought perhaps you were in danger. So I told you things I would never normally speak of."

"Thank you," I said since it seemed appropriate. "But it all sounds like riddles."

"Then sit down," said the abbot. "Sit quietly and listen to the small part of the past I'm prepared to explain."

I sat on the stool by his side. He turned to face me. His breath was a little heavy and smelled of garlic but his eyes were as warm as before and I felt impelled to trust him. He inhaled deeply and puffed out his fat little chest as though he was remembering what he would rather forget. "I'm Italian, as everyone knows. I come from the great Republica di Venezia. It was where I met Vespasian. I was an aspiring prelate, studying theology. Vespasian was a young man of unusual charisma. He was travelling through Italy, coming from the University of Bologna, but drawn to Venezia as all wise men are. He was already an alchemist of some power of course, and he invited me to study with him. I abandoned theology and turned to magic." He paused, drumming his fingertips on his knee.

"What happened?" I asked, impatient. "What about Vespasian?"

"I was his pupil for two years," sighed the abbot. "I learned a great deal and became adept. Then I repented and returned to God and Christ's mercy and that's all I'm prepared to tell you of myself. As for Vespasian, I know very little that I care to repeat. He was the son of the Baron de Vrais then, his family were wealthy and he was heir to a title and a fortune. But when I was sent to England some years ago as the abbot to this convent, I met him again, this time as a veritable pauper with the name Vespasian. I did not ask questions. Those who dabble in the dark arts may often lose everything. He gave me few explanations, but he kept in touch. I imagine he thought he might one day make use of me. From Christian charity, I never turned him away."

"Thank you," I said again. He hadn't told me very much but it fitted neatly with what Thomas Cambio had told me that night sitting in my own living room in my other world. I got up to go.

"You must take this with you," said the abbot, pointing to the carved snake. He still refused to touch it.

"I'd sooner not," I said. "I think I saw someone. I told you. A man I hate, who must have put it in my room. Won't you keep it? Won't you destroy it?"

"You cannot destroy infinity," said the abbot. "And I will not keep a symbol of alchemy in my room."

Reluctantly I picked it up. It felt warm. I folded it back within my skirts. "Can I come back and see you tomorrow?" I asked. "And if I see this man again, can you protect me?"

The abbot stared at me in silence for a few minutes. "No," he said eventually. "I felt a movement through the spirit veils, something that troubled me. But there's been no other traveller here, no young man, no strange visitor. I cannot protect you from either an apparition or from pagan alchemy, and I will not have shadows threatening this sacred house. Therefore you should leave this convent immediately."

"I've nowhere to go," I said, blinking back tears.

"That's not my concern," he said. "You bring evil with you and it has no place in a house of God."

"If any power can protect me from evil, then surely God can," whispered Tilda.

The humour and light in Abbot Bernados eyes had gone cold. What had once been his charm and had inspired my trust, had entirely disappeared. "No doubt," said the abbot, "but you have stayed here long enough. Now you must leave. And take that serpent with you." He waved a dimpled hand at me. He wore one ring, gold and heavy and carved in the shape of a goat's head. It gleamed suddenly in the candle light and flashed ruddy.

"Thank you then, for all your previous hospitality," Tilda said. She got up, still clutching the circular carving, and slowly left the room without turning around.

Back in my room I put the coiled snake on its peg on the wall and stood at the window, looking at nothing. I was trying to make sense of matters which were simply nonsensical. Then I opened the small chest and began to pack a parcel of the few belongings I had brought with me. I did not take the wooden snake, symbol of infinity, but left it where it hung. Instead I took the wooden cross, and felt no guilt at the theft. The abbot would not give me protection, but God might. I walked the long passage from the guests' quarters to the great hall and I left the convent, unlocking the door for the second time, and trudging out through the wet grassy slopes and back down into Grub Street towards the mire of London. I arrived as the Cripplegate was unlocked and the portcullis raised, the bells of St. Thomas ringing out from the Jewish quarter. It was the nineteenth of October.

The streets were mostly empty though a few folk wandered, as I did. One elderly man was sluicing down the gutters outside his shop. I knew him vaguely. He was famed as the best goldsmith in the city and kept his premises clean for rich customers. The shit he washed away collected in cold heaps further down the street, where the raykers would eventually clear it. His window, the shutters let down on chains to form the counter, was wide and above it was painted his guild's arms. It was the road of the goldsmiths and fine workers in silver and pewter, the rich quarter leading to Cheapside's markets. I turned the corner where the streets narrowed and cobbles gave way to beaten earth, walking on until my calf muscles ached. Leather Lane, Fletchers Alley, on down to Coopers Street and from there to the river and the wharfs. I went up again by the bath houses and entered the darker streets under the arch of the old broken aqueduct.

Two whores leaned against the doorway of the Chandler's Tavern but they took me for a lady and sniffed down at their bare feet and ragged hems as I passed. The inn was open but the singing had long finished and I knew old Alan Pomfrey would be inside alone, polishing his bar, spreading sawdust and watering down his ale.

I walked up to the next rise where the two wider roads intersected, one running up, the other down, with St. Mark's Holy Church and its beautiful wooden spire between them guarding the old crossing of the ways. I took the down and followed it back towards the river, approaching London Bridge. With the reek of the Thames salty in my nostrils, I reached my old house and its barred doorway. I used the stolen cross, and I broke through the barricade and smashed the lock. Then I pushed open the lopsided door from its rust damaged hinges and went indoors. I was home again.

It was damp and the rats were nesting in every corner. I swept and cleaned as I had not done for months and I even climbed into the rafters and tied up the wandering thatch. I chased out spiders and beetles. I made up a bed from the fallen rushes although I knew it was flea infested, and I tucked it all up with my own two bed covers from the forest house and a blanket that I'd stolen from the convent.

I put out five big pans to catch rain water since the water barrel was smashed in and I hung the convent's cross beside them. I hoped it might deter the sheriff should he remember the house had been commandeered. Then I crawled upstairs, lay down on my comfy new bed, curled up with the daylight dancing through the ripped velum, and fell asleep.

It was some hours later and the bustle in the street outside was at its busiest when I woke with something pricking my side. I shifted, pushing away the straw that could sometimes be sharp and was penetrating my clothes, but the discomfort continued and jabbed at me wherever I moved. I suspected cockroaches and rolled over but the thorn pricked my other side. With a yawn and an unwilling stretch, I sat up, rummaging for whatever was so persistent. My hand touched something warm and hard and I pulled it out. It was the little coiled serpent that ate its own tail.

CHAPTER THIRTY-TWO

For two days I tried to return to Molly. It was not fear, nor even for simple escape. I wanted to see Thomas Cambio. He was the only person I now believed I could trust, and I needed answers. I wanted someone prepared to explain without speaking in riddles. I called to him and I practised the same rituals he'd taught me for entering Tilda's world, but nothing happened. I didn't have the granules he'd given me, the most essential ingredient. Besides, Thomas had taught me how to get back to the medieval, but he'd never told me how to get back to Molly. The secret was keeping the door between worlds open he said, but I didn't know how to swing in reverse. I sat with the little snake in the palm of my hand and wondered how I could have left out such an essential equation.

"Vespasian's a man of great power," Thomas had told me that night, "and power is always amoral. I've some power myself of course. I know I'm not above suspicion. But I've journeyed a long way through time and space, and now I'm here to educate and protect you."

"Me? Why me?"

I had been emerging from the intoxication of an evening with my cosy counsellor when she drank Earl Grey tea and I drank God knows how many glasses of an average vintage. Coffee with Thomas sobered me slowly and that helped. I was able to accept what would otherwise have seemed too absurd. "Because that is what I do," said Thomas. "I help whoever's in need, and you, my dear young lady, have a need that supersedes any other."

University professor material, wise eyed and silver haired with a wide smiling mouth, but discussing magic as if it was a recipe for porridge. "You're telling me that you're a time traveller?" I said. "A sort of cosmic angel?"

"Oh dear me no," said Thomas. "In fact, in many ways I'm just an ordinary man who lives in the here and now. Just down the road in fact, though I don't believe in coincidences – there is no such thing of course – and where I live was surely arranged by other powers. But I discovered when I was quite young that I had a strange gift. I've developed it over the years and now I use it to delight myself, and to help others. That seems far more satisfying than just helping oneself, you know."

Now I sat on my straw bed and stared at the carving and at the dust in the corners and the rip in the window and the broken shutters and remembered every word of a conversation that would not take place for a thousand years.

"But you know Vespasian. You say you've met him," I'd answered.

"Yes, that's right," said Thomas. "He's a remarkable personality and I imagine anyone journeying back to that particular era would end up meeting him. He's the hub, you might say."

"Please, please tell me about him." I was scrunched up in the chair with my head beginning to hurt and all around me floated the milky rainbows that Thomas had produced from his walking stick.

"Drink your coffee," suggested Thomas. "It'll clear your head and take away the nausea."

The colours kept swirling. "How do you know I've a headache and feel sick?" I'd asked, obediently sipping the coffee.

"Oh, no magic about that," smiled Thomas. "I'm afraid inebriation usually has that affect. Besides, you were looking quite pale. Now I believe things are warming up."

The room had been cold, left empty all day with a frosty autumn wind outside. Now the sun was shining inside although it was past midnight and I was beginning to feel wide awake and very comfortable indeed. "Yes, you certainly have a remarkable walking stick. Is it your magician's wand?"

He laughed. "No, I'm afraid not. I'm just creating a disturbance in the veils to help calm the atmosphere. Now, shall we begin with the explanations?" He leaned forwards. "You were asking about Vespasian? And a few other things need to be explained, I imagine."

I wanted that sort of help again. If I couldn't go to him, then it was possible that he might come to me. As an experienced time journeyer, he could manipulate his travels where I could not. But I'd never asked him if he kept the same appearance in different places. Few would recognise Molly as Tilda. Thomas Cambio might be equally disguised.

So I got up and put the little snake on the old chest under the window. It seemed to settle, coiling tighter, basking in the pale sunshine. I left it there. If it refused to leave me, then I would ignore it.

For two days I rearranged my life back into London routine. I went to the market and I stole. Tilda felt a strange complacency, a renewal of identity as she returned to the old life. She stole food and a slim purse from a fat housewife. With the few pennies I bought a hen, a new lock for the door and a new pair of shoes. I went to see Jack Saddler and made some excuses and told some lies. "I'll stay just a little while," said Tilda, "until I decide where to go. Back to the village where I was born perhaps. Then the house is all yours again. The sheriff doesn't seem to be interested."

"Don't you worry, miss," said Jack. "You keep warm and look after yourself. Tell me when you reckon on leaving and I'll be off to the sheriff myself and ask for occupancy. Meantime, come Sunday after church. We set a good dinner, Sundays."

It was him I bought the shoes from. He wasn't a cobbler but he was a fine leather worker and he made the shoes for all his own family and half the street too. They were black and soft like gloves, and Tilda was proud to own them. They peeped out from the fifthly hem of my tunic and gleamed like little silk slippers.

So I had a good Sunday lunch of peas pottage and sardines in oatmeal, with spiced ale and endless talk about the state of the nation and King John's latest scandals. In an effort to reclaim the French lands he'd lost in battle to the wretched Philip, he'd taken hostages and now, against all the laws of chivalry and Christian decency, they were treated appallingly, poor souls. One seven year old child had been hanged. Another young man died after being castrated, without recourse to either medicine or the clergy. It was also common knowledge, so they said, that some years back the king had starved his own nephew to death. Rumour, of course, was all we had, and rumour wove gruesome stories.

"He's fond of mutilations and castrations, is our good gentle king," said Jack through his mouthful of peas.

"No good criticising the nobility," said his wife. "Gets you nowhere except into the dungeons, mighty quick."

"No one can't hear me in me own house," said Jack. "I doubt the king's too fond of London city. Knows we're an independent lot. And what about Vespasian, Tilda? Never did understand why you all moved so sudden. The sheriff never knew you was all thieving, you know."

"Better safe than sorry," I muttered.

"Except for poor Isabel," said Agatha.

"Well, we're careful not to hunt the king's deer," I said quickly. "There's plenty to eat without risking the gibbet."

"Castration's the latest fashion," muttered Jack. "Castration for poaching too. Lose your privates for a few morsels to quiet a starving belly, I've not heard naught more wicked. Now, talking about the gibbet, there's a new body in the square. Red Ralf, most feared highway robber on the Fosse Way, they reckon. All his guts is hanging out and spoils the fruit for a half mile around. But they didn't dare castrate the bugger."

I clamped my mouth shut. Jack was discussing the consequence of law and order, but it brought images of Muriel Bunting hanging upside down in the little church in my West Country village, with her skirts around her neck and her entrails on the mosaics. Thinking of Muriel would bring back memories of Sammie and I had to avoid that if I could. Agatha wanted me to stay the night but their room was already well crowded and the youngest child Mabel was a brat who picked her nose and wiped it on my skirts if she could squeeze close enough. So I said thank you but no thanks to Agatha though I took the jug of ale she offered me and the remains of the pottage for tomorrow's breakfast.

I walked home slowly, little more than a few steps around the corner but long enough to feel the delicious bite of frost in the wind and enjoy the moonshine on my forehead. It was five nights since the new moon and already its silver crescent was bright as a Saracen's knife through the scud of clouds.

That night, warm in my straw bed with the rats scuffling overhead in the thatch, I dreamed. It was the night of October the twenty second. I dreamed of Thomas Cambio. I could not see his face but I saw his long slim hands and heard his voice. "It is the symbol of infinity," he said, "and is not an evil sign."

"I know that," I whispered. "I was told. But why does it haunt me? How can it cling to me, however hard I try to distance myself?"

"You could try and burn it," said Thomas, "but fire and alchemy make a powerful combination."

"Now you talk in riddles, like all the others," I complained. "I wanted you to come because you speak plain. I need answers, not more puzzles."

But the dream faded and I woke to a cold morning. It was October the twenty third.

CHAPTER THIRTY-THREE

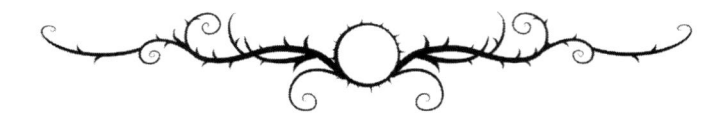

It was Walter who came to see me. I was out at the time and came home with an armful of stolen food to find him sitting in the kitchen waiting for me. He had picked the lock, something he had always been particularly good at. He was talking to the hen.

"Her name's Molly," said Tilda, putting the bag of barley and the onions and leeks on the table beside the small leafy cabbage and the three turnips.

"Well, you're not starving I see," said Water, nodding to the table. "Vespasian said you wouldn't be."

"You're not angry with me then?" I offered him an apple.

"No, of course not. But I don't want that. It's stale and soft. We eat far better than that in the forest." So he was angry, after all. "For God's sake Tilda, you frightened the life out of us at first. We thought you'd been taken off like Isabel and Richard. I thought you might be dead."

"I'm sorry." I ate the apple.

"Vespasian said it wasn't that. He said you were alright, you'd just decided to leave. You'd run away."

I nodded. "Yes," I said. "I really am sorry, but I had to go. I took all my clothes and my blankets. It was pretty easy to see I hadn't been stolen away in the night."

"You should have left a note. A letter."

"Don't be silly," said Tilda. "I can't write and you can't read."

"Vespasian can read and you can write a little bit, I've seen you," said Walter. "Anyway, then I was worried that you'd gone because of me. It wasn't, was it? Because I wanted you to marry me? Vespasian said it wasn't that either."

"He was right," I said. "It wasn't that."

"He said it was because of him," said Walter, "but he wouldn't say why. He didn't ask you to marry him as well, did he?"

Tilda sniggered. "No, certainly not." A few explanations went through my head but I wasn't going to tell the truth. "I can't talk about it Walter, really. I just had to get away."

"It's to do with what happened in the castle, isn't it?" he persisted. "When you were gone for an hour and you said you'd been gone for weeks. You said Vespasian tortured you. That's impossible. But something happened. You're angry with him, aren't you?"

He grabbed my left hand as I picked over the core of the apple, and held it up. The burn marks were fading but the palm was ridged and discoloured. I nodded. "Yes, alright, it is something to do with all that. It's magic, Walter. I don't really understand any more than you do. Please don't let's talk about it now." It was strangely pleasurable to see him – old company and friendship in a lonely place.

We had lunch together and he helped me cook it. I discovered laughter again as he tripped up carrying in one of the pans of rain water from outside and startled the hen. He'd brought me a gift of wine, stolen of course, and it was the weak, sweet yellow English stuff I disliked, but we drank it and laughed even more. He told me the gossip and the tattle from the forest house.

"Gerald's puzzled 'cos Vespasian won't take him back to visit his grandmother. He won't let him claim his title either. Gerald's gone sort of quiet."

"Sulking."

"Maybe. He seems sort of sad and I think I might feel the same in his boots. Anyway, he doesn't talk much, especially to Vespasian. But we carry on training, even more now. You know Tilda, this new life, with manners and swords and riding, well I reckon that's really for Gerald, for when he's accepted as a baron. He'll need to know all those things. We won't, but that's the reason he teaches us whether Vespasian admits it or not."

"Perhaps one day you'll be a great knight," I said. I felt I owed him some sort of gentle flattery.

"Don't be stupid," said Walter. "But I want to be able to defend myself. Who knows, one day I might go and crusade if I can afford it."

"Well, at least Vespasian's a good tutor." I thought of what else Vespasian had taught. How to steal. And the black arts to an Italian priest.

"I hope you don't mind," said Walter, saying goodnight to me from the straw bundle he made up on the other side of the room. "But I don't think I want to marry you anymore."

I felt ridiculously rejected. "Why? I mean, that's good, because I don't want to marry you either. Or anyone else, either. But why?"

"It sounds soppy now," muttered Walter into the straw. "But Vespasian talked to me quite a lot after you'd gone. He talked about love. You know Richard used to go on about romance and chivalry. Of course, he thought he was in love with you too, poor Richard. Well Vespasian says that's all silly. Just part of growing up, he said. He told me a lot about what he calls real love and how it's different to chivalry and courting and then passion and wanting – well, you know. Though when you're young you think it's all the same thing. He helped me understand, man to man. I feel different now. I'm – sort of – grown up."

"Good," I said. It was a conversation I would have liked to overhear. Vespasian's attitude to sex was something I already wanted to kill him for.

"You've got a strange round wooden thing on the chest over there," said Walter suddenly. "I don't remember seeing that here before."

"I found it," I said. "Go to sleep Walter. We can talk in the morning."

I wasn't sure if sleeping with a young man alone in the same room was considered appropriate for a girl my age in medieval days, but it didn't seem to bother Tilda. She saw Walter as a brother. I curled up and watched the moon rise through the torn window parchment. It was misty white, now a half moon at the end of its first quarter. It was the night of the twenty third of October.

He stayed two days and I enjoyed most of it. We acted like the kids we were, threw the milk at each other when it went sour and clotted, burned the pottage while trying to reheat it without adding water, chased the hen when she laid an egg under my stool and I stood on it, and sat around the kitchen hearth to tell stories, like old times.

"Stephen's getting bigger at last," said Walter.

"He's fourteen years old," I said, "or maybe fifteen. He can't have stopped growing yet."

"It's experience really, isn't it, that makes you grow up," said Walter. "Anyway, he's got more sense than you'd think. He gave me a message for you. He says you ought to come home."

"I am home," I pointed out.

"Back to the forest house. Stephen says we all miss you and worry about you and it's really dangerous for you to be on your own now."

"I'm not coming back," I said.

Walter sighed. "Stephen says you got all uncomfortable because things had changed and we weren't just piglets snuffling together anymore. Talking of marriage, and murder and everything, well, it made you feel like the odd one out and maybe you thought you were spoiling things for the rest of us too. So you left."

"Well, that's astute of Stephen," I admitted. "Actually, he was the first to start avoiding me after you went on and on about marriage. So I'm glad he worked that out. Perhaps Vespasian talked to him too. But I can't come back. Not yet anyway."

"I'd never live in London again," said Walter. "It's better in the forest. I love it. It smells so sweet. I love the birds singing and the wind in the tree tops."

"You're getting poetic." Then I thought of something, and how odd it was he'd come if he didn't like London anymore. "How did you know I was here? Did Vespasian send you?"

Walter squirmed, blushing. "He did suggest it," he admitted. "He says you're in danger."

"If I am," I said distantly, "then it's as much from him as anything else. I won't come back."

"Well, I just thought I ought to try," said Walter. "I mean, Vespasian wasn't especially vehement about it. He told me I'd find you back here in the old house though I don't know how he knew. Guessed I suppose. So the danger can't be that bad."

"If he really wanted me back," I sniffed, "he would have come and got me himself."

It was early on the morning of the twenty sixth of October that Walter left. He broke fast with me first. Being winter, Molly wasn't laying much, but we managed a boiled egg each, stale rye bread and half a mug of ale. We sat at the kitchen table with the hen clucking fretfully under our feet and the sun knocking at the grime on the oiled window cloth. He had a long walk and wanted to get off early. There was the smell of burned out ashes and mutton tallow from last night's candle. Walter had stolen me a whole sling full of candles but I wish he'd managed to get the expensive beeswax instead of tallow, which stank and spluttered and spat rank smut and kept going out.

"I'll miss you," I said, which was quite true.

"Then come with me, silly girl," he said. "It's a good life in the forest even if we are outlaws. What happens if the sheriff turns up here and arrests you? Asks about Vespasian? Or you get caught stealing and there's no one to come and help?"

"I'll move on soon," I said. "I promised Jack Saddler I would and I know I'm not really safe here."

"Stick with your pride and your silly ideas then," said Walter, standing up. "I'm off." He said one more thing before he went, standing on the doorstep in the pale sunshine, with his small pack slung over his shoulder and his dark hair in a mess. "I do love you in a way, Tilda," he said. "I'm not even embarrassed to say it. You've changed a lot in the months since we left London. If you ever need anything – you know – a special friend or something, then tell me. I'll do what I can."

"Thank you, Walter," said Tilda. "I hope I see you again soon. And I hope you find someone nice to marry one day. Please don't go off to the crusades."

He marched away down the road with a grin, shaking his head as if I was a lost cause and not worth answering. I never did see him again.

CHAPTER THIRTY-FOUR

I left Tilda sweeping out another mouse nest from the kitchen corner. The mice were nibbling at everything and the rats were stealing the eggs. She was bare foot, trying to protect her new shoes, and she was missing Walter. She wasn't admitting to herself what else she was missing.

With a lurch of vertigo I separated, saw her small pale face and the aura of long brown curls fade into the shadows while absurd noises jangled inside my head. The telephone was ringing, the hen squawked as it dashed from the broom, the kettle was steaming furiously as it clicked off, Tilda stubbed her toe and sneezed as feathers flew, one or both of us got the hiccups, then there was Brahms playing somewhere. I was Molly again.

I tried to ignore the telephone but it kept on. Finally I pulled myself into the present and answered it. It was Bertie and he was fine and thought he might come back if I'd have him back into the spare room and he promised he'd be no trouble. As if! I hiccupped Tilda's hiccups and said O.K. I supposed he was a bit like Walter though twice his age and half his intelligence but any company was good sometimes.

I took the tea I made into the living room and sat staring at the blank television screen. A few days before I had wanted to revert to Molly because I'd needed the explanations I thought I could only get in this world. Now I was here, I wished I wasn't. My mind was a medieval mind and I was an eighteen year old medieval girl with a destiny she feared. I, she, her, there was a confusion of mental spirals. Although as Tilda I spoke an ancient form of English barely intelligible to a modern ear, my mind always spoke and heard in the language I knew. Now, for the first time perhaps, I found I was thinking in antique words and had to force myself into modern Molly again. A slow apathy of timeless inertia imposed. So I did nothing for several hours and allowed myself unconscious rest.

Then finally I took the mug of tea, which had gone stone cold in my hand, and shoved it in the microwave. I checked the date on the local newspaper which had been pushed through my letter box and still lay folded on the passage carpet. It said the twenty sixth of October. I rustled through the pages. There was no mention of murder, police enquiries or magical occurrences. When the microwave bleated, I retrieved my reheated tea and went back into the living room where I sat and stared at the blank television screen until my cup went cold again.

It was then I noticed, hanging small and quite unobtrusive on the wall over the fireplace, the little wooden carving of a snake that ate its own tail. I accepted its presence completely. I had almost known it would be there.

At about five thirty when it was already getting vaguely dark outside, I switched on the repaired central heating, which I should have done before because it was freezing, searched for my mug of tea which I eventually found, equally freezing, still in the microwave, and turned the television on. Something about the insistent modern blare and the platitudinous self importance of the programme finally woke me up and I was home, Molly again, and ready for action.

I wrapped up, scarf, coat, gloves, thinking just how much warmer life in medieval times had been, and went out. I trotted down over the little bridge and behind the Post Office to the Smith and Joker and ordered a hot toddy. Then I sat with it in the alcove and waited for Thomas Cambio to turn up.

He arrived all tweed and dark green mackintosh as I remembered him. He saw me at once and brought his drink over, just as though we'd had an appointment. "You look cold," he said. "Wouldn't you like to come and sit by the fire?"

"No thank you. I've decided that close contact with real fires makes me positively dizzy. But I'm delighted to see you again. I was really hoping you'd be here tonight."

"Perhaps," he suggested, sipping his whisky, "we could have this one drink and then you might like to come back to my place for a long talk. That's why you came, isn't it?"

I nodded. "I'd be interested to see your place."

"I shall walk you home afterwards of course," he said. "Unless you decide to go straight back to Merrie Olde England."

I said, "It's not so merry at the moment."

He had a very tiny cottage not far from mine and even closer to my counsellor, Ruth Ableside, who I had decided not to see again. We wiped our boots on his hedgehog mat and he unlocked a door so tiny that he had to bend to fit inside. He turned on the electric light and lemon welcome sprang into life. There was flowered wallpaper and a rose patterned carpet. It looked like the country cottage of an ancient and genteel old lady. It certainly didn't look like anything this man would have chosen. For a moment it reminded me of something designed by a film studio, a clichéd representation of country charm. "Come in, come in," he said. "Tea, or coffee?"

"I remember you make lovely coffee," I said.

He smiled, hanging up the mackintosh. "I spent a lot of time in Italy you know and they're fanatical about their coffee there. Venice. I loved it. Lived there for a few years."

"In which century?" I wondered.

"Several," he said, quite seriously. "And of course, it was where I first met Vespasian, though by a different name."

The couch was chintz and deeply cushioned. I nursed my coffee, Wedgwood china and a chocolate biscuit. "I dreamed," I said, "a few nights ago. I wanted very much to ask you about something and I dreamed about you and you answered me. Was that just a dream?"

"Just a dream?" He sat opposite me. There was a small fire which had burned low. He poked at it and released the reluctant flare, adding another log until the fire turned huge and filled all my eyes. Then he put his feet up on a padded stool and raised his coffee cup. "My dear young lady, we must never speak of just dreams. Yes, I dreamed of you as you dreamed of me. I answered your question. I would have come over to you, but I was a little caught up you might say, too busy, in another time."

"So that snake thing's a symbol? In alchemy? Something magic?" I leaned forward and found myself whispering. "Would you be surprised if I told you it followed me here? It's in my own living room now. Nothing's ever come backwards or forwards with me before. Only daisies – and injuries – and this."

For the very first time, I thought he looked distinctly surprised. His face was suddenly animated and he blinked twice. Then he quickly shut the emotions off. "Surprised? No, not at all. You say it was placed in your convent room by this person Malcolm? A powerful alchemist, I assume. So most unwise, I think, to touch this thing."

I felt I was missing something. "Would you? You have such amazing power. Would you destroy it for me?"

He frowned. "I should like to help, but no, I think not. It's probably better left alone. In the meantime," he smiled again, brightening, "tell me what you've been up to."

I told him. I particularly told him about the convent and the Abbot in some detail. Then I took a deep breath, which was increasingly difficult in the suffocating heat of the tiny room, and said, "Dear Mister Cambio, I really don't want to sound as if I'm trying to be clever. I trust you. You're the only person who understands all this and really helps me. But you go back to the same time and places I do, and you must become someone there, just like me. Are you, is it possible, when you go over there, are you Abbot Bernado?"

He took a moment, as if he was unsure whether to be pleased or not. "Well, you've a remarkable instinct indeed," he said eventually. "I hadn't expected you to guess so quickly. But of course, when I'm him, he has his own personality and isn't totally under my control – just as you find with your friend Tilda. Unfortunately, Abbot Bernado sometimes has his own ideas and I was sorry to be so inhospitable, dear Molly. I should certainly never have asked you to leave the convent, especially at such a difficult time. I shall try and make it up to you."

I smiled and relaxed. Knowing about the Abbot explained a lot and gave me confidence. Tilda didn't always listen to me either. "That doesn't matter at all. I understand. It's just nice to know."

"Then let's move on from the coffee to the wine," said Thomas. "And relax a little further. What else can I tell you? What else can I help you with?"

"Oh, with Vespasian," I said at once. "Tell me more about him and fill in the blanks."

I hadn't noticed when it happened, or even how, but the electric light had diminished into fire flicker. Shadows crept close. "Forgive me, but I'd have thought dear Vespasian is hardly the point here," Thomas said quietly. "He's almost irrelevant now. It's these other people, Arthur, Malcolm and the rest of that sinister group, which you need to concentrate on."

"But you said you don't know any of them," I pointed out, almost apologetically. "Besides, she's busy trying to hide the fact, even from herself, but Tilda's obsessed with Vespasian. She's been in love with him for years."

Thomas raised his brows. "I understood from you that she wanted to kill him?"

"Well, perhaps she does. And I do too – though I couldn't really, of course. Not actual murder. I doubt if she could either, but she'd like to." I looked into my lap and played with the stem of my wine glass. "But that doesn't stop her feeling what she's always felt for him."

"Ah, young ladies," smiled Thomas. "Will we ever understand them?" He sounded just like the Abbot.

"But," I said, "you always seemed to like Vespasian. You warned me he was – dangerous. But you said you respected him. You called him the hub and said he was fascinating and charismatic. But Abbot Bernado doesn't like him at all and says he's capable of great evil. So, which is which?"

"Both perhaps," said Thomas. "Remember that the Abbot is a practising prelate and believes in organised religion. He's now heartily ashamed of his previous associations and his knowledge of alchemy. If the bishop discovered his past, he might be excommunicated."

I finished my wine. "You keep talking about alchemy but it sounds like magic to me. I read up a bit from the library on the old pagan beliefs before the church moved in, but none of it sounded very scientific. I mean," I knew I was missing the point somewhere, "it seemed to be all about nature spirits and trees and herbs and the magic of sacred groves, a bit – well, fanciful and sixties hippy. Vespasian believes in herbs and potions but alchemy's about the philosopher's stone and turning base metals into gold and discovering science."

Thomas refilled my wine glass. "Oh dear me no," he said. "I'm amazed you have the facts quite so muddled. And you so closely involved, too! I really must put you right."

It seemed to be the heat of the fire and the movement of the flames that made me sleepy, rather than the wine which was light and fruity and I was pleased to find that it wasn't going to my head at all. Yet somehow I found it hard to concentrate on Thomas's explanations. He seemed to be sitting closer and occasionally patted my hand, which I found sweet but strangely disconcerting. "Most believe alchemy began in ancient Egypt, once known as Al-Kemia of course," he said, "though some say it came originally from Atlantis. The Greeks learned from the Egyptians when Alexander the Great conquered the great civilisations. Plato and Pythagoras were naturally both adepts but they merely adopted the Egyptian teachings of Thoth. Then the knowledge grew more sophisticated through the early Jews who incorporated it into the Cabala, and finally with the Arabs of the middle ages. They were quite the most civilised peoples during our medieval times you know. The original Zoroastrians developed the mysteries and much Asian knowledge and yoga was absorbed. Then the Knights Templar of course. There have been enormous strides forward since then, the Rosicrucians and naturally the Masonic Lodge, with Newton, Blake and even a certain Mr. Jung, but that is all quite irrelevant to your story, for we must stop with Tilda, Vespasian and my dear Abbot. Besides, as history raced forward, so the alchemic association with the old pagan spirits began to wane, and that changed its course considerably." His voice was almost a chant. I could hardly follow it, yet it also drew me in. It felt hypnotic. "Venice was the great trading power of the west at that time and the Venetians adopted much of the more profound knowledge, both mystic and chemical, of the Arabs and Persians. I believe that's where Vespasian honed his studies. He was originally sent to the University of Bologna as a very young man when his father the baron was still alive. Vespasian's mother was Italian. Perhaps you knew?"

I shook my head. "He looks rather Italian perhaps."

"Well, that's of no matter," continued Thomas. "He was an only child I believe and heir to the title of course, but his parents were alive and wealthy and in good health, close to the throne and friends of King Richard's mother. A difficult woman, Eleanor of Aquitaine, but that's another story.

At that time, I was already slipping in and out of the mind and body of one Bernado Schiavone, who was studying theology in Venice and was ambitious. So when he met Jasper, son of the English Baron de Vrais, half Norman, half Italian and a young man of seductive charisma, I became as interested in alchemy as Bernado.

The principles of alchemy have since been kidnapped by Christianity with such stolen symbolism as the Holy Grail, but at that time it was still pure mysticism. Of course, there were those obsessed with medicine, gold and chemistry, the desire for wealth of course, but also the desire for understanding and knowledge. Base metals into gold – well, some dabbled with the idea. But the real foundation of alchemy was the desire for eternal life, not of the body as some now suppose, but of the spirit."

"I thought the soul was more what the Christian church preaches," I muttered.

"Indeed," he said. "But alchemy encompasses a great deal more than puritanical beliefs based on hope and faith. It is the study of utter control through higher knowledge."

"The philosopher's stone?"

"Not a stone at all, naturally. It relates to the Opus Magnum and is the achievement of divine consciousness. But I really cannot give a thesis on such an enormous concept in just a few hours."

I was extremely tired though the clock on the mantelpiece ticked off at just nine o'clock. I didn't feel that a comprehensive knowledge of alchemy was necessary at all. "You've told me enough," I said with as much of a smile of gratitude as I could stretch to. "I always seem to be tired these days. It can be most inconvenient."

"Very normal, please don't let it worry you," smiled Thomas. "The result of time travel of course and only to be expected. It fades as you become more accustomed."

"Thank you as usual," I said. "It's just this serpent. You say it's the symbol of infinity. How can it follow me? Why does it? What should I do about it? And," something else broke through the fogs of sleep, "you talk about divinity and Christianity and purity. But these people believe in torture and evil."

"Ah yes," said Thomas. "Well, of course, wherever you get the possibility of great power and wealth, as Vespasian proves very well, you will always get the dark side."

"Like Star Wars?" I mumbled.

"Oh dear me no," smiled Thomas. "Much, much more realistic and disturbing than that."

But I had to go. I was falling asleep as usual and I apologised and asked if we could meet up another evening. He offered me his spare room if I wanted to stay the night but I told him Bertie was coming back the next morning, so I couldn't. He frowned slightly. It seemed he would have liked my company though I doubted if a man could be lonely who travelled time as some people travelled the local bus routes. He patted the sofa. "It is far too cold to walk home," he said with genial patience. "My spare room is very warm and comfy. You'd be most welcome." I thought he was going to try and pressurise me but then he seemed to think better of it and shrugged. We walked back to my place together, Thomas seeing me home as usual. The paths were moonlit though the night sky was a little overcast and the village stream reflected more cloud than stars. It made my world a smaller place, enclosed and limited. I liked the boundaries. They felt safe. An absurd delusion but one I encouraged.

It wasn't until I was back in my own home and curled up in bed with a cup of cocoa to take away the after taste of the wine, that I realised Thomas had once again avoided the question of the coiled snake that ate its own tail.

CHAPTER THIRTY-FIVE

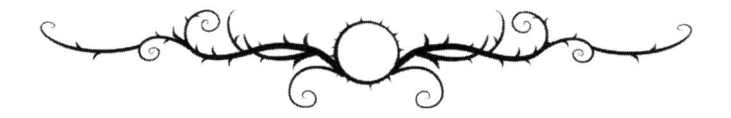

I slept deeply without dreaming. It was very early the next morning, being the twenty seventh of October, that I was woken by something tapping on my bedroom window. At first I could not remember who I was or what world I was in. Then I decided I was Molly and that my life was a gentler, safer life and I could risk getting up to see what had disturbed my silences.

I expected Bertie sometime later in the day but he had his own key and certainly wasn't agile enough to climb up the wisteria outside up as far as my attic. Thomas Cambio might be a wandering spirit which made him ageless but he inhabited a seventy year old body and I didn't believe it could be him either. I hoped it might just be an early rising magpie. I got up and shuffled over to the window. The tapping continued without pause.

My window was a double casement and opened outwards into the last dewy chestnut leaves and the pale graspers of the leafless wisteria. The sky was still dark and starless now though the moon in my modern times was slowly approaching climax and shone smooth. There was no one outside at all. No one had climbed my tree, no one was trying to attract my attention. I sat on the padded window seat, shivered and peered out. The autumn damp slunk into my room and filled up the corners. I closed the window and went back to bed. The tapping had stopped. I decided it must have been a loose branch, twigs in the wind, fronds of climbing greenery. I pulled the quilt around my ears and tried to gain back all the warmth I had lost. Then the whispering came directly into my ear. The voices intermingled but I heard every soft inflection. I lay in a sweat of ice and could not escape because I had opened my home to them and now they were in my head.

"I will turn the cards for you," whispered the woman. "First you must cut the pack." I did not recognise her voice and I saw no one. I saw only shifting darkness in my room and squeezing my eyes tight shut made no difference. The voice repeated, "You must first cut the pack."

"I can't see you," I whispered back. "I can't see the cards. I don't want my future told."

"Oh, this is not your future I foretell," said the voice, "it is your past."

"You mean Tilda?" I pleaded. "Please, she's suffered enough. Please leave her alone."

"You must cut the pack," said the voice.

I curled up tightly, my knees beneath my chin, my head under the covers – a petrified child. Then another voice interrupted the woman's sibilance. The new voice was as soft and malicious as a frosted breeze over low grass and I recognised it at once. "I will cut for her," said Vespasian.

"You have no right. She has not appointed you," said the woman.

"I took that right," said Vespasian. "It was claimed in blood and is indisputable. It cannot be denied."

"Very well. I believe it was properly witnessed by one of the common folk and therefore I acknowledge your right," said the woman. "Now cut the cards."

I was shivering like a fool. I had become such a part of enduring magic I should not have been afraid, but I was terrified. Then

Vespasian said, "The card is the number eighteen. It is the card of The Moon."

"That is appropriate," said the woman. "It is the Arabic nine and represents the cycle of reincarnation."

There was another voice which interrupted her, harsh and ugly and gloating, neither masculine nor feminine. It gathered force, reverberating into a snarl. "That is the card which represents the final stage of the quest when rationality must be sacrificed for instinct and the material state surrendered during the first acknowledgement of spirit. It is the card which challenges courage and opens the paths of the dead. It is true then, who she is and what you have done to her."

"It is quicksilver," said Vespasian, soft as the dying echo of threat. "It is the mercury which changes body into soul. It represents not only death but also rebirth. And so – the reintroduction of incarnation both into body and into spirit."

"With this card," said the woman who had first spoken, "the girl is surely alone. I do not take her part. She relies only on her own faith."

"She is not alone. I will stand in her place whenever I choose," said Vespasian. "None of you can deny me. Even her. Even you."

"I will deny you," hissed the second voice. "And I will claim both of you. You will both wish for death and I will deny you reincarnation, rebirth, and death itself. You have challenged me for too long. The card is The Moon. The full moon peaks this Samhain. There are just five days to wait before I eat you both."

"Then continue to chew on your hunger," said Vespasian and I could hear the malice in his smile thicken like treacle poured on honey. "But do not anticipate torture, for the girl is under my protection, and me you will never touch again. I was never the acolyte you thought me and I do not swive with filth."

I still saw nothing but I heard her spring. At the same moment I heard Vespasian laugh. The wind rushed around me like winged creatures on an invisible battlefield.

The first voice said, her voice bland beneath the rushing wings, "The law stands, whoever chooses to disregard it. The human's claim is just. His actions were not challenged at the time, for he understood when others did not. Therefore, now he has the right to take this female's place whenever he wishes."

The angry hiss spat back. "Law? Rule? I make the law. I rule over this arrogant striding fool who thinks himself powerful, when he is as human as all the rest. I will eat his prick, and drink his eyes. I will bend him over my altar and flay his hide from his puny bones."

I heard Vespasian's laugh again, very soft, from close by my side. "Evil is always ignorant," he said. "You call me human. You call the girl human. You understand nothing. But I will teach you, and you will learn."

The shadows hurtled huge and swamped me. I thought I had fainted but when I woke, the normality of sunshine was streaming through the window, the curtains were drawn back, and the catch was rattling loose. My bedroom was swathed in a dazzle of glistening dust – the brightest autumn morning this year. I sat up and rubbed the disbelief from my eyes, then brought back a semblance of reality in the shower. I had just put the kettle on when Bertie arrived and I almost kissed him.

The Davidsons had finally become a little tedious or perhaps that was how they were beginning to find Bertie. He unpacked his case in the spare room and handed me a box of chocolates. I disliked chocolates, something he had never been able to grasp through seven years of marriage. As far as Bertie was concerned, women all liked chocolate and that is what you were supposed to give them.

"You're not still all vague, are you?" he demanded, eating the first of the chocolates himself. "You're no company at all these days, you know."

I knew what he meant. When I was being Tilda, it left Molly without personality or coherence. "No, I'm sort of myself at the moment, if that makes sense." I yawned. "Mind you," I added with a slight shiver, "I had a very disturbed night so I dare say I'll only be half awake today."

"Bad dreams?" It was what he was no doubt still suffering from himself.

I shook my head. "Perhaps, but it didn't seem like a dream. There was something tapping on my window and I had to get up and see what it was."

"Quoth the raven, 'Nevermore'?"

I allowed myself a smile. "There wasn't anything there at all. Just the chestnut tree in the wind I suppose."

"You ought to get it pruned," said Bertie. "By the way, I like your little carved snake over the fireplace. I saw something like that in the antique shop down Tramper's Lane a few months ago. I nearly bought it for you. I know you like funny old stuff like that. But this isn't the same one, is it? That one was much more modern looking. Yours is better carved and has nicer eyes."

"I didn't know you ever took any notice of that sort of thing," I said, surprised.

"Well," said Bertie, "it just goes to show, doesn't it? You underestimate me as usual. Anyway, I like your one, it looks really old. Where did you find it?"

"Just hanging around," I said.

I walked off and left Bertie in the kitchen with the chocolates. I swaddled myself into my coat, scarf and gloves and walked quickly down to Thomas Cambio's cottage but he was out. I was bitterly disappointed. I assumed he was off walking on the hills as he often did and as we'd first met but I didn't feel like walking in the drizzle and mist. There was a sense of threat closing tighter around me, magic was no longer a strange interruption in my life but a constant companion, my own shadow and a part of myself. Fear had moved into my gut, a black stone of tremendous weight. I had little reason to trust anyone, even myself, for I was two people and felt more unbalanced than those around me with their unsettling menace.

Instinct told me Thomas was a safe guide and his other self, the abbot, a man of kindness however intolerant his age had made him. But when I needed him, he had gone and I was all alone. I returned home and unwrapped myself back into the warmth. Bertie was making lunch so I went upstairs.

Back in my bedroom I sat on the unmade bed and remembered

what I could from the night's messages. I examined the catch on the window which would no longer close tight, yet before it had always clasped snug. Now its rattle persisted when I pushed at it. Then I got up and went downstairs to search the house, for once a very long time ago I'd bought a pack of tarot cards. They had appealed because of the designs rather than their possible and improbable meanings. I had no book of divination or explanation, I had bought only the cards and now I couldn't remember where I'd put them. I had never, ever used them. My book shelves were cluttered and disorganised but, even though I hadn't seen or thought of these cards for years, I found them at once. They were tight wedged in the very first place I looked. The carved serpent watched me from the wall.

I undid the dust grimed cellophane from the box and sat with the cards on my leather chair by the empty fire place. They were colourful and held a certain fascination, though they looked somewhat different to the few others I had ever seen in my life. These had been designed by one Aleister Crowley whose name seemed familiar, and they were called the Tarot Cards of Thoth, which sounded even more familiar, though I couldn't remember why. I shuffled them, then cut the pack. I turned over the next card. It was the card of The Moon.

I sat there for a long time with the card face up, staring at the picture. When I looked up from it, my walls had faded and I was sitting on the dew damp grass beside the cold pool I loved, in the medieval forest where Richard had been buried and where I had sat as Tilda so many times before. Through the silvering trees, my book shelves, the window and its sunshine reflections all paled but were visible all the same in a combination of worlds. I was Molly and my room remained, but within it the forest of a thousand years ago stretched in translucent autumn glory. Richard's burial mound had been decorated with vervain, periwinkle and henbane. Then I realised the rest of the flowers were in my lap and I had been the one who had strewn them across the grave. Beneath the little piles of green herb and tiny purple flowers, was the card of Thoth, number eighteen in the major arcana – The Moon.

I heard him behind me as he walked up through the trees. This time I was expecting him. I knew he stood and looked over my shoulder for a moment before he spoke. "I see you have found your card," said Vespasian. Then he walked forward until I could look up and see him. "It is dangerous for you here. You should go back to your own time."

"I'm still in my time. But I know this place too," I said, "although I've never been here as myself before. I didn't ask to come and I don't know how to leave. But I feel at home. You don't recognise me?"

"Recognise you? Are we playing word games?" inquired Vespasian with his usual soft malice. "I doubt we have time for that. I've seen you occasionally in your own place, and I'm hardly likely to forget who I've met there. I know who you are and I know who you are not. You are not my Tilda, but you merge with her. You bring her into great danger."

He was standing over me and I had to strain my neck to look up at him. He was dressed in the old dust-worn clothes of before and his hair was untrimmed. I was in modern clothes, a loose dress and cardigan and my own hair was probably more of a mess than his. Once again, aware of his gaze, I was conscious of the length of my modern skirt and tried to tug it down over my legs. "That's ridiculous," I said. "It's you who bring her danger." I was angry and reminded of everything I hated him for.

He didn't seem annoyed at all. "Perhaps," he said, half smiling, "that's partially true. It has been true. Do you want me to explain? Perhaps you are the one to help her, and it's time I told someone the truth." And quite suddenly he sat beside me, stretching out his long legs on the grass, leaning back on one elbow, his face raised a little to the mild sunshine. I could see the holes in the dust faded black of his woollen hose and the frayed edge of his tunic. The little handle of his hunting knife was visible tucked into the cuff of one of his boots. I could feel the warmth of his breath on my cheek.

"Then answer these questions," I demanded, sitting upright and a little rigid. I was blushing, feeling uncovered, but most of all I was angry. "You come into both worlds," I hurried on. "Why? What do you come for? Is it to kill?"

He leaned over, stretching out his arm. I thought he wanted to touch me, and tensed. Instead he picked the tarot card of The Moon from my lap and held it up to the light. "This is not made by hand," he said. "It seems that the world of the future takes what it wishes from the past, turning knowledge into progress. Then is magic more accepted in your time?"

"No, it isn't," I said. "Less. But you haven't answered my question."

He looked across at me and grinned. "You look so fierce, Mistress Molly, woman of the future. Do I kill? What a question to ask a God fearing man."

"I doubt if you fear God or anyone else," I muttered, increasingly irritated by his prevarications and pretence at good humour.

"Now there you are wrong," he said. "I do not fear God because God is love, although sometimes love might be fearful to some, and real love is inevitably awesome. But there are men I fear and forces I fear even more. However, that was not your question and it is not your business."

"It's my business who you murder," I said, glaring at him. "Three women have died in my time and one of them was my cousin. I loved her. She was slaughtered in my own home. I have to know if it was you. So how much were you involved?"

"I am sorry if you lost someone you loved," he said, his voice soft again, without the underlying thread of threat. He looked away from me and across to the silver shadows of the forest pool. His fingers were in the vervain I had spread on Richard's grave. "I know how that feels," he continued, his voice little more than a whisper in drifting memory. "They killed my wife. She was the first, many, many years ago. I know how you feel and I am sorry."

I was silent. I waited for him to go on. This time I knew he would.

"No," he said, looking back at me. "I kill, when I have to. But I did not kill your cousin or any other woman in your world. I do not torture or kill for pleasure. I do not lust for blood or hunger for pain.

My pleasure is not the suffering of others and torture disgusts me. That is not my sickness or my vice."

I believed him immediately. The relief was incredible. I stopped shivering and my shoulders relaxed, but I wasn't entirely satisfied yet. "Aren't you one of them? Part of the group? Arthur and Malcolm and the others – you work with them or for them. They tortured Isabel. They killed Richard." I suddenly realised then just how much I longed to trust him.

I thought he might ignore me but then his own face relaxed and his voice was gentle again. "Arthur, and his cult are my enemies," he said, "as they are Tilda's. I am not one of any group. I have no group. I work alone."

I took a deep breath and said what I had not intended to say. "But you raped Tilda."

His voice altered again. "Listen to me now," he said, "I have warned you as I have warned her. You are in great danger. You should not meddle. There are far worse dangers than torture, rape and death."

"I can't think of any," I objected. "But I don't choose to meddle, and I didn't want any of this. I got sucked in and I haven't the faintest idea why. Have you heard of reincarnation?"

He smiled as if I was a two year old who had just discovered his first book and asked his parents if they knew anything about reading and writing. "You think Tilda might be your past? It's a possible explanation," he said. He was still holding my tarot card. "This is the symbol of reincarnation."

"Yes. I think you said that last night," I nodded. "I heard you though I didn't see you. Did you know that was me, and not Tilda?" And then, as an urgent afterthought, "And who were the other two people?"

"They are beings of great power and evil," said Vespasian. "You cannot have met either directly, though no doubt you will, unless you choose now to step away. Mine is a game you can neither comprehend, nor hope to control."

I sighed. "Everyone speaks in riddles," I said. "I'd hoped you might help me understand everything."

"Everything?" He smiled. "That would be expecting a little too much."

"Well, at least something," I muttered. "You've told me you didn't murder Sammie. Although a murderer would lie in any case, I do believe you. Strangely enough when you bother to talk sense at all, I usually believe you. But there's such a confusion in my head and I desperately need to understand."

"A pathetic and sad assumption," he smiled absently. "What is happening is not of this logical, material world and yet you expect to understand it with a logical, material intellect." He was lying back now, his head resting on his clasped hands, surrounded by the little dark tangle of the wild thyme and the fronds of the fennel. Beyond the rise and fall of his slow breathing, I watched the pool ripple silver as the fish jumped and the leaves floated dark red from the overhanging branches. Further, part glimpsed through the trees, my living room still stood like an alien boundary, a doorway between worlds and a reminder of the magic that surrounded us. Vespasian was right. No logical explanation would serve, nor bring understanding.

"I know someone," I said. "In my world, he's called Thomas Cambio. He's told me a great deal and he doesn't talk in code like you do. In your world he's Abbot Bernado of the convent of The Little Sisters of Angelica and you knew him in Italy."

Vespasian twisted around and stared at me, frowning. "I know the abbot," he said. "How do you know him?"

"Tilda knows him in your time," I answered, "and she went to his convent, but he told her to leave. But in my time he's Thomas Cambio."

Vespasian sat up, looking intently at me from beneath hooded lids. "I doubt the abbot has the capability of either transmutation or metamorphosis, though there are other systems of alteration and absorption less pleasant, such as the incubi and succubae." He paused a moment. "Thomas stands for doubt. Cambio means change. I do not trust the sound of your friend."

"Names don't have to mean anything," I said crossly. "You appear to change your own whenever you want to."

Vespasian seemed to relax, settling back again. "And time I changed it again," he smiled at the sky. "Poor Jasper, Baron de Vrais had to disappear, wanted for the terrible slaughter of his wife. Now Vespasian is wanted for murders just as foul. The Roman Emperor Vespasian was a man who believed in inspiration and peace after centuries of war, but it seems that peace eludes me. And Fairweather? Well, the weather is fair no longer."

"Because you're a magician," I accused. "You study black magic."

"I am not a magician, I am an alchemist," he corrected me. "Alchemy is perhaps the highest goal a man can aspire to. And names do matter. Remember symbolism, even if you choose to forget most else. Until you can be sure, if you are capable of such judgement, I suggest it would be better not to let this man Thomas into either your confidence or your life, especially on any more – intimate basis."

I glared. "Are you trying," I demanded, "in a rare diplomatic manner, to try and tell me not to welcome this man into my bed? Because, let me tell you, apart from being a disgusting thought and none of your damned business, Thomas is very elderly and a gentleman." I was going to try and be dignified and leave it at that, but I couldn't resist a final remark. "And I," I said, still glaring, "am a lady."

He laughed. "The hypocrisy of any woman's ladylike behaviour impresses me no more than that of diplomacy," he said, now smiling at me with the usual sardonic malice that irritated me so much. "So, you have a title, or simply claim lady as a symbol of refinement. Absurd. I spoke of what I know to be important, but you are a comparative stranger to me and I've no authority to order you. Besides," his smile widened, "it seems in this future time of yours, men have abandoned authority over all the women in their lives. A form of equality has been established. I consider it delightfully challenging. I am fully aware, of course, that you and your attitudes have a quite fascinating influence on my innocent Tilda."

"I would like to influence her more. She still obeys you too often."

He frowned, though did not turn to look at me. "At the time which has come, and that which is coming, obedience to existing wisdom is greatly advisable, and you would do well to copy Tilda's." Then he did turn, and looked straight at me. His eyes were so black and I read a haunting sadness, which contradicted the amused malice of his voice. "As a woman capable of travel between worlds," he said, "and with the power of transmutation, holding within her my Tilda's life, and the existence of others far greater, I am puzzled by your ignorance. I am rarely puzzled by anything anymore. But you lack understanding. How does power and ignorance blend?"

Now he had asked me a question I could not answer. I mumbled, "But it's you who misunderstand. I have no power at all," and stared back at him.

He sighed, and stretched. "So now, dear Mistress Molly, I have to leave you, before your time pulls me further in. There's a great deal I have yet to do. A climax is closing in on my world, and it's there I expect to meet you again. You claim neither power nor knowledge, but you travel where you should not, and have skills you should not have. Just remember what I've told you, whether you consider it my business or not." He stood up and I hurried to scramble up beside him.

"Hang on," I said. "There's so much more. What climax? Why should I be there? And the snake, the little wooden carving of the serpent that eats its own tail. Do you know about that? How do I destroy it?"

"The ouroboros," Vespasian said. His voice remained soft but his eyes were stern. "And you must not attempt to destroy it, though I doubt you could, however much you tried. It is there to protect you."

"But it's – horrible," I said, dismayed. "Malcolm put it in my room."

"He did not," said Vespasian. "He does not have that power."

My own world was moving inwards and the forest fading. The bookshelves had pushed back the trees and the colours of my carpet were under my feet, the scent of the herbs lost. "Then who, what?" I demanded. "What is it? Where did it come from? What did you call it?"

"The ouroboros is the alchemic symbol of infinite eternity," said

Vespasian, "and it was I who sent it to you. Now it is bound to you. It would be wise not to trust those who are afraid to touch it."

"But I'm afraid to touch it," I said, my voice rising in panic as Vespasian began to disappear into the growing shadows.

"Ah yes," he said, very faint now, "but you see, you are one of the most dangerous of us all."

I was left standing in my ordinary modern living room feeling absurdly out of breath and clutching a handful of little dead flower heads, periwinkle, vervain and henbane, and a pack of damp tarot cards with number eighteen, the card of The Moon missing.

CHAPTER THIRTY-SIX

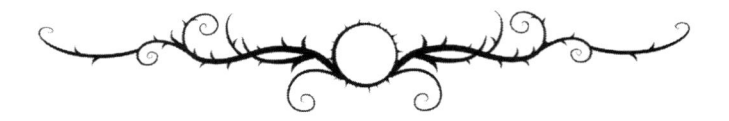

It felt shockingly mundane at first, and terribly flat, as if four dimensions had suddenly shrunk into two. I tugged my old cardigan tightly across my shoulders and sighed. All the lights seemed to have gone out. The air smelled stale. Then Bertie rumbled in with lunch on a tray and I had to be myself again. I mumbled at him with my mouth full for half an hour before extricating myself and trudging back upstairs. I sat on the little couch beside the window in my bedroom and looked out at the chestnut tree. It seemed absurd that such a peaceful world was just a veneer hiding a thousand dangers. 'Peace eludes me,' Vespasian had said. Indeed, it was barely a memory.

I had brought the tarot cards upstairs with me and I spread them out on the bed, looking at their design. Then something occurred to me and I turned them back, shuffled them, and cut the pack. I picked up the card I had cut. It was number eighteen of the major arcana, the card of The Moon. I smiled. The card was no longer there for Vespasian had still been holding it when he disappeared into his own time and I into mine. Downstairs, back in my own living room, this card had been missing. Now it was back. Everything was unreal. Reality had taken a different shape.

I scattered the cards onto the floor, letting them fall as they wished, some turned upwards, others down. Then I climbed into bed and closed my eyes. I would not use Thomas Cambio's system for returning to Tilda. Her life was in increasing danger and I needed to build up strength and understanding before going back to help her. So I slept and hoped to dream.

It was not the dream I expected. I did not dream of my other self, nor of any of the people I had met as her. I did not link to Thomas, to Vespasian or to anything that explained the things I so desperately wished to know. I went back to my own childhood.

My mother was standing over me with the knife upraised. I was nine years old and huddled cold in bed, the sheets soaked beneath me where I had urinated. The knife caught the sudden moonlight like a white fire. It was almost a full moon, half way perhaps between the turn of its first quarter and its halfway peak. My bedroom curtains were flimsy and never fully closed, and the moon often lit my nights; a friend when other friends left.

I screamed for my father. When he was at home, he protected me while my mother raved into manic excess. But I knew now what I had not known on that night when I was nine and my mother appeared at my side, that in fact my father had already left for good. I never blamed him. He had tried very hard for many years and he was a simple soul. Such a small, tired man to cope with a crazy woman and a sad little girl who needed so much more than he could give. I don't think she ever tried to kill him – only me – but he just couldn't bear it any longer, and he ran away. Just like Tilda.

My mother hadn't tried to kill me that night, though I expected her to. Wild eyed, drooling and spitting, she had cut all around me, splitting open the pillow beneath my head so that a thousand feathers spun around, into my eyes, my nose and my gasping, crying mouth until I was half suffocated and half delirious. She had cut the blankets into shreds of thin, unravelling wool. She had ripped at my nightdress and sliced through the curls of my hair. Then, when the mood left her, she had slumped at my bedside and begun to heave until she choked and vomited at my feet. She had fallen asleep there.

When I was sure she slept, I had crept downstairs and that's when I found my father gone, all his clothes taken, his pipe from the table, his slippers from beside the chair, his coat from the peg. I telephoned the police and they came and took my mother away. She was still in the same hospital where they had taken her all those years ago. I never saw my father again.

My dream retraced each step, each heartbeat. I woke crying and it was half past six in the evening and the stars outside were already clear and bright. The moon was all shimmer and almost full, halfway between the turn of its first quarter and its halfway peak.

I got up and washed my face. Bertie had gone out and left me a cold dinner beside the microwave. I didn't bother to heat it up. I put my coat on, turned up the collar and went down to the Smith and Joker. Thomas Cambio was already sitting beside the fire, talking to Ruth Ableside and another woman. I bought myself a tomato juice and went over to them. They made room for me at the table and I sat down.

The woman I did not know stretched out her paisley shawled arm and shook my hand. "I'm Sarah Ableside," she said. "Ruth's sister. I'm a counsellor too in my spare time but during the day I work at the little herbal nursery just outside the village."

I wanted to talk to Thomas alone but I thought perhaps he would walk me home afterwards, and I could ask him in for coffee and we could talk then. In the meantime, I tried to be polite. I'd liked that pretty perfumed nursery once, it had a good reputation and I knew Wattle had bought some of her aromatherapy supplies there. "I buy pots of basil at that place every summer," I said. "I used to love cooking with basil, though I rarely bother cooking anything anymore."

"Oh you should," smiled Ruth. "It's so rewarding, amongst the sweetest pleasures of life." Everyone was smiling. The conversation pattered inanely into smiling platitudes. All the time Thomas watched me patiently from his corner and the firelight turned the pupils of his eyes red with dancing shadows. I stuck it out until closing time. By then I had added vodka to the tomato juices and was drinking Bloody Marys. I had a headache.

When finally the pub shut and its customers drifted off into the darkness, I expected the two cherubic sisters to trot off together but Thomas took an arm each and insisted on walking them home. With increasing unchristian irritability, I trudged behind. At their front door, they turned with a glow of genteel generosity heightened by an evening of sherry around the pub fire.

"Please come in," said Ruth, "and have a little something with us before you have to go home in the cold again."

"It would be so nice," said Sarah. "We left the fire burning low, so the room will be nice and toasty."

"We have our own elderberry wine," said Ruth, "and a little of last year's nettle wine too. Do come, we'd be so pleased."

"I made gingerbread earlier," said Sarah, "and I'll make a pot of camomile tea."

It all sounded hideous. "I can't, really," I said. "It's already late. Thank you, but no."

Then Thomas messed it all up by saying, "But why not? My dear Molly, I'm sure it would do you good. We won't stay long and then I'll walk you home afterwards." So I scowled and turned it into a smile and tramped back into the William Morris cottage which I had not intended to visit ever again.

It was while I was sipping the nettle wine and pretending that I liked it but no thank you I really didn't want anymore, that I ended up staring at the mantelshelf. I had not been listening to the chatter. I had been thinking about my mother. The dream had brought back all the dull misery that had infused my childhood. It was two full years or more since I had visited my mother in the asylum and I wondered if I was being sent a sign that I should go again. Symbolism, said Vespasian. I should look for symbols.

The sisters had built up the fire again. The heat flickered, distorting visibility of everything close so the carriage clock and the green vase of dried rosemary and pussy willow all appeared to shimmer and move. In the centre of the little row of ornaments, between two brass elephants, was a small wooden carving of a serpent that ate its own tail.

"I see you're looking at my little ouroboros," said Ruth. "Do you like it? It's quite a rarity. I found it in the antique shop in Tramper's Lane a couple of days ago."

"Yes," I said. "I like it. What did you call it again?"

"The ouroboros," said Sarah. "The symbol of infinity. I'm sure you know about such things."

I stared at her. "Why should I?" I demanded.

"Because," smiled Ruth, all dimples, "we believe you are the veleda my dear. More nettle wine? Or shall I make more tea?"

I stared at her. "I've never heard of a Veleda."

"The veleda," interrupted Thomas, leaning back in his chair and watching me closely from his flaring shadows, "was the seer and channeller who lived during the reign of the Roman Emperor Titus Flavius Vespasian, in the year 74 A.D. She was considered divine, but although she was a powerful alchemist, I'm afraid divinity actually escaped her at the end."

"I have no idea what any of you are talking about," I said, panic rising like bile.

Thomas sat forward suddenly with a reassuring smile. "I'm sorry to have broken your confidences without your permission," he said, "but Ruth and Sarah are great friends of mine. I've known them for many years. I always come to them to recount my experiences when I return from my – how would you call them – journeys into time. You can trust them as you trust me, of course. We will help you with anything we can."

"Trust isn't that easy," I pointed out. "If I make mistakes about who to trust then it could be very dangerous."

"How true," said Sarah. "You are quite right. And of course, Ruth and I don't have the power to go travelling and inhabiting other people in history as you and Thomas do, so we're just small fry in the scheme of things. But we can still help."

"You see," continued Thomas, between sips of elderberry wine which made his pale lips glossy crimson, "the veleda, searching for different paths to ultimate divinity, became associated with Janus, the keeper of the gates."

"The gates of the Underworld, and those doorways separating times and worlds and dimensions," said Sarah, "which must be kept open, of course, for you inspiring travellers."

I was silent. I knew nothing of Janus or the veleda, but I knew something about opening doors and the passages between times. Thomas said he had given me the secret grains for just that reason.

"I could start by doing your astrology," said Ruth, getting up. Behind her chair the small bookshelf held some thick papers. She pulled out a very large book. "Do you know your exact time of birth, my dear?"

"Muriel Bunting used to do astrology," I said vaguely. "She used to give lessons. Then she was killed and hung upside down in the church."

"A terrible, terrible thing," agreed Ruth, flicking through the wafer thin pages, "though not a subject for tonight, I think. In fact, it was I who taught Muriel astrology originally, quite some years ago. Now, your date of birth?"

I considered saying I had forgotten and then realised that I was being absurd. This was exactly what I had wanted. I was about to get answers to questions I hadn't even thought of asking. "Is astrology connected to alchemy too?"

"Oh, indeed it is," smiled Thomas. "For perhaps a thousand years' astrology and astronomy were considered to be the same thing. Astrology echoes the macrocosm in microcosm, as it is above, so it is below. I would guess that your horoscope makes up the perfect star, fire and water."

"Water," I said. "I'm Pisces." I gave the full details. I knew my time of birth to the nearest few minutes, for my mother had told me. She'd never forgiven me for the pain I caused her. I had taken my first breath just as the moon had shone through her hospital window.

"Sagittarius rising," said Ruth after a moment, "and the Moon four days past its peak in Scorpio in the twelfth house. How interesting, my dear."

"Very interesting indeed," said Thomas, smile fixed. "As I expected, the perfect six pointed star of combined fire and water."

"But Tilda isn't," I said. "She was born in mid August sometime in the day, during a storm."

"Leo I suppose but my books wouldn't give me the maths for her chart anyway," said Ruth. "The calendar changed you know, and dates are different in medieval times, though I daresay I could work it out if I wanted to. But it doesn't matter anyway. It's you who controls all this, don't you see, not her. You go into her body. She isn't even really aware of you."

"How do you know?" I asked suddenly. In fact, Tilda was very much more aware of me these days. "How can you know anything about her?"

"Well, of course, we don't really," Sarah smiled quickly. "Just from what you told Thomas, and Thomas has told us."

I was surrounded by smiles. "So what does my chart say?" I asked.

"Leave it with me," nodded the smiling Ruth, "and I'll do your whole horoscope for you tomorrow."

"In the meantime," said Thomas, "perhaps it's time we were leaving."

It took us some time to get away after all. The sisters helped us wrap up, "It'll seem so cold outside after being in a warm room like this," and insisted on talking for ages on their front step, thus ensuring that we caught cold after all.

"It's late October so Scorpio now, isn't it?" I said. "You said my moon was in Scorpio."

"Yes, and it's nearly a full moon," said Sarah, pointing up at the sky. The moon was huge behind the top of her bare branched Ash. "Though of course, this full moon will be in Taurus."

"Taurus," said Thomas, "is my birth sign as it happens. I'm afraid that makes me much more of a plodder than you, dear Molly. Pisces is the sign of the psychic you know."

"I'm not psychic," I said, shivering on the doorstep. "I may have strange adventures, but I talk to people who are very much alive, not those who are dead."

"That, "said Ruth, with her eternal smile, "can always change, you know."

CHAPTER THIRTY-SEVEN

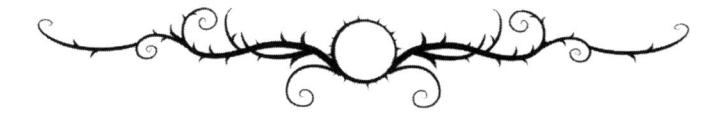

The dawn poured over my valley like a rose pink promise. I scrambled out of bed. At some time during the night I had been injected with energy and optimism. I clattered downstairs and then slowed at the halfway mark. It was early and Bertie was still asleep. He hardly ever seemed to work anymore and had let his private insurance brokerage lapse during all the depression, but he still needed his sleep. So I tiptoed outside, put the front door on the latch, and went to sit in the hammock under the chestnut tree. The leaves had almost gone though some curled brown foliage still clung to the safety of their branches. I swung a little, dew bottomed and damp but uncaring. I thought about Sammie who had loved to sit here, and I thought about my mother and whether there was any point in visiting her. She didn't recognise who I was any longer and it only left me depressed and weary for the following week. But my dream had sent me yearning. I had loved her, even if she had never been capable of loving me. I even wondered where my father was all these years later and if he was finally dead and at peace. It certainly couldn't have been any fun being married to my mother and I suppose he had only stayed for me, stubbornly silent regarding the shame of mental illness and raging violence. After the police had committed her to the asylum outside London, I had been sent to a foster home in the West Country, which I had adored. It had been bliss. I still associated bliss with these windswept hills and wind trapped valleys, with the dry stone walls and the thatched cottages, tiny streams and tourist beloved villages. So I lived here now and was successful, whatever that meant. Except that I didn't write anymore because I had forgotten how to. I lived it all instead.

It was the bright, cold morning of October the twenty eighth and I felt very well indeed.

I made breakfast and coffee and the smell of frying bacon should have woken Bertie but it did not so I knocked on the door of my spare bedroom and called him. There wasn't any answer so I pushed open the door and peeped in. He wasn't there and his bed hadn't been slept in, unless he had risen even earlier than I had, and uncharacteristically made his bed before leaving the house. It was a surprise but what Bertie did wasn't my business anymore so I went back into the kitchen and ate what I had cooked, double helpings.

On the kitchen table my laptop sat smart black and unused. My agent didn't ring anymore. As far as he was concerned I was still having a nervous breakdown after the murder of my cousin and I wondered if I actually was. Then I wondered, not for the first time, if I had inherited my mother's illness. The police had surely considered that too although they'd tried to be subtle about it, but before being thrust into the care of the counsellor, they had sent me to the police psychologist. I assumed he had decided on my sanity. He could have been wrong.

I hadn't done any housework in days and little enough for weeks. Bertie had tried to help but he had masculine dust blindness and didn't know how to work the vacuum cleaner. It was autumn but I began to spring-clean. I was blowing the cobwebs from my own brain. Symbolism perhaps. I even vacuumed the stairs, which I hated doing because of all the little corners. In the bedroom I had to crawl around and collect the tarot cards that I had scattered the day before. I searched in the fluff under the bed and behind the cushions of the window seat and in every possible shadow. Then I boxed them neatly and counted them out before returning them to their container. Number eighteen of the major arcana, the card of The Moon, was missing again. All the others were there. I made the bed and then brought the cards downstairs with me and put them back in the bookshelf, squashing them in hard, and deciding they would stay there.

I looked at my wall above the mantelshelf where Vespasian's small ouroboros hung. I reached out a finger and smoothed it along the carved wooden surface. It didn't frighten me anymore and now I saw its beauty instead of its ugliness. Its eyes watched me back. They should have been blank. They weren't. I was delighted that Ruth and Sarah had one similar, presumably the one from the antique shop which Bertie said he nearly bought me. I was glad he had not, because seeing it in the little William Morris cottage had been my sign that these people were truly safe and to be trusted. Vespasian had said. And Vespasian talked of symbols. So I knew.

I wondered who I should visit first, Thomas or the sisters. I decided I would start with Thomas and only go directly to Ruth and Sarah if Thomas was not at home. We had made no particular appointment the night before, but meeting again was a natural assumption. By nine o'clock I decided that it was already a reasonable hour to go visiting and I put the dishwasher on, brushed my hair and grabbed my coat.

My excitement was like a scurrying mouse, the flutter of butterflies or the unfolding of magnolia petals. I now had three people whom I trusted in my own world and who wanted to help not only me but Tilda too, and who knew the secrets of the magic that had possessed me. They were, slowly perhaps, introducing me to the knowledge I needed. Today I expected to find out a great deal more.

I was out of the house and half way down the street when I heard the sirens.

Three police cars screeched past me and up into the narrow road behind my cottage, going in the same direction as I was. I stood very still for a moment and then started to run. I got to Thomas's house and found the cars parked in a clump outside his door. I saw

Constable Peterson, whom I recognised, trying to keep the neighbours back. Amongst the twitter of horrified onlookers were Ruth and Sarah Ableside, still in their rosebud nightdresses and hugging their dressing gowns around them, tear stains on their little round faces. I couldn't get close enough to Thomas's house to see what had happened. I was so lost in panic that I thought I'd be sick. I was already heaving when Ruth saw me and pushed over to my side. She put her arm around my shoulders. "Sometime this morning," she gulped. "We were still in bed. We didn't hear a thing."

"It's Thomas?"

She nodded, still hugging me. "In the front garden. Right in full view." The knot of police and forensic experts now hid everything from the street. An ambulance squeezed up into the remaining space, shuddering to a halt on the cobbles, doors flung open. Everyone moved back.

"Is he like the others?" How did you say something like that? "I mean, was he murdered? Tortured?"

"He was murdered," said Ruth, "that we know. As for the details, well, I'm not sure and I don't think I want to know yet."

"Then it's my fault," I said.

Ruth stared at me through her tears. "What makes you think such a thing? That's a terrible thing to think. And it certainly isn't true."

"I open doors," I said, though my voice didn't obey my mind. "You said it yourself, last night. I never mean to, but that's what happens. I open doors. I open windows. Evil gets through. Them."

"Them?"

"Yes, them," I said.

I hugged Ruth and told her I'd come back and see her later. She went back to Sarah and the police. She was Thomas's closest and longest surviving friend she said, and he had no living relatives. She would be spending all day at the police station. I expected a visit from the police myself. I had spent all the previous evening with Thomas, Ruth and Sarah and the whole pub had seen us leave together. The police would certainly want to talk about that. I would tell them that we had gone on afterwards to Ruth's house and spent almost two hours there and that then Thomas had walked me home before going home himself. Worried for my own safety, he had pressed me to let him stay the night, but I had refused and now I was sorry. I was the last person to see him alive except for the murderer and the police would certainly be wanting to talk to me. I doubted if they would be quite so sympathetic this time. This was the fourth murder and I was linked to three of them.

I walked back around the corner and sat on my front doorstep waiting for the police. They didn't come for some time and it started to drizzle so I went indoors and put the kettle on. Bertie hadn't come home. I presumed he had found yet another girlfriend.

My house was all bright and shining and polished clean and reminded me of my early scrubbed optimism. Now I felt guilty, as if I had been dancing around the house with a feather duster at precisely the same time that someone had killed Thomas Cambio. The dishwasher was just finishing its cycle and spitting steam. I took my mug of tea into the living room and put it on the mantelshelf. Then I took down Vespasian's ouroboros and held it tight. I wished it had been Thomas who had bought the other one, instead of the Ableside sisters. He had needed the protection after all, he who had seemed to need it the least. With all his amazing powers and experience, he had died before me. All his knowledge and magic was dissipated into nothing, lost to me, who needed his answers, and to the world which had few precious souls like him.

I was thinking about Vespasian when the police turned up. I had left my front door open for them. They knocked and I called out, "Please come in. I knew you'd be coming."

I offered them tea but they wanted me down at the station, so I took my coat back off its iron peg in the hall and put the little coiled serpent, which I was still clutching, in the pocket. Whether I understood it or not, the ouroboros might be my only hope of safety. A street of neighbours watched as the police held the car door open for me. I sat in the back with my coat collar turned up and my eyes a watery pink. I wondered if the curious and concerned would think I was being arrested and I wondered if later I actually would be.

Wanted for questioning, helping the police with their inquiries, would they offer me the proverbial one phone call and what on earth was my solicitor's name. Come to think of it, he wasn't a criminal lawyer anyway, he'd helped sort out my legal affairs from time to time, publisher's contracts, selling my mother's house, complications with her committal, my father's continued non-existence and my divorce. No use at all with murder and accusations of black magic. I huddled into the back corner of the car and felt that I had been better off as Tilda after all. I wished with all my heart that Vespasian would come and rescue me again but I was in the wrong world.

I was all day at the station. I heard the rain pelting outside and bouncing off the vine that clambered around the windows. I was given take-away egg and tomato sandwiches for lunch which I didn't eat because the bread was soggy white cardboard and my throat was closed with fear and unhappiness. By the evening I was still sitting on the same chair with my bum going numb and my head throbbing. I was given a tin plate of atrocious food for dinner and several mugs of very stewed tea. Constable Peterson went out and got me a donut which was sweet of him even if I didn't like donuts. Finally, at ten past ten, they drove me home. Bertie still wasn't there. I crawled into bed and dreamed of Vespasian.

CHAPTER THIRTY-EIGHT

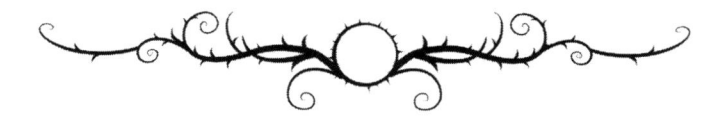

It was still raining when I woke and I still had the headache. I was also starving since I had eaten nothing except a burnt sausage and half a donut since yesterday's breakfast.

I scrambled eggs and ate them standing up. Then I slung on my coat and hurried off to Ruth's. I went the long way around and picked up a Cotswold Daily Express from the newsagents by the bridge. I was served by the marijuana smoking son who was scratching his pubescent pimples and had blood under his finger nails. It made me feel suddenly ill. "Getting exciting, isn't it?" he said, pointing to Thomas's photograph on the front page.

I didn't answer, took the paper, and went back over the bridge to Ruth and Sarah's house. I began to read the article as I waited for someone to answer their front door. The police had told me very little yesterday. They had been asking questions, not answering them, so the details in the newspaper were mostly new to me. Thomas Cambio had been found in his own little front garden, killed sometime the previous night. The exact time of death was hard to judge since hours of cold and rain had obscured the evidence. There was no doubt that he had been murdered. He had been killed by six deep wounds to the chest and neck. The murder weapon was presumed to be a very heavy bladed knife of some kind, possibly a double edged sword of antique design. Mysteriously, he had been discovered – by the postman at eight thirty in the morning – wrapped in an ancient cloak, in excellent condition in spite of being rain soaked. Several people had been questioned but no arrests had been made.

Sarah answered the door. She was still in her nighty and looked as if she had been crying since the previous morning.

"He wasn't tortured," I said. "It sounds like a quick death."

"We don't know if the police are covering up any of the details," sniffed Sarah. "You know, to help catch the killer, the way they often do. They wouldn't tell us much yesterday. Come in anyway, my dear, Ruth's making boiled eggs and soldiers. Would you join us? Here, I'll hang your coat up for you, it's very wet."

"I've had breakfast already," I said, shrugging off the coat and holding it out to her. She reached out to take it and then seemed to change her mind, rather suddenly. She withdrew her hand, shuddered slightly and retreated a step. I smiled. "Sorry, yes, it's dripping isn't it? Shall I put it in the bathroom?"

Sarah pointed to the curly carved coat and umbrella rack in the little hall. "It'll be alright there. Just hang it up and it'll soon dry off."

I followed her into the kitchen and sat at the table. A condensation of steam hung under the ceiling. The little toaster rattled, the saucepan of dancing water jangled on the spotless old cooker and the kettle was boiling with a faint whistle. Ruth was buttering toast. I watched their aging innocence, wondering just what sort of danger we might all be in.

"I haven't known Thomas long," I said. "It must be terrible for both of you. You've known him for years, haven't you? He said you were his oldest friends."

Ruth nodded, nibbling on her toast. "He was our dearest, our very dearest friend. Just like a brother. Of course, we share the same interests and shared knowledge too, although he had such tremendous power and we do not. "

"Oh, nothing like him," said Sarah with a sigh. "Not that there is anyone like him. He was so talented you know. He travelled into medieval times of course, as the good Abbot Bernado, and knew your Vespasian. But he travelled into other centuries too, Egyptian dynasties where he learned the original secrets of Thoth, to ancient Greece and Alexandria and studied the arts of Hermes Trismegistus. He was one of the first to translate the Emerald Tablet. He was an amazing man. We shall never see the likes of him again."

"He knew Zoroaster," said Ruth, pushing away the shell of her egg. "He met many of the greatest scientists in history. He was friends with Jung I believe. He even hinted once that he met Moses."

I stared. "If all that's true," I said, "how can they have killed him? I mean, he was too powerful. He had far more power than they do. What about the philosopher's stone? What about everlasting life?"

"Oh, we wouldn't know," said Sarah, shaking her head. "We aren't adepts, like Thomas. We only really know what he told us."

"And what if he exaggerated?" I said, aware of sounding unavoidably rude. "I mean – sorry – especially now. But it's such a fantastic story. It's not that I disbelieve it, after all, I'm no one, though I go back to medieval times myself. I haven't even any control, I just do it. But how can a man who knew everyone and done everything and has the control too – how can he be killed so easily? It doesn't make sense."

"He was too trusting," sighed Ruth. "He was kind and loving and believed in humanity's intrinsic goodness. Clearly he was taken quite by surprise."

"He was amazing," I said. "But how could such a man be too trusting? If anyone understood the dangers and the evil, then he did. It frightens me, thinking about who killed him. Whoever had the power to murder a man with Thomas's powers, then the killer must be a devil indeed."

"That," said Sarah, "is what frightens us too."

I didn't stay long. Although these were the only people left who could help me understand what I desperately wanted to grasp, it seemed they knew less than I had supposed. I had believed they were second only to Thomas in their powers or knowledge but suddenly they were just two sweet little ladies, cosy in their thatched cottage with their roses and their William Morris curtains and paisley cushions. They knew about astrology and had bought a modern copy of an ouroboros as a curio. They seemed to have shrunk. Thomas's death had left them diminished.

They saw me out to the hall. I struggled back into my coat which was still extremely wet. The sisters stood back a little while I flung rain drops around. "One last thing," I said, as Ruth opened the front door for me, reaching out her arm from a slight distance. I could hardly blame her for not wanting to touch me. I was so cold and wet. "The newspaper says Thomas was found wrapped in an old cloak. That seems so odd. Bizarre. Did he get it from his travels? Do you know anything about it?"

They shook their prim cherubic heads. Sarah smiled reluctantly. "Hardly the only odd thing about it all, is it? Perhaps the cloak came from your Tilda's time."

"After all," said Ruth, "we can assume it had something to do with the man you call Arthur. He sounds like the devil himself. Either him – or Vespasian."

I trudged back home in the rain and was sorry not to find Bertie waiting there for me with a hot drunk and his inane smile. I needed silly remarks and a new perspective on everything. I needed someone who thought the latest sports car on the market was more important than black magic and who would just want to sit by the fire and tell me about his new romance and how tiny her waist was and big and blue her eyes. The house seemed very cold and the chill hung from the ceiling like the condensation in Ruth and Sarah's kitchen. I sat down on the white fluffy rug beside the hearth and started to lay the logs. I was using the newspaper I had bought to screw up into spills for lighting the fire, when I noticed an article I thought vaguely interesting. Three days ago the antique shop in Tramper's Lane had been badly damaged by a small explosion, and the cause remained mysterious. Quite a few valuable articles had been scorched and a Louis XIII writing desk had been reduced to ashes.

I read the article three times, decided it wasn't relevant after all, twisted the page into a screw and shoved it in amongst the kindling. I held a match to the paper and it flared, bringing instant colour and the beginning of warmth. Then I wandered into the kitchen and opened a tin of soup. I felt I ought to be doing something more important, something that I had forgotten, or been too stupid to think of. I knew myself insipid and useless and I flopped onto my couch in front of the fire with the bowl of soup. It tasted chemical, without the rich, natural flavour of medieval pottage. I wondered where Bertie was. I wondered what Vespasian was doing and then reminded myself how absurd it was to think about that when he had been gone from this world more than eight hundred years ago. I watched the flames of my fire rise and stretch, shimmering into a thousand shades of red and golden sulphur.

I had dozed, woken, and dozed again when I thought of something I could do. I rolled off the couch, put my knee in the bowl of soup which spilled pea green and sludgy across my carpet, and went off to clean myself up. It had stopped raining but it was damned damp and cold outside so I got back into my coat and walked up to the police station. Detective Constable Peterson, the Met guy who I felt comfortable with, wasn't on duty so I spoke to the local inspector who had been both kind and helpful to me once before. It seemed a long, long time ago now but he remembered it.

"I told you at the time, Miss Susans, that I could hardly make a habit of confiding police secrets to you." I had not seen him during my exhausting questioning the day before but now he invited me to sit down in his office, not in the bare interview room. I knew he was going to be interesting or I wouldn't be sitting there with a cup of tea and taking up his extremely valuable time. "You must realise that, unfortunately, you are now under suspicion yourself."

"Yes," I agreed, "I know, but you know I didn't do anything wrong."

I had my hands deep in my coat pockets and wondered momentarily what on earth the strange hard thing was that I was automatically clutching. Then I realised it was the ouroboros, which I had forgotten was still there.

"That's as may be, Miss Susans," said the inspector. "As it happens, I'm beginning to believe that you're involved after all, though probably without knowing it yourself. Do you believe in coincidences, Miss Susans?"

"No." I shook my head. Not anymore I didn't.

"A close connection to three out of the four victims of very unpleasant murders, now that could be a coincidence." The inspector brought the tips of his fingers of both hands together and tapped them as if he was keeping time to a fast tune in his head. "This is a small community and of course, everyone seems to know everyone else. But your involvement is a lot more interesting than that. It would seem likely that you were the last person to see three of these persons alive."

"Apart from the murderer."

"Of course."

"I know," I said, because I did, "that it looks bad. I feel bad, extremely bad. I liked Thomas very much. He was a newish friend but I was beginning to think the world of him. My cousin – well – I don't even want to talk about that anymore. I actually came for a very different reason."

"I'm listening," he said, lighting a cigarette and squinting through the smoke.

"It's the cloak," I said. "I might know something about it." I knew I was taking a risk but I really wanted to find out about it and I would only find out by asking. "Could I see it?"

"I'm afraid that's out of the question," he said, lifting both eyebrows. "It's the most valuable piece of evidence we have and is being examined by forensic experts. Now tell me, honestly please, why are you interested? What might you know?"

I was disappointed. "Then describe it to me."

He was puffing cigarette smoke and thinking almost audibly. I watched his brain click. Then he made a quick decision. "Tell me exactly what you know first," he said, "and then I shall."

"Nothing that remarkable," I prevaricated. Silly, quick lies, a habit most writers acquire. "Just that Thomas had one, a copy of a medieval cloak. He was terribly interested in medieval times. I only went to his cottage once, but he showed it to me. It looked very old but he said it had been specially made as a copy."

I don't think the inspector believed me at all and the suspicion in his eyes deepened into a heavy frown. "What was it like?" he demanded. "In as much detail as you can remember, if you don't mind."

"Green," I said at once. "Dark green with sort of embroidered fleur-de-lis around the collar."

The inspector stared at me under thickening brows. His cigarette was burning down and about to drop a long stem of ash which he had forgotten all about. "We found nothing like that in Mr. Cambio's home," he said. "No cloak of any kind. The one the body was wrapped in was quite different."

Well, of course it was. I had made the other one up. "Sorry. So, what was it like?"

He didn't want to tell me but he'd made a bargain and finally he decided it wouldn't hurt. "It was dark brown," he said, "coarse wool and dyed in the ancient manner with natural bark and herbs. It had no hood and clasped under the chin with an old leather buckle. It was trimmed with rather threadbare fox fur. Well worn but in basically good condition even though it appeared to be extremely old. Our experts seem to think it might be genuinely medieval, or a very clever copy using original materials."

He had described Hugh's cloak. The cloak that Hugh had lent me when I went through the forest to try and find Gerald and Vespasian, but which had been taken from me, or lost. I had left it behind in Vespasian's castle by the river.

"Thank you," I said, a little breathless and deeply dismayed. I had expected the cloak to be genuine and I had wanted to know if I recognised it. I had wondered if it might be one I remembered Malcolm wearing. I had not expected it to be Hugh's. "I'm sorry to have troubled you."

"As, it happens," said the inspector, "you trouble me quite considerably, Miss Susans. I am now perfectly sure you know more than you're telling us. Withholding information is illegal of course, but the actual mischief you could cause is far greater than that. Do you know who committed these murders?"

I shook my head, a little wildly. "Honestly, I don't. I don't know anything. I wish I did."

"I hope you realise it's your duty to tell us anything you do know," continued the inspector, his voice deepening. "You may think you're protecting someone, but you could be allowing a killer free license to murder again. Can you live with that on your conscience, Miss Susans?"

I gulped. "Yes, I understand why you're all so suspicious of me, but I promise I don't know who did it." I tried terribly hard to look innocent but I doubt if it worked.

"We can always take you into custody you know, for further questioning." I liked the man but he was getting angry.

"Truly I don't. know anything," I repeated. "I'm a writer. I knew three of the victims, as you keep reminding me. I've written crime thrillers in the past. I just want to know all the facts so that I can try and come up with solutions myself."

"That," said the inspector, "would be a pointless and very dangerous game, Miss Susans. Unless you already have some clue – or know the actual truth."

I nodded. The inspector wasn't the only person who kept warning me of the danger and telling me to keep out of things. Someone else had warned me to back away from the game. The trouble was, I was very deeply involved indeed and I had no idea how to get out at all.

CHAPTER THIRTY-NINE

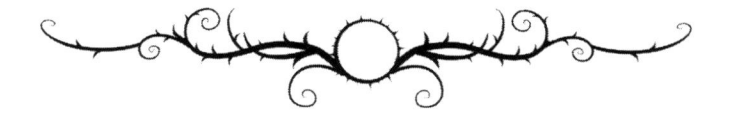

I sat clutching the little pewter jar that Thomas had given me, container for the granules which would help me control my return to Tilda should it not occur naturally. It was the only thing I had of Thomas, the only link left, and I cuddled it as if it was a comforter or a photograph. It was quite unadorned and smooth as if polished. It looked old. The pewter was so dark it was almost black and the lid was just a little bent as though fingers had pressed into it many times over many years, but it still closed perfectly and the waxy seal inside kept the strange contents safe.

The granules smelled unpleasant. The smell reminded me of volcanoes and decay. Sulphur and rot. But I got up and began to prepare the elixir that Thomas had taught me. There was no point staying as Molly now. I did not believe there was anything I could learn from the Ableside sisters. Without Thomas they seemed lost, and so was I.

The stars shed glitter across the huge blackness of the night sky. This was country England and a big horizon, bare October trees and a moon closing in on full majesty. At exactly midnight as one day swung into another, I collected dew in the little glass pot that had once held marmite. Back in the kitchen I transferred the liquid into a small bowl containing one teaspoon of sea salt. I had already chopped fresh rosemary, thyme and betony. Then I added hot water and finally one grain of Thomas's mixture.

I took the thing into the living room and sat with it, preparing last thoughts before drinking. There was the temptation of staying. I did not know what might be happening to Tilda. But I knew that, whatever I decided first, I would end up going. I had to.

It was one o'clock in the morning of October the thirtieth and the night was glowing, moonspun and cold. The liquid I was ready to drink was sludge green and had a quality of slime. It smelled bad and there was no tinge of herbal aroma. I held the drink in one hand, Thomas's pewter jar in the other and then I heard the front door slam. Bertie had come back.

He came marching into the living room appearing tired, even haggard and looked at me without surprise. I was feeling guilty but there was nowhere to hide what I was holding. "I have to talk to you," he said.

I nodded. "Open a bottle of something if you want. Maybe a drink would do me good as well."

He didn't seem interested in the fact that I was already glass in hand and the drink it contained looked and smelled disgusting. "I'll have a brandy. You too?"

I nodded again and put both Thomas's jar and the glass of green liquid on the small coffee table. Bertie handed me a large brandy which smelled a lot better, and drank his own in two gulps. "Go on then," I said. "Tell me about it. Is she nice? Beautiful? Local?"

"Nothing to do with women," said Bertie. "Not this time. It's me. I'm going mad and you have to help." He stared at me, looming over me, looking helpless and threatening all at the same time. I stared back up at him.

"You've just been terribly upset," I said, groping for words. "Wattle and then Sammie. I mean, we all feel we've been going mad. Did you know there's been another murder?"

Bertie poured himself another brandy and drank it. "Yes, I heard," he said, "but I never knew the guy so it's different. In fact, it's totally different. Would you like to know why?" He was glaring at me, trying to make a challenge out of nothing.

"Bertie, hush," I said. It was rare for him to become so belligerent. I wished he would go away. He was interrupting something far more important. "I've known you for ten years and I don't think I've ever seen you quite like this before. Perhaps you're having a nervous breakdown. You ought to go to bed."

"Don't be so fucking patronising," said Bertie. "I asked you a question. Do you want to know why this latest murder is different?"

"Alright." I had to calm him down and get rid of him.

"Because I didn't kill this one. But I killed the other three," he said.

If I hadn't already been sitting, I would have fallen. "Don't be stupid," I whispered. "Besides," voice stronger, "it's not true." I couldn't tell him that I already knew who had done it with some certainty. "Tell me what on earth makes you think such a thing."

He flopped onto the couch, clutching a third brandy. "Because I keep dreaming it," he said, almost shouting at me. "I dream all the details. I know everything and how it was done. I feel knives in my hands and I feel all the warmth of the blood. It's revolting and hideous and I feel every bit of it. I'm frightened to go to bed. I daren't sleep. Shall I go on?"

"You have to get help," I mumbled, "a psychiatrist." I wondered about Ruth Ableside but she wasn't sufficiently qualified. "You know it couldn't have been you. Bertie, you know you couldn't do anything like that. You loved Wattle. You loved Sammie. You're a nice person."

"I loved Muriel too," he said, still glaring at me. "I never told you but she was an old girlfriend. Older than me of course, but I was just a kid at the time, before I met you. Behind the church in the shrubbery by the old gravestones when I was fifteen."

"Good heavens." Muriel had just seemed a nice little old lady, an overgrown hippie, daft and kind. "You mean, she was your very first?"

And then it happened. Bertie's face rolled back, all the heavy jowls and faded handsome squareness, the soft blue eyes and the shining hair, it all rolled back like the tide from the beach. There was someone else behind. Inside. "But not the first I killed," smiled the other voice in the new eyes. "Not even the most enjoyable. I didn't bother raping her, she'd become scrawny, but the kill was pleasant enough."

I couldn't move. "Who are you?" I croaked but the words stuck. My thoughts fled into mental delirium. I wondered if I could reach Thomas's elixir and escape. I was terrified that the thing inside Bertie would now kill and torture me, for I was the other woman who had meant something to him. Then I was terrified of who it was inside. Arthur – or Vespasian. I no longer believed this was Bertie at all.

"Oh yes, you know me," said the thing. The face continued to change, a dissembling and rearranging of flesh into falling, flaking skin, flaying of features, burning eyes. First in soft shadow but then in virulent detail, the bones rose like worms in a skeleton, cracking and joining across the brow, pitted blood soaked sinew, sliced muscle and blueing veins like coiled snakes. I sat in horror and watched.

Bertie's clothes and body disappeared into the blur of insubstantial memory. It was a woman crouched before me, a woman I had never seen before. I had not expected a woman. "No," I whispered. "I don't know you. I have never known you."

She grinned and showed all her teeth, big mule's teeth in front, huge tiger's canines at the sides. Bertie had gone completely and was not anywhere there at all. The woman squatted before me, knees bent out, fingers balanced on the floor, spider like. Then she stood, looming upwards until she towered in black immensity. She wore a medieval cloak, embroidered in black pearls and gold thread. The clasp of the cloak was a goat's head carved in gold. "You know me, whether you realise it or not," and I recognised the harsh sexless voice of the woman in the night who had been present at my tarot reading and had threatened Vespasian.

"I know you now," I said, cringing. "But I don't know who you are."

"I have used many bodies," she said, "but they are only shells. They call me Lilith and adore me. They call me Baphomet and fear me. I have been Sekmet and Medusa. I am the monster of Bagdad, the giant of Saxony, and the vampire of Transylvania. You cannot truly know me. No mortal can."

"If you kill me," I said, "I'll go back to Tilda. I won't feel your torture. You'll gain no pleasure at all from me."

"I have no intention of killing you," she smiled, stretching gums. Her teeth clicked into the widening gaps. "You are the Gateway. I shall use you, not kill you. I enjoyed murder when that tired old body could be pushed to rape and kill the women he'd loved, but torture is a passing plaything. You are only useful to me fully alive."

"What about Thomas?" I demanded. "Why did you kill him? Bertie never even knew Thomas, let alone love him. Thomas was much cleverer than me. You could have used him instead. Why did you kill him?"

"I did not," said the giant woman, a low growl, the words coming not from the palate but from the throat. "Your lover killed Thomas Cambio."

"I don't have a lover. Bertie and I were divorced ages ago," I yelled at her, clinging to sanity.

"Your dark lover," spat the woman. "Your dabbler in alchemy. And tomorrow I shall kill him and eat him, and perhaps your child self too."

"I know who you are," I said. "You're the devil. You're Satan. Lucifer. Evil."

She laughed at me, all genuine glee at my stupidity. She was still laughing when the face changed back. With a grinding of jaw and lips and eyes, Bertie came flooding into life and took back his face. Great tears were tumbling down his cheeks and collecting across the creases of his fear and pain. "You see," he muttered, as if his tongue was only slowly becoming his own again. "I dream but the nightmares are all real. I killed them, those dear friends, but I don't know how I did it. I have to be locked away before I can do anything else. You have to take me to the police. I have to be in an asylum, like your mother."

"Like my mother?" I couldn't grasp reality because there wasn't any reality. "Bertie dear, for God's sake, stop talking. It wasn't you. Listen, and I'll try and explain things."

I had been desperate for someone to explain to me and now I had to explain to Bertie, whose nightmare was even worse than mine. We were both standing up now, shivering like idiots, staring at each other. I leaned forwards and hugged him, to console and reassure him, making myself touch what I was frightened to touch because within him somewhere was the creature who terrified and disgusted me. If she inhabited him at will, as I lived sometimes within Tilda, then perhaps it had indeed been Bertie who had murdered and tortured three women.

But not Thomas. The woman had denied killing Thomas. If she gloated over the other more visceral murders, then denial of one would likely be true. She said Vespasian had killed Thomas. It was something I didn't want to think about.

"Explain? You can't," Bertie shouted into my face. "What in hell can you know about all this?" He wriggled away from my reassurance and reached out, quite slowly and deliberately, and picked up the pewter jar and the little bowl of green elixir. I watched him as if it was slow motion and I was paralysed.

"Don't touch," I managed to say.

He smiled, not his own smile, and he had mule's teeth all yellow grained and tiger's canines huge and curved behind. "The jar is mine," he said, though it was not his voice, and he put it in his pocket. He drank the liquid and licked his lips with a tongue tip that was long and thin and blue. Then I watched the animation quickly disappear from his face and body and he tumbled at my feet like an empty coat. I was crying and screaming and choking altogether. The glass marmite jar fell and smashed on the tiles of the hearth. I bent down over Bertie's sagging unconsciousness but I could see he was still breathing. I knelt beside him but the room spun like dust in a storm. I had not drunk the elixir but I was leaving. I hung onto my head with both hands as if it might be left behind. I felt sick and dizzy.

Thomas's recipe which I had prepared and Bertie had drunk, still smelled rank and sulphurous and the stink of it swelled, infecting me too. Then I welcomed it and breathed it in because its effect was taking me back to Tilda. It was slow but I sat still and small on my own hearth rug and let it swim into me, breathing deeply now and aware of one world leaving as the other moved in. I did not feel I moved or changed but my surroundings leapt into silhouette and then back into swirling colour.

I was sitting on the hard earth floor of our old house in medieval London. The chicken was clucking in the corner and I could hear a small scuffle in the wattle and daub, rats scurrying up to the thatch. The fire was lit huge and blazed in a rage of scarlet heat, spitting soot from the logs and flinging vast shadows across the room. Neither Bertie nor the monster within him were in the room. Opposite me, beside the fire and on his old straight backed chair with the carved arms and the threadbare padding, sat Vespasian.

I swear he actually saw me enter Tilda's consciousness.

"Welcome home," he said, stretching his legs. "We have a lot to talk about and then there is a lot to do. There is only one day left."

CHAPTER FORTY

Tilda sat cross legged, folded her hands in her lap and looked up at him. His boots were stretched beside me and his face was lost part in dancing shadow, part in the distortion of reflected flame.

As usual, his voice was soft, like a breeze among leaves, but carrying the first threat of storm. I had to strain to hear him above the crackle and spark of fire. "There are few gifts I am free to give you," he was saying, "but some comprehension and coherence is one that I owe you. I avoid explaining myself when I can, but this time I will answer some of your questions should you have any."

I felt Tilda's heart beating in my chest, or perhaps it was mine in hers. She was both frightened and excited. He had come to get her. She had wanted him to for so long, yet had not expected it. But out of the darkness he had come, just for her. "I have a thousand questions," she murmured. Now I wished I could speak for her. She had a thousand questions but I had a million.

"It is late," answered Vespasian. "Far too late, but we must use what time we have. Ask what you wish of me and then we must sleep for the few hours that we need. When we wake again, I shall take you back to the convent."

Tilda looked down at her lap, playing nervously with her fingers. It was only then that I realised she was holding Vespasian's ouroboros. It was nestled in her palm, curled neat into shadow, her thumb through its central circle. "This," she began. "I thought Malcolm had sent it but now you say it's yours. I was so frightened of it. The Abbot didn't want to touch it."

"When I sent it to you," he said, "I didn't know exactly where you were. I believed it likely you'd gone directly to the London house, and stayed here. It didn't matter. It would have found you, wherever you were. I had something to do, and to arrange for Gerald, which could not be delayed. So I sent you the purest symbol of protection I had, to keep you safe until I could come myself."

"How?" she mumbled, "do you send a thing – like this," and she held it up, "through the air? And say it will reach the right person, wherever that person is?"

Vespasian's smile was very faint, just a tuck in that dark suntanned skin. He said, "My dear child, do you expect me to explain something like that at a time such as this? I have a power – as I think you know. But it took many years to hone, and cannot be explained in minutes. Perhaps, on the way to the convent, I can tell a little more."

She looked up at him suddenly. "I don't want to go back to the convent," she said. "I want to stay with you."

He smiled again, this time a rare smile that touched his eyes. "No. I must take you to a place of relative safety. Where I am going will be the most dangerous of all." He leaned forward unexpectedly and flicked a long tangled curl back from my face. "You're a forgiving child, Tilda." He smiled again. "I'm sorry I hurt you so much before, but there are some things I cannot explain and that is another of them. Now, ask what else you wish. Then we must rest."

I said, avoiding his eyes, "That – about what you said – and what you did – would be the most important question."

He shook his head. "I cannot answer you, nor will I, only to assure you that I do little without purpose, and my purpose was neither lust nor cruelty. Ask another."

"The abbot told me to leave," she said, plaintive, "but you want to take me back there. The prioress hates me."

"Abbot Bernado," said Vespasian, his voice drifting into the slow murmur of memory, "was a pupil of mine many years ago in Italy. I taught him the fundamentals of alchemy. He was an eager student. Although he returned to orthodox Christianity, he remains grateful to me for what I taught him. And very wealthy. Riches bring power. He has used his power within the church."

"You taught him how to be rich?" Tilda was intrigued. "If you knew how to be rich, why we were always so poor?"

"I taught the good Bernado how to turn base metals into gold," smiled Vespasian. "A useful trick and one of the basic principles of alchemy which he has utilised now for many years. That's why the prioress, whose name I have forgotten and who is without interest, will not denounce him although she hates him and is terrified of the dark powers she assumes that wealth involves. Power corrupts. All that is utterly unimportant. Bernado will take you back if I ask him personally, and you'll be safe there. True Christianity creates an aura which cannot be breached by evil, and in spite of his greed, the convent remains within a strong ring of sacred protection."

"You never seemed very interested in Christianity," said Tilda wistfully. "I thought you followed the old religions."

"Yes, alchemy is far older than the Christ," said Vespasian. "That doesn't mean that the son of the Father is not the holder of a power greater than the enemy. I don't mean the slaughter and wanton cruelties of the crusades or the rigidity and wilful misrepresentations of the growing church. I speak, as the Christ taught, of the power of love. Those who understand these things are already uniting alchemy with Christianity. They call it the Grail. But that is not my path. I do not have the time."

I shivered. "That sounds so final."

He was still smiling a little, patiently waiting for Tilda's questions. I knew it was kind of him. It was the only gift he felt he could give her. She said, "So why don't you make gold for yourself? Why weren't we rich in London?"

He took a deep breath, holding it for a moment before speaking. "Arthur murdered my wife," he said, and his eyes glazed, shutting off warmth. "She was his step daughter, Joanna's child. They tortured and murdered her and left her in my bed." He wasn't looking at me anymore, but into the depths of the fire. Then he looked back briefly at me and frowned. "This is not your story and not something I intend to tell you in any detail. Suffice it to say I was accused of her death. I had to disappear. King Richard's justice was no more inspired than John's and at the time, John was regent. I gave up my title and became Vespasian. To then become a wealthy man would have attracted attention. I chose to live in the shadows. Only once, in the forest house a few months ago, did I finally make gold and then only enough for the existing emergencies."

"You adopted all the children," I wondered. "Was that simple kindness?"

He smiled again, amused. "Does that seem so unlikely?"

I shook my head. "No. Well, yes. I mean, you taught us to steal."

"Gerald was very young," he said. "He was my step-son, my wife's child from her first, arranged marriage to a man already within Arthur's circle until his death. Arthur and my wife's mother intended bringing up Gerald according to their beliefs. I owed it to Ingrid to save her son so I extricated him from them and took him away with me. It was necessary to live in anonymity, watching them but unseen. Never having trained as a useful man, I had few ways of making money without drawing attention to myself. I stole. Not being a good Christian follower of the Ten Commandments, I found this made us a reasonable living."

I smiled too. I couldn't imagine Vespasian worrying about breaking such a minor thing as an entire moral code. "And then you found a hoard of orphaned brats, begging and stealing across the city. You already had one boy. So you took in others."

"I felt a little sympathy, perhaps," he admitted, almost as if it were a confession. "Gerald's identity could be more easily hidden within a crowd. Besides, the streets of London can be a dismal place for a small child to live and starve. I'd recently undergone some experience of misery myself. I was more susceptible, perhaps, to the difficulties of others."

"We all hero-worshipped you," stuttered Tilda, embarrassed. "The boys still do."

He looked down at me and stretched out his hand, lifting my chin so that he looked into my eyes. "But not you, meus carus?" he asked softly. "Not anymore?"

She couldn't say that it was no longer hero-worship but something much stronger. I felt her cheeks flush but in the bright firelight hoped it wouldn't be noticeable. "It's confusing," she said. "It's all to do with what's happened. I just don't understand about alchemy and torture and magic. It's like trying to peer through fog and just when you think you can make out shapes, then the smoke moves in and it's hidden even deeper. Will you explain all that? Can you make me understand?"

"I cannot," sighed Vespasian, "not entirely. Symbolism is the reason for everything, as I've told you. You try to see in terms of solid fact, but that's not how the world turns. Facts only exist because symbolism shaped them. That's why you're frustrated by what you call confusion and riddles. I speak not in code but in the only truth which we can grasp on our level, which is the symbolism of spirit."

I stared. "I still don't understand," said Tilda.

"I would frighten you further," said Vespasian, "if I told you the greater truths." His voice had faded again into lost murmurings and the pale reflections of moonshine. "And now I believe it's time we rested. There is a lot to be done when we wake and a long road for both of us."

"Oh, please," Tilda sat up straight, gazing up at him with a desperate determination. She sat at his feet and the heat of the fire was calming, but now she wasn't calm at all. "Not yet," she pleaded. "Sleeping isn't important and I don't want to go back to the convent anyway. First you have to tell me more." It seemed miraculous that Vespasian was talking at all and I valued it as much as she did. The ouroboros still lay in her lap and she continued to clutch and finger its curves. "First tell me about Arthur and Malcolm and who they are," she begged. "Why do they do the terrible things they do? Is evil so mindless? You were there, in the house. Joanna and Arthur, they talked as if you were one of their group. What you did to me – so you won't explain that – but you saw what they did and you were with them. Did you want to hurt me too?" Tilda was dizzy and utterly miserable. As she choked back her tears, for a moment I was myself and able to speak quite clearly. I saw Vespasian narrow his eyes as he watched me. He recognised my presence. "I wonder which of you is the devil," I said, "and which the saviour. Or if there are two devils and no saviour at all."

He knew at once they were Molly's words. He leaned towards me and his face became stone. "Answer me first," he said, emotionless, "and then I will decide whether to answer you." I couldn't look away from him. His eyes, or something behind them, gripped me. "And you will tell me the truth," he continued, "or you will discover I have more power than you can possibly imagine." I couldn't even blink. "Now tell me," he said, "are you the veleda?"

The spell snapped like stretched elastic and Tilda gulped. "I don't understand," she whispered. "You know who I am. I know no one called Veleda. You frighten me."

Vespasian relaxed. "There's no need to be afraid – not yet," he said. "Since you cannot understand the absolute truth, I shall speak in terms of the distortions you call reality." He sighed, and put his hand gently on my shoulder. "The veleda was the seer who lived during the Emperor Vespasian's reign in ancient Rome. She studied alchemy and was a great sorceress. When I took Vespasian's name as symbolic of inspirational peace within power, I called to her. She has come many times, and she has opened the gates."

I stared. It was me he meant. He thought Molly was the opener of gates. Now I believed he was possibly, probably, quite right. I'd been the gatekeeper for the thing that had taken Bertie and killed in both worlds. I wished I could push Tilda aside long enough to ask Vespasian about Thomas Cambio. But Tilda was crying. I wanted to hold her and comfort her myself. She seemed so very young. "I'm sorry," she was whispering. "I'm so sorry. I know I don't understand anything even though I should. I'd help if I knew how."

And then, to my utter amazement, I felt myself crushed deeply within Vespasian's arms as he lifted Tilda from the ground where she sat, and wrapped her in his embrace. "Foolish child," he whispered in my ear. "Quiet the trembling and the fear. You mustn't try to help me, little one, nor could you if you tried. When, previously, you came to help me, you created more problems for us both. I was forced to do something to you that appalled me, and you suffered great injury and pain." His cheek was against mine, his long fingered hands strong around me. "Enough now," he soothed. "Now is the time for sleep and golden dreams," and he carried me carefully across the room to the narrow wooden staircase and up the steps. He seemed to find Tilda's weight so inconsequential that she was like a small bird against his chest, all crushed skirts and long curls, just a tangle of childish interruptions and a tear stained face.

"Please –" she whispered, her mouth crushed against the dark wool of his cotte.

"Hush," he interrupted her. "The time for questions has passed."

Two beds remained upstairs, one which Tilda had made herself from fallen thatch and roughly gathered straw. The other pallet Walter had bundled up when he came to stay. Vespasian knelt and laid me carefully on my bed, pulling the cover up around my chin. Then he went across to the other side of the room, gathered up the rushes from Walter's pallet and carried them over, kicked into some semblance of shape alongside mine and covered with his own cloak. Then, looking down at me, he slowly began to undress.

Tilda lay in bed, breathing a little ragged, and watched the man who had once raped her and said nothing. Through her eyes I watched him too and for a few moments there was no one else in the world. Vespasian slowly removed his heavy padded cotte, jet buttoned and stiff with overlaid panels. He dropped it casually on the floor beside the bed and laid his sword and long tongued belt on top. He shrugged off the deep burgundy tunic which he wore beneath and stood in his loose white shirt, black hose and boots, looking down at me. He pulled the knife from his boots and laid it across the sword. Then he sat beside me and tugged off the boots. I watched every movement and wondered what Tilda should do.

He smiled suddenly, fully aware of my thoughts. "I've no intention of doing you further harm," he said, voice soft in the long shadows. "What I do now is simply for your protection."

I was absurdly aware of a vague disappointment. I turned and closed my eyes, cuddling down into the straw's rustle and scratch. I was fully dressed and had made no attempt to remove my tunic, though I was barefoot. I felt Vespasian climb onto the bed beside me, the long warm strength of his body against my back. He flung one arm across my waist, closed his fingers around me, and settled, stretching. I could feel his breath on my neck.

Tilda was exhausted but I couldn't sleep. Vespasian seemed to have quickly fallen into dreaming and his breathing became deep and slow and steady. I lay still, unable to turn because of the weight of his arm around me. I loved his closeness and I didn't want to wake him. The moon was full, almost at its height and the light turned all the room to silver sheen, each detail clear in its strange cold illumination. Tucking my chin down on my chest, I squinted at the hand clasped just below my breasts. I studied each finger, long and olive skinned, deep tanned after constant exposure to the weather. The nails were clean, short and square. The knuckles were prominent, a fighter's hands, but the fingers were flexible and long phalanxed with an expansive spread. His ring was heavy and the ruby glinted through the shadows.

"Stop examining my hand," smiled Vespasian softly into my ear, "and go to sleep."

I stifled a giggle. "You're not asleep either?"

"Hush," he said, "if we do not rest now, we'll not have the strength to cope with the dangers of tomorrow."

They were not the most reassuring words to help me doze, but within minutes I was dreaming.

CHAPTER FORTY-ONE

Vespasian's ugly brown horse showed me its teeth and snorted, all wide nostrils and bravado, but I smiled as Vespasian helped me up onto the saddle. I had come to know the horse well while we lived in the forest house and I knew that in truth it was better natured than its master. Vespasian adjusted the stirrups for me and tightened the bit. Then he took the reins himself and led us down the narrow streets away from the house and all its memories. The midday sun was autumn pale between the rooftops.

Once past the winding tangle of lanes, the jutting eaves, beamed buttresses, bustle, squash and dirt, Vespasian lengthened the stirrups and climbed up behind me. I leaned back a little, enjoying the support of his body. Tilda had long desired intimacy. Now after a short night of his fraternal warmth, we were tight squeezed with the edge of the pommel pushing me firmly back into his grip. I could feel his tension, arms and thigh muscles taut as he guided the horse, and his chin was against my forehead. Vespasian spoke softly, squeezing his knees behind mine, and immediately we gained speed. The hooves made little sound except the slosh of dark yellow from the gutters and the clipped clatter on the beaten earth as we cantered to higher ground. The horse's rhythmic pace lulled me deep into Vespasian's embrace.

The wind was in his black hair, sweeping it across my cheek, and although I was bundled in his arms, the bite of frost was in my face and against my body. "Are you cold?" he said, his soft voice almost blown away.

I was surprised he was thinking about me at all. "No," I said at once. "Though Hugh's cloak would have been warmer than mine. He lent it to me but I lost it, you know, in the castle by the river."

He paused. I could guess his thoughts. "Yes," he said. "I found it. I used it for – another purpose. But that's something else I cannot explain to you. At least, not yet."

"It doesn't matter," said Tilda. "Hugh wouldn't object." I smiled to myself because Hugh had always objected about everything, though he'd been patient enough about the loss of his precious cloak. My private knowledge of the purpose the cape had served and what Vespasian had done with it, was lost in Tilda's shivers.

"If you're cold," said Vespasian, "pull the ends of my own cloak around you. It's thicker than yours." It was blue-night velvet and heavy sable lined. I caught its corners round me and cuddled cosy back to Vespasian's body.

The town's scavenging dogs squealed and hurried away from us into the unpaved side streets, the kites and ravens flapped up to the roof tops, the bony little pigs and the busy chickens hopped from our path. A goat, bleating like a baby, turned and ran. Up past the tall arches of London's principal conduit, on through the narrow alleys and the wider roads of the main cheap, finally we left the city walls beneath the low portcullis and huge shadow of Cripplegate. The road headed north.

Beyond London and away from the buildings, the sun opened our horizons. The air smelled sweet, leaving behind the stench of sewerage. As the ground rose I looked down, seeing the snake glitter-caught twist of the Thames dazzled with autumn sunshine and spanned in columned stone. I had crossed that bridge many times, with many memories. Beneath its cold wet shadows Vespasian had found Tilda nearly eight years ago, and taken her under his protection. Then less than a year ago, it was where she had found

Isabel and all the nightmare had begun. The serpentine sheen reminded her. "I still have the little carved snake. Now I know it comes from you, I promise not to lose it."

"I doubt you could, even if you tried," said Vespasian. "I have bound it to you."

We were within sight of the convent wall. "Is this what Malcolm was looking for then," said Tilda, "if it's so precious? I thought it was his and he'd left it in my room on purpose. I thought it was evil. But since it isn't, why did Malcolm come?"

Then quite suddenly and deliberately Vespasian pulled on the reins and the horse stopped, feet firm on the thick grass. The stillness was momentarily pronounced. Then he spoke directly into my ear. "So – tell me again, why did you think the ouroboros came from Malcolm?"

I twisted around to look up at him. The menace was back in his voice. Tilda thought she had angered him. I wanted her to say she'd told him about this already, quite distinctly, and he'd either not bothered listening or had not taken her seriously. But instead Tilda said, "Was I stupid? I thought I saw Malcolm come from my sleeping chamber in the convent. Perhaps I was dreaming."

"You'd been asleep?" It wasn't like Vespasian to repeat my words. He always understood what I was saying before I said it.

"There's a room there in the traveller's wing, where I went to sit by the fire," stuttered Tilda. "It was morning, but I fell into such a deep sleep, when I woke I felt sick. I saw Malcolm coming from the direction of my little room back towards the courtyard. He didn't see me. When I went to lie down on my own bed, I saw the snake on the wall. So of course, I thought he'd put it there."

We were standing quite still now. Vespasian's grip on the reins at my waist appeared unnaturally tight. He said, "Did you explain this to Bernado?"

I nodded. "The Abbot said he'd felt an unnatural disturbance in the air, something unpleasant. But then he said no one else had come to stay at the convent so it couldn't have been Malcolm. But that was strange because it's a convent so of course it's all women and no men ever visit, except the abbot himself of course. When I asked him to take the carving because I thought it was evil, he wouldn't touch it and that was when he told me to leave."

"You speak specifically of Malcolm," said Vespasian slowly. "Do you remember him so well? You were unconscious or delirious most of the time in that house. I made sure you were completely oblivious when he flogged you and I doubt you ever saw him clearly." Vespasian paused. "How can you be so sure it was him?"

"Because I nearly stole his purse once in the market," I said, a little breathless. I hadn't previously realised exactly what Malcolm had done to me. "Just before, you know," I said. "Finding Isabel. Arthur caught me. Arthur, his wife, Uta and Malcolm, so of course I recognised them at your castle. I'll never forget them now."

I thought Vespasian was going to change his mind and take me away. I expected him to turn the horse but he didn't and I was disappointed. After a moment, he flicked the reins and the horse walked on. We rode up to the high wall and then at the convent gate, Vespasian dismounted. He looked up at me before ringing the heavy brass bell. "You will not be staying here after all," he said. "Listen carefully, because this is important and I will not tolerate mistakes."

I felt Tilda's heartbeat race. "I promise. Whatever you say."

"I believe the good abbot has been dabbling beyond his powers," said Vespasian. "I believe it may no longer be safe to leave you here. When I sent the ouroboros to find you, Bernado must have felt its arrival, but instead of recognising alchemic purity, it seems he spoke only of an unpleasant disturbance. Malcolm's presence, undoubtedly sanctioned, is an even greater wickedness. Now there are things that must be said, and things I must collect, so we will go in and face him. You will stay extremely close to me and you will not leave my side for any reason whatsoever. Do you understand?"

I did. "I don't want to be left here. I'm glad."

"You should not be glad," he said, "for where I will take you will be far less pleasant and my company is something you should neither choose nor welcome. However, if in what you've told me is right, I must adjust my plans."

"I saw Malcolm," I repeated. "I know I did."

"Perhaps your prioress has more to be frightened of than I realised," said Vespasian. "However, that does not interest me now. You must promise not to leave my side, whatever happens. Hold to my cotte if you wish. And if possible, do not speak unless I tell you to."

"I'll do whatever you say," said Tilda.

Vespasian smiled, more amusement than malice. "You were once an obedient child," he said, "though less so since you became inspired with ideas of chivalry and adventure."

"Was that wrong of me?" said Tilda, chin up. "My friends were being murdered. You seemed to be in danger. I wanted to help."

"I had told you not to."

"You might have been dead," said Tilda.

"In which case," said Vespasian crossly, "you could hardly have helped me. Besides, when I die you will know it because I shall come back to haunt you."

"Then it was because you were so angry with me," continued Tilda, looking at her feet, hanging loose above the stirrups, "that I had to run away from the forest house. That – and what you did. The things you told me and what you refused to explain. Then Walter and the others as well. But mostly you."

"I know that," said Vespasian, taking the convent bell in one hand, his other still holding the horse's bridle. "Which is why I came to get you myself, once I was free to do so. But the past is no longer relevant. Quiet now and keep the sword I gave you close."

A scurrying novice came to open the gates. We followed her up the pathway to the main building, a well dressed knight leading his lady on their horse, a normal and respectable couple travelling north. A young stable boy came from behind the building, dancing at Vespasian's heels, ready to take the reins. Vespasian helped me dismount and threw the boy a penny. "Don't stable him," he ordered. "Wait here and hold him. If he frets, walk him. I shall be back shortly."

Once into the shadows of the long hall, the novice turned. "Has the lady come to stay, lord? I will take you both to our prioress, Sister Rosamund."

"No," said Vespasian shortly. "I wish to see your abbot. There's no need to come with us. I know the way."

Vespasian's manner was as usual imperious and the little novice blinked and backed off, leaving us alone. I followed his swirl of cloak along the cool corridor, coming directly to Bernado's study. Without knocking, Vespasian pushed open the door and we walked briskly inside.

The abbot looked up, nose over papers, eyes protruding. He opened his mouth to complain but then clamped his moist lips shut with a snap. He stared at us for a moment, then clasped his plump fingers before him, managed a hesitant smile and waited patiently for Vespasian to speak.

Vespasian put both hands flat on the abbot's desk and leaned forward, speaking low and quiet but distinctly so that the words seemed to vibrate, heavy with controlled malevolence. "I hear you have been playing a new and very dangerous game, Bernado," he said. "Did you think I wouldn't find out?"

The abbot hurriedly cleared his throat. "As always, Jasper, it's a pleasure to see you. But I've no idea what you're accusing me of. Perhaps we should discuss this over a glass of wine." He was looking at Vespasian but his eyes flicked aside to me.

"Don't be a fool," said Vespasian. "You know I will not drink anything you offer me now. I want only explanations. And I will recognise the truth, Schiavone. You should remember this, since you value your comfortable life."

The abbot's Italian became more accented, exaggerated by nerves. "La giovane? I must apologise for asking her to leave, but you must understand my friend, I have a position to uphold. Already she stayed far longer than we normally accept visitors. Gia, naturalmente, al inizio era una considerazione – solo per – yourself."

"You told her to leave when you saw the ouroboros," said Vespasian. "Why?" He was leaning right over the little man now, both hands still gripping the desk.

"Most intimidating, Jasper," agreed Abbot Bernado, moving back with a scrape of the chair legs. "And quite unnecessary. You know I cannot risk having pagan talismans here. I could be excommunicated. A very simple explanation, don't you think?"

Vespasian spoke softer still. I was clutching his cloak, but I shivered. "If you imagine, Bernado, that I am such a fool, perhaps I should prove to you that I am not. Would you like me to do that? Shall I offer you proof, here and now, that you must not try to play alchemic dice with me?"

The abbot cringed. "Jasper, please. Tell me exactly what the matter is and I shall do my best to put it right. I've always shown you my gratitude. I know how much I owe you."

"Indeed?" smiled Vespasian. "Then why are you now dealing with Arthur d'Estropier? Hasn't gold been enough for you? Now you want spiritual as well as material power?"

"What has the girl said?" glowered the abbot, hunched beneath Vespasian's gaze. "What nonsense has she told you? I have nothing to do with the black arts."

I stood and stared and said nothing. Vespasian was still smiling. "You make too many mistakes," he said. "You see, I believe explicitly whatever my young friend tells me. Now your prevarications and absurd disclaimers increase my mistrust."

The abbot was breathing deeply. "I've been a friend of yours for many years, my dear de Vrais," he puffed. "I've kept the bailiff from your door and the wolf from your back. I may have talked to Arthur on a few occasions, since it's always wise to know your enemy. You deal with him yourself. It is impossible to avoid him. It's in the nature of our work."

"I deal with him because I intend to destroy him," said Vespasian softly. "Why has Malcolm d'Estropier been permitted to enter this place?"

The Abbot scowled. "The girl's wrong," he said, though his eyes remained on his papers. "No one of that circle could enter here. This is a house of God."

"So I once believed," said Vespasian. "But it seems your corruption is deeper than I'd supposed. If you were speaking the truth, Bernado, you would look into my eyes. In fact, you can barely face me. Look at me now."

The demand was so sudden and pronounced that I jumped. The abbot's head snapped up and he glared directly at Vespasian as ordered. "You can't destroy me, de Vrais," he said. "Your power may go beyond my own, but you stand alone. I have all the collective power of the group behind me."

"Not at the moment," smiled Vespasian. "You still underestimate me. I have been where you can never go and I am not limited by greed or the desire for reputation and the good opinion of men. My knowledge comes from Araby and Spain, from Persia and Egypt, and not Italy alone. My power comes from the future as well as from the past. You have one last chance, Schiavone. Give me back the papers of Jabir Ibn Hayyan and the seal of Thoth that I entrusted to you. Then I shall consider what to do with you next."

The abbot visibly trembled, though with a great effort he looked up again and smiled weakly. "Of course, Jasper. These things are yours. I'd never deny it. But I have them in safe keeping and not here in this chamber. You'll have to give me leave to go and get them."

Vespasian laughed. "Not alone," he said. "We will come with you."

Abbot Bernado climbed from his stool and stood small before us. He looked up at Vespasian, then glanced briefly towards me. I had trusted this man. I had trusted Thomas Cambio and had thought them to be the same occupying life force. Now all the warmth I had once thought so genuine had turned to animosity in his eyes and all my belief shrivelled. What I had read in his face had been quite false and maintained only by the mask of magic. Now the mask crumbled and turned to hatred. I had ruined his friendship with the man who had been his mentor and whose power could destroy him. I looked quickly away and kept close beside Vespasian.

We followed the abbot into a small room leading off beyond the study and reached through a narrow opening behind the desk. Without window, it was heavy with dust and gloom. Another desk stood central. On this a massive bible was opened at the Gospel of St. John. The pages were beautifully illuminated and the first letter was scrolled in vibrant and glorious colours. 'In the beginning was the word and the word was with God and the word was God.' It was written in Latin which neither I nor Tilda understood, but I knew the words off by heart. I would have loved to turn the vellum pages and see more of its ancient beauty but the abbot was rummaging in the cupboard beneath. He reappeared, squinting, dust in his eyes and his tonsure capped in cobwebs. He cradled a small package, held in parchment and tied with gold thread, and he appeared to be breathless with the weight, either material or spiritual. As he looked up at Vespasian, his expression changed and I read regret. "It's all here," he said, words tapering off into shame. "I'm sorry Jasper. Truly I'm sorry. I never meant it to be this way."

"Instead of your desires empowering you, you allowed them power over you," Vespasian said. "It is a common weakness. Now, tell me the truth." As he relinquished the package the abbot breathed relief. Then the spite returned to his eyes and his mouth tightened.

"Anything," Bernado said. "Ask anything of me, dear friend." As he spoke he brought his hands together, clasping them tightly across his chest, breathing deeply as if excited. I could see the sweat on his upper lip and his mouth moved fractionally as if he spoke some other word, lost in silence. Then, fingers still entwined, he stroked the ring he wore, engraved with the goat's head. I felt Vespasian stiffen, while watching the other man closely.

The room had been dark and stuffy. Then time coughed and blinked and missed its tide. I felt it. Something was happening and a black threat moved and came alive. The shade deepened and the gathering dust spiralled and scattered. I was standing as close to Vespasian as I could. I felt hot wind, though all doors were closed. I clutched again at Vespasian's cloak.

Vespasian's voice dropped soft like the barely heard murmurings of water over sand. "If you bring that thing any closer," he said, "I will destroy this convent and you with it."

There was a pause. The darkening in the corner hesitated. I couldn't breathe. Then I felt Vespasian reach to my hand, his fingers probing my tight closed fist. I knew what he wanted and I gave it to him. He took the ouroboros and held it up. It was just a little wooden thing, smooth and blind, but in the lightless shadows it glowed rich golden with a sheen that came from nowhere.

"No," screeched the abbot. "You'll kill us all. Use that, and your whore dies and you too."

"As usual, you are mistaken in many things," said Vespasian, still smiling. Then he leaned over and gripped the abbot's wrist, dragging him forwards. The swirl of darkening menace in the room gathered speed and height. I could not look away from it. Then the abbot screamed and everything happened at once.

Vespasian had forced the ouroboros against Bernado's pale forehead and for a second the little serpent seemed to curl there, burrowing into the skin below the tonsure until the abbot's eyes were filled with pouring blood. I was sickened and couldn't find breath, for there was no air left in the room. It was leached by some mounting horror. Beside me Vespasian held the struggling abbot. They were momentarily united, the coiled snake joining them as fire sears flesh to bone and the stench of burning exploded into black sparks and flying ash.

The smoke stank. The roof above us split. A slashing light so white that it crackled, sprang down from above, raging power in one single blow straight through the beautiful pages of the bible, the table beneath it and the cupboard below. The abbot fell to the ground, clutching his chest as Vespasian flung him away like a broken cup. Vespasian turned to me and swung me quickly around to face him. "This whole place will burn," he shouted above the turmoil of mounting and terrifying confusion. "Take these and guard them if you can. They are utterly precious." He pressed the wrapped package and the ouroboros into my hands. "Now, run," he demanded.

I hesitated one moment but he had moved away from me and into the awful tumult. I ran.

CHAPTER FORTY-TWO

There were ashes in my mouth and my lungs were hot and filled with fire. There was also something more horrible than fire. I raced through the corridors and into the great hall where a cluster of nuns watched me in alarm. I screamed at them, "Get out. The convent's burning."

I didn't wait to see if anyone followed me. Then I heard the bells. The main doors were open and I ran towards them, clutching up the frayed and grimed hems of my palla and skirts, the ouroboros stuffed down my bodice, Vespasian's parcel under one arm, and my sword firm in my other hand. Then I heard the grinding of the falling beam and saw its long shadow spin as it tumbled directly in front of me. The flames shot up all along its length like little lizard's tongues. The heat billowed into my face, though the sensation I felt was of sudden ice. My hair caught first and then my clothes.

I whirled through vermillion, blood garnet, sulphur and raging golden fury. Yet nothing else in the hall burned. The attack was direct and this time against me alone. Against me, and what I carried. I lifted my cloak and threw it over my head, stifling the flames, still running for the doors. Then the larger blaze was all around me and the fire engulfed us all.

I was unaware of pain. Vespasian had told me once, pain didn't matter. There were other places where one could go, where pain could not exist. Now I stood outside on the long grassy slopes of those peaceful gardens where once I had tried to destroy the ouroboros, and I watched the building's destruction, walls disintegrating in huge thundering flames as the roof cascaded inwards. Tiles and plaster and furnishings all crumbled. Beside me and in front of me the multitude of nuns gathered like fluttering flapping blackbirds, staring around, lost without the guiding discipline of routine. Others still ran squealing from the fires.

"Lightning," muttered one of the nuns to my left. "I saw it from the buttery. Lightning struck straight to the heart of the abbot's chambers. But look, there's no storm at all."

"God's retribution," whispered the other, her voice hardly audible above the roaring blaze, though we now stood far enough away.

"But the storm's coming," said an older woman. She pointed up and I looked with the others. The peaceful autumn blue was churning into black cloud.

"That rain will put out the fire," I said. The nuns looked at me in a muttering of suspicion. Many recognised me, knowing my reappearance coincided with this sudden violence in their lives. Very carefully they moved away, banding tightly, distancing themselves from me.

"She looks badly hurt," whispered one to another. "Should we help?" I remembered the novice who had sat next to me at mealtimes and whose trencher I had shared.

"That's also God's retribution," said the older woman. "She brought the devil into God's house." I took no notice. I had put my sword away, the little wooden snake was safe between my breasts, and I clutched Vespasian's parcel safe. Now I peered into the chaos below, searching for signs of him. That was all I cared about now.

I heard the voice behind me before I heard the horse. "You should have moved further back, or did you think I might need saving again?" Vespasian was leading the horse up across the grass behind me. He put his hand on my shoulder and I swirled around, relieved and delighted. Then I realised my legs could no longer hold me and I crumpled, as if a dream were dissolving into wakefulness. He caught me, arms around my waist. He lifted me up and cradled me for a moment, looking deeply into my eyes. "Are you badly hurt? How did this happen? You should have been well clear before the flames took hold."

I wanted to close my eyes but I couldn't. All the pain I'd ignored, waiting to be sure he was safe, now surged through every muscle. I burned as though the flames were still around me, coursing my veins. I could have fainted. It would have been a sweet escape, but Vespasian held me centred. He would not permit unconsciousness until he was sure of me. "In the main hall," I whispered, as if he'd ordered an explanation and even controlled my tongue. "The beam fell. It was the only thing on fire in a cold room. It fell just onto me."

"His final vengeance," murmured Vespasian, "before he died. Bernado was a fool. He overestimated his power, but at the end he managed to call up something that might have ruined us all."

"The lightning?"

"Ah no." Vespasian smiled, and it curved right into his mouth and eyes as I had rarely seen him. "That was another source altogether. You and I, Tilda, and the abbot too, we were audience to far greater powers than ours. The lightning blasted directly through the open pages of the bible. Only God has the force to strike His own. They were the words of St. John and one of the purest oracles of alchemy. The destruction of the lightning was God's anger for His word defiled."

"And the other thing? Something dark and horrible came into the abbot's chambers."

"He tried to summon one of the lesser demons," said Vespasian softly, still holding me tight. "That rank presence in the holy room was a direct invocation to God's fury. So the demon fled the place of sacred retribution, and found you, it seems. Its malevolence was directed at you from the beginning since Bernado blamed you for my discovering his treachery. But you held the ouroboros, and the seal of Thoth. You could not have been badly hurt, I think."

"I'm getting used to pain," sighed Tilda, leaning her head against the support of his shoulder. I had the devil of a headache.

"Once again I'm afraid much of the blame is mine," said Vespasian. "We have very little time, but I'll do what I can to heal you first."

A hundred nuns clustered on the slopes but they kept apart from us, afraid to come too close. I saw the prioress among them. "And the abbot?" I asked.

"He is quite dead," said Vespasian, "but not by my hand. He was a good man once and I knew his value while he trusted me. Corruption travels along strange paths. It was his own Christian God who killed him."

I nodded. I was remembering the abbot's eye sockets filling with blood as Vespasian forced the little serpent against his forehead. Vespasian may not have killed Bernado, but he had tortured him first.

"What now?" I sighed, closing my own eyes.

"Now?" said Vespasian. "Now it all begins. Now I will be tested at last and you will finally discover all the things I have long refused to tell you, which you should never know. Clearly it is destined that you be tested at my side. It is what I wished to avoid although knowing I have no power to alter the path of destiny, neither mine nor yours. But first, I must make you strong again." He lifted me onto his horse and climbed quickly up behind me. He pulled on the reins and the horse wheeled, heading into the longer grass and leaping into a sudden gallop. I leaned back against Vespasian, his parcel safe between us, and the wind in my face was fresh and clean and cold, both relief and salve.

I felt we flew. I hadn't expected such speed from Vespasian's tired old horse. Nestled safe, the rhythm eased the pain, but I kept my eyes open. I wanted to know where he was taking me. The pale sun was low in a lowering sky and each passing tree threw a long dark stripe across our path, disappearing beneath the horse's galloping hooves like the rungs of a ladder. I'd thought the poor beast ugly, with his ribs all jagged and his eyes rolling like a drunken clown. Now he was sleek and beautiful and virile.

The convent's destruction was way behind us, even the rank

scorched stench wind blown, and the black cloud that rolled over it like God's wrath had disappeared. We were thundering into a silky twilight within a velvet night. I hoped we were going back to the forest house.

Then I woke without having known that I slept, and we were not in the forest house at all.

There were whisperings and soft murmurs and voices in the dark. "But she looks so badly injured," said someone whose voice I recognised but could not place. I was on a soft bed and the curtains enclosed me. I couldn't see beyond them but a candle was flickering to my side and the hangings shimmered deep crimson in the tiny flame.

"They're only surface burns," said Vespasian. "She's not as badly hurt as she seems."

"I don't understand, my lord," said the voice. "You said it would be too dangerous to bring her back here. You said she'd be safe at the convent."

"I cannot always be right," answered Vespasian. I was sure he was smiling. "You must accustom yourself to my occasional fallibility."

"On the contrary. I believe – you – you're perfect my lord," said the younger voice. "Just tell me what to do – and I'll do it." Now I knew it was Gerald. He was trying very hard to be polite. He sounded desperately nervous.

"The time to prove your courage has not yet arrived," said Vespasian softly. "For the moment just be my squire and bring me water. Cold water from the deepest well. Then leave me alone with her, and go to your own bed. Tomorrow is the day of trial."

I heard Gerald leave and I tried to sit up. I was extremely stiff. My head pounded and when I put my hand to my forehead, it came away smeared with ashes and soot. The bed curtains snatched open and Vespasian looked down at me. He had not changed his clothes and looked sweat stained and travel creased, but his eyes were very bright. Behind him I saw details in candlelit relief, vivid colours, a hundred tapestries and a floor tiled in mosaic. It was the most beautiful room I had ever seen but I was afraid he'd brought me back to his castle by the river. He shook his head. He seemed to know exactly what I thought as if it was written in the soot on my face. "No," he said, quite gently. "This is the estate of the Baron Tennaton and now belongs to Gerald. We are way north of the forest and far from my own southern estates." He frowned then, holding the candle up to see me clearly. "Now, how do you feel?"

"Better," I lied. "Please tell me why we're here?"

"You are not better," he said. "And just because I once offered to answer all your questions, doesn't mean I intend to continue the service indefinitely. However, I'll tell you this. Your burns are superficial. I'll treat them, and then leave you. There's something I have to do. You'll stay with Gerald and be safe in this house until morning, when I shall return. In the meantime, you'll sleep and not waste your strength with gossip. Do you understand me?"

"Of course, I do," I replied rather tartly. "You're telling me to shut up and mind my own business and you'll be back tomorrow."

He grinned. "Exactly. Remember it." He put his arm behind me, lifting me against the piled pillows, goose down in fine linen and a soft support.

"That hurts," I mumbled. Pain tore across my chest and neck. I felt as though my head had split open.

He didn't apologise. "Evidently knowing me brings pain to many. And always to you," he said softly. "Seemingly this is something I can no longer control. But I can be your nurse, as I have before against far greater abuses."

Gerald came back with a pail of water, hauling it two handed, staggering across to the bed and spilling a good deal. "You're awake," he said to me, huge with surprised smile. "Isn't this incredible?"

I couldn't nod, because everything hurt. "You have a grand house," I mumbled. "You're a baron. That's definitely incredible."

"Oh, I didn't mean all that," he said at once. "I meant Vespasian, I mean, Jasper. His Lordship. And you. It's amazing."

"That's enough," Vespasian interrupted him. "Bed, now my boy. And don't come creeping back in here after I'm gone. I'll be back with the dawn."

Gerald put the bucket of water beside the bed and left, looking back with a wave. Vespasian had begun ripping strips of linen and dipping them into the water. The room was warm but the water looked icy.

"I can wash myself," I said, watching him.

"You cannot," said Vespasian, continuing unperturbed. "Since the pain is doubtless comprehensive, you can neither judge nor see where the burns are most invasive. You'd soak the bed rather than yourself. And besides," he did not even smile, "I enjoy undressing you."

CHAPTER FORTY-THREE

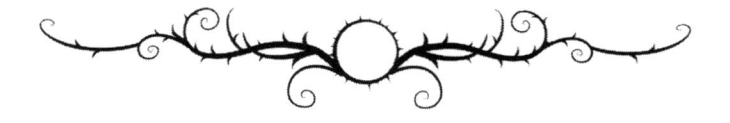

One side of my body had been singed by the flames, and now the cold water across my skin was bliss. Fragments of scorched material peeled back, still attached to my flesh. I turned my head away, breathed deeply and closed my eyes.

Vespasian had stripped my clothes from my upper body, carefully removing the charred and ruined tunic, stolla and camise. I was burned in one narrow strip from the waist up across my left breast and shoulder, the width of the beam which had hurtled onto me. As his hands eased away each garment, then caressing with cool wet fingers, I struggled silently with my private mixture of pleasure and embarrassment. Though I flinched and sometimes trembled, Vespasian continued gently, ignoring what he certainly must have understood.

The pain had already subsided. This was no equal to the far greater nightmare when Vespasian had nursed me in his tower by the river, gradually healing the results of persistent torture. But those marks still remained. I felt his eyes on me and on the thin silver scars that reminded us both of what had been done before. His eyes penetrated, so darkly intense that they also burned; they were more small flames amongst the sooty wounds. Then Vespasian paused. I opened my eyes. His gaze snapped to mine. I thought the pupils opened suddenly huge and black like tunnels. Inside the tunnels lay something so terrible that I couldn't, and wouldn't, comprehend.

He lowered his eyes. "The burns are minor," he said quite gently, "and these marks will fade quickly. I can take most of the pain away, and sleep will heal the rest. The charms you held protected you. But the danger does not end here. You must always keep my talisman close." The carved serpent lay on the small table beside the bed from where the fat beeswax candle cast its light. But he was still watching me. "These other scars from the past," and he lightly touched the longest which still ran deep in a smooth white worm from my navel up across my ribs, between my breasts and up to the right shoulder, "will fade more slowly. Some may remain forever."

His touch was light but I flinched. "The memory remains," I said.

He frowned. "You were not conscious," he replied. "I placed you under trance. I doubt you remember what was actually done."

"Fragments," I muttered. "Strange, horrible pieces like broken mosaic. One scrap of memory brings back another, like ripples on water."

He was again gazing so deeply into my eyes, I thought he was trying to read my mind. "Tell me," he said.

"I don't want to," I whispered. "I don't want to talk about it."

He sighed. "In the future, if I'm still here and you have the courage, tell me your nightmares. I can wash them away as surely as I wash these burns. I can eliminate the last fragments of memory, if you wish."

I blinked. It sounded almost menacing. Tilda demanded, "You can influence my memory? Wash inside my mind?"

He was rinsing out the cloth he was using, but looked up again as I spoke, and nodded. "Of course. Though only with your permission – and cooperation. Did you think my powers nothing more than bravado?"

"I never understood them at all," Tilda said. "I don't know anything about alchemy or mysticism, the old gods or the new. It frightens me."

He was sitting on the edge of the bed, facing me as I lay half propped up against the pillows. He'd removed his cotte and sword but still wore his travelling clothes. I was deeply conscious of my partial nakedness as he watched me and touched me. This wasn't the first time, but that did very little to ease the inevitable discomfiture. "The church," he said, as if recounting lessons to a child just as he once taught me how to steal or to cast an arrow straight up into the heart of a bird, "disguises God's power behind dogma, elitism and rules. Rules limit individual thought. They offer the safety of mindless regulation. That hides what is beautiful as well as what is fearful. Safe boundaries attract the simple and repel the complex. Spirit is complex. So the church becomes a material power, with only the semblance of spirit. Instead, true religion is a limitless chasm. Why should you not be frightened?"

"It's what happened to Bernado, isn't it?" I said. "He forgot spirit."

"He chose to grasp at spirit through materialism, instead of approaching materialism through spirit," Vespasian said.

Tilda slumped down, trying to tug the velvet bedcover up around her but it was taut where Vespasian sat and she couldn't cover herself. He made no attempt to move and he continued to watch her. Because I knew he did nothing by mistake, I also knew he was keeping me vulnerable. Both the nagging pain and Vespasian's immovable regard made me increasingly irritated. "So you could wash away my memories," I said. "Out of kindness? Or to stop me realising just how involved you really were? Not just hide what they did, but hide how much you did too?"

He raised his eyebrows as if my remarks were barely worth the answer. "If I am a man capable of inflicting torture," he said, "why should I be a man who would deny it?"

I felt weak and naked and exposed and increasingly hot. The flickering candle at my side reminded me of the convent flames. Now Vespasian sat so calmly with the cloths in the water at his feet, and I was scorched all over again by shame. I was deeply agitated. "Sometimes you are kind," I said. He was prepared to explain some obscure theory of religion, but never the simple truth about himself.

"You've protected me many, many times," I persisted. "But the danger was always because of you in the first place. And the pain. And the fear. So tell me now, without riddles or codes, did you torture me? Did you help them with what they did? I know it was your house. I know you hurt me – that one particular way." Tilda didn't even want to say the word 'rape'. She continued, "So what else did you do?" I glared at him, determined to force an answer. "And if you think all that pain's just forgotten, then you're mistaken. Waves of it come back, all the time, and remind me. So what happened there, for pity's sake? And what part of it all was your part?"

He did, as usual, the thing I least expected. He leaned forwards very slowly and kissed me gently on the forehead. I barely breathed. Never had he shown such affection and I lay still and stared back at him in total amazement. The brush of his lips had been dry and brief. Now he sat straight and gazed directly into my eyes. "I'll tell you the truth, since that's what you ask of me," he said, "though you will mistake and misunderstand. The truth, when told in fragments, can be mightily misleading. One day, perhaps, if you're still in my life and I in yours, I'll explain what I cannot tell you now. It would take me days to speak of the truth behind the truth and even then, it would do you no good at all."

I took a deep breath. "Tell me anyway," I said.

So he smiled without any hint of malice and leaning forward, gently traced those strange dark scars still clearly visible on the lower inside curve of my left breast. His direct touch was so suddenly intimate that I shivered, though his fingers were warm. I knew what he touched although I was watching his eyes and not his hand. It was the design of the little dragon which lay deep and red immediately over my heart.

"I've told you before," and his words were now so soft that I had to strain to hear him and the small patter of the candle flame was louder. He said, "I am not seduced by pain or attracted to blood and the cruelty of one man to another. That is not my path. The violence done to you for pleasure was not done by me and I used a method to remove you from your own body while that pain was inflicted."

"But you didn't stop them. Arthur and Malcolm and the others. You didn't stop them."

"No," he agreed. "I did not stop them. I was one amongst many and I am not all powerful. Indeed, I was also a partial prisoner, and could influence very little, only ensure your mind and spirit slept. Unable to give you physical release, instead I gave you unconsciousness. But then what I did to you myself was in many ways the worst of all." He had been tracing the mark on my breast, as if he found it beautiful, and his fingers gently followed the outline of its wings and snout and claws. I had stared at it myself many times in revulsion. I knew exactly what he traced. Now he looked up and back into my eyes. His own were huge and black again, flooding out emotion. "I was no part of any other violence done to you, but I raped you, as you know," he continued without pause, "and I did this."

"That?" Having challenged him to tell me the truth, now I was bitterly sorry, and hated what he'd said.

He answered as softly as ever, as if what he said was an endearment instead of a violation. "I branded you with the sign of the fifth essence which is the inner fire," he said. "And these are scars which will never fade. You will carry this for the rest of your life." Then he stood up abruptly, and pulled the bedcover over me and up to my chin. I was still staring at him. "Remember in future," he said, now quite curt, "not to ask what you do not really wish to know."

I turned my head away. I couldn't look at him. "It's all so frightening," whispered Tilda into the pillow. "You frighten me."

He stood at the side of the bed, the wavering candle light illuminating his face from below, seeming suddenly demonic. Then he leaned forwards and blew out the flame. The immediate darkness fell muffled and warm and I heard only the soft silken murmur of his voice as he moved away. "Good. You should be frightened," he said. "And if you fear me, then that is best. Remember fear. It may protect you when a sword cannot." The bed curtains rustled and I heard the door close softly behind him as he left me.

I lay in the dark and shivered like a fool. I couldn't calm my own body and it stuttered and boiled as if I was possessed with more than my own panic and confusion. I closed my eyes and placed my hand carefully over the mark of the dragon, still the one remaining place on my body where the unhealed scars jabbed more viciously than the other old wounds. No ordinary tattoo, it had been drawn in flame and for weeks it had blistered. It still stabbed like a knife in my heart.

But he had kissed me. A father's kiss perhaps, or a brother's, but a kiss all the same, and deep with tenderness. The heat of his breath and the touch of his lips now seemed as etched to my forehead as the dragon he had branded on my breast.

I'd always recognised his danger. I knew him as a ruthless man, capable of causing pain. Even before he said that he raped me, I'd been sure I had reason to fear him. I'd suspected him of every violation except those which he'd eventually admitted. Once I'd even thought him involved in the murder and torture of the sad dead women in Molly's world and yet, absurdly, I had never expected what he finally told me.

It must have been an hour or more that I curled in bed, unable to sleep or even to think. I could hear myself crying. Tilda was sobbing into the pillow but I was Molly and my misery was mixed with bitter anger.

When I heard the door open again I expected Vespasian's return. I turned away towards the wall and pulled the woollen cover up around my ears. But it wasn't Vespasian.

"I shouldn't have come," said Gerald, whispering into the shadows. "He ordered me not to. But he's left now and I wanted so very much to talk to you. Are you asleep?"

"Yes," I said. I wiped my eyes on the pillow slip and tried to keep the sniff out of my voice.

"Shall I go away?" he asked.

I managed to sit up a little, peering out into the darkness. I could see his blonde dishevelled head bobbing uncertainly, worried that I'd tell him off perhaps, or worried about Vespasian's anger when he found out. "Come and sit down," I said. "Tell me what's happened since I went away."

"Most of it's beyond guessing," he snorted, that old familiar derision. "The whole world's gone mad. Vespasian – of course I ought to call him Lord Jasper de Vrais – he's my step-father and that's weird enough, but he won't discuss things and doesn't explain anything and I've been longing to talk to you."

CHAPTER FORTY-FOUR

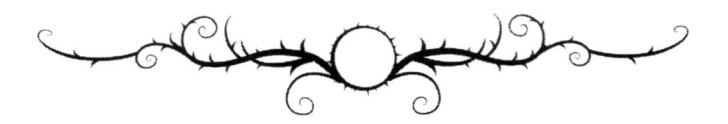

I dreamed. Once Gerald left me I thought there'd be no time for sleep and supposed my own disquiet wouldn't allow it. But pain didn't keep me awake and my dreams were vivid.

It was the men I feared. Yet now asleep, I was surrounded by women. I didn't see Vespasian, nor Arthur or his brood. My consciousness held no lingering trace of the things Gerald had told me. Instead I stood in a cold dark place all alone and voices whispered around my head like wind in clouds.

I knew the woman's voice I most hated. "You must cut the cards," she said. "It is time to cut the pack again."

"I'm dreaming," I answered her. "What happens in a dream cannot have validity. I will not play your game."

There were other women. One had a small, sweet voice like a loving aunt or a kindly neighbour. "Oh dear me," she said, "dreaming doesn't protect you at all, you know. You mustn't think you understand all the rules."

"It's the church that has rules," I said, grasping at vague memories. "Only the church makes boundaries. Spirit is a chasm."

"Cut the cards," said the creature that had killed my cousin and decimated her body and ruined my life. "You will see them the moment you cut the pack."

I clasped my hands tight, determined to resist. "Are you Satan?" I demanded. "Or are you," grasping at memory again, "the veleda?"

"You speak without understanding," said a third voice. It was low and deep and practical, emotionless but still feminine and I thought I recognised Joanna, Arthur's woman and the mother of Vespasian's murdered wife. "You are ignorant and lack intelligence. You are not worthy of your own position."

"What is my position?" I whispered.

"Dear child, don't you even know?" sniggered the maidenly voice, all artifice and false sweetness. "Why, you're the Holder of the Portal, my dear. The veleda has set you in her place, though it's not through merit, I'm sure. You are certainly no alchemist."

"And nor are you," I said, without knowing why or even what I was really saying. "Alchemy isn't evil. You all practise evil. You're necromancers, not alchemists. That thing who speaks of the tarot is without humanity and utterly evil."

And as if I had introduced her, the voice said, "For the third time I order you to cut the cards. This time there is no one to take your place for we have your interfering blasphemer involved elsewhere. We have you alone. You must do it yourself."

Each word felt like a blow. The compulsion to obey was overwhelming. I searched for the protection of the ouroboros but I was dreaming and in my dream I truly stood alone. But now I experienced a strange duplicity, for I stood holding tightly to my own wrists and yet I saw one hand reach out obediently to take the cards I could not see.

As she had said, when my fingers touched, the pack appeared. Their backs were all fire with a whirling myriad of black and gold like a cross of thorns against an eclipsed sun. They spun all around me, intertwining with the voices. In the instant of touch, I had chosen one.

It turned with a snap and flew towards me, growing huge and spitting fire. I thought it would smother me and tried to step away from it. I stumbled and fell backwards. Then the card landed small in my lap. The voices had gone and there was a silence without echo. I looked at the card that I did not know I had chosen. It had no number and it was the card of The Fool.

I woke and sat up. A pale cold light was forcing through the unlined bed curtains.

"It is the thirty-first of October and the day of the Samhain," said Vespasian. "Tonight is All Hallow's Eve and there is a great deal to be done." He stood in front of me looking desperately tired. Beneath the magnetism of his eyes, the lower lids appeared bruised.

"I dreamed," I said. The dream fingers still clutched at me and I was shaking. "There were three women. I had to cut the cards. I didn't want to but they made me. My arm went out even when I held on to it."

He sat quickly on the edge of my bed and looked searchingly at me. "Do you know," he asked, which was not what I had hoped he would say, "which tarocchi card you picked?"

I nodded. I had wanted him to tell me that dreams didn't matter and whatever I'd seen was of no relevance at all. Instead I said, "The card of The Fool. Except they called the cards tarot and not – what you said."

"Tarot – tarocchi – it's the same thing." He seemed greatly relieved. "The card you chose was a good one. They may leave you in peace for the moment, before the final choice."

I stopped shaking. "I talked to Gerald before I slept," I said. "Please don't tell him off. When you tell me things, it frightens me. But he told me so much and he was able to explain so I actually understood. It helped a lot."

Vespasian smiled, heavy with the old malefic gleam. "That means," he said, "that nothing he told you was of any use. Nor could it be. My dear step-son knows only facts and nothing of the truth behind them."

"I wanted facts," I said. "That's what helped."

"And you were soothed and distracted sufficiently by these pointless facts," he said, "to spin you directly into the unprotected malevolence of Lilith's dream." I must suddenly have looked terrified.

He smiled again and his own malice faded a little. "No matter," he said. "The card you chose was Innocence."

"The Fool," I sniffed. I couldn't do Gerald's snort. "But I'm not a fool. You may think it, and perhaps sometimes I am, but I'm really not stupid at all."

And then he flashed me such a smile of malefic spite that I shrank right back against my pillows. "Ah, but I do not think you foolish at all," he said. "You hold as many secrets as I do, dear Tilda, though you cannot yet understand them fully yourself, and the danger you bring to us all may be guileless but it is a threat as great as any you suspect of me." He lifted my chin with one finger, forcing me to look up at him. "Don't quake when I speak to you. Remember your courage for you are going to need it."

"You frighten me," I whispered.

"So you keep informing me," he said. "But that is not yet my concern. If we survive this night, perhaps I'll attempt to overcome that in the future. In the meantime, know that the tarocchi Fool is not a foolish symbol, but represents the traveller through destiny and the soul open to experience through the innocence of hope. His hope transforms not only himself but the world he travels through. He is the butterfly and the dove, the white rose and spirit in purity." His eyes were calm and hooded again. "Do you still think you chose a foolish card?"

I wondered if he was telling me the truth and then decided that whatever else, it was now always the truth he told me. "Does it all matter so much?" I said. "It wasn't as if I chose the card, it came to me as I touched it. The woman told me she kept you out of the way so that I had to cut the cards myself."

"She did," said Vespasian. "I had no choice, though it seems this time you needed neither my presence nor protection. The Tarocchi Fool is your true card, Tilda, and you chose it because it recognised its mistress. The next situation is unlikely to be so benign. When I next demand the right to act in your stead, it will be to save both our lives."

I should have questioned his ability to travel into my dreams but instead I took a very deep breath. "I know my life's in danger. But yours too?"

Vespasian smiled and a glint of the old malice was back. "Though Arthur would cause my death if he could," he said, "it is you who are my principle danger. You may easily take my life, Tilda, before this night is out."

I thought it absurd. "I don't suppose you'll explain that," I said crossly.

"Quite right," he said. "I won't. Now, your own clothes are once again ruined and there are no woman's garments in this house. There've been few servants left here for some years and certainly no lady of the estate. I've therefore borrowed some clothes for you, if you call it borrowing. However, few if any may fit. You must do the best you can." He had tipped a pile of assorted materials into my lap. He had not asked me how I felt. "Dress quickly now," he said. "We must leave soon."

Wherever he had stolen these from, it was a very odd assortment and in spite of his having removed my clothes on several occasions, it showed that his actual knowledge of woman's attire was sadly lacking. I struggled to dress, still stiff with the ache of the burns, but it was the fire in my head that slowed me most. A ragtaggle collection of half understood information chased itself around my mind. I thought of Bernado and the foul thing he'd somehow conjured, then the far greater evil of the woman who had possessed Bertie, murdered and tortured in my own world, and now forced herself into my dreams. I did not understand the relevance of the tarot pack. To me it seemed childish as if playing with paper could influence a life. What Vespasian had done remained with me like heaving nausea, but in spite of the horror that surrounded him, he was still my only protection within an increasing threat of manic power.

Gerald had explained the mundane things that Vespasian would never stoop to tell me, of his history and how all this had begun. At least Tilda could now feel the earth solid beneath her feet. So I concentrated on Gerald's tales while dressing, squeezing out the darker shadows from the edges of my mind.

Vespasian's step-son had sat on my bed and whispered to me all the things that he had discovered, and which excited him so much. He hadn't lit the candle. We sat together in the dark, telling stories as once all of us had in far greater innocence, back around the fire on long evenings. I felt a sweet nostalgia and a terrible sadness for lost simplicity, which at first spoiled Gerald's enthusiasm.

"All these years," Gerald told me, "before you came of course, for I was with him at the first, I thought of Vespasian as a remarkable man. I always loved him. He was my father and my hero and my saviour but I never thought he might truly prove to be my father. He seemed such a powerful man, but he actually had no power at all. That was the puzzle."

"So," I had whispered into the darkness, clutching my bedcover up around my neck, "I suppose you were too much of a baby to remember anything before the London house. But we know some of it now."

"That he's the Baron de Vrais and my step father. Yes, that's right." Gerald had brought me wine from the estate's cellars. We had a cup each, sitting there in Gerald's great house on the bed with its soft expensive mattress, sipping Greek Malmsey and whispering in the dark. "He was the only child of the old Norman Baron de Vrais, and his mother was the lady Bianca, Italian nobility from Venice. I expect he was always unusual and terribly clever. He was sent off to university in Italy at Bologna when he was fourteen and spent a couple of years there studying, but then he took off travelling far and wide. Do you know he speaks a hundred languages?"

"A hundred?" I smiled. "How enterprising of him."

"Well," grinned Gerald, "French and Latin and English of course, like all the noble lords. But he speaks Italian and Castilian and Greek as well, – and Persian and Arabic too because he spent years in all those countries and he's translated all sorts of learned documents from one to the other. He spent months with the Arabs in the libraries of Toledo. Do you know his works are still held in monasteries all across Europe?"

I remembered the package that Vespasian had demanded from

Bernado before the place burned. He had mentioned papers with some Arabic name. "He started studying alchemy, not languages," I said.

"He won't talk about the magic," said Gerald. "I suppose everything went together. He knows how to make gold from iron."

"Did he show you?" I asked, greatly intrigued.

Gerald laughed. "Not even a peep. He says I'm never to have anything to do with alchemy. But I won't need to anyway. My family are terribly rich if I can claim my lands back from Arthur. Then there's Vespasian's real wealth, which he's lost but he says he'll leave everything to me if he ever gets it back."

"He might have children of his own one day," I said without thinking.

"He says he counts me as his own child," said Gerald proudly. "He really loved my mother you know. She was Ingrid, Baroness Tennaton and she and my proper father were one of the few families with real Saxon blood, instead of being Norman descent like Vespasian. You are too, aren't you?"

The question had taken me by surprise. After all, I was Molly and my lineage was probably as bastard as any modern Englishwoman. "Saxon? Yes, I suppose so," said Tilda. "But my parents were serfs."

"Well, that's because of the Normans too," said Gerald with a sniff of sympathy. "Anyway, Vespasian says his family wouldn't keep serfs. They made them all freemen. Mind you, I don't think it was all kindness. He says they worked harder that way, because it wasn't grudged."

"So Vespasian came back from all his travels and got married."

"My real father was killed in a sword fight resisting Arthur, who was the man who'd married my mother's mother," Gerald told me. "So my mother was widowed with this little baby who was me of course, and already under Arthur's control. He took over all the lands and property she inherited and practically locked her up in his house. My grandmother, that's Joanna, she helped him do it. I thought she was so kind and beautiful when I met her, but she's a terrible woman. How can anyone kill their own daughter?"

Vespasian had told Gerald a lot about his parents and what had happened to them. As he had once given me the gift of answers to my questions, so he had given Gerald the gift of all the information due to him regarding his heritage. Now Gerald buzzed with the knowledge of his own rightful importance. He was to be Baron Tennaton and if Arthur and Joanna died, then the probability of a brilliant future might come back into his hands.

"When we were living in London," Gerald went on, "Vespasian started stepping back into the King's good graces. Do you remember? All that was for me." Gerald was grinning and even in the dark I could see the flash of his teeth. "He was incognito of course, and called himself Vespasian Fairweather instead of Jasper de Vrais, but he started building up the reputation of an honest man, going to fight with the King and getting known for his courage, so that King John would accept him and then knight him, and that would open doors for me again. I bet Vespasian hated being summoned for silly hunting trips and things, but he went, didn't he? If he'd had a little longer, his plan would have worked and he could have helped me claim my title."

"The king didn't recognise him?"

"No, he hadn't known the king before, not personally. As Jasper, he'd only known the old King Richard. The other court nobility, well I think many of them knew and either turned a blind eye, or actually encouraged it. I expect lots of them were really pleased to see him back, whatever he called himself. You know how overpowering Vespasian is. He could influence people just with a smile."

"He never smiles, except when he's being nasty."

"Alright, just by looking down his nose at them then," said Gerald.

"I want to know about your mother," I told him. "Tell me about her."

"They met in England after he came back from his travels," continued Gerald. "He was called home when his father died, and his mother died very soon afterwards I think. So Vespasian, I mean Jasper, he was the baron himself and terribly rich and powerful and into all this alchemy stuff. I'm not sure, I mean – he isn't going to tell me all that, is he? – but I think he was sort of getting into the blacker side himself when he met up with Arthur. Vespasian was much younger so perhaps he was impressed with Arthur, or maybe it was the other way round. Anyway, he joined him and all the others too. There's this foul man called Malcolm, well he's Arthur's son by his first wife. Then there's a whole brood of both commoners and nobles, and Vespasian became one of them. He wanted dark power I expect, but he wouldn't do everything Arthur wanted him to. He wouldn't obey and insisted on going his own way. Then he met my mother Ingrid, who was hidden away in Arthur's house, and they fell in love of course and got married. Chivalry and romance in the middle of the wickedness. That trapped Vespasian – I ought to call him Jasper – and pulled him further into the clan."

"There seems to be a great deal of variety between practitioners of alchemy," I sniffed. "Vespasian believes in the old Earth Magic. Arthur follows black magic and that's not really alchemy at all, though I suppose it's related."

"Well, Vespasian knew so much, he taught the others," said Gerald, "so they kept him and tried not to let him go. But then he discovered they were into some really brutal stuff. He found out Arthur had killed my father. So Vespasian took my mother and me and they ran away. Being Baron de Vrais, he had all these estates but they were up in the north and west of England and too near Arthur's lands which were north east so they came down south to the estates my mother inherited from her father. My grandfather had been a rich merchant, and one of the first to bring cotton in from France. He was Joanna's first husband and a good man I think. He went down with his ship outside Calais."

The small castle on the river where Arthur had taken Gerald and where I had gone and then been imprisoned and tortured, had in fact been Ingrid's home. Much of the adjoining land, not at that time classified as royal forest, had belonged to Ingrid and therefore passed to her new husband. What belonged to a wife became her husband's property so Jasper, Baron de Vrais, his young wife and his step son travelled south and took up residence on her estate. They built a smaller house among the trees where they often stayed to keep out of the way of any unwelcome visitors when Arthur was looking for them. They opened a leper hospital in the woods, introduced new practises on their farmlands and freed their serfs. Vespasian refused to join the crusades but they travelled a little, to Normandy and Anjou. They had, perhaps, a few short years of happiness together.

Eventually, feeling safe at last I suppose, they moved north and went to live on the grand de Vrais estates in Staffordshire. Then Arthur and Joanna came one dark night, just like Arthur came later on to take Gerald. Vespasian was called away on a royal summons at court. He found afterwards the summons was falsified by Arthur. But when Vespasian returned, he found his step-son taken and his wife murdered in their bed.

Ingrid had been killed in exactly the same way that later they had murdered Isabel, except that Ingrid lay on the velvet majesty of the huge marriage bed, so blood soaked that Vespasian could smell it and knew what had happened as soon as he entered the house. The servants knew nothing. Arthur had grown in power.

Vespasian found his beautiful wife with her eyes blinded and knives stabbed through each. Her nose had been sliced from her face. Her naked body had been sliced down with the sternum split. One small hand and one delicate foot and ankle had been flayed with all the skin peeled back from the flesh. Her stomach had been cut open to see whether she was carrying Vespasian's child. Vespasian never knew how much agony had been done to her before she died. Such torture would have taken a long time, unless achieved purely by magic. Hopefully she was already dead before such pain.

Joanna and Arthur publicly accused the Baron de Vrais of murdering his own wife and the Regent John, never having known Vespasian personally, accepted the expediency of the accusation. Arthur was financing many of John's own luxuries, so his word held authority. Vespasian stayed only to bury his wife and burn the bed. Then he travelled east to Arthur's estates. He stole back his step son and immediately went into hiding. For some years, no one heard what had become of the wicked Baron de Vrais, sorcerer and magician, who had committed murder most foul.

Arthur, in Joanna's name, claimed Ingrid's lands which had all been confiscated by the crown in Vespasian's absence, and the woods around the leper hospital were designated royal forest. Vespasian was left in absolute poverty, exiled and wanted for murder and unnatural practises.

"The torture," I asked Gerald. "Why? Is it part of black magic?" I had never told Gerald exactly what had been done to me, but he must have known some of it. All the boys in the forest house had talked about it.

"I honestly don't know," Gerald had said. "I told you, it's that sort of thing Vespasian won't talk about. But he told me other stuff about Arthur and that group. They'd been searching for Vespasian for ages when they found out where he was. Then Malcolm secretly made advances to Isabel. Well, you know what she was like, poor Issy. She was silly and vain and I suppose she was flattered by Malcolm's tricks. After all, he'd have seemed awfully grand to her, a fine young lord who might have wanted to marry her."

"How wretched," I sighed. I had grieved so much for all the others, but I was suddenly conscious that I'd never truly mourned Isabel. "After all, Vespasian might have bedded her, but he certainly never gave her any hope he'd marry her."

"Oh well, you know what she was," nodded Gerald. "Or perhaps you don't, you weren't around. Well, Vespasian found her whoring outside the Cock Tavern when she was just nine years old and such a skinny little thing and brought her back to the house. There was just him and me and Walter and Issy for ages."

"Then Vespasian shouldn't have taken advantage of her," I said primly into my blankets, trying not to sniff.

"You have some awfully funny ideas sometimes, Tilda," said Gerald, eyeing me with suspicion. "You're not going to cry, are you? You can hardly accuse Vespasian of improper seduction, knowing Isabel. He certainly never touched her for years till she grew up, I can tell you that. And it wasn't as though he was hard up. Didn't you ever notice? I suppose you were too much of a kid. Well, women of all kinds used to flock around."

"You think that's an excuse?" I demanded. "I suppose you think it's normal for a man not even bothering to be faithful?"

Gerald sighed. "I'm not getting into that sort of argument now," he said. "Especially with you. Anyway, listen, if you want me to finish the story. Vespasian soon knew what was going on but he admits he didn't stop it because he wanted to find out exactly what Malcolm and Arthur were up to. I don't suppose he cared much what Isabel did, as long as he could get to Arthur. She was trapped in the middle, poor Issy. But it was her own fault really."

"My God, she didn't deserve what she got," I said in horror. "So Arthur murdered her in exactly the same way as your poor mother, to send Vespasian a message?"

"Yes, that's right," said Gerald.

Which was why Vespasian had been following Isabel that day, and had found her body at the same time I had. I had collapsed into his arms and he had been kind to me and horrified at Isabel's fate. But he had been partially responsible for her death, as he had been for most of what had later happened to me, the torture and the pain, whether he had done it personally or not.

CHAPTER FORTY-FIVE

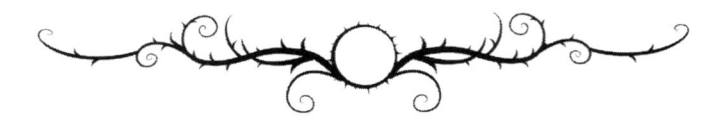

But Gerald knew even less about what was to happen next than I did. Vespasian would face not only Arthur, but mystery, sorcery and greater powers of which Gerald knew nothing at all.

And that ignorance, though I could hardly tell Gerald, was less true for me. I'd faced evil and knew something of its terror though nothing of its origins and less of its meaning. But I knew that I myself was one of the dangers. Vespasian had made that frequently clear. But even before he had spoken, I had begun to guess. Tilda-Molly, the holder of the portals, as they'd called me in the dream. Gatekeeper. I opened the way between worlds, not only for my own passage but for the thing which followed, and killed. Vespasian had long guessed, but Arthur had only recently recognised it. Gerald was Joanna's blood and forfeit to their cult but now they wanted me for a whole different reason.

The other boys stayed at the forest house and Vespasian had left them a good deal of money but no guarantee that he would return. If he was not back within the week, he told them to divide the money between them, go back to London and make their own fortunes. Gerald, of course, had promised to take them all as brothers onto his estates if he ever officially became Baron Tennaton again. If he was even alive to claim the title. Stephen had promised to find wolves and do battle at last and impress Vespasian when he came back, and Walter had passed a message for me, sending his regards and saying he wished me well and would willingly do me any service in the future that I might call on him to do. Osbert and Hugh were itching to be off and make their own way in the world but they had promised to stay for the week and mind Stephen and the house. Then Vespasian and Gerald had ridden off into the night and the forest had whispered around them like warnings in the wind.

"One last thing," Gerald had said to me before creeping back to bed. "You know that beautiful little pool with the falls and the stream, where you told the others to bury Richard, and they did. My mother's buried there too."

That had awakened murmurings of understanding. "Yes, Vespasian often went there. It had magic, I always knew that. He said it meant something to him too, though he never told me what."

"First they buried her all grand in the churchyard with the priest and Latin services. But afterwards Vespasian ordered her body removed and two of his men secretly carried the coffin all the way down south to the forest. Vespasian took me to her grave. It's right next to Richard's, though the mound is flattened now. It's covered in the wild herbs Vespasian planted there. He says it's holy ground and not being consecrated by the church doesn't matter at all."

I said, "I'm glad I've been visiting your mother's grave even if I didn't know it."

Now I dressed in the mismatched garments that Vespasian had brought me, buckled my sword with a garish red leather baldric and tucked the ouroboros into my belt. I walked down the wide staircase and joined Gerald at the main doorway to the hall. He was more grandly dressed than I had ever seen him. "Vespasian bought me all these," he said, somewhat apologetically. "You'd already run off to London. He took me to the market and we didn't steal a thing. He chose all the materials himself and ordered this cotte made. He said I had to look the part when we faced Arthur."

I wondered what part I'd look myself. Even Gerald eyed me with some amusement. My white stolla was too long and I had to hitch it up and although the bliaud was grand and red velvet with gold embroidery, it was three sizes too large and the neck so wide that it fell off my shoulders. At least I had a good leather belt to hold it all together and the baldric helped. The cloak was red too though a little too short, and lined with otter pelts. I thought it particularly beautiful and useful too, since it covered my other ill fitting clothes. There had been no camise so now the stolla's stiff fabric scratched my breasts, but at least I had new shoes that fitted fine.

I was admiring Gerald's powder blue finery while embarrassed by my own oddments, when Vespasian strode out from the hall. I stared at him in amazement. I was used to seeing him scruffy and uncaring, his clothes often threadbare, stained and dust clogged, though sometimes lately I had seen him grand and loved his occasional beauty. Now he looked like a king. He was dressed in dark blue and gold, breath taking and majestic. The glint of his cuirass was visible beneath his embroidered cotte, then the wide leather stripe of the baldric across his right shoulder. My mouth must have been open in surprise. He looked back at me and his mouth twitched slightly, black eyes bright.

"It isn't funny," I said. "You and Gerald are putting on a glorious spectacle and I look like the forgotten serving girl."

"Not in that cloak," interrupted Gerald kindly. "It's really nice."

"My dear Tilda," said Vespasian, "what you wear will be of little consequence I assure you. You may prove to be the most important of us all."

I waved that aside and thought he was teasing me. "You wanted to leave me at the convent," I pointed out.

"It would have been far better had I been able to do so," he said, and he was serious again. "But there's nowhere else of safety I can leave you, so you will have to come with me and play out your not insubstantial part, as is inevitably destined."

I had been frightened that he might want to leave me alone at Gerald's house so now I was happy enough to ignore the irony in his voice. "If only you'd explain what I'm expected to do, then I might be more use to you," I said and Gerald at my side nodded agreement at once.

As usual Vespasian avoided what I said and answered my silent thoughts. "I cannot leave you where you'd have no protection, and equally, where I would have none from you," he said. "There are servants here on the land, but few of them and no one I can trust. You will both therefore behave yourselves like well mannered and obedient children, and keep quiet until I tell you to speak."

"Yes, my lord," said Gerald, who was easily overawed. I resisted Tilda's urge to giggle and said nothing. Vespasian led us out through the big studded doors and they clanged shut behind us with an echo I found somehow ominous.

It was the last day of October but outside the sun was warm. Gerald's farm lands stretched wide and distant, golden behind their scrawny hedges. A vegetable garden had grown a little wild. The estates had not been well looked after, hardly surprising in the absence of any master. Some steward had probably been leaching the profits for himself. Now Vespasian had installed new staff and there was a sense of bustle while abandoned land was being reclaimed. A stable boy was waiting patiently with two horses ready bridled. Neither one of them was the horse we had ridden from the convent the day before. These were well groomed beasts who would snort down their nostrils at Vespasian's ugly brown gelding. I glared at both of them.

Gerald mounted the grey from the block and Vespasian tossed me up into the saddle of the other. He was black and glossy and all pride but he nuzzled Vespasian's hand with pleasure so I forgave the stallion his snobbery. Vespasian mounted behind me. "Where have you kept the ouroboros?" Vespasian asked and I realised he didn't want Gerald to hear. I tapped my belt. "You cannot lose it easily," he said, which I had certainly found to be true. "But make sure to keep it safe. Solve et coagula. You should always be conscious of where it is."

We set off slowly with Vespasian leading but once into the narrow country lanes between the fields, we quickened to a canter. The peasants turned their heads to watch us ride past. It must have been strange gossip for them to see their lord appear, little more than a boy, after so long a time after the previous baron's death. The harvest was already in, the wheat was heavy in the sheds and it was the time for sowing the winter grains. The harnessed oxen trudged furrowed fields, wide patient heads to the earth, dragging the cut of the plough and guided by the ploughman in his mud clogged boots. The sudden splash of scarlet autumn poppy flung sideways from its roots was like blood in the sun.

With the day mellow on my face, the strength of Vespasian's arms around me, his body tall at my back and the fur lined cloak muffling me against the wind, I cuddled more hot than warm. The marks of yesterday's burns were still uncomfortable on my left cheek and I tried not to think of what was inevitable and imminent. Since Vespasian had, as usual, refused to explain what was coming, I accepted that the ignorance I loathed might instead prove the basis of my own protection.

The morning was balmy and the sun's warmth muted though it fluttered brilliant in the glorious autumn leaf above our heads. Hazel, ash and oak, willow, birch and alder waved scarlet and bronze above, their shadows striping the path. We rode for some hours through lane, pasture and forest, across the gentle roll of placid hills and splashing through the shallow sparkle of woody streams. I counted time as the sun rose high into the tree tops, and then, announcing afternoon, began to slide down against the blue. I saw we were travelling west. With the dazzle in my eyes I almost dozed, but then, unexpectedly, Vespasian began to speak. "In last night's dream," he said, his voice careful as if he did not want to alarm me, or perhaps not give away clues he would rather keep to himself, "you cut the tarocchi pack. Did you see the creature that held the cards?"

"No," I said, a little sleepily. "I saw nothing until the cards came whizzing towards me. But there were three voices. One of them, I think, was Joanna."

"What else?" he demanded. "They named you portal keeper, or holder of the gates?"

That made me wake up. "You've called me that yourself. And yes, they did." I couldn't look him in the face because he was behind me and the horse was making a good speed, so I sat still and took a deep breath. "So, what doors do I open?" I said. "What gate do you all talk about and how do I open it? And who is Veleda?"

"You will find all that out this evening," he said, almost casually, as if discussing the weather. "You will celebrate Samhain as you have never done before."

I could hardly tell him that I had never celebrated it at all and had no idea what it was. "Now you want to frighten me," I accused him. "Will it be so terrible?"

Vespasian did not answer me at first. There was a silence and I could hear only the steady thud of the horse's hooves, the bright wind in the trees and somewhere a blackbird which sang of its prowess and its home. Each creature claiming its title, as Gerald wished to do. Then Vespasian said, "Do you remember the first card that was cut, when the tarocchi pack was shown to you, but when it was I who took the card in your place?"

"The card of The Moon," I said. Then I remembered that I was confusing Tilda with Molly and Vespasian had led me into a trick, to make me admit more of myself. I wondered how much I should say. "The woman in the dream told me," I prevaricated quickly, "before I chose The Fool."

"If you lie to me," said Vespasian pleasantly, "I shall happily torture you again, and this time on my own initiative. Now, tell me the truth."

"It was the card of The Moon," I said under my breath. The blackbird continued to sing as if all the serenity of the countryside was his own, and without evil or complicity or magic. "You know that because you cut it. But I know it because I was there too."

"Very well, that is better," said Vespasian. "But this is a conversation we shall continue once we arrive. In the meantime, you have slept very little through several much interrupted nights. Sleep now if you can. But remember brat, that I am not one of your naïve child admirers and I know almost all your story. You would be wise not to try and lie to me."

I had no answer and for once no desire to ask questions. It seemed we both had our secrets, both denied each other our true stories, and both distrusted the other. I slumped down and closed my eyes.

When I woke, the sun was dipping from afternoon to evening, a vapour hung like silver mist all around us and the nightmare had already begun.

CHAPTER FORTY-SIX

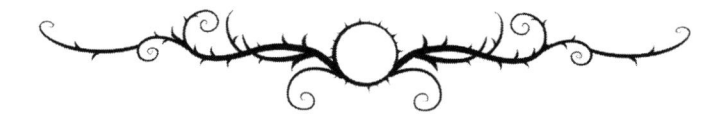

It had become very cold and there was a sparkle of light rain across the grass. The two horses stood in the glowing haze of different worlds. Beside me Gerald sat wooden, holding so tight to his reins that his knuckles were as blue as his smart new cloak. His hood was up against the drizzle and I could not see his face. Behind me and sitting straight and quite still, Vespasian supported me, the reins of our horse loose in his gloved hands. I took a deep breath and held it. The world around us did not clarify.

Vespasian spoke softly to me, his mouth against my hair. I was sure Gerald could not hear him. "This is the place I prepared for us," Vespasian said, "and why I was not present in what you call your dream. Do not be frightened. It will seem strange, but the power of nature is our friend. This is the ultimate nemeton, sweet and clean without vice. I did not want this final confrontation to take place in the soiled cellars of necromancy."

I thought I saw the clearing in the forest by the remains of Ingrid's burial mound and where the cold pool I loved banked Richard's grave. I saw the wild flowers and wandering herbs and I saw the silver ripples of the water. Then, in lingering shadows and towering from roots knarred and mossed, I saw the yew tree that was from Molly's world and had no place in the southern woods of old England. I had met Vespasian there once when he slipped through the doorway I must have opened myself. So he knew the yew tree, as I did. It was old enough to have been young in medieval days, not here but in the west country where Molly lived. Then I saw the chestnut tree from my own Cotswold garden and the blurred hint of a striped hammock looped beneath. Other trees twined branches, the ash whose strong branches had served as our first arrows when Vespasian taught us archery, the full green summer oak from behind the forest house, a floating whisper of willow reaching its leaf into the reflecting water and the grasping gloss of a strangling fig, all hollowed by the tree it had once killed and eaten. There was the stream that divided east and west in my own Gloucestershire village but the little Tudor bridge was gone, and a now beech paddled its roots amongst its own russet leaf fall. Beside it an alder stretched, clad in mistletoe, all thick with glossy white berries. Yet the alder waved fresh summer leaf while the mistletoe displayed proud winter fruit. The ancient yew yawned its shade above us all. In my time it was an empty giant and had lost half its heart. Now here in the majesty of its prime, it was solid and strong and wide. I thought, for just a moment, I could hear its song.

"It is two worlds," I said.

"It is all worlds," said Vespasian.

He dismounted, nodded to Gerald to do the same, and held out his arms to me. I tumbled into them like a child, all crumpled and shivering. He set me on my feet and stood looking at us both. The horses snorted and tossed their heads, frightened by intangibility. Vespasian tethered them both to a hornbeam branch just beyond the edge of the clearing beside the stream, where they bent to drink and gradually calmed. He strode back to me, removing his gloves and tucking them into his belt.

The pool was both pools and perhaps more, for under the huge yew tree there was also forest water and here the edges merged as if a hundred silver ribbons plaited back through the Earth's memory. Beneath my feet was a tracery of perfume from the herbs Vespasian had once told us to collect. I could smell the colours and the fresh washed sky and the worms ploughing underground and the secrets of the whispering trees. I could smell lavender and betony and harewort. There was dock and pretty purple vervain in the shadow. I stood on fronded fennel and chervil, white thyme, golden buttercup and bright periwinkle. I lifted up my face but there was no warmth in the air, the wind stung and the sky was almost hidden. The leaf of a thousand trees encompassed all seasons. There were autumn cascades in carmine, rust, ruddy orange and fading purple. There was winter's burnished copper falling from bare etched branch. There was the soft lemon green of spring's new birth and above it, the canopy of rich summer emerald.

I thought Gerald would misunderstand but he was lost in the misted magic. I looked straight back at Vespasian who was watching me closely. "Tell me about Molly," I said.

He smiled quite gently and I realised he was surprised. "I thought you would deny her," he said.

"How could I?" I answered. "You've brought her world into this one." I nodded towards the chestnut tree and the vague striped outline of the hammock. Beneath lay medieval fern and bracken, slick with sliding rain drops. Its patter was a hundred muffled voices deadened in the gloaming. Wet earth, wet leaf, the moisture of drinking growth.

I was waiting, hoping that Vespasian would speak again, but Gerald interrupted us. "It's my mother's grave," he said. He was bending down, his beautiful blue silk knees in the grass. There was a white rose lying where the mound had once been.

"She has a right to be here," Vespasian said. "She was the first they slaughtered. She was tortured and mutilated because of me but she was sacrificed to Lilith. She was the beginning and has a right to see the end."

"Richard's grave is here too," I said. Henbane and strawberry runners had grown over its grassy hillock.

"You may see him again before this night is over," said Vespasian. I stared at him but he didn't explain.

"Will I see my mother?" gasped Gerald, bright eyed, but Vespasian shook his head.

"I do not believe so, child. It's more than twelve years and she's gone too far on," he said. "But she'll hear the echoes of this night's work and what happens will ease her passing into the next great adventure." I wished quite suddenly, as I knew Gerald was wishing, that I had known this woman who Vespasian had loved so much. He was not a man who would give his love easily.

Since Vespasian had not answered me about Molly, I walked over to the edge of the pools with their interspersed banks and pebbled shallows, and looked down through the varied levels of water to the flurry of fishes and the strange, sudden leggy hop of tadpole into frog. As I watched, the dragonfly emerged from its larvae, wet drooping winged from the silvered surface, the water beetle scurried busy across the ripples and the snail clung to the weedy fronds below. This was all pools and all seasons as the trees were all trees. Then the sun came out and the rain turned to rainbow.

I watched the reflections on the water slither into brilliant refraction and the spectrum repeat in all the million droplets amongst the undergrowth. I saw a hologram of rainbows, shimmering multicoloured candles in the wind. Our stage was lit.

I heard Vespasian behind me but he put his hands on my shoulders and kept me facing outwards. "As this is a combination of many worlds," he said and his voice crept like a hint on the breeze without malice, "so you are many people. You should feel at home here."

"I do," I said. "It's beautiful."

The sting of cold had flown with the sun's arrival. A buzz of warmth was birthing up in the high leaves, accentuated in the dazzle. Vespasian said, "Do you still switch, you and her, or are you now always combined?"

"I thought you knew everything," I said.

He spun me round quite suddenly and looked down at me, still holding me firm by the shoulders. I felt the force of his hands and wondered if he could break me if he wanted, but the strength in his face wasn't anger. It seemed more like hunger. "What I know, and you do not," he said, still soft, "is that within you, the two innocents are united by danger. Molly is represented by the tarocchi card of The

Moon, Tilda by The Fool, which is the sweetest card of all. But soon you will be told to cut the final card, which is that of the Path Holder."

It was warm now but I shivered. "I would have told you everything I knew before, if you'd asked me," I said. "And if I'd realised how much you knew already. But you frightened me and hurt me and talked in riddles. And I – me – Tilda – didn't fully recognise Molly until a few months ago. I'm not trying to hide anything, really I'm not. I'm not a danger and I don't want to harm anyone."

He sighed. "I dissuaded confessions," he admitted. "Keeping Tilda in ignorance was her protection and her right. Besides," his voice softened further into only the rustle of echoes. "I would not let the gatekeeper into my house, my secrets or my heart, for you could have destroyed everything and all my hopes with it."

"I never thought of you as having hopes," I said stupidly. "I think of you as always getting what you want."

"With my wife slaughtered in my bed and my future dragged into solitude and grime?" He frowned. "For a woman of three worlds, you show remarkable ignorance in this one." The malice was back in his voice. "Are you equally absurd in the others?"

"I'm sorry," I said, "but I probably am." Tilda was always ready to admit inadequacy and I was beginning to feel that way myself. Most of all I wondered what was the third world he referred to, and whether I would ever understand. And then I thought of something else. I asked him, "Why did you murder Thomas Cambio?"

His eyes were suddenly inky with suspicion. "Don't you know?" Then his hands gripped me so violently that all the sting of the burns burst back. "I warned the woman Molly. Did she," he stared into my eyes, reading the truth in case I lied, "the future you – ever bed this creature?"

I shook my head so vehemently that I was dizzy again. "That's ridiculous," I said. "She – I told you before. Thomas was an old man. I liked him and I trusted him and I was shocked when the evil thing told me you'd killed him. At first I thought he'd been murdered like all the others."

Vespasian relaxed his grip. "You liked him either because of stupidity, because your own darker self tricked you, or because he tricked you himself." I remembered when I first met Thomas in the mist on the hills, how I'd meant to avoid him and then found myself vacuously agreeing to immediate friendship. How I'd always ended up doing what I had never intended doing, speaking words that had never been in my mind and how one drink and the flare of a hot fire had sent me into a trance, and him into my confidence.

"So it was you who killed him?"

"You should have known that from the start," said Vespasian. "I left you a message."

I nodded, though in fact I'd mistaken the clue. "You wrapped his body in Hugh's cloak."

"When Molly alerted me," said Vespasian. "I followed your Thomas Cambio. Even the name symbolised what he was, the wer-myth and one of Lilith's shells. But I killed him too quickly and the spirit fled the body before it was done. I had little choice. Lilith has other flesh she can inhabit at will and she cannot be so easily tamed."

I felt something crawling over me, a realisation of filth and disgust. "The thing I've met," I whispered, "the foul thing that comes into other bodies and tortures and kills and controls the tarot and wants to control me. That was inside Thomas? From the very start? And you ask if I made love to it?"

"No," said Vespasian. "I asked if it fucked you."

It was an inopportune moment for Gerald to appear at my side. He had been kneeling beside his mother's grave and was now bent and tired. "I'm interrupting you," he said, "but I have to talk to someone. I never thought much about my mother until now. I mean, as far as I knew, I had no parents at all. I was split from an egg like a chicken without a past. Now it all starts feeling real."

I looked around us at the flicker of lights, diamonds and misty worlds colliding. "But it's so unreal," I said. "More unreal than any dream."

"No, Gerald is right," said Vespasian. He had taken his hands from my shoulders at last and it felt as though he'd released me from an inquisition. "This is the truth behind the symbolism of simple fact. We stand within the soul of nature instead of its material illusion."

Gerald nodded as if he understood very well. "I can feel it," he said. He looked up, his wide blue eyes gazing into Vespasian's black intensity. "Have you brought me here as a sacrifice, my Lord? Is that why we've come?"

Vespasian smiled and I thought it was the gentlest smile I had ever seen, transforming the harshness of his face into tender and wistful affection. "No, my child," he said. "You have come here to know who you are and to claim your freedom and your future. It is I who am the sacrifice."

CHAPTER FORTY-SEVEN

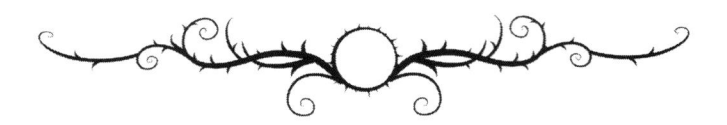

The glimmer of fallen rain still caught the long low rays of prismatic sunshine, but a pale twilight slunk close. I knew now what Samhain was and in this past age of mysticism and old faiths, All Hallows Eve was the night when gates opened from one world into another, the crossroads of the afterlife spun in upon themselves and justice could be done between spirit and creator. As the holder of gates, I had been summoned.

A zenith moon was huge above the tree tops. Where the sky before had been hidden now it was all light. A great white blazing circle reflected in the pool. The smooth water turned pearly silver. The night was not yet dark but the moon, perfectly full at the height of her second phase, had risen early, watching over us all.

"When will they come?" I whispered.

"When you call them," he said.

There had been birds in our forest glade. In the spring cool of the willow and chestnut I had heard the co-coo-cooing of the woodpigeon. The blue tit had bobbed along the lower branches of the hazel, the lark had swooped and trilled and blackbirds had sung their fluting love calls, liquid as the silver pool. But now as first shadow silhouetted the darkening leaves, the silence hushed us all.

"I'm aware of being Tilda." Frightened to break the suspenseful quiet, I spoke as soft as Vespasian. "I'm aware of being Molly. But you call me the gatekeeper and I'm not aware of that at all. There isn't anyone else I recognise inside me. There's no third personality."

Vespasian frowned, eyelids heavy. "That has been a puzzle to us all," he said, "even to Lilith herself. As it has been in the past, she expected the veleda to open the doors. That is why she forces you to cut the cards. The next card you pull from the pack will be that which represents the way holder. But I will not allow you to choose. I will not lose you to utter evil and I can influence the card I pick where you cannot. I will stand in your place."

"Thank you." I was shivering again. "I freely give you that right."

"But you cannot give it," he said. "It cannot be done voluntarily. Indeed, I have taken the right and no one can now deny it to me."

I understood so little and wanted to understand so much, so I argued over what didn't matter. "How can you demand to stand in my place if I haven't chosen to let you?" I said. "If I've no choice, how is it you to take my place, and not another?"

He stared down at me, expressionless. "I stole that right," he said. "It can be done no other way."

"How?" I demanded.

"Can't you guess?" he said, very soft.

Suddenly, I realised, through trembling, this was indeed the answer to that which Vespasian had always refused to explain. It was not something I wanted to think about now, though I'd longed to understand for months. I was beginning, perhaps, to appreciate why he could never have told me the truth before.

We still stood, all facing each other like three tired travellers waiting for the storm. Gerald stood peaceably by my side, following what little he could. He looked even younger than he was, all pretty in his powder blue. He said, "Am I in your way? Would you talk better without me?"

"Arthur will be here soon," Vespasian said. "And then there can be nothing hidden."

"Who else is coming?" asked Gerald. "Will my grandmother come?"

"All that brood will come," nodded Vespasian. "And others too. You will stand beside or behind me, my son, and keep absolute quiet unless I tell you otherwise. If you speak out of turn, I will strike you. Do you understand?"

Gerald blushed meekly beneath his tousled flaxen hair. "Yes, my lord," he murmured.

"And another thing," said Vespasian, again acerbic, "You will immediately cease calling me my lord like some idiot child brought up to do so by his strumpet of a wet nurse in his father's castle. You will do me the favour of calling me Vespasian, as you have always known me before you discovered I was someone else."

Gerald relaxed. "Excuse me, my lord," he said, all dimples.

I hoped Vespasian would laugh, but he didn't. "You may wish to call me something else altogether before this night is over," he said. "Remember only this. You must not speak unless I order it. You may be asked many questions, or encouraged to talk by those other than myself, but you will obey only me. It is important."

"I understand," said Gerald, looking at his feet.

"And me?" I asked. "Must I be mute?"

He looked searchingly at me. "Molly will speak for herself as always," he said. "Tilda should keep as quiet as possible and will undoubtedly wish to do so. The gatekeeper will have a great deal to say, I imagine, before I claim the right I already hold to speak in her place."

Gerald stared from Vespasian to myself. "So we're just three," he said, "and one just a girl. And they will be twenty or more."

"They will be more than that," said Vespasian. "Eighty, a hundred perhaps. But among them will come creatures who supersede mere number. It's of no matter how many there are. And we are not just three and one of us is not just a girl. You underestimate us, Gerald."

"Is someone else coming then, who's on our side?" asked Gerald hopefully.

"Our allies are already here," smiled Vespasian. He swept his arm towards the whispering trees and the grave mounds, the waters, flowers and herbs. "Hush now, the sun is sinking and Samhain has arrived."

The sunlight, already diffused, had dipped below the last young saplings of our horizon and with its passing the moon seemed brighter and even hungrier and the shadows crept longer. In the deepening twilight the rainbow glitter was transfused with moonshine. Gerald held his breath and then let it out in a frightened gasp. Along all the edges of our mist shrouded glade and wandering boundaries, the people were already thick under the trees.

I could see no faces for they hesitated, just shadows themselves in their dark cloaks. I waited for Arthur to stride forwards and face us. I expected immediate attack. But there was only hesitation. "They are waiting for you, and for Lilith," Vespasian said softly in my ear. "And even Lilith waits for you."

My pulse was so fast that it burned and all my panic rose like vomit in my throat. I still was not sure who Lilith truly was, nor of any of the questions I had meant to ask. The drifting lassitude and dream state in the glade had seemed timeless. I thought nothing would happen until I was prepared, but now it had begun and I was as unprepared as I had ever been. I stared up at Vespasian, who stood tall and supportive beside me. I reached out and clutched at his hand, slipping my fingers into his cupped palm. My hand was very cold, my blood immobile in its veins. Vespasian's fingers were warm and dry and hard. I felt the banded ridge of his palm from his long hours in the saddle, the wearisome pull on the hands from guiding the reins. Then crossed like a star, the weals across his palm from combat and the weight of the sword. A man whose hands told their own stories of action and attack, of defence and of the long, bitter years of solitary planning. They were hands that could kill, but he held mine tight and warm as I pleaded silently for his help.

He smiled down at me, a real smile, tucked with genuine tenderness. "We all wait on you," he said, still whispers on the breeze, "and yet you beg for comfort and cling to childhood."

Tilda had often wanted to rest against him, to hold to his hand and shelter in the protection of his touch. When I was young, I wished for my own parents to offer me such a cocoon of safety and affection, but had never received it. I sighed. "Lilith is the thing I met?" I asked. "She took over Thomas, and inhabited another man I knew. The thing that killed and tortured in Molly's world?"

He continued smiling, an even greater reassurance than the clasp of his hand. "Yes, you have met her undisguised," he said, "as few ever do. She is the tarocchi reader, malignant guardian of destinies and the reveller in human agony and blood. She is the oldest demon of them all, split off from creation in the first instance when good became fused in positive concentration and evil became scattered in negative fragments. Throughout history we have called her Lilith, but she has no name for herself and is hermaphrodite, being neither male nor female though often both – for she represents dissociation and chaos, as does all evil."

"It was Lilith that Arthur was waiting for," I murmured, remembering, "in the tower when he tortured me."

"Indeed," said Vespasian. "At first as sacrifice. He intended your pain and eventually your death as a gift in her honour. Then, perhaps because of me, he recognised your use as a lever. Then slowly he began to suspect your true power. Finally, through torture and blood he hoped to summon, control and dominate the gatekeeper. He needed you to open the path."

"And so did you," I sighed. "He lost, didn't he? But because of what you did to me, you succeeded. That's how you have the right to stand in my place?"

"This is not the time to explain the past," said Vespasian. "You must now face the future."

Arthur had entered the circle. I smelled his breath before I realised he'd come.

He was not as tall as Vespasian, but was all muscled threat and imposing swagger, supporting a square head so cruelly lined that the skin slunk in folds from cheek to jowls and from hooked nose to the gaping corners of his eyes. Like Vespasian, he was very dark, black eyed and olive skinned, but his crow hair was thinning and his beard was clipped silvery stubble in a wide bruise across his jaw. He looked at me as I looked back at him but he did not come too close.

"So, de Vrais," he sneered. "Have you yet discovered your own whore's identity? Is this the veleda indeed, or just the bitch at the gate?"

Vespasian kept my hand in his, but he lounged at my side, all casual insolence. "Come and find out, d'Estropier, if you dare. You failed miserably before. Do you have any virility remaining to make the attempt again?" As usual, his voice drifted soft, forcing the other man to stand silently, straining to hear each word.

Arthur didn't have the control Vespasian had naturally and I saw the fury flicker in his eyes. "I'll kill you this night, Jasper. I should have done it long ago, but I was tricked into believing you useful. Tonight we bring out the sacrament and the altar and I'll break every bone into small pieces before your soul's allowed free of its sacking."

"I thought it was my soul you wanted," said Vespasian pleasantly.

"I no longer want any part of you," snarled Arthur, "only the pleasure of killing you, as slowly as I wish." His right hand rested on his sword hilt. I saw the sword was curved like a scimitar and embossed in gold. I couldn't see what the ornate design represented for the dark clawed fingers held it in shadow.

Then, though I was Tilda with my child's hand tucked into the safety of Vespasian's, and I was Molly watching in silent horror, my voice spoke words I did not even understand, much less expect. "Keep back. I have not yet cleared the way," I said, quite clearly from a second throat, not gulping in fear like my own. "Gloat in consequence, not anticipation, or the sword swings back upon its owner."

"Then clear the way now," said Joanna. She had moved up behind her husband and now stepped forward into the moonlit aura. Her pale head was sleek and she looked polished, dressed in black with jewels high at her neck, elegant and severe. "Make the way clear for Lilith. She can command you, if we cannot."

Gerald stood to Vespasian's other side. I looked across at him. I felt his misery, staring at his grandmother. She ignored him. Now the mist was crowding in on us, a silver fog all spangled with refraction, closing off the trees and the pool and the crowd who stood on the edges.

"It takes great power," Vespasian explained to me briefly, "for any one of them to enter into the nemeton that I have prepared here. But there are many of them who have that power. Eventually many will succeed, Uta and Malcolm and the others. Some will shrink away and all will suffer the weight of natural beauty pushing against them. It will slow them and weaken them. It will help us." He had released my hand and was easing his fingers back into his heavy leather gloves, steel reinforced and ready for battle.

"The veleda will come," I said, in someone else's voice. "She is almost here."

Vespasian's hand closed again on mine but he did not look at me. "Ah yes," he sighed. "I thought she might."

A heavy dew was bringing shimmer and soft sodden whispers. Amongst the crowd, now barely visible under the hush of the trees, a few were trying to push forward into the opening. One or two came a few steps and more behind them, taking courage from the first. They were all dark cloaked like ravens ready for the scavenge, but I thought I knew Malcolm with his thin legs trembling, and Uta taking his arm to lead him forwards. I could not see at first why they were so reluctant. They could have rushed in on us and killed us all, easily overpowering us where we stood. I was used to Vespasian's power and his foresight, the glazed sardonic arrogance that made others step back and listen only to him, but I did not believe that he alone could intimidate such a brood as this. I clung to Vespasian and thought I'd scream, biting my lips to hold onto my courage.

"Don't be frightened," he whispered and the encouragement of his voice was huge. "You're quite safe, for this is the gate you have opened yourself. It is the way to the Underworld. But you can always close what you have opened. Remember that."

"To hell and beyond?" I stuttered. It was impossible to believe I had any hand in the monstrous terror taking shape before me. I had touched nothing and said nothing. I had turned no handles and spoken no incantations. "If I don't know how I've opened anything, how can I close it?"

"I will help with that, if you ask it." Then he put his arm warm and strong and close around me and all my terror turned to safety and relief. "Stand tall," he commanded, "for the night is just beginning."

Then, as I stared ahead the yew tree parted as if fractured and all its width and its length splayed out with thunder and roaring like the splitting of the earth. A shadow far blacker than the night was released. The moonlight neither illuminated nor entered it. And, from the cradle of Vespasian's embrace and my vulnerability, the voice that was recognisably not my own, said clearly, "Lybbestre, Mistress Alchimia and divine veleda, it is hallowed Samhain and with moon phosphorus, we have prepared the portals of the way. When you wish it, I will part all the gates."

A woman stepped from the black pillar of lightlessness within the yew. She was wearing long and shapeless white, her hair was white and her eyes were milky, like pearls within the oyster's shadow. Her mouth was thin and wide and stern and her face was all bone, both womanly and masculine. She walked, head high, into the glade and she looked only at Vespasian. She was my mother.

CHAPTER FORTY-EIGHT

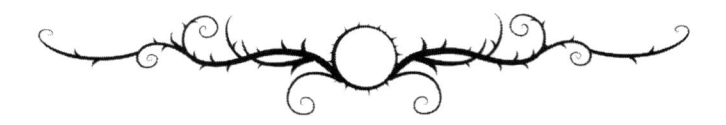

It was more than two years since I had seen my mother but she had changed very little. Even her milky half blind eyes had neither relinquished more of their colour, nor cleared to full sight.

She took no notice of me at all but I had been used to that since a child. She spoke only to Vespasian. Had she spoken to me, I could not have answered. I was paralysed by shock.

"You are not Vespasian," she said to him. I knew her voice. It was the same, flat and a little harsh, sentences ending unbalanced with a hint of madness.

He looked at her impassively, unblinking and without emotion, but his eyelids were heavy and the curved lashes hid the glitter. He was poised for either defence or attack and probably for both. "In this life I am Jasper Cesare," he said, announcing himself as softly as always. Even a demon could be forced to listen. "I am Baron de Vrais of Demis-Bayeux, Gloucester and Stourbury. I am holder of the seal of Thoth and you know me, for it is many years since I first called you. Vespasian is a name I took, because of its association. Its symbolism binds us. You have always known it is not who I am now, though perhaps it is who I once was."

The group around Arthur had grown, each creeping forward to

cross the hidden boundaries, sword gripped with whitening knuckles. Then the quick release of breath once under the open moonlight, and still alive within the glade. I stood a little behind Vespasian now, sheltering in his shadow and clutching at his gloved hand. Gerald stood to his other side, very still and silent as he had been ordered and also because he could not have spoken even if it were asked of him, but his sword was unsheathed.

My mother lifted her chin and said, "Yes, I know who you are and you know me." Then, for the first time, she looked around.

She was taller, perhaps, than I remembered her. For all the years in the asylum I had seen her only in bed, sometimes apathetic, always incoherent and then later comatose. I had forgotten that she towered over me. Now she looked down on me and her wild white hair echoed the moon's aura. She shook it back from her face, ghost's mane, uncombed in twenty years, a thorn bush without obedience to gravity. I stared back at her and she gazed on me as if a spark of curiosity wavered behind the milk smear of her pupils. But she was not blind. She saw me clearly and completely as she saw all of us. Then, to my utter amazement, she smiled. It was like a lizard smiling, a stretching of the wide thin lips, an exercise that the mouth had forgotten or perhaps had never known and was utterly unpractised. It was, incredibly, more than an acknowledgement, it was approval. "The daughter they gave me," she addressed me, "when I asked. The daughter to keep the gates. You have opened them for me many times when I commanded you. But I see you have grown beyond such simple servitude. The man at your side has empowered himself through violence, taking the right to stand in your place, to close the gates as he wills it and to move your destiny. But he cannot always keep the paths. Without you in his presence, he would need to replenish the power constantly through force. Do you know that, with or without him, you can still open and close the doorway of your own volition?"

I stared at her with my mouth open and my head thumping and all my heart and my brains bundled together in dishevelled confusion. I risked speaking. "No," I said, as clearly as I could with my tongue twice its size and seemingly stuck to my palette. "I understand not one single word of what you tell me. It was always like this. I never understood you."

"How could you have?" said the veleda, looking down on me through my mother's face. "I am seer and diviner, I am goddess and prophet and represent alchemy at source. I have reincarnated many times. I was called back once more into the life we shared by this man who calls himself Vespasian. With the dark power and the light, he summoned me from my grave beyond graves. At his call I returned to life, but no human body could hold me. I took one that I would discard at will, but one that could birth a daughter. When you were sent, I received you, deciding it would suffice, and I taught you to swim between worlds. Through your small child's heart, I spun you back here many times. I taught you to open the way."

"He called you?" I whispered, looking from Vespasian to my mother.

"And Lilith used the way, whenever it opened," Arthur said, interrupting from behind me. "She used it for her own pleasure and patronage and glory." He moved closer and I felt the brush of his sleeve as he pushed past me, facing the veleda, the sorceress who had been my mother. I cringed, hating his proximity and the stink of his voice, yet his face shone in awe of the divinity before him. "You made no attempt to close the doors to Lilith," he addressed the veleda. "So tell me, which do you support? Do you stand for the Blood or the Dragon?"

The veleda stared at him from her greater height, all impassive majesty. "Lilith allows no other to speak in her place. She will ask me herself when she comes, if she wishes to know. I do not acknowledge her slaves. I will not speak to the worms who worship her. She is on the path now, for her way has been opened."

"But you will answer me," Vespasian interrupted, soft and gentle as the rain that was now falling, and even to her there was the hint of threat in his voice, "for you are here only because of me, and because I summoned you, and it is my power that determined your rebirth. Now tell me, why did you use this child? Throughout history and in all your incarnations, you have always opened the gateways yourself."

"All history is beyond your scope," she said, turning back to him. "You cannot judge my choices. But that one choice, in your ignorance, was yours. It was you, human dabbler, demanding my return in human form, even though I have grown so far beyond you all that of necessity a human body could not support my strength. You summoned me and so I was reborn, but the body fractured into madness. I required a living representative. The daughter I created was strong and sane and would obey me. She will still obey, for she has not yet discovered all the powers I have given her."

"I have no powers," I said, though she had not spoken to me.

"You have many," she answered, turning back to me and the little reptilian smile flicked across her mouth. "Do you think I'd bring a foetal reflection into my womb? You will discover all your powers, in time. I give you the freedom to exercise them for good or evil, as you desire. There is joy in both."

I looked away from her and put my free hand against the hard leather of my belt, behind which nestled the ouroboros. The rain was sleety and the sun had sunk into total dissolution. It was rich black around the moon's halo, and the rain caught the light in webs and snail slime. The glade was drenched in promise. My cloak sheltered me but I was bitterly cold.

"It is the witching hour," I quoted softly to my toes, "and Hell itself breathes out contagion to this world."

"Yes," said my mother's voice. "There have been many who knew the secrets, and practised the art without the knowledge of the simple bluff world they inhabited." Although I still understood little of what she said, it was the first time we had communicated so clearly since I was a small child at her skirts.

"Who is Lilith?" I asked her. The silence around me now shivered into breathless excitement. I had asked the question for myself but the answer would be for them all.

The veleda continued to look at me with interest and a vague approval. "Adam's first partner, his and all men's shadow and the eternal threat," said my mother. "She has other names. Baphomet, the hermaphrodite deity is one. She is a power of evil far greater than Lucifer, for he was only angelic subterfuge and simple corruption, the pallid disguise which slipped into wickedness for fear of Good. Lilith has never known anything other than evil."

Arthur stepped forward again, and Joanna came beside him. They dared to face my mother. "Lilith is the greatest power," said Arthur, all pride. "She personifies it. She and evil, they are united."

The veleda smiled her frog smile and looked from her white eyes down her white nose at the man, black hooded, black breathed, who stared up at her. "Evil does not unite," she said in contempt. "Evil scatters, for it hates and mistrusts everything including itself. Evil supports no follower. Beware evil until your own power grows."

"We have all the power we need," said Joanna coolly. "And if Lilith uses us, because we wish her to, then we also use her gifts."

"Lilith sells, but she makes no gifts," said the veleda. "And her power is not ultimate. Even I and my door keeper can refuse her entrance between the worlds."

And my voice moved away from my mind as it did when the gatekeeper spoke, and I said to my mother, "Then stand aside, for she is coming and you will welcome her, as you have always done, for she is your mother as you are mine."

She came through the broken yew as the veleda had, but she came with a snarl, leaping and huge. I stumbled and would have fallen if Vespasian had not supported me. Even Arthur, Joanna and the few of his group who had so far entered the magic glade, scurried backwards. She was a great gleaming toad, legs bent up, knees apart and feet together, balanced forwards on her clawed finger tips. She had the mule teeth and the curved ripe canines I had seen before, and her eyes were seeping blood, striped like crackling scarlet patina with a crocodile pupil. Her nose was smashed hog-like into her bones but her hands were clawed and long, each finger twisting independent like snakes crawling from her palm. At first I thought she was clothed in fire but then I saw her skin was a chameleon's and although sometimes she was explicitly visible in naked hermaphrodite duplicity, then she merged with the darkness and the grasses and the rain and became both sexes and all things, for she was everything's darkest shadow.

Had she not demanded I look at her, I could not have faced what disgusted me so deeply. I kept forgetting to breathe. But it was, absurdly, exactly as Vespasian had told me, for I stood central to them all. Arthur and Joanna, with the others crowding excitedly around them, were ignored.

"So, the little bitch is the keeper, as was established without precedence." Lilith straightened, unbending and rising, gradually becoming the woman. She turned to face my mother. "And you, emperor's whore, you have never shared your power before. Why now?"

It was what Vespasian had asked her, but faced with Lilith, my mother gave a different answer. "To anger you," she said.

Which is when Vespasian, who still held my hand hot and crushed in his grip, spoke loud and very distinctly for the first time that I ever remembered. His voice carried, wind born, with stark clarity. It sounded more incantation than conversation. "Hell's debris, swiving excrement of forgotten and obsolete kingdoms," he said, looking at both creatures. "Many years ago when I summoned the veleda and the gate was opened for Lilith, I gained what knowledge and power I sought and you took the payment you demanded, which I have given fully and without retaliation, being a just purse. Your jealousies and bickering are now futile, for in the end you service one master or another, and hate us all. Meanwhile, my repayment is witnessed, upheld and completed. Now I have my own price to demand, for I hold the gatekeeper and through her, the path. This night I demand the destruction of the forces of destruction. Neither of you have seen your danger."

Lilith turned back to us with a screech, black leather wings appeared from her shoulders and she squatted like a harpy, spitting flame. "Be still," she said. "You cannot challenge me," but she looked to the yew and its rigid, rapidly narrowing shadow.

"I have closed the pathway," said Vespasian, his voice sinking back to its usual malefic hush. "I hold you both within this nemeton. You cannot leave. Unless you pay my price."

The tree had closed with a snap like the sudden breaking of thick glass. The rain streamed through its spiky tangle of leaf and the pool shuddered with rippled reflections from moon and magic. I looked at Vespasian. I had thought his clasp on my hand was for my protection but it had been much more. With the gatekeeper's power between his fingers and the right he had previously forced on her and ripped from me, he had now shut the gates between worlds.

"The sweet arrogance of humanity," said my mother without visible rancour. "But the power over the pathway is not yours by right. You have stolen the place from my appointed daughter and soon you must repay it."

"I will take payment now," said Lilith. "The time has come to take the last card."

The two creatures stood and looked down on me, one all creased and dirty white like the woman I remembered from the asylum, the other flowing folds of crocodile skin. I was symbolic of deity myself and could look back without lowering my eyes, though I had once again forgotten to breathe. Vespasian's strength beside me seemed increasingly immense. To his other side Gerald continued to stand straight, all young princeling, waiting for his turn. He faced the horrors that must have astonished him, with a courage I admired and had not expected. Arthur and his huddled clan seemed quite superfluous, having neither voice nor presence. Joanna was muttering to her husband but he waited, as we all did, to see what would happen.

The dark closed in darker and the silver shrank, now just a simple round moon in a deep October sky. "Cut the pack," said Lilith.

This time I could see the tarot cards and they were my own. The pack of Thoth designed by Aleister Crowley was held out to me, face downwards, with their coloured crosses bright in the rain sparkle. "Do not touch the cards," Vespasian said at once. "Stand apart and do not touch the pack."

Lilith's claws cupped the tarot, curved and gilt. She grinned into Vespasian's face. "Then take the card for her," she said, all sudden sweetness, her claws still tight gripped. "You sweated and grunted, claiming this right. I do not deny it. I watched you. So be her puppet now, and choose the card. I am waiting."

"Then wait," said Vespasian, "for I will not cut a tarocchi pack that you have spoiled and slimed. Some of these cards are missing. Bring the pack of Hermes, and I will cut it for the path-holder."

"I am the diviner of the cards," breathed Lilith with a growl. "I do not desecrate my own tools. Be careful what you accuse me of, human. I am waiting. Cut the pack."

For a moment he let me go. In releasing my hand, I felt a chill like ice moving into my veins, as if my support had left me boneless. Vespasian stepped towards Lilith and struck her hand upwards. I could not believe he had done it. I could not believe he had touched her. Then, in seconds, he was back with me and had briefly retaken my hand, his other arm around my shoulders, and my blood heaved back into the easy warmth of normal circulation.

Hurtling and spinning, Lilith's cards scattered. Colours in a fountain, tumbling one on another around our feet and the tufted wet grass. I heard such a gasp from Arthur and his followers, like waves on a beach. Myself, I was still barely breathing at all.

Lilith sprang, teeth and nails bared, but she never reached us. Vespasian faced her, sword in one hand and the seal of Thoth raised towards her in the other. Beside him, on Vespasian's orders I had drawn my own sword and the ouroboros I held up in my other hand. I saw Gerald, half dazed, also raise his sword high and it caught the moon shine and seemed to sing.

To my complete amazement, Lilith cowered back, dropping again to toad squatting, eyes glaring but lowered. "I do not have the cards of Hermes," she said. I believed it to be an acknowledgement that Vespasian was right. The cards she'd offered had been doctored.

"But I have," said Vespasian clearly. "I have the pack of Hermes here."

CHAPTER FORTY-NINE

They were around us now, almost half perhaps of the crow clad worshippers, Arthur's cult and Lilith's adorers. Steadily overpowering the forces of the nemeton, breathing in the presence of the dark, shuffling closer like circling wolves though shifting uncertainly, many now summoned strength to pass the threat of the boundaries. Now they waited only to see what their leader would do to us.

The veleda stood aside as if she had little interest in the play of forces beyond her vision. She neither judged nor showed emotion, but she watched and something behind the flickering pale eyes proved intent. I did not look at her. Intimidating as she had always seemed to me, I could not trust her detachment nor her equanimity. I realised then that though Lilith was evil itself, the veleda represented neither love nor hate, but absolute amorality which would not attack nor support me.

Gerald, myself and Vespasian faced Lilith as she took the pack of cards that Vespasian handed her. It seemed she disliked their touch. Between her claws I could see their parchment beauty, hand painted in gold leaf with raised mercurial lines, liquid, slithering and smooth.

They smelled of something that reminded me of home. It was another sort of power. Happiness, perhaps.

Beneath my feet spread the scattered tumble of the cards of Thoth, my own, now just wet cardboard. Lilith held out the cards that Vespasian had given her. "If you touch me again," she spat at him, "I will flay you from prick to knee. Now, cut the pack." And Vespasian smiled, leaned forward, and took a card.

He turned it over. It was number seventeen of the major arcana, the card of The Star.

The card was me. I saw myself in his hands, kneeling on the banks of the cold pool I loved, half into the water which was silver ripples around my legs. I was naked as Vespasian had found me there before, and my brown hair, sun tinted, curled like a cloak across my shoulders. Behind me eight stars glistened so vividly that they blinded, card to eye. One star was the larger and I looked up to the sky above the glade and saw it shine also there. The tarocchi stars moved in an arc through paper and ink, and the paper water swung around my paper knees. I looked from the card to the pool among the trees, for it was also there, and the gentle ripples were the same.

I felt great peace and sighed, looking up at Vespasian. The card's spangled stars were so bright, they under lit his cheekbones. But it was not until I saw the sincerity of his smile that I realised he had not been completely confident of picking the right number.

A bitter wind was building, swirled and curling in the trees above our heads. I heard its force and watched its anger turn to fury, so that black leaf scattered across the moon and hurled screeching into the glade. A witch's wind, a turmoil of infuriation, and the branches swayed and crashed one against the other, creaking as if to break and whipping up the leaves that had already blown. The gale cannoned into tornadoes of stinging twig, bark and foliage.

I tugged my cloak around myself as the hood was flung from my head. Vespasian held me tighter. Gerald moved closer. We all recognised the increasing threat of something coming, more than wind or storm, but heralded by the powers of nature.

Arthur jostled, furious, striding over, his own cloak slapped against his body and streamed behind him. "I deny your right to take the card for the path-holder," he shouted over the tumult. "I challenge your place. Make her pick the card for herself. Make her cut the pack again."

"Fool," said Lilith, turning momentarily to Arthur. Her long tails of thin hair were in her face, tangled into the blood oozing from her eyes. "You dare challenge? You accuse me of ignorance? Is destiny not mine and tarocchi not my slave? Everything has been done according to the rites." She stretched out her clawed arm and Arthur was swept aside like loose parchment. The card of The Star lay on the grass at our feet. Above it, Lilith snarled, still spitting, at Vespasian. "But now I claim you," she growled, "and I will eat you this night as I told you I would. Yes, you have paid the price demanded for once worshipping at my altar and for the power I gave you and the knowledge I taught you. I took your wife in splendid sacrifice and I received your earthly ruin, all sweetly ravished by my new acolytes. That debt is paid. But you are still a foresworn traitor and now I come for you."

Vespasian stood unmoving, his legs straight and a little apart, well balanced. In one hand he still held his sword, in the other, the seal of Thoth. Fiery hieroglyphs raced across the intaglio. The mark of the Ibis was clear white within the etched triangle, and the triangle within the square, the square within the circle. The flames did not burn but they lit his hand so it seemed they danced by his control.

"Yes, I have come as the final sacrifice." He spoke very clearly, his voice again raised. "But first you must learn how to claim me. If you touch me now, you will burn. Already your source is stifled. I have closed the gates and you have no recourse to the Underworld. Look to your black breath before it is choked from you. I am holder of the seal of Thoth and this is my witness. I stand in place of the Way-Holder and she is my witness. My power is greater than any other human here, and you are my witness."

My hands were shaking and if someone had attacked me, my sword would have struck only grass. I gripped the little circular snake tightly and watched Lilith hesitate and step back, the heavy folds of her skin swaying. Then I could feel someone behind me and when something touched me on the shoulder, I jumped as though beaten. When I whirled around I saw Uta. I could still see why I had once wanted to be like her.

The steely drizzle had become flying ice and although Uta's hair was wet and her blonde plaits swung and curved like little plump eels twisting around her head, the rain made them gleam and she remained beautiful. Her eyes were almond, blue, soft, and filled with shining tears from the sting of the wind. "Do you know," she said sweetly, "why Jasper can demand the right to take the card in your place? He chose a card that saved your destiny, but not for your own salvation. He now has the power to control the paths between what is above and what is below, though only while you're placid, too stupid and cowed to fight him. He believes he's beaten and conquered the gatekeeper and now all the power is his, but do you know how you were tamed? Can you imagine what he did to you in Arthur's castle?"

I shivered. I should have ignored her but I couldn't. "Yes, I know," I answered.

"I'll tell you anyway," she said, "because I don't believe you know."

I looked up at Vespasian. "She will tell you the truth," he said softly, still aware of my presence though his eyes were on Lilith and not on me, and I knew he was ready for her. He had waited many long years for this night. He knew and welcomed whatever it would bring. "Let her tell you, if you wish it," he murmured. "You have always demanded answers to your questions and I have always denied them. I'll risk your hatred. Perhaps now it is time you knew everything."

Time seemed to stand very still and the stars arched and spun as they had in my tarot card. I felt terribly alone, separated from everything else so that now I saw neither Vespasian nor any of the others except Uta. I looked at my feet. Between my shoes and their wet, bedraggled bows, and amongst the scattered spread of the tarocchi pack Vespasian had discredited, was a single white rose. I was standing on Ingrid's grave.

I turned to Uta. "I don't care what Vespasian did," I shouted at her. "I don't care if he still craves power. He's welcome to mine."

"Because you lust after him, but he pledged himself to me," hissed

Uta. "Arthur held him chained in the dungeons but he swore he'd be mine if I released him, and I did. He swore on Lilith's altar but he left me and went to you. Now he's foresworn and that's why she's claiming him now. So I have asked, and Lilith has agreed. She will eat him at midnight."

I hated her so much it hurt. "He doesn't seem overawed at the prospect," I said. I could no longer see him but I could hear him. Somewhere distant I could hear his laugh. I wondered what he could possibly have to laugh at.

"Do you know, I watched while he raped you?" smiled Uta. She licked her lips. She only wanted to disgust me but I believed her. "Did you think he'd do it without an audience? He wanted a witness and I stood at his side."

Over the mounting winds, I could hear her. "I don't care," I yelled in her face, though I lied, and I cared with all my heart. "He told me. I know why he did what he had to do. I won't listen to you."

"You will," said Uta. "You have the power of the gatekeeper but no magic and no alchemy. You will listen to every word because I tell you to."

I held tightly to the ouroboros, my sword still in the other hand. "I am protected too," I said. "There is also magic in my life."

"He stripped you," she persisted, "and strapped you to the pillars of Lilith's altar. I watched. He was vicious. So brutal. I thought he would break your back. He climbed on the great stone slab and straddled you. Then he whipped and burned you before he raped you. Were you a virgin? Of course you were. I watched you sob and bleed."

Through the screaming gale the mists rolled briefly back and I saw the black hunched crowd of Arthur's people, moving, massing, rushing from the edges of the glade to its centre. The storm had weakened the power of the trees.

There was more Uta wanted to tell me, all plumply eager with her delicious memories, like the miller's daughter drawing the hot, crusty loaves from the depths of her oven. I was saved by my mother. She interrupted, saying, "They are coming closer. Soon the two realms will touch. You have given your power to the mortal and he has closed the gates, but if you do not reopen them, the collision will kill you both."

I stared back at her. "I trust Vespasian," I said. "I'll do nothing without him." But I was no longer sure I trusted Vespasian. What Uta said had hurt. Knowing it, and hearing it from her, was very different.

Now I wondered if this was Vespasian's plan, to annihilate Arthur and all his brood, ourselves, the power of alchemy which he now repudiated, and Lilith in our midst. It was a sad ambition but I was prepared to die for a thirst like that. I was prepared to lose my life, as Vespasian was, if all this evil and the horror that was Lilith died with us. But the mists in my mind were thicker than those in the glade, with no moonshine in my thoughts.

"Perhaps you're right to trust him," my mother said, looking over my head at Lilith's shadow and the focus of the storm. "He chose the right card, though Lilith had hoped for others. She tried to influence his hand. He avoided her malice."

So I had realised. "What did she want me to pick?" I whispered.

"The Devil of course," said the veleda. "Or perhaps Death. Even The Tower would have served her purpose and put you into her power. Best of all would have been The World, for that is her own card and personal to her."

"And if I had?"

"As the gate-keeper, you would have belonged to her," said my mother, "as she believes you should by right."

"Do you cut cards?" I asked. "Is life just a game?"

She nodded. "I cut the pack, when she demands it," she said. "We all walk a fate symbolised by Lilith's cards of destiny. I am The Priestess and that is my card. I know my path."

I was adjusting. Uta had gone, running to Malcolm's side at my mother's appearance. I was isolated now, a pocket of time that held just myself and the veleda. The glade could tighten or remove us as it wished. Even Lilith's storm now barely touched us, just a flurry and an echo of the roar beyond. "So," I said, trying to keep my breath steady. "May I ask the same question that Arthur asked of you at the beginning? Whose side are you on? His, or Vespasian's?"

"I take no sides," she said. "There is no such thing as side. Life is the challenge of growth fulfilling potential, an endless clamber towards perfection, whether the perfection of beauty and love, or of perfect malefic evil. True spirit is beyond right and wrong. That is what alchemy is all about. Your lover knows this."

"He's not my lover," I sighed. "He's never made love to me. He raped me, just to gain power."

"Of course," she said. "What else could he do? Are you squeamish about such things?"

I stared at her. I reminded myself she was inhuman, and even less my mother than the mad woman I'd once known her to be. "Yes," I said dully. "I'm strangely prejudiced about such things. So tell me, why did he have to do it?"

"You delay me," she said, frowning down her long nose. "You remind me of the daughter I once let you be. You ask questions that are not your business to ask."

"It's not my business to know why I was raped?" The wind was leaking through the hushed walls of our isolation. I had to raise my voice.

"To dominate the gatekeeper takes great control. It must be done with pain and violence and intimidation," said my mother, watching the shimmer of the rain from the wild black sky. We were once again entering the storm. "Your essence could never be taken by any creature or any assault unworthy of you. Holding you prisoner, Arthur imposed pain in blood. To take you from Arthur, Vespasian exercised the only greater and more personal violence that exists. Had he not done this, as the gatekeeper you would have become Arthur's, and the servant of Lilith. The man you call Vespasian saw what the creature Arthur had done to you, and so to take you as his own, exerted a greater torture to supersede and overwhelm that which had already been done in Lilith's name. Perhaps in your humanity you whine in self pity, but the Way Holder I called upon to represent me between the worlds, can only be subjugated by a dominance as lofty as her own."

"I'm Molly," I said, shouting now over the newly released winds.

"I'm Tilda too, who is not your daughter. I feel nothing inside me of this other creature, this keeper of gates, this thing you call me."

"I allowed you too much humanity," sneered the veleda. "So, he hurt you, this pitiful man, and you complain? Yet he took you so easily. What of a little suffering? Many humans live by it and wallow in it. The suscipient of torture is flattered by the torturer's concentrated attention. His delight in her is ultimate. Lilith brings pleasure to many through pain, both to bestow and to receive."

I winced. "I know why you don't take sides." I shuddered. "You see beauty where I feel revulsion. And Vespasian takes no pleasure in – causing pain."

"And if he lies?" suggested my mother. "All humanity lies and especially to themselves. This is the man that once called me from the peace of my grave, to answer his own craving for knowledge. At that time the judgement between good and evil was not one he chose to make. You must know he is capable of cruelty, even though he believes in a higher motive than mere pleasure. What of it? As your mother I taught you pain and the strength it brings. You've weakened since I left you."

"You taught me hate," I said, sounding childish and sullen.

She smiled, same lizard lip stretch and a flick of the tongue. "I will tell you one more thing," she said, "before we must return to the battle. This pathetic sensitivity and your physical denial of sweet degradation does not interest me in the least. My body birthed yours but that does not unite us, nor bind me to responsibility. In some previous life long ago, you might have been my mother. You will never know. It's as my spiritual representative by the Gateway that we are united, and my watcher by the path does not snivel about a little discomfort. She also, like the pallid child Mathilda, was virgin. None had ripped her integrity from her before. Now she respects the dominance that stole her power by force. But power you still have, and will always have. So the one last thing I tell you, before I take my place at Lilith's shoulder, is this. When you return to the body of my physical daughter, come to visit me before I die. I have arranged my end and it will come quickly, so you will have to hurry. I have a gift for you, which I will give you when you come to witness my physical disintegration. A special gift. It is not any longer the gift of pain which taught you strength, nor one of love, which I have never had to give. But it is a gift you will value as you have valued no other."

I began to answer, but she had gone. So I stood there, staring into the blizzard, with my eyes half blind and my hair all tangled around my head. I was still clutching the ouroboros but it was offering me no protection against the wilderness of attack and the battering of wind, rain and ice. I could not see Vespasian. I could not even see Arthur, Uta, or any of them. The air was filled with flying debris and the manic swirl of leaf and branch. I heard the creak of falling trees but all I saw was Lilith.

She squatted and the flesh of her thighs rolled to the ground around her like a frill of skirts. Her body continued to change, swollen and discoloured. The storm centred her, snatched from nature, an indiscriminate attack, a great heaving tidal sea of pulsing violence. She was still summoning turmoil as the veleda went back to her side, standing calmly within the tornado. Almost untouched by the chaos, my mother looked across at me, speaking again without emotion. "The collision that must occur if you do not take back the power to open the ways, will destroy you," she said. "And that is not the destiny of The Star."

"I don't know how," I screamed back at her. I couldn't even hear my own voice over the screech of the wind, but I could hear hers.

"Fool," she said to me. "Know yourself. Know your strengths and take them within you. Intend it and the gates will open."

I couldn't hold onto intention nor onto anything except the ouroboros. I was lifted by the storm and felt myself fly. My cloak turned to ice and I dropped my sword.

I faced the stars. For a moment I didn't know if I was looking at my tarocchi card or the real night sky and whether the smashing trees around me were fantasy or nightmare. I even wondered if this was only the dark sadness that always came after an interlude with my mother, sending me as usual into my other world, my secret place, that was secret no longer.

Then I saw Uta. Her mouth was huge, a scarlet circle of terror filling her face as the same wind that lifted me, lifted her. But not quite the same wind. I had thought the ouroboros was no match for the storm but the violence that spun Uta, carried me gently below her as though I drifted on breezes like an uncrushed autumn leaf. Instead, as I watched her, she was gripped and pirouetted by a bizarre and horrifying force. I continued to watch as her hair, those two gorgeous plaits I'd once imagined around my own face, were torn from her head in swirls of blood. Her scalp was left bare and white, but razed crimson in a thousand cut ribbons. I could not hear her scream though I saw her throat swell with it. She sped on and up, still spinning, a maniacal puppet caught in a frenzied hurricane, battered now by hail that tore at her flayed skin, the clothes swept from her, and finally, as I still watched because I could do nothing else, both flailing arms revolved in their sockets and were ripped loose, spinning free, grasping alone at the cloud blurred stars.

Distorted, naked, armless, hairless and dissolving in blood, she continued up. I had always thought the underworld to be down. I had been wrong.

I floated back to earth, soft as a duckling feather.

Joanna and Arthur stood together, facing Lilith and my mother and between them they held Gerald. I had no idea what had happened to Vespasian. For one crazy, stunning moment I imagined him flying, armless and screaming, in the gigantic horror of the storm above us. Then I blinked and turned to Gerald. "They can't keep you," I said to him. I pointed the ouroboros at Arthur. "Let him go."

With a snort of derision, Joanna grabbed Gerald around the throat. I could see the pointed spikes of her finger nails pressing into the young, pink skin. Gerald choked. Arthur stood beside his wife, gripping Gerald by shoulder and wrist. "Open the gates," said Arthur, "or we'll kill him."

"You've no power over me," said my voice, which was not my voice. "You dare not touch me. What interest does the holder of the paths have for a human child? Your power is a puny thing compared to mine. You cannot do or say anything to make me obey you."

"That is true," said a soft voice directly behind me. "But I believe I can." And as I sank back against Vespasian in relief and delight, the point of his knife came slipping very sharp and bright and cold around my neck and pressed taught against my throat, its point pricking deep into the skin. "Now," he said, lost malice blown in the retiring force of the winds, "if you do not obey exactly what I tell you, immediately and in explicit detail, I shall kill you at once."

CHAPTER FIFTY

I stood very still with my pulse racing, leopard ambush, jungle fever. I was lost in unknown territory. I was more Tilda now than Molly, and wanted to cry out to him, *but I love you*.

He held me, his long knife against my neck and his arm now fast around my chest, crushing my breasts as he gripped me tightly back against him. My breathing was restricted and my gasping burned with a taste of sulphur and mercury, the poisons of alchemy in my mouth.

Around us two dozen bodies or more were scattered, decapitated and ripped in pieces across the wet grass, gutted moans in the dark. I saw that Uta had not been the only one slaughtered in muddy, bloody and devastating dislocation. I believed Lilith had happily murdered her own supporters. She stood before us now, stone gargoyle, immovable snarl.

It was still raining but the wind had slowed to a groan, wood creaking and the gentle rumble of turbulence through the remaining leaves. I was frightened to move. "You will speak no word of any kind," Vespasian said to me. "You will not order the merging of the ways or the parting of the Styx. You will not unite the worlds and you will not open the gates. You will be silent, or I will kill you."

Joanna still clutched Gerald, one hand hooked into the collar of his cloak, the other tight around his neck. "You'll not kill her," she said to Vespasian, glaring white faced in the moonlight. "She's your whore. You've not the courage to kill her."

Vespasian's voice came calmly from just a little behind and above my ear. "And you, who killed your own daughter in a welter of agony and the bloody flaying of flesh, could not understand my painless execution of a demon's daughter?"

The moon, released from the confines of the storm, glowed brighter now behind the lacery of tree branches. "If you kill her," croaked Arthur, furiously, "you condemn us all. Why would you die yourself, only to spite us?"

"Oh," said Vespasian and I knew that he would be smiling, "my desire for your utter annihilation is not spite, I assure you. My wish comes from a holy determination and I will not be crossed. Your death will come tonight, whether it includes my own or not."

"I don't believe you," rasped Arthur. "You've never planned your own death."

"As usual, you are wrong," said Vespasian, so softly that I could barely hear him and I was as close to him as I had ever been. "I have never feared pain or hardship, least of all, the grave. Death stands in every one of Lilith's cards, not only the black painted skeleton of the tarocchi. Now you can choose your own death, d'Estropier, since control is what you long for. Stay as you are, and it will be at your own connivance. Or, if you are not yet prepared to die, let go my son."

The pressure of his knife edge, sharpened and honed like a cock's spurs for the fight, cut a little deeper and stung like the devil. The point gouged a little further up and under my chin. My jaw was forced upwards, or my neck would have been slit. I smelled the warmth of my own blood.

Joanna was wrenching at Gerald's wrist as he began to struggle, but she was trying to keep her dignity. "If we let my grandson return to you," she said, "will you open the door between the worlds? Will you do it at once?"

Gerald, in wretched and puzzled misery, opened his mouth to speak. I wasn't sure if he would beg Joanna for his own life, or

Vespasian for mine. Vespasian looked at him, cold and implacable. "You will say nothing," he ordered him. "You will be silent." Gerald bowed his head and sighed, becoming still.

Under my feet, and way beyond the pain of Vespasian's knife, I felt the rumble and quake of the collision mounting. I heard the echoed calling of the souls approaching on the path, half way to us and crying that they were blocked and the way turned against them. Hallowe'en's ghosts had arrived, with nowhere to go. I could hear them knocking. Their anger and their lost confusion vibrated through my toes and up through the pulse of my heart, down my fingers and spun through my head. My own needs swam the same wave with theirs as they called on their gatekeeper to open the way, all wistful, desperate supplication. I heard them and could not answer. They were streaming through the valley, pushing forwards, their part blind eyes peering through the mists towards the doorway where the shine of their past lives should have been opening brightness to them, but I had muted the moon voice and their way was hushed. I began to cry. I leaned out to ease their shuddering but my mind could not touch them. Their yearning for the warmth was blocked. I stood useless, with tears pouring down my face and mixing, salt sting, with the blood on my neck.

Vespasian said to Arthur and Joanna, "You will release the boy, and once he is back at my side, I will open the gate and we shall all be saved, for the moment. But first you must swear his freedom. On Lilith's eyes, swear you will make no further claim on Gerald, either by blood or by birth, by title or by greed. Otherwise I will kill the keeper and you will be lost forever, even though I shall join you on the highway. Hell's gates are wide enough to accept you all and they do not need me to open them for you."

As Arthur muttered his agreement, Joanna released Gerald. It was so sudden that he stumbled, but quickly regained his boots, and, grabbing his sword, turned back to his grandmother. His voice was unsteady. "You killed my mother. I think you killed my father."

"But it is your step father that just wanted to kill you," said Joanna.

"Come here," interrupted Vespasian. "I will not tell you twice. Come here, beside me."

Gerald stared around, and lowered his sword. Meekly, he went to Vespasian's other side, all the time trying not to look at me. Then he stood solid, sword in hand, glaring at his grandparents. "I hope I get the chance to kill you myself, before the end," he said, but they were already backing away.

"Now," spat Arthur, "open the gates."

Vespasian removed his knife from my throat and turned me at once in his arms, so that my head was against his shoulder, my blood on his mantle and my body crushed against the silky velvet of his cotte. I was still crying on his pearls when, with the knife tucked back into the cuff of his boots, he moved his free hand up into my hair, holding me steady, caressingly close.

"Are you ready for this?" he whispered to me.

I had not been ready for any of it. "They are calling at the gates," I said in a desperation I could neither control nor understand. "You must let them in. It is the utmost misery. Don't you hear them? Don't you pity them?"

For one astonishing moment I thought he kissed the top of my hair. "I am sorry, piccina," he whispered, "for all that I do to you." Then, without letting me go, I heard him speak the incantation, very softly so that it became a chant, hazy in my mind. "As it is above, so it is below, and let them be combined this night. Samhain, hallowed gateway of the Underworld, let them through. In the name of Janus and of the veleda, part the river and let them through. Without coinage or challenge, on this one midnight toll, Charon roll back the Styx and let them through. I have the Right, I hold the staff and I demand the gates flung wide. I open the way to all worlds and as the falling horizon no longer divides the macrocosm from the microcosm, let all be one."

And so they came. They did not come through the yew tree or from the small graves beside the pools. They came from beyond the nemeton, drifting past us like the melting of candle wax, soft colours all lost in swirls of fog, shining faces and happy eyes, the gift of breath for one last night, they came and they passed by us, wandering out into the heaths and the woods and the fields, searching for those they had once loved, and lost.

I sighed, standing back for them to pass. My tears had dried, but Vespasian still held me tight. "Do you see them?" I asked him gently. "Do you see the light in their smiles? This is how it must be. You cannot bolt the door. Not on Samhain for the worlds revolve too close and must intertwine."

"I see them," Vespasian answered me. "But in shadows, the passing light within the shade. I may have taken the right to your place and your power, child, but I do not share all your magic."

Slowly they faded also from my eyes, and I was Tilda once more. I breathed deeply again. "Would you really have killed me?" I asked him, "if Arthur and Joanna had not let Gerald go?"

He did not look into my eyes. "Perhaps," he said to the air. "There are some things more important than life."

"And you had to convince them so – emphatically? I wish it had been more nominal and less explicit." The pain of the cut stung insistently.

"You do realise, don't you, zuleikha," he said softly, "that this night we might all die, whatever I am able to do? It is important only that Arthur and all his people also perish."

"And Lilith?" I whispered.

I heard her. She was behind me, and I thought she was laughing. "No human can kill me," she was cackling and slime leaked from her snout. But she had been suffocating. I had seen her and felt it. When Vespasian had closed the gates against her, she had suffered, confined, drowning in bubbles of her own poison. She had crept quietly to a corner of the glade, unseen and small shadowed. Now she could breathe again and was swelling with budding strength. "Your fool of a human thought he killed me when he stabbed the body of my fetch. But Thomas Cambio was no more myself than the other thousand bodies I've inhabited."

The divinity in me sprang again. I was losing my grasp on the knowledge my other self held, but the spirit of the path keeper remained. I stared up at Lilith. "If the gates had not been unlocked, you would have strangled in your own bile," I said. "Not death, perhaps, but paralysis until I myself died, my person replaced by another opener of the way."

She had not yet returned to her full self. "Ignorant bitch," she said. "You think because I lost you in the cutting of the cards, I've no further weapons against you? I can still claim you. The man who stands in your place and now controls the doorway, has yet to cut the cards himself. But this time, as he chooses for you, you shall take it for him."

The glade had changed. All around us the trees leaned down, listening to everything we said, trunks bending in the darkness, creaking and yawning in the echoes of the wind. Many had broken in the storm, now shattered branches and torn bark. The others had closed in and the space left to us, where the pools still gleamed their misted banks, was narrowing. Within now stood the remains of Arthur's cult, decimated by those many killed in the storm. Arthur stood directly behind Lilith, with Joanna to one side and Malcolm to the other, more than sixty others at his back. They had waited a long time for Lilith to finish her games and lead them. Without her orders they would do nothing, but they were itching to fight. They had come for many reasons, but most of all to kill Vespasian, and myself.

I faced Lilith and this time I no longer sheltered in Vespasian's shadow but stood before him and his hand rested on my shoulder. I had lost my sword. I felt no need of it but I held the ouroboros which I had never relinquished. Beside Vespasian, Gerald stood, breathing heavily, half in trance. Though struggling with his courage and disbelief, he was determined to prove his value.

I could not see my mother. The march of the ghosts passed between us, mostly unseen except by those few who stared in horror at the shimmer of pale souls coming past the pool, from the tree shadows and from the lost intangibles, through our solid bodies and on towards their own private dreams, called by memory, hurrying to the warmth, silvered transparencies in the night, eager now and thankful that finally the blessed gate was opened and they could fulfil the promise.

No one waited now for me. It was Lilith they waited on again. I stood very still and let the dead pass through me as they went on their own paths, away from us. I could still see them and felt the shiver of pleasure as their souls connected with my own. I said to Lilith, "I will take the card for him, if you order it, but you shall not have what you want. Show me them." Lilith showed her teeth. From the folds of her skin, she pulled out Vespasian's pack of cards which he called the tarocchi of Hermes. They glittered, a welcome and not a threat. I reached out my hand.

Behind me, Vespasian said softly, "You hold my life in your hands, little one. Do you know that?"

I was concentrating, and no space for panic. I must not be Tilda, who would cower to Lilith's control. I must not be Molly, who would snatch and choose at random. I must be the gatekeeper, who could influence the cards and dismantle Lilith's trance. "I will not give you over to evil," I said, a whisper as soft as his own. "But I cannot disobey my mistress and I must cut the cards as she orders me. What must I take?"

He answered me calmly, his voice even, his hand on my shoulder unpressured. "There are many which will evade both her cunning and her hunger," he said, little more than a murmur against my hair. "If you have the power to choose, then take The Aeon or Judgement, which is the number twenty, for this is my card and has been my destiny until now. But if you cannot cut what you will, it is of no matter. If you give me to her, try and get away yourself. Save Gerald if you can, and leave me. I risked Lilith's vengeance many years ago, and was lucky to escape her then. Perhaps now is my time. I am prepared for sacrifice."

"Fool," hissed Lilith. "Be quiet while the divinities choose your fate." She pushed the cards towards me. I tucked the ouroboros back into my belt, and leaned forwards. I felt the switch. I was no longer myself. I knew I would pick the right card.

As it touched my fingers it felt cold and silky, and sparked with electricity. As though making the choice itself, it sprang into my hand. I turned it over. It was number twenty of the major arcana, Judgment, or as Vespasian had called it, The Aeon. Though I had been so sure, the idiocy of confidence slipped away and I thought I might faint. Vespasian said softly into my ear, "Thank you." He sounded, quite suddenly and for the first time, desperately tired. "I am grateful, cielo mine. Lilith eats those who are fed to her. And she chews – slowly."

Lilith had darted back in fury, turning away from us. I breathed relief. For one moment, the air felt fresh. I leaned against Vespasian. He was grateful, he said. But I believed he was still in danger. "Uta's dead," I told him. "But before she died in the storm, she said you were foresworn, to her and to Lilith. She said what you said – about Lilith eating her sacrifices. Is your life still forfeit?"

"Not anymore," said Vespasian. "What Uta told you that I did, I did. At the end of this night I would have stood alone, and battled Lilith, and lost. You have just saved me. Do I deserve it?"

"Judgement is your card, not mine," I said.

Lilith's anger did not wait on our conversation. On the turning of the card which denied her, she had sprung back. Now she began to bloat, filling the sky and obliterating the stars and the moon and its fragile aura. The trees pulled back in fluttering revulsion, nature's consternation. Their own magic was obliterated by Lilith's.

She started to scream, both arms flailing in a hundred grasping joints. Her grinning liplessness and huge tusked snarl lunged down, her claws in Vespasian's hair, around his neck and in his eyes. I thought he would be blinded. I thought he would be dead. Blood poured down his cheek and from the knotted veins in his neck, but he dropped from beneath her, rolled and rebounded, facing her again. He stood panting as she swung towards him. "You cannot deny the card," he said. "It has been decided. My forfeit is cancelled."

"I do not deny it," she said, all gaping growl. "But no puny human, once prick deep in homage to my divinity, dare think to wound the very force he once adored. Your destiny is judgement and now I judge you."

Vespasian waited, slowly sheathed his sword and held up again the seal of Thoth. Once more the geometric pattern and hieroglyphs sprang into flame. "But it is I who judge," said Vespasian. "Not you, who have neither capability nor objectivity. Judgement is beyond you, for you know only evil."

Lilith hesitated. She was breaking her own laws, and knew it. Even I knew it. But she leapt suddenly forwards, stopped, feinting, and lunged. Her claws spread out and lanced his arm, ripped through his cotte and into the muscle, streaming dark blood. Vespasian stepped aside and flung the seal. It spun in whirling sparks and struck her, piercing the side of her throat against the jugular. She roared and belched and squealed, and falling backwards, clutched her neck. Between her trembling, grappling frog fingers slime oozed. She bent low, stamping on the fallen seal, shattering its flames into invisible fragments, the power of its magic into decomposed dust in the grass. She screamed again. This time it was a call to her followers.

The battle had begun.

CHAPTER FIFTY-ONE

They rushed us. They had been waiting for more than two hours, pent up with the thrill of suspended excitement, every nerve and every muscle bent like the bow string. They had watched and waited through the brutal shock of the storm and its wild destruction, returning gradually, adrenalin again under control, to more suspense and the struggle for patience. Until Lilith called them, they did not dare advance. At first kept at distance by the sacred trees and the magic of the water and the blending of the worlds, they had been unable to approach, but now all but a very few wretched and dismal weaklings were inside the nemeton and Arthur led the sixty three men and women remaining alive who had followed him and worshipped Lilith for many years. As Lilith screamed her own challenge, they raised their swords in shouts of glee and hatred, at last into action.

Most threw off their cloaks as they ran and I saw the gleam of armour beneath their dark tunics, steel breastplates and full hauberk, chain mail from scrawny neck to knees. They were all around us and we were three people only, but if we had been a hundred and three it would not have mattered because there was Lilith. Already I believed she'd killed more than twenty in the storm, an appetiser perhaps, a war dance to excite her own anticipation. Injured by the Seal of Thoth but with her avarice for pain not yet assuaged, she stormed up to the clouds and covered the moon, pitching us into total dark.

Vespasian stood central, his sword in one hand, the long knife pulled again from his boot in the other. Although he was bleeding from huge wounds, he showed no obvious exhaustion or pain. Beside him stood Gerald. I heard Gerald's breath like a kettle boiling but it seemed that Vespasian did not breathe at all. He was searching for Arthur in the shadows. He would destroy Arthur before they killed him. Unleashed now, he sliced the head from the first man who approached, a swing so vigorous it pulled him quite around and the decapitated head spurted blood and bounced and tumbled on the grass, spitting teeth. Vespasian fought with dagger and sword, with feet and shoulder, elbow and knee, and with the speed and balance of his spring. His blades flashed in the gloom. As he lunged with the long sword, so his dagger maimed another. At first Gerald covered his back and they fought in rhythm. I watched Vespasian's concentration, his focus on each enemy's eyes, interpreting the direction of the man's intention, the stab or the feint, always reacting first so that every attack against him was met, repulsed and failed.

It seemed, even now, the trees fought as our allies. Within the strange waving shadows, I could not see if men were taken or killed. But the trees moved in, creating avenues and barriers so that no crush of more than a few adversaries could approach together. Then Gerald was grappling with a short, stocky creature, and took the man's knife in his cheek. Vespasian swung back to help him, and was taken almost at once by four, two on each side, who lunged and broke him to the ground. I saw one man's sword go through Vespasian's arm and come out the other side, clots of bloody flesh in the light of Lilith's watching eyes. His arm hanging stiff but not useless and still wielding the knife, Vespasian bent low and ricocheted the attacker over his shoulders, twisted both boots into the slip of the mud and was back on top. A worm of torn muscle hung from the wound, but wrenched from its owner's grasp, he pulled the short sword from the weeping hole. He twisted, and buried it to the hilt in the other man's heart.

Within the staggering confusion, I thought I saw a branch, a huge oak arm as gnarled as dragon jaws, heave down on one man's head, caving it into smashed and oozing fragments. Then the whole trunk stepped forwards, blocking other paths, rattling its acorns in a rolling giant's gait.

But Arthur's people were on top of Vespasian like fleas, swarming over him, scurrying out from the trees towards him. Though Vespasian threw them off with fists and sword and knife and five were dead before they got him down, he was pushed steadily under. Gerald was half beneath him, just alive.

Arthur looked down on Vespasian and said, "So, it was not so hard in the end," and kicked him hard between the legs.

I had not done a thing. I had not resisted my enemies, nor been attacked, not hurt nor even winded. I was standing beside the silver pool with my arms behind me, deep under my mother's spell. My feet were so rooted to the ground that I expected to grow leaf and the birds to nest in my armpits. I was utterly removed and completely impotent. But I could hear and see and speak.

Though doubled with pain, Vespasian rolled and sprang, but I watched as he was hurled to the ground a third time. I stood, still as a pillar all marbled and cold, begging my mother, absurdly, to let me go and help. I watched as Vespasian, with his knife thrust in one man's heel and his sword through another's calf, struggled upright once again, and spinning away from Arthur's thrust, grabbed Joanna, first by the edges of her cloak, then her arm, and finally her throat. Then he held her as recently he had held me except that his hand was squeezing around her neck, and his knife was half buried in her breast above her heart.

Joanna squeaked and wheezed, kicking back against him, but she hooked herself deeper onto his knife point and his fingers were so tightly pinned into her creamy little neck that her flailing feet were raised from the earth and she floundered there, swinging a little, while he strangled the life slowly from her. "Will you do nothing then, to save her?" asked Vespasian while Arthur stood before him, mouth open, and for the first time Vespasian was breathless and gasping between words. But Arthur, in the moment of reaching out for both his wife and his enemy, was caught by Gerald from the ground, and stabbed sword point to young fingers on the hilt, up through the groin to the pelvis and belly.

A restless, churning reluctance battered the rest of Arthur's clan, fearful of losing both their leaders, they stood, sword arms hanging limp, leaning over to catch their breath and their wits, peering through the swirling mists and pounding branches.

Arthur fell heavily, pumping hot gore from the top of his thigh. The great slick of blood mixed with the scarlet sticky grass in the rising dew. He was slipping forward, unable to keep his balance. He had fallen on Richard's burial mound. Gerald shouted, still little more than a child's voice desperate to be heard above the heavy groans and the hoarse breathing. "In barter for taking my friend's life, for ruining that of my step-father, and most of all for murdering my mother, I demand your death."

Arthur was in spasms of pain, twisted on the ground, his sword lost amongst the dark shadows of the longer grass, trying to stifle the shame of his own screaming. He looked up into Vespasian's eyes, and Vespasian smiled.

"Kill him," murmured Vespasian. Gerald stood, just one moment of pause, not for pity but for pride. He watched his step-grandfather quiver in pain as his life slipped slowly away through the pumping blood from his thigh and groin. Then Gerald swung his sword slanted across Arthur's head so that the face split in two down the nose and through one eye, and the snarl was the last movement the mouth made before it fell apart. His brains rushed out like gruel on the grass.

Vespasian waited until Joanna had seen her husband's face cut through and his tongue loll from the gaping hole, and then snapped her neck with a quick twist and the tightening of his fingers, like a chicken in the farmyard, ready for the pot. He threw her down and her body slumped across Arthur's still twitching legs.

Then Gerald and Vespasian turned to face the rest.

Many, twenty perhaps, now crept away. Gone quickly between the far trees, silently disappearing back into the world of men. But others remained, some eager and defiant, some cautious. Vespasian swung his sword, already black with blood and lung and flesh, and many of them died. Gerald killed one from behind with a thrust through the gut while Vespasian brought his own knife up between the same man's ribs and I heard them crack.

The noise came in waves, the shouting and the screams and all the great clashes of sword on sword and sword on bone. Then, because I was able to count almost as if detached, there were just eleven of her followers left when Lilith finally regained her power, recovered her strength and decided to move.

Vespasian was bleeding heavily from the deep gash below his left elbow where the sword had pierced him, sliced between ulna and radius, smashing muscle but missing bone. His forehead was cut and there was dark blood in his eyes, his jaw deeply grazed, his neck slashed by Lilith's claws and both hands pitted and cut through his gloves to the bare knuckles within. Gerald bent almost double, heaving, breath finished, his pretty blue clothes so bloodstained that it was impossible to see which was his own, and which from his enemies. They stood together and looked up at Lilith's face looming over them, her mouth gloating. She had watched and enjoyed the spectacle of death. The pain and destruction of her own followers still delighted her. But forced apart and made impotent by Thoth's seal, she had needed time to rearrange her powers. Now she walked forward and the earth vibrated.

Of the eleven remaining, six, already exhausted and wounded, turned and ran, dropping their swords, more terrified of their own goddess than their enemies. The crunch of their escape was muffled by the dark mist. Of those few remaining, five summoned courage and grouped at Lilith's knees, eyes shining with pride and exhilaration. The first was Malcolm. Beside him was a woman. The other three were tall men, strong in age and shoulder. Against terrible odds, Gerald and Vespasian had been almost victorious. With skill, with courage, and with magic, they had almost tasted success. Now they waited, accepting the final failure. They did not expect to master Lilith.

I had seen Malcolm enter the glade some hours back and I had seen his thin legs tremble with the effort of passing the tree thick boundary. Now he was all swagger, though his long bladed sword was clean. I didn't recognise the dark haired woman at his side, but I knew one of the men. I remembered him from Vespasian's castle, the sweated excitement of sadism clear in the candle light. "Will you continue with the girl today?" he had asked Arthur, panting for my torture to begin. "Will you still prepare the sacrifice?" I had smelled his lust and hunger.

From within my mother's hypnotic trance, I remained without pulse or breath or any power of movement. My eyes could not blink and my throat could not swallow but my brain was still my own. I stared at the man I remembered and the words of his delight in my agony echoed in my memory. I still stared as he cuddled back to Lilith's fat toad legs and their fluid, chameleon leathered hide. I watched him swing out with his sword. I concentrated and I found my own answer to the question my mother had refused to answer. The gatekeeper had a force I was beginning at last to understand.

I killed the man with the short sword who had wanted to watch me tortured and who had pleaded with Arthur to prepare me as the sacrifice. From a distance of many feet and without moving, I killed him. The wife of Janus smiled and exercised her vengeance.

With a squawk of sudden pain, the man gasped, fell to his knees and clutched his chest, throwing down his sword. He wore chain mail and a thick black tunic, but through it all his lungs exploded, gushing white and red and yellow with the stench of rotting and corrupted bile. The man died slowly as Vespasian and Gerald stared. Then Vespasian looked across at me. He knew, and I was ashamed.

It was then I realised I had killed Uta too. Unaware and undirected, I had caused the death of many during the battle. The storm that had maimed and killed had not been Lilith's. It had been mine. More than twenty had been ripped apart by gale and ice. And when Vespasian and Gerald fought, I had, from my trance, been there beside them. I had killed without sword, but with devastation. Vespasian had always warned me of the danger of the gatekeeper.

Malcolm leapt away from the man dying at his side, while Lilith looked down and licked her lipless mouth.

"Four left," I said silently in my mind, and my mother answered, also in my thoughts, "At last. You are waking up."

The odds now stood four against two, one little more than an inexperienced child though learning fast, while Vespasian, ignoring the overpowering threat of Lilith's presence, rushed immediately on Malcolm. Their swords met in brilliance, steel on steel, reflecting moon light in flashes of storm. Then Malcolm's blade shattered in shivering, buckling shards. He stared back for a second at Vespasian's, his weapon in his face, and at the man inexplicably dead at his side. Then dropping the broken hilt from limp fingers, Malcolm turned abruptly and ran. Vespasian sighed.

He turned and thrust his sword through the next man's heart, but when his blade turned aside, scraping as it glanced sideways against the metal breast plate, Vespasian slung the sword and grabbed the man with both hands, thumbs pressing up beneath the jaw and against the larynx, quickly breaking his neck.

Gerald held the dark haired woman against a tree, sword pressed to her throat. She gasped, begging for her life. Gerald stood in terrible uncertainty, unable to complete the kill. Vespasian killed the last man, though took longer, the other man's knife slashing down Vespasian's cheek before he threw him off. Knocking him down with the blunt weight of his sword hilt, Vespasian ran him through the ear with the full length of his knife.

Only the woman remained. Vespasian bent down and wiped both his sword and his knife blade clean on the wet grass near the rise of his wife's grave. The woman facing Gerald was hysterical. "Kill her," said Vespasian, looking up briefly. "You only prolong her pain."

"I can't do it," said Gerald though he held his sword still poised.

"I said you must obey me this night," said Vespasian, standing again, and sheathing his own sword. "Now, kill her."

Gerald tightened his grip but couldn't press home the blade. "I can't," he muttered. "I can't kill – a woman – like this."

"You only make her suffer more," said Vespasian, impatient. He strode to Gerald's side, again removed the long thin knife from his boot, and in one quick movement, slit the woman's throat. As her blood spilled, she slid down the tree trunk and curled at its roots. Vespasian bent once more to clean his blade. "It's finished," he said. "Now we discover what Lilith has planned for us all."

CHAPTER FIFTY-TWO

My mother let me go. I melted from the nose down in fluid ripples of painful release. Each muscle accepted back its life with grateful, and throbbing, humility. I stumbled but didn't fall. I didn't look back. I went at once to join Vespasian.

Gerald was bouncing. Through the desperate tiredness and all the blood, the adrenalin and pride still spun. Impossibly, they had won. "You were under a spell, weren't you," Gerald said. "Like being tied up in a sort of web. You were practically hidden. I bet you wished you could fight too. But we won anyway. We didn't need any help after all."

"You did not see her, but she fought too," said Vespasian softly. He put his hand on my shoulder, as if taking me back into his possession. "And her help was – invaluable." I was sorry that he understood so well. The vengeance of the path keeper had been so ugly.

"Well, it was magic of course," grinned Gerald. "I'll never, ever believe all this once we're out of it. It'll always seem like just a dream."

"But it is a dream," spat Lilith from above us. "Did you think this was anything as mundane as reality? This is truth and truth is as far beyond your concept of reality as is my power beyond yours."

Gerald shrank, losing his golden grin and paling to grey in the moonlight. No one had forgotten Lilith but, clutching the wound in her throat and wallowing in the resentment of injury, she had been forced from the battle, weak and strangely impartial. She had still gloated over the agony. Perhaps it was the welter of death that had renewed her strength.

"Let us go," Gerald said, peering up into the tower of her shadows, with as much courage as his youth allowed him. "We won the battle. Now let us go."

"I may allow you life a while longer," Lilith answered him, "for you do not interest me at all. I am here for hotter blood." Without touching him, Lilith waved her claws and Gerald fell, immediately unconscious, into the mud. Vespasian took my hand. He did not look at me nor I at him.

Midnight had passed but it would be some time until dawn. My mother came quietly to stand by Lilith, unchanged as she had been throughout. But Lilith was a giantess, monstrously swollen with her head in the clouds and the moon beneath her shoulder blades. I couldn't know if Lilith had ever expected Vespasian to succeed against so many, though perhaps, understanding the precarious balance of good against evil, she had. Now she wanted Vespasian for herself.

The veleda said, "The sacrament and the altar are ready but you know the risks."

Lilith lunged downwards, squatting back onto her haunches. "I always take risks," she said. "This is my food and my water and my sleep and my breath. If I must be refused all these, then all my existence becomes shadow. He will not refuse me these two. I have been patient. He cannot refuse me now."

"They did not take the cards you wanted," said the veleda calmly. "Their destinies are not in your hands. They fought your acolytes and won. By all the laws of nature, they are free. They are no longer your rightful sacrifice. They belong to Him."

I wanted to run away. I wanted to run like Malcolm had run, but Vespasian stood quite still, with my hand clasped in his, his sword and knife sheathed and his back straight. He knew, I believe, that he faced death and certain torture but his face was passive and almost serene.

He'd achieved all and more than he'd hoped. I knew he was right and escape would be impossible. Lilith could stamp me out with one flick of her toes, but it was standing and waiting that made me ill.

"I still have a claim," hissed Lilith, "which even He cannot deny. I call on past dues. This is a creature which once swore me his life, and now has the temerity to strike me. Will you fight for your door stop?"

My mother stared back at Lilith with her milky pale eyes, the pupil barely visible, like a shallow black scar just caught in the centre. There was no expression in her face at all. "No," she said. "But I doubt you can take her. As you have seen, she holds powers of her own."

"I shall suck them up," snapped Lilith. "Power spices flesh."

My mother shrugged. "You are breaking the rules."

"My existence is an eternal challenge to Him," Lilith muttered, for the first time subdued. "And I will challenge again, and again. He must look to His rules, and I to mine. And my rule is clear, for no prick-filth human can flout me – can profit from my power and teaching and then turn against me – can swear an oath on my altar and then renounce that oath without suffering my revenge. I will have him, and I will reach him through your own pitiful creation."

"Yet she owes you nothing and is not forsworn to you." My mother was actually standing up for me?

Lilith grinned, which I found terrifying. "You may hate me, but you keep your place and stand apart. You are impartial. Yet this puny egg, laid from your own rebirth, takes side and fights openly for Him. So I will claim them both."

Lilith was fingering the air, commanding the shadows, shaping ribbons of shade and fountains of darkness, until we were all enclosed. The trees had gone, and the pool, and the grasses, herbs and sweet moonshine. All the bodies of the dead had gone and their scattered weapons, the clotting and mangled remains of their varied endings, the spread of their blood and the echoes of their lives. The wind had gone and even the little breeze. The sky had gone and the stars and the huge white moon. We were, truly, very much alone, standing on short tufted gorse which was all that Lilith had left of our glade. In less than a minute, she had destroyed Vespasian's nemeton.

But behind us and very close in our confined space, was a plinth of some dull stone, a plain block of something colourless and rank. It was entirely undecorated but was high and wide and sad.

"It is the altar of Lilith," said Vespasian, "and I have seen it before."

"Indeed, several times," agreed Lilith. She had shrunk back to human size and stood to my right, almost a woman, pig faced and crocodile skinned, who spoke clearly and had the light of unfathomable expectation and delight in her eyes. My mother had moved behind the block and simply watched. Lilith continued to speak to Vespasian. "I am always present when my worshippers sacrifice to me, even if I am not seen. I know your past, Baron de Vrais, once a more precious priest of mine than the sycophant Arthur d'Estropier could ever be. I know what you did for me and respected you for it. But then you turned away. In ignominy and the platitudes of pathetic guilt, you changed direction. Now I intend reminding you of what you lost."

I remained speechless. Vespasian said, "You have broken the seal, but I am not without other powers, and not all of them learned from you. I can hurt you before you kill me."

"A new experience. There have been few with that ability," crowed Lilith.

"She fears only the wrath of the One," said the veleda, from her distant stance. "She has forgotten how to be afraid."

"It is a shame," said Lilith, ignoring my mother, "not to kill the man first, and see the suffering of the watching woman." She was speaking to herself, but the speech was for Vespasian. She wanted him broken. "But the gatekeeper must be subdued," Lilith licked her lips. Her tongue was blue. "Once the female is subjugated, her power is also denied to the man who would otherwise claim it. Without her, he will simply become himself." Lilith looked up, staring at Vespasian. "You should appreciate my artistry. You once tortured her yourself. I'll show you how it should be done."

She was still speaking, but the sudden echo of a whistle pierced me and the darkness, within which we already stood, became a far greater darkness. Before I could even be conscious of fear, Lilith's touch or the beginning of the last journey, I was abruptly removed.

There were rooms in my head, all empty. Some were filled with light and others were deeply lost in shadow, while one was sinister with murmurings and huge corners. I wandered through them all, calling someone's name, but I had forgotten who I called. I could not feel my body and I supposed I was naked. I circled endlessly, restlessly wandering, continually searching for a purpose that I could not any longer understand. It was in the chamber all dazzling in brightness that I stopped at last. I sat in the middle of the spangled floor to watch, while all the glorious light became a crimson sunset and then a burning so fierce that its colour became a thousand shades of white. The flames swept up from the base of the walls and sucked out the air. The fire didn't worry me and I curled my toes, bathed in light and drank in the heat.

Before me, resting on the ground and between my legs, I saw the coil of the wooden serpent, the ouroboros which had stayed with me now for so long. I reached out in affection to touch it and hold it to my face, but it caught the little licking flames and all around it flickered blue, falling slowly into the tiny black scattered ashes of absolute disintegration.

I cried then, because I had lost what Vespasian had given me and had told me to keep safe.

Then there was neither pain nor pleasure but a delicious knowledge of release and overwhelming peace. Now I could breathe again. I breathed freedom and lassitude and the promise of forgetfulness. Death seemed such sweet contentment.

Someone was screaming at me. I recognised those screams from before, from many dreams and many awakenings. I recognised the voice. It was my own. The screams shattered the peace, ordering me to escape the flames and search for the water. I smiled to myself. There was no water. The advice was absurd. I couldn't find water in rooms which were dry of life and love and held only the lost fingerprints of past effort, now utterly pointless and buried deep in pale regret. I lay back, stretching my spine against the hard floor, feeling the stone under my shoulders and the heat on my breasts. Then I looked up, eyes wide open, as the roof became a rivered conflagration and streaming, flying ashes all alight. I was still smiling as they fell around me, thinking, now I shall never be cold again.

Someone slapped my face with such force that I swore. The room tumbled away from me and the walls shivered into splinters and above me was sky, not flame nor sun nor moon but sweet fresh, fresh breathing air, and Vespasian yelling in my ears.

Instead of the warmth of somnambulism and death in delicious apathy, I was pummelled back into wakefulness and an awareness of a cold wind and one bright star above the tree tops. I gulped in the air I had forgotten how to breathe and turned, sudden spasms of pain jolting me from dream-state into a reality I had no wish to join.

"It will hurt like the devil," said Vespasian, "but you must now return and endure it."

I could see him clearly. More, I could feel him, for now I was in his arms. The hot stone of my bed had gone and was replaced by a cradle in motion and the support of his body against my cheek. "Why?" I whispered. I was surprised at my own voice, which I could barely hear, sounding like a little child's moan, just a feather puff of lost weariness.

"Because, if you leave me now, the world will never be the same," he whispered back to me, words drifting on the warmth of his breath. "And though our world would be the better for change and should not be the same indeed, without you in it, it has no chance of reconciliation for me."

He could not be talking to me. I was lost anyway and had no idea who I was, or could be, or had been, and whether I wanted to be anyone at all. "I would like to go home," I managed to say.

"All in good time," he said gently, "when I discover where home is to be."

CHAPTER FIFTY-THREE

Memory came back very slowly and some of it I was never to remember at all. And that was a good thing.

We were still in the restricted glade, confined within the limits that Lilith had created, a bubble within Vespasian's sacred nemeton. The altar remained. It was a vile, stained block of threatening stone, and I had lain there until Vespasian had carried me away, cradling me on the ground within the crook of his arm. I was wrapped tight in his cloak and the fur was wonderfully soft and pleasant against my skin. I was uncomfortably aware that beneath it, I was wearing no clothes of any kind.

But there was no sign of Lilith, nor of my mother. Besides myself and Vespasian, just two others knelt amongst the scrubby grass and smiled at me. One was Gerald, and the other was Richard.

He was so beautiful and so alive, that I knew at once Richard must be a ghost returned, even before I remembered the drama of his death.

I turned back to Vespasian. His eyes reflected such terrible exhaustion that I wondered if he was dying himself. There was no glitter of wise knowledge and bright intelligence, nor of humour or even of malice. There remained a tired glaze of caring patience but his face seemed bloodless. Instead, beneath me, I was aware of the strength and support of his arms and knew that in spite of it all, he was still in control.

Gerald thrust his bright tousled head down beside me. "I can't believe you're alive. My God, Tilda, you should be dead. But then," and he grinned back at Richard, "what do we know about death, after all? It's not what I thought it was."

"Gerald," Vespasian informed me softly, "has been more fully unconscious throughout the past hour than even you have been. Lilith can produce deeper trances than I, and Gerald knows nothing, as usual, of what happened. Though even when awake, his consciousness can be a little mute, as we are all aware."

Gerald continued to grin wide enough to catch dragonflies. "That creature Lilith knocked me out. Well, how can a monster like that be anything but a dream? But I felt the blow alright. I came to just a little while ago and found Richard sitting beside me like a candle flame, all shining. I thought I had to be dead myself and then he started talking and everything began to make sense after all."

"Forget about sense," Vespasian told him, "of which you know nothing in any case. This is all about truth and that is a very different matter."

"You mustn't avoid explaining what happened to me," I begged, gazing up at him, trying to put more feeling into my eyes than I could manage in my voice. "You won't protect me by telling me nothing. I have to know or my own imagination will send me mad."

"There is time," murmured Vespasian. "Perhaps once the pain is passed."

"I was lost in rooms in my head," I struggled up a little, speaking as clearly as I now could. "I'm still not really aware of pain. At least, it comes and goes. Did the veleda put me under another spell?"

His eyes were kinder than I remembered them. "No. The spell was mine," he said. "I told you there were places in your head, where pain could not reach you. Once before, when you were to face Arthur's torture, I put you into trance. This time the trance was of necessity a little deeper."

Richard came closer then, and put out one tentative finger and touched my cheek. I felt his warmth. Gerald had been right. Richard was a candle flame. "Vespasian and Richard rescued you between them," said Gerald, still unable to contain the grin now inhabiting his face. "Vespasian's amazing. He did strange things like a magician and he called Richard. Sort of conjured him up. But I only saw the last bit. That's just as well. I couldn't have borne seeing you hurt."

"I came through the door you opened," Richard said to me. His voice glimmered like starlight and was not the child's voice I remembered.

"Vespasian opened it," I said. "He took that right."

"You must forgive him for that," smiled Richard. "It was well intended. He was able to call on me and I challenged Lilith." I thought his face so charmed and thrilling that I didn't expect anything could brighten it further, until he smiled, and showed me that it could. But he was still in child's form and looked even younger than before. I could not believe he had challenged Lilith.

"How?" I asked.

His bright red hair flopped down into his eyes as it had when alive. "Oh," he said, "that's nothing special. I brought a message, that's all. I don't even know who the message was from, though of course it was from the other side. What you call Paradise. It told Lilith she couldn't have either of you. She was forfeiting her own power, by trying to take one of His."

"How do you bring a message from Paradise?"

"Well, not on parchment," laughed Gerald, "though I wish it had been. Now there's a keepsake I'd prize forever."

"The message didn't need to be spoken or written," said Richard, brushing his bright hair back from his forehead. "It existed just in my presence, and in facing her, coming from His realm. My appearance was the message. That was enough."

"You always wanted to do something gloriously chivalrous," I said, attempting a smile. "Now you've done something far more exciting and romantic than anyone could ever have imagined."

"I could do it, because I always loved you," said Richard. "It doesn't have much to do with chivalry. After all, Lilith couldn't kill me, could she?"

"She could have carried you off to Hell," I said, remembering the tarot cards.

Richard shook his head. "I already have my place allotted elsewhere."

I was getting better at the smile. "I think you're telling me you saved my life. That makes me feel I matter. And best of all – it's wonderful to see you again."

Richard nodded. "For me even more. But I have to go. Samhain's filtering into dawn. I can't outstay my time."

I had the strength of Vespasian's cradling arms. "You don't miss the life you had?" I said. "The souls that came back at midnight, all the multitude I saw pressing on the gates, they wanted so much to come back."

"Not me," smiled Richard. "They carry guilt or sorrow, love left unspoken and duty left undone. It's been beautifully satisfying to see you again, Tilda, but where I live now, it's more beautiful by far. Will you come then, and see me off?"

I looked up at him. "I'm the gatekeeper, not the boatman," I said. "I think I'll never see you again."

The dawn touched the tree tops in a shimmer of pale rose, a cold tinge of promise. Light then leaked back into the sky with such pale hesitancy that I wasn't sure if it was truly sunrise, the moon's aura returned, or maybe just the echo of the stars. But when I looked back, Richard had gone.

Gerald was rubbing his eyes. "Was that all real?" he whispered.

"One day," Vespasian said, "you'll learn to make your own definition of reality. In the meantime, my child, I wish to talk to Tilda alone. You must rest, before a long journey."

"Rest?" complained Gerald. "But I've been asleep for an hour or more."

"Being knocked unconscious is hardly the same thing as sleep," said Vespasian with a welcome return to the acerbity I enjoyed. "And you will do as you are told, or I shall knock you out again. Take your cloak to the edge of the tree line, stay there and close your eyes. Don't worry, I shall not forget you."

Gerald grinned, trudging off to the roots of the trees now faintly visible in the growing light. The birds were wakening and the leaf flutter was dew lit. I watched Gerald's small shadow diminish into the taller shadows. All the grove and its glade were shifting, again encompassing the magic of Vespasian's creation. I heard the soft ripple of water catching the first breezes.

As the early rose deepened into soft lilac and the bird song began all around us, I looked back to Vespasian. "Please tell me," I said.

"If I described it all," he frowned, "there would have been little benefit in removing you from it and putting you in trance in the first place. I shall tell you only the indispensable."

"It doesn't frighten me," I said, though the pain was now filtering back.

"I understand," he said, watching me. "The pain will return and while it's as its worst, I will not move you. We'll stay here until you're strong enough to travel. Then I'll open the glade and take us out, back into the world you recognise as real. In the meantime, you're utterly safe. Neither Lilith nor the veleda can return here." He held me tighter, as if with his strength he might stop my bones falling apart. Over his shoulder the low winter sun now spread a sallow and greenish light behind the trees. The colours coagulated into a sickly morning, releasing the distant forest from its silhouettes.

The pain was spasmodic but I shuddered as it took me. I said, "So tell me now, before it gets any worse, what Lilith did."

He shook his head slightly. "She meant to kill you," he murmured. "She attempted to ruin your body and absorb your soul. But she was stopped. Is that not enough?"

"No," I whispered. "Or it will haunt me for the rest of my life."

"Very well," he sighed. His eyes were all huge black pupils and I could see the throbbing pulse at his temples. "I must tell you something first, Tilda, which is not now easy to speak of, but who I am and have been is unfortunately an integral part of this explanation. So simply this. Perhaps I'd always been wilful as a child. I found it easy learning skills and strategies, and that is dangerous for a young boy. I also had a certain talent for hedonism, among other things, and I believed in indulging my potential. At university in Italy where my father sent me, I discovered there was more to power than a long sword and a sack of money. I began a study of alchemy which took me across half the world and into the deepest esoteric delights of magic. My tarocchi card is Judgement. For long years, I did not judge, even between good and evil. I accepted a world in which all things seemed equal. I worshipped the old religion, which condones many of the mysteries so frightening now to the church. I discovered Lilith." He was watching for my reaction, but I was too tired to make one.

"Because of that, when I returned to England after my father's death, I met d'Estropier," he continued. "I was titled and rich, though money meant nothing to me by then, since I could create my own. I knew more than Arthur. I taught him. That is a terrible thing to admit, and it disgusts me, to have instructed the perverted in the black arts. Tonight you and I between us, Tilda, killed all those who were once my own students, and I their tutor."

I looked away. "I killed no one," I mumbled. "I was paralysed."

He smiled. "You may believe that if you prefer," he said. "Though you ask for truth and should accept your own, as I do mine. For we took the search for spiritual power on Earth too far, Arthur and I, and I chose to reawaken the veleda."

That was a subject I wasn't so sure I wanted to understand any further. "For greater power. Alright, I know. She told me herself. Tell me about tonight."

"Even though you picked a tarot destiny for me that denied Lilith both my body and my soul, she decided my past still entitled her claim. I'd paid the price demanded of me at the time, fully understanding, and accepting it. I paid with my ruin and my solitude. It is many years now since I learned to judge, and chose to take the path away from amorality. But I'm still capable, it seems, of cruelty in pursuit of power. Lilith knew this and demanded the forfeit. Perhaps her claim was just."

"Richard says it wasn't," I insisted.

"But," smiled Vespasian, "with the same power learned from the veleda and used in the past, it was I who summoned Richard."

I suppose I gasped. "The message – from Him – was ordered by you?"

"Of course," he said, quite without humility. "Designed and franked. But remember this – no one speaks in God's name without His sanction. Had He denied me and repudiated my message, I would not have survived the attempt. I would have become Lilith's property with more surety than you can possibly imagine."

I could not in any manner appreciate or consider such a danger. "But you took that risk? I cannot even think about that."

"There's no need to think about it," Vespasian told me, sardonic again. "I took that risk. It's done." I was still warm in his embrace. He smiled down at me and brushed the tickle of fur from my chin. "As for the rest, I'll not tell you everything Lilith did. Her altar's stained with your blood, but that will fade, as all her gluttony does in Time. When the trance I put you in begins to loosen further, some memory may return, but most will not. I will tell you only that first she needed to dominate whatever power you had as the veleda's gatekeeper. As a substitute for divinity and subjugated to humanity, she thought she could eat you alive. She was wrong about two things."

"She underestimated you," I said.

"Indeed," he agreed. "Us both. Her conceit is monstrous. Evil always underestimates its enemy. She had not appreciated what power I'd gained after leaving her priesthood, and she did not realise how well I had protected you."

"Oh," I managed to smile. "The ouroboros?"

He shook his head and the cold black silk of his hair brushed across my burning forehead. "She took that from you and burned it. It was a small thing, a talisman against lesser powers than hers, and had already served its purpose. But then she saw and touched the dragon."

The pain was returning rapidly. I was losing coherence as my focus wandered. Now past the sharp shadows of Vespasian's cheekbones, the trees had reassembled. Again I saw my chestnut tree swinging its striped hammock, entwined with the creeping fingers of wisteria from my eaves. When we'd first arrived in Vespasian's grove, my chestnut had worn her green summer petticoats. Now she blushed sweet russet and gold. Behind the willow I heard the faint lustre of running water and knew the cold pool and her jumping fish had also returned. I saw the huge girth of the yew tree, quite healed and whole and bristling growth, gnarled branches spread and a blackbird calling between his arms.

Reality, yet so unreal. The confusion was in my head. I could not remember a dragon, though my memory was filled with flame and dragon's breath. "There isn't any dragon," I said, pitifully vague. "Just bird song."

Vespasian's black eyes were pouring over me. "The dragon I gave you," he whispered. "Another journey into pain, my child. But you've listened enough. It is time to sleep and heal, although I shall not remove you entirely. No burning rooms in your mind, just the soft music of the new day."

CHAPTER FIFTY-FOUR

At first it seemed the gift of Vespasian's sleep, instead of taking me forward into hope and peace, took me backwards into memory. I remembered vestiges of what I had asked to know, and no longer wished to.

I had been placed on the altar without ropes or chains but I could not move. Around me I smelled an eternity of old bloodshed in misery and terrible pain and the reek of it suffocated me. My fingers touched dried clotting, all that remained of many thousand years and many thousand souls, all lost to Lilith.

I surrendered to lethargy and the acceptance of inevitability. It was such a relief, not to struggle anymore. I wondered what Hell would be like.

I heard myself scream even as Vespasian's trance transported me from nightmare into fantasy. But now I also saw a little of what Lilith had done to make me scream.

I turned away from the desecration of my body and watched Vespasian. He stood at the foot of the altar. He was trapped in consciousness, eyes wide and mind aware, but unable to move, or blink, or speak. I believe it was my mother's spell, as she had previously held me. He was weeping. His wounds continued to bleed but it was not for himself that he wept. I had never imagined him so vulnerable. Now I saw my sacrificial ruin but felt myself blessed, because Vespasian wept for me.

Quickly my dream swept me into sweet rose flavoured fields, cherry blossom and sunbeams. The horror in the glade faded. Happily, I let go, when something pulled me back. A howling, yowling, awesome screaming, all beast and nothing of humanity, and as the altar cracked beneath me, so Lilith cracked, a wound she'd not suffered for an aeon. I was still there, writhing in pain, but she sprang away. Her claws, deep in my blood, had touched the brand of the dragon, the tattoo on my breast above my heart, mark of the fifth essence and symbol of the inner sacred fire. The metamorphosis of dedication to the Ultimate Purity had entered into her own being and, as she had done to others, it had flayed her hand.

Flung back from the altar, her fingers in flying streamers of flesh, Lilith's spine snapped through its centre. At that moment Vespasian slipped free. He called on salvation and summoned Richard. And, sanctioned by Paradise, Richard had come. It was Lilith's final failure. With a screech of abject fury, she had disappeared and taken the veleda with her.

I drifted through star milk. The night was deliciously empowering. It smelled like chocolate and vanilla, kisses and warm summer afternoons under the vines with the sun turning the grapes dark purple, pale polished with a white sugary blush. I could smell the tiny sweet jasmine flowers and clustered orange blossom, huge cream gardenias slowly opening each petal, and black velvet roses, dew fresh. I could smell soft puffed downy pillows and crisp white cotton sheets and someone in the bed beside me who breathed my name and searched gently for me with his wish filled hands.

Then as I melted into dreamlessness, Vespasian's gift of sleep healed my memory and my mind.

Vespasian brought me back again. His voice cut through the soft pink shadows and I opened my eyes. "It's time to go," he said. "The glade is falling around us and the world is creeping back."

I was on the ground, still wrapped tight in his cloak, with his supporting hand behind my head. My chestnut tree had gone and so had the yew. A march of dark spruce lined their points between me and the sky, returning reality. It was quite light though I felt little warmth from the sun. Vespasian was kneeling beside me, watching me intently, reading my eyes, deciding whether I was stronger, or failing. Then I realised beneath the fur and velvet swathes of his cloak, I was now dressed. I wondered what I was clothed in and decided I could feel Vespasian's own woollen shirt, still warm from his body, though ripped where he'd been wounded. Above this I was covered by the long tunic he'd stolen for me before Samhain. I was wearing loosely laced hose but they were not my own gartered stockings, being too long and too thick and the feet, instead of being tucked into shoes, were around my ankles in creases.

"Am I," I peeped up at him, "wearing your clothes?"

The tucked dimples of his smile were barely controlled. "The fit is hardly a perfect one," he said, "but your own were destroyed. We face a long journey. I've the power to increase a horse's stamina but not indefinitely, so I must change horses twice at least. I've small inclination to carry a naked woman through the countryside or into the posting taverns." He'd started to smile after all. "Something I've not tried before, but I imagine it might confuse the innkeepers." He flicked my damp hair back from my face, approving my appearance perhaps. "I had no wish to embarrass you with the clothes of our dead enemies," he murmured, "blood stained and foul with their disgrace. So I gave you mine. Thick with my blood of course, and sweat, and the stains of battle. But I had no others to offer you."

So the dead had returned. Now that the sacred grove had paled into mundane reality, the bodies remanifested, rotting flesh in undug graves, strewn for the wolves and the ravens.

"So you mean to travel naked yourself?"

"I think you will notice," he said and the smile hovered, "that I am dressed, though not, I admit, very attractively. I've taken what I needed from the slain, those of my size. I can change once we reach my own home."

"Which home? London? The forest?" I hoped it would be the forest.

He shook his head. "I'm taking you to my hunting lodge in the west country, part of the de Vrais estates," he said, "where you have never been. It is many years since I lived there myself. The land was confiscated by the crown but the people remember me and my return is already prepared. We will stay there while I reclaim what's mine. Now that Arthur is dead, I shall discredit his accusations easily enough."

I could hear horses snorting and looked up. Gerald had come from between the trees, leading the black and grey hunters by their bridles, the two horses which had brought us to the glade. I had forgotten about them. "I never saw them, during the fighting," I said.

"You would not have," said Vespasian. "They were excluded. I had them tethered beyond the circle of magic. Now, are you ready, my child?"

I had no idea. "Yes," I said, "I can ride."

"Since you did not know how to ride before," he said, "it's highly unlikely that you can do so now. I was asking merely if you have the strength to be lifted, and to travel. I shall take you up before me."

Gerald, smiling at me with what he thought was sympathy and encouragement but which looked more like boyish excitement, mounted the grey. Vespasian carried me and set me carefully on the tall stallion's saddle where I clung, trying to ignore the dizziness and nausea. Vespasian quickly mounted behind me and took the reins. I leaned back against him, calming both stomach and head. The horse tossed his mane, snorting and rolling his eyes as Vespasian tightened his thighs and turning, headed for open ground. Then the trees were behind us and the grove was just a tiny blur in the distance, a small mistake in the passage of time.

We went slowly at first, walking steadily through open woodland, careful of rabbit warrens and ditches and the sudden startled flush of pheasants. It was well past midday and the sun was wintry and low without heat. I tried to close my eyes but the steady jolt of the horse kept me alert. Then, with a blast of fresh air in my face and

Vespasian's words in my ears, "Hold on. Now we must make more speed," the whole horizon opened up and the horses sprang directly from walk to Canterbury canter and from canter suddenly into a wild, free gallop.

I heard the vibrating thud of Gerald's mare behind me and the wild beat of the horse I rode, deliciously exhilarating though the cold wind stung my eyes. I extricated one tentative arm and tugged Vespasian's hood over my head, warm silken fur on my cheek. The passing miles became as much an incantation as the spells in the grove. At one time, miles turning into hours and time into space, I thought I slept. Vespasian's voice had murmured through my thoughts like a song of enchantment and carried me away into long lost lands. But I returned again to pain and bilious wakefulness.

It had been autumn when I entered the sacred nemeton, the last day of October, Samhain and Lilith's nightmare. Now I became aware of winter. The passage of the seasons had been swallowed and thrown aside. I saw the muddied slick of old snow in the shallow gullies and the horse's hooves splashed through slush, sleet and briar before heaving up again to ice hard ground and the glower of a pasty, rain heavy sky.

Then we were under trees once more, a web of bare branches in an endless spindly flurry above my head, a waving delirium, an eternity of passing cloud, blurred by speed. Either side of us were fields all grey in the deepening twilight, their ploughed furrows like dark drains, slick with collected water and flecked with white, drenched from recent rain and hail and snow. A partridge, frightened from its roadside cover, dashed suddenly across our path and another rose up, wings struggling for height, and flew off into the increasing shadows.

Beyond the hillocks and the bushes and the stretched farmlands, a village snuggled warm in its hollow, safe sheltered from the wind. I saw a cosy neighbourliness of thatched roofs and first candle flicker behind the parchment windows, all clustered around their church spire and faith in a safe God.

We slowed to a tired trot and clattered into the village as the sun dropped a final slanting light and the crescent moon came up behind the clouds. It waited to rain until we were under the tavern's porch and then tipped down with an echo of thunder and sleet. Vespasian dismounted and lifted me down, signalling to Gerald to support me. I could barely stand, but I thought Gerald fairly unsteady too. It had been a long, long time in the saddle. The ostler came to take the steaming horses while Vespasian spoke to the innkeeper. Then we were led directly inside to a backroom with a big curtained bed, two pallets and a blazing fire on the central hearth. Vespasian took three candles, lit them from the fire, and replaced them in their sconces. Then he took me from Gerald's guiding arm and helped me at once to the bed.

I sat propped against the pillows which he wedged behind me. I couldn't lie flat or the nausea pitched in. I heard the steady strum of the rain pelting outside and then the draught whistled down the chimney hole and all the smoke from the fire gusted back on us. I coughed, eyes stinging. I felt wretched and rising bile made me heave. Vespasian came instantly to my side, his hand to my forehead. He'd brought a bowl. I was violently sick. He leaned over me as I retched, carefully holding my hair back from my face. Then he turned to Gerald and spoke quietly. "Fetch water and the best hypocras. Afterwards go to the hall and order food for yourself. I know you're tired, but you have to eat and I need to be alone with Tilda for a while. When you can't keep your eyes open, you may come back and sleep on the far pallet. I'll wake you early tomorrow morning."

Vespasian turned back to me. I was shivering uncontrollably though I saw the fire, high scarlet flames and felt the heat. The sour stench of vomit invaded the bed. "You've ruined my good shirt," he said with an unexpected grin. I felt ridiculously comforted.

Gerald came bustling back with a pitcher of aromatic spiced wine, a bowl and a heap of linen strips. Behind him a small grubby boy shuffled and staggered with two buckets of warm water. The child peeped at me with curiosity but dared not speak. Vespasian dismissed him with a nod. Gerald crouched beside the fire, watching me. "You're not going to die, are you?" he asked encouragingly.

"She is not," said Vespasian. "But she's going to be extremely sick for another hour at least, and no doubt she'd prefer you not to be her audience. There's nothing more you can do to help." He looked back at me briefly with the remains of the smile. "Probably she'd prefer I wasn't part of the audience either, but she hasn't the strength to throw me out and I've no intention of leaving."

"Then I'll go and eat," said Gerald. "There's roast pig, piping hot, and cabbage boiled in milk. It smells amazing. Well, you haven't fed us the whole day, have you! Shall I bring some for you and Tilda?"

Vespasian shook his head and the sheen of his black hair reflected scarlet flames from the fire. "She'd never keep it down," he said, "and I'm not interested in food as yet. You may eat enough for all of us. Clearly you've forgotten the discipline of hard living and fighting on an empty stomach. Once you get full royal recognition and your title back, you'll have to start your knight's training. That'll include a regimen of starvation all over again."

"You'll be my trainer, I hope," said Gerald with a tentative bounce. "Yes, I know, you want me out of the way now. I'm going. But I have to keep this damned hot cloak round me or everyone will stare. My clothes are all torn and bloody."

"And very little of it your own," said Vespasian, "so go and look after yourself for a few hours and leave me to me look after Tilda."

I had a blinding headache. My stomach churned, my eyes saw only stripes and sparks and I felt utterly broken. "I think," I managed to say, though my voice sounded a long way off, mumbling like a drunkard's, "I'm going to be sick again."

When it was over, and my head, bathed in warm water, seemed to settle and my eyes saw just one of Vespasian's frowns, he indicated the rank and spoiled clothes I was wearing, and his own cotte, all rich blue velvet and gold trimming ruined, first with blood, and now sticky with my vomit.

"This has to go," he said, and shrugged the sleeves from his arms, pulling apart the torn lacing and flinging the pearl broach from the shoulder. Beneath it, neither the bliaud nor the shirt were his own. Both were too tight. He ripped them over his head, and quickly sluiced down his chest and forearms in clean water. He remained in his borrowed hose, their points now unlaced and falling loose around his hips. His left arm was striped with wounds still partially open and bleeding. A hundred other injuries patterned his body but he gave them no attention as he washed the sweat, blood and vomit from his torso. Leaning back weakly on the pillows, I watched him from half closed eyes. Strangely, in all the years that Tilda had known Vespasian, she had never before seen him stripped even to the waist. I found him extraordinarily beautiful.

He came back then and sat on the bed beside me. "Now it is your turn," he said. "I'll buy some serving girl's clothes for you tomorrow morning but in the meantime you must sleep naked. Can you raise your arms? Then I'll help you undress."

I bit my lip. "Can't I stay as I am?"

He leaned over me, brushing back the curls of sweat tangled hair from my wet forehead. "My dear child," he said patiently, "it may not be the most diplomatic moment to remind you, but I have already seen every part of you and touched every part of you and there are no secrets between us. You must now let me undress and wash you and then you can drink something, which will help, I think. After that, I believe you will sleep. These clothes will have to be burned."

It felt strange and not uncomfortable to lie quite naked on the big feather mattress with the cover replaced by cloths, while Vespasian washed my body very carefully, sensitive to the places where the injuries were deep and had to be avoided, and attentive to my own trembling, which I could not control. Then he dried me with equal care, removed the damp cloths beneath me, and pulled the cover up to my chin, tucking me in.

Eventually he fed me a little spiced wine. It tasted hot and warmed me wonderfully inside. "But I think I'll only bring it back," I mumbled.

"Not this one," said Vespasian softly. "This one, I have doctored."

And so I slept again and did not dream at all.

CHAPTER FIFTY-FIVE

Vespasian told the inn keeper he was father to us both, Gerald and I, and that we'd been overtaken by thieves on the road. We had all put up a fight, hence our bloody injuries, but although we'd managed to keep hold of two of our three horses and Vespasian's jewels and encrusted cotte, we'd lost all our baggage. This was also supposed to explain my unkempt and nauseous state. Feminine hysteria no doubt. "We are obviously most inept fighters," sighed Vespasian absently. "We shall have to try harder next time."

Gerald was sulky about the fabrication. "You've just beaten fifty men or more, not to mention those – well – what were they? Demons," he said with his impressive snort. "And I don't think I did too badly myself. And now you let people think we're cowards? My God, you were incredible, Vespasian. I mean, my lord. We were incredible. And now this robbery story makes me look stupid."

"Courage and cowardice are merely absurdities of circumstance." Vespasian shrugged, a pewter mug of breakfast ale in one hand and a wedge of dark bread in the other. "It's those too frightened to be cowards who practise courage for safety's sake." It was a little past dawn and he'd arranged food to be served in our chamber. The rain had cleared and the day looked brighter. Gerald was tucking into a large platter of goose egg pancakes with honey and I felt my stomach lurch. I was not eating.

"That sounds mighty prim and pompous," said Gerald, forgetting his new found filial respect, "but it's all been so exciting and there's not a soul I can tell."

"Don't talk with your mouth full," said Vespasian, "and don't wipe your mouth on your sleeve, there's a napkin to your right. Your training for knighthood is obviously going to be a long one. Besides, once you send for Osbert and Steven and Walter, you can show off your new grandeur to your heart's content. Only remember they're unlikely to believe everything you tell them. In the meantime, we've two more day's riding in front of us so I intend making an early start. I can give the horses strength and endurance, but all magic has its limits, and the horses must travel at a speed they recognise."

Gerald looked up at his step-father. "You're not taking me with you all the way, are you?" he asked. "You mean to leave me at the Tennaton estate."

"You must put your own house in order, and I, mine," Vespasian nodded. "I shall take Tilda with me to Gloucestershire but we'll both come down to visit you once she's fully recovered. The new manager I've installed is a good man. He'll look after you."

I felt strong enough for the first few miles. Flax country, we passed quickly between shorn fields in silence until the sun rose up higher into a soft golden haze. Fresh washed now, everything glistened and the air smelled good. I was wearing the rough linen of a serving girl's clothes from the inn and I thought Vespasian might have stolen them until I saw that his pearl broach was missing. Some of his own clothes were new as well, though his cotte had been steamed and cleaned with fuller's earth and must have been brushed with sand for three hours at least, until all marks of my rebellious stomach had gone. Some of the blood remained and the material was hacked and damaged, including a great slash down the left arm. It would take many hours to mend. He wore a thin brown woollen mantle like a journeyman's which contrasted strangely with the ornate cotte, but I was still wrapped in his own luxurious fur cloak.

The new palfreys, though fresh, were stubborn and slow to speed. Vespasian spurred forwards once we came to open ground and the horses reluctantly pressed into a rhythmic canter, their ears back, heavy hoofed. They tired quickly and when we slowed again Gerald came up to ride abreast and began to talk. "You look better Tilda. Yesterday you were green and yellow. This morning you look almost pink. How do you feel?"

Vespasian had not asked me how I felt. In fact, I was not feeling well at all. The nausea was churning back bile again and all across my body the pain concentrated, burning up to the top of my head where it pounded like hoof beats. "Yes, I'm all right," I said.

"Everything starts to fade, doesn't it?" Gerald said. His bright hair was pretty in the winter sun and he looked remarkably healthy himself. "I mean, now I even wonder if it was all a dream."

"But that's what Lilith said, isn't it," I told him. "It was a dream. A true one. Nothing so true could be as mundane as reality."

"Yes, but that's trickery," sniffed Gerald. "Those sorts of things don't make sense. When I'm a great knight perhaps I'll look back and understand it and tell stories to my grandchildren."

I had thought Vespasian lost in his own thoughts but now he interrupted. "Greatness is the result of transcendence," he said, as soft as the hill's breeze in our faces. "To transcend, it is necessary to rise beyond. And only by returning to the beginning, can one go beyond. Then, to return to the beginning, it is necessary to transcend."

"You see," said Gerald to me, "that's the sort of thing he says. I just can't make head nor tail of it."

"That's something to do with alchemy," I said, almost as if I understood although in fact I did not. "Don't think about all that. Tell me about your grandchildren."

He laughed, but it reminded him of something. "You know, in the middle of the battle, when I wasn't nimble enough and my grandmother got hold of me and Vespasian grabbed you and there was all that talk about letting me go or he'd kill you and shut the gates, well I didn't understand a word of that either. It was horrible."

"It was all horrible," I said. "Perhaps it's better if we don't understand."

Gerald's horse had dropped behind and he trotted up quickly beside me. "It'll be wonderful to explore my own house, but I wish you were both coming with me," he said rather sadly. "It'll be dreadfully lonely being left on my own. I've never been alone, you know. Not ever. Vespasian's always looked after me. Of course if I'd been a normal baron's son, I'd have been sent away from home when I was seven and I'm glad that didn't happen. I'd have been sent to some boring family for training, and probably swapped for their poor son. It's a horrid idea, if you ask me."

"I imagine it's supposed to teach independence," I suggested.

Gerald sighed. "I don't want to be independent yet. I just wish you were both coming to stay with me."

"Vespasian has to start claiming back his own estates."

"Which may end up being mine too," Gerald said, cheerful again. "Unless he has children of his own with you, Tilda."

I felt the blush rising from my ears inwards. "Don't be stupid."

"Sorry. I won't tease you." Gerald was aware of Vespasian pretending not to listen. "But it'll feel mighty odd having you for a step-mother." Then he caught my glare and sniggered. "I'll be quiet," he said. "Besides, I suppose I ought to start thinking about tonight. Before Vespasian brought you from London, he set me up with new staff. There's a farm manager and an estate manager who mutters in French, and a grand steward and a secretary who seems to do nothing but talk Latin. I can't understand any of them. Then there's loads of new servants, including a cook, would you believe? We used to spend half the year starving and now I'm going to have my very own cook. I suppose the place will soon feel like my own, but there's a lot to learn."

"So you're officially the baron already?"

"I suppose I always was without knowing," said Gerald. "Now Arthur's dead, well – it's all just there for picking."

"And all organised before the fight with Arthur and Lilith? He must have been very certain we were going to win." I looked up at the underside of Vespasian's jaw, which was soft and indicated a smile.

"Had we lost," said Vespasian, "I doubt the futility of my arrangements would have concerned us within the greater scheme of heavenly priorities."

Gerald sniffed, "You mean we'd have all been dead."

"Precisely," he said. "It was always the likeliest probability."

The day was warming and the sun had turned apricot. It was approaching midday and the horses were already tired. Vespasian let them slow to an amble, enjoying the warmth on our faces. We took a long lane between orchards and Gerald reached up and grabbed two little apples, left late to ripen on their stubby tree, smelling sharp and strong. The rest had been harvested long before.

There were hives under the trees, little wooden industries waiting for the next year's cherry and pear blossoms. Along the hedge tops, sheets had been spread to dry like wild swans stretched on a green tapestry, all crisp in the sunshine. There were cottages tucked into the countryside, chimney holes gusting peat smoke through the thatch, a sudden flock of great white geese hissing at the horses from the other side of a weedy green pond. Serfs, husband and wife, were tending their own strip and planting peas against thin canes. The manor house straddled the hill behind the steady sounds of someone chopping wood. The bare tree branches were thin stitcheries of empty embroidery against the washed out sky but the lattice of holly prickles along the hedges was house to the lark and the robin, the field mouse and the wandering weasel, hiding entrances to the badger's set and the tunnel to mole's loamy hole.

I heard movement and life. I felt part of the season, aware of the scuffle of little surreptitious daytime hunting and the patient snore of hibernation. I heard all things and was part of everything. I felt magic in my veins and wild mysteries rushing like streams in my head. I still felt the pain, but it was subjugated to pleasure.

Gerald's words tumbled me back. "Isn't it dinner time?"

"You still have your knife," said Vespasian. "Catch yourself a hare."

"And eat it raw? Besides, I'm not nearly quick enough for that sort of hunting and you probably wouldn't even wait for me." Gerald lapsed again into silence. I was glad. Something was happening to me and I wanted it to go on. Then Gerald spoke to me again and all the fantasy was gone. "The people Vespasian put on my estates, he'd known them years before," said Gerald. "He went around and found people he trusted. I suppose he had lots of staff and retainers and everything before he changed his name and went into hiding."

"Did you think I was born an outlaw and hermit?" Vespasian interrupted, his voice brushing the top of my hair. "I was able to trace those I previously employed." I had flung back the hood of his cloak and the sun was increasingly sweet.

"I suppose you had real friends once," agreed Gerald with interest.

"I seem to remember some." Vespasian laughed, a peaceful chuckle half lost behind the sound of the horses blowing the lane's dust from their nostrils. His smiles and gentleness soothed me. His wounds were untreated, the long riding must have strained every bruised muscle, but this was the first time in all the years since his wife's murder that he knew absolute satisfaction and the joy of serenity. In unexpected abundance, he'd achieved the amazing totality of his ambition. Arthur's evil had been utterly destroyed from the world.

It was another hour before we rode into Gerald's grand forecourt. I'd admired his beautiful new home before, when brought there from the burning convent. But now I could appreciate nothing. I was increasingly weak and the long journey was turning into another nightmare. The pain had become constant. Vespasian, watching me always, understood. He spent little time settling Gerald. "Tomorrow your men can send the horse back to the inn and retrieve your own," said Vespasian. "There's nothing more I can do for you at the moment except give you my blessing. You're a child no longer, my son. Go and order your life as you wish, eat well and then rest. But I've no intention of deserting you for long. Perhaps, before they think they're deserted themselves, you should collect the rest of the boys. I believe most still remain at the forest house."

"How do you know?" demanded Gerald, stamping mud from his boots and striding around his own courtyard with all the pride of the young lord he was about to become. "That night in the glade feels like a month ago and time's part of the magic, isn't it? I mean, we went in for Hallowe'en but now it's December at least."

"Yesterday was Candlemas," said Vespasian. "The day of my own birth. It is now symbolic of rebirth. And you must not question how I know what I know, my child. It is beyond you. Just accept that I know it."

We left Gerald standing at his own grand doorway, beaming at us in the sunshine. I managed to smile and wave before sinking back heavily against Vespasian's support. I thought I might faint. He turned the horse slowly, and headed back onto the low blueing heaths. "Close your eyes, and sleep," he told me. "I cannot ride too carefully, or we will never reach a place where I can help you properly, piccina. If the pain becomes insupportable, you must tell me."

I thought I heard him singing. At first I believed it was his own happiness, and then I slept, and understood.

When I awoke again to astonishing pain, we were already under cover of dark, the trees were ghosts in the moonlight and I was cold. Vespasian felt me stir and spoke softly. "Another few minutes and we stop for the night. I'll take you to the nearest tavern, though it isn't respectable. No matter, I think it unwise to travel further tonight. The poison's crawling deeper. You'll be warm there, and I can look after you."

The sky was deepest black and the moon just a sliver to the east. Above me the enormity of star spangle drifted like spilled milk, one star huge above the horizon like the star on my tarot card. For a moment I wondered if reality had blurred, as Vespasian had done in the sacred glade.

Then a small white wind flew suddenly over my head between me and the starlight, a barn owl out on the hunt, and I was back in the world I recognised. I heard another owl calling softly to his moon, and then the unexpected jolt of four golden eyes under the trees. "They'll not harm us," Vespasian's voice seemed to drift like the star gleam. "The wolves are hungry and tired too but we're surrounded by my magic and they fear us."

The tavern was outside the village on the turn of the highway, squat under a bare oak tree. Vespasian dismounted first and carried me down in his arms. I could not have walked and he seemed to know. The horse was led away, froth on his dull flanks. Vespasian ordered a private chamber and carried me to it. It was small with several disordered pallets and an old uncurtained bed, a lumpy mattress on a low palliasse. There was no hearth but two tallow candles were lit and a brazier of hot coals stood by the window. I expected lice but it seemed clean enough. "I shall fetch you gruel if they have it," he said. "It is too long since you ate."

"You haven't eaten either," I mumbled. I felt dreadful and I certainly wasn't hungry. "And I should treat your wounds too."

He ignored me and went to find the innkeeper. It was a far busier tavern than before, with noises of bustle. I heard loud drunken singing, laughter and someone shouting, answered with the sound of blows. I buried my ears in the pillows. Vespasian came back with a serving girl, food, wine, and more hot coals for the brazier. "We'll doubtless be disturbed this night," he said, coming to sit beside me with a bowl of pottage and a spoon. "This inn serves as a wayside brothel, as many of them do around here. But I've told them my lady is ill. If we aren't left in peace, I've promised to cut the tavern keeper's throat and feed him to the wolves. I think he believes me." Personally, so would I.

The steam from the bowl and its heady perfume were bringing back the nausea. I was sinking into blackness. There were knives in the black, and shudders of pain. Vespasian frowned, put the food back on the floor and leaned over me, both eyes and hands examining. I tried to speak but my voice wasn't there. Vespasian put his finger to my lips and shook his head. "Hush now my quicksilver child, and let me explore," he said, just whispers in the dark.

There was no time to be timid, and I was in too much pain. He searched my body and I felt his warm strong hands beneath my clothes. But I abandoned consciousness and once again entered the sleep he granted me.

CHAPTER FIFTY-SIX

I dreamed that he slept close, his body curled to mine and his arm around me. But when I woke with a narrow beam of sun in my eyes from the slit above the window shutters, he was on the far side of the bed outstretched and propped up on one elbow, looking across at me.

I yawned and stretched and watched his slow smile. His voice was barely there. "It seems last night's doctoring helped, little one."

"I don't remember much," I said. "But this morning feels like a good morning."

"Then you will break fast, with some bread and ale at least," he said, "and afterwards we'll take the road. There's a fresh horse waiting and a warm sun. With nothing to delay us, we should reach my home by early afternoon."

The horse was placid and the sun sped our ride, fair weather for my Fairweather. We came to his hunting lodge shortly after midday and I saw it like a fairy palace, pale stone glittering in the winter sun, surrounded by trees and nestled in the tuck of two little hills. We rode down to it from the higher ground and coming nearer saw the stream flash like silvered onyx and the turn of the mill creaking between house and banks. Behind was a square of vineyard, shorn now in its tidy rows, a small orchard and a courtyard of outbuildings and stables leading to the kitchen garden. Then stretched the great sweep of ploughed farmland beyond.

I leaned forward over the pummel, impatient for the first glimpses. "But it's so big," I said into the swirl of his cloak. "You called it a hunting lodge. I imagined small and cosy."

"There is nothing small about the de Vrais barony," he answered me in the soft voice of apology, "and nothing you might choose to call cosy. My ancestors were never known for their humility."

I believed that without any difficulty. "But it's beautiful."

"I am glad you like it," he said simply.

I wondered if he had previously sent notice of his arrival, and if his people had been hired to set things in order as they had for Gerald. I soon learned they had. Now I also knew what had taken Vespasian such a long time before coming to get me in London.

There were six stable boys and a head groom as we clattered into a cobbled courtyard. Feeling dull and horribly crumpled in my serving woman's linen beneath a man's cloak while knowing my complexion to be unfashionably tanned and disgustingly sickly, I insisted on dismounting unaided. I walked slowly across to the doorway held open for me and into the shadows within. Vespasian stood back a little, understanding. There were servants at the step but he dismissed them all, took my elbow, and together we went inside.

Vespasian's house welcomed me with long slanting sunbeams across marble tiles. The high walls were lined with tapestries so vivid at first I thought they were windows. But I was allowed no time to look around. Through the great hall, up five stone steps, still watched by the bobbing huddle of servants, Vespasian led me directly to the master chamber. Intimidated by such unaccustomed grandeur and desperately shy, I hesitated, but he guided me across to the high curtained bed, closing the door behind him. To him of course, I was as transparent as always. "Don't be a fool," he told me softly. "Would you sooner faint on the bed or in my arms? Lie still and close your eyes."

It was some time before he returned. I knew I must have slept again, for the long windows let in only a muted darkness and a streak of moonshine. Vespasian sat on the huge carved chest under the window, one foot up and his elbow on his knee.

"Here we go again," I said wearily.

"Did you expect to recover more quickly?" he said. "I'm afraid that would be impossible. Didn't you realise you were poisoned?"

I hadn't realised, but of course, it made sense. Not that any of it made sense. Vespasian had nursed me so many times, I had been wounded so many times, pain and torture had become the habit of my life, and my body was a patchwork of injuries, old and new. As usual he seemed to know what I was thinking. "Before there was only the spite of a human hand," he said. "This time, you were tormented with all the malicious barbarity and malevolence of Lilith herself. You cannot possibly conceive what that entails."

"No," I whispered. "Not really. You put me into a trance."

"But now," he said, "I have all the tools of healing around me. Before I had nothing more than hot water, a piss pot for you to vomit into and the power of my own hands. But this house is a study of alchemy, of medicine, of potions and magic." He was watching me, and thinking aloud. "I will not dose you with poppy syrup if I can avoid it. Opiates can also enslave the patients they cure." He paused, and smiled. "It might be easier to get you drunk."

I wondered if he'd gone quite mad, and stared. "Drunk? But I'll just be sick again."

He said, "You need an anaesthetic of some kind, piccina. Lilith's splinter is buried inside the dragon. I must remove it but the pain will be far too much for you to bear alone."

"I thought," it was so hard to think at all, "the dragon brand frightened her. That's why you put it there, isn't it? You said it burned her and cut her hands."

There was a corner hearth with a proper chimney and over the flames a domed copper hood gleamed with dancing reflections. Two long windows flanked the hearth and Vespasian drew heavy tapestries across the shutters, enclosing the warmth and colour and leaping firelight. As the master chamber, there was only one bed with a truckle rolled beneath. The velvet hangings were pulled back, their heavy golden folds disguising the patterns of the embroidery. The mattress was wide enough for several people and so thick and softly padded that in spite of the pain, I had never known a bed so comfortable. The high beamed ceiling now sprang with light from fire and candle. The beeswax was sweet scented. I barely recognised the difference between dream and reality anymore and this seemed to encompass both.

He came and sat close to me on the bed, looking down at me. "Lilith's nail entered your breast," he said softly. "That's when she touched the dragon. She was hurled backwards and the altar split but she left the point of her claw in your body. It's been worming inwards and poisoning you ever since. It would kill you, if I left it. I've treated most of the other wounds during our journey, but until now, this was beyond me." He put his palm to my forehead. His fingers were icy and I shivered. "Now I must not wait any longer," he told me.

I knew I was feverish. I was also sick with disgust, knowing some part of Lilith was still inside me. "Can I – sleep?" I asked, "while you do – whatever you do? Won't you make me unconscious again?"

He shook his head. His eyes reflected the firelight. I knew he was worried. "This isn't simple nursing, piccina," he said. "My power challenges hers. This time your heart is her battlefield, your body the altar. I will not risk you dying under trance. I might not even know, until it was too late."

He gave me heavily spiced wine and propped me up while he held the cup. The wine was dark red, almost black in the curtain shadows, and tasted glorious. It was unlike anything I'd ever drunk before. Tilda wasn't used to strong alcohol but I was, so I was surprised when I realised, very quickly, I was intoxicated. Vespasian watched me intently while I drank, and when the cup was empty, he refilled it. "I've had – enough," I said and my voice sounded absurdly plaintive.

He smiled with a trace of the old malice. "What an easy conquest you would have been, had my intentions been otherwise." I thought it an unwise subject for him to tease me with.

"You've drugged the wine," I accused. Now my words were slurred.

He lifted the cup to my mouth, insisting I drink again. "Of course."

He removed some of my pillows so I lay almost flat. "The wine is doctored," he said, "though not with the poppy. It will help, a little."

Carefully, one by one, he removed my clothes, though left my tunic bundled around my hips and over my belly, groin and legs. Then he unwound the bandaging he'd tied during our journey. I lay back on his bed, uncovered to the waist. I was now used to being undressed in his presence, but even half drunk and half drugged, I was timid at the intimacy of his fingers brushing across my breasts. I'd liked the warmth of his own soft shirt against me, but now my sudden nakedness made me tremble. I closed my eyes.

While I was partially naked, Vespasian wore a new linen shirt belted over his hose. One sleeve was ripped up to the shoulder, exposing his left arm, now heavily bandaged. I counted the small wounds still scratched across his face and hands. I wondered if either of us would ever be free of Lilith's battle scars.

I couldn't look down at myself now, but I knew what lay there. Over the long months, the dragon brand had sunk into flat lines like dark embroidery. Now plunging deep into its snarl, was a black hole which bled continuously, leaking a pinkish slime. My breast was red and inflamed. It hurt like the devil.

Vespasian washed me with herbal salves. Then he stretched his long fingers, hot from the water, and began to massage around the outline of the dragon. The pain flared at once. I gasped and held my breath. "Breathe," he ordered me. "Breathe deep, little one. I cannot be quick."

I'd always liked the hard strength of his hands. Now his fingertips felt like iron. His palms rubbed against my nipples but he ignored my discomfort. He probed close to the dragon's wings, watching both where his fingers worked, and then my face, constantly reading my expression. He was not gentle at all. Spasms of pain raged through me. He spoke often, or chanted, first with words I couldn't understand though I thought the language might be Greek or Arabic, then softly in English, and sometimes directly to me. If he hoped to distract me from the agony he himself was now inflicting, then it was quite in vain. I didn't dare flinch. I bit my lips and stayed very still, staring up at him as if I could enter his eyes. "I cannot hurt you less," he said. "I am sorry."

His hands roamed. He pressed deeper. For a moment it seemed his fingers were groping inside my body, always searching for the splinter. He traced it from the dragon's tiny snout, along its relentless passage into my flesh. Now I could imagine it in me, wriggling ever closer towards my heart.

Then at last I felt it inside and screamed. "It is nearly over," he said, and leaned across me. His breath was in my eyes. A magical promise, with one brief moment's relief. Then something plunged red hot into my breast. I screamed again, and with the point of a long curved silver needle, he hooked the splinter and plied it out.

He held it up to me. It was green as a jewel and burned with a small wisp of foul smelling steam. "It is finished," he said. "There is nothing more."

I slumped, gasping for breath. For a moment I was fainting. Then his breath was in my eyes again and in spite of weakness, I felt a delicious sensation like sleep and invigoration all mixed up together. "It feels – wonderfully – better already." I sounded drunk.

Vespasian grinned. I saw the sweat beads gleaming on his forehead and forearms, gathering along the creases of his own dark scars. He looked utterly exhausted, and totally happy.

He still held the needle. It was slick with my blood and tiny points of weeping flesh. Its length had pierced the tip of the splinter, now quickly disappearing into smoke. He flung it into a small pewter bowl and watched until it burned to ashes. Then he threw the ashes on the fire. Spitting into tiny green flares, they spluttered, then died, and were gone. Vespasian washed his hands in the herb scented water and then came back beside me. He began to wash my breast. The hole in the dragon's face gaped red and ugly.

Vespasian took a small metal object with a narrow blunt end, and thrust it for some moments into the heart of the fire. When he returned to the bed, he leaned over me again, his eyes inches from my own.

"One last torment, piccina," he said softly, and instantly brought the red hot metal onto my skin at the point of the wound. I smelled burned flesh and thought I'd faint. The mark on my breast singed and puckered. Then it closed into a tiny dark keyhole.

Vespasian used a soft blue ointment and began to cover the face of the dragon. He pushed some very gently into the cauterized wound with the tip of his finger. Finally, with patience and care, he bandaged all across my chest, tucking my breasts into the linen binding.

I thought he'd tell me to sleep. I could see the deep bruises of exhaustion around his eyes and white pain around the edges of his lips. I was so tired I knew I couldn't have moved from the bed if Lilith herself had appeared. I whispered, "Thank you," and nothing else because I had no voice left.

He ripped the last bandage, tying the ends around me in a quick knot, testing its resilience. He looked up at me over his busy fingers. "This will heal slowly," he said. "But the poison is gone. The splinter is gone. Gradually, the pain will be gone." He lifted me slightly, his hand at my back, wedging pillows again behind my head. It seemed he was purposefully avoiding my eyes. He stood and I thought I heard him breathe more deeply. Then what he said was so shockingly abrupt, I was sure I was dreaming.

"But now," he frowned, choosing his words with more care than usual, "within the next few days, if you will accept it Tilda, I believe I must find you a husband."

I was completely inebriated, which wasn't helping. Then all the tiredness and the desire to sleep fled away. I opened my mouth and no words came out at all. Finally, I managed to squeak, "What?"

But he had already left the room with an armful of unguents and bandages, and I knew perfectly well that he'd intentionally spoken at the moment of leaving and that he wouldn't allow me conversation on the subject until I was stronger, when he would not be able to avoid it.

CHAPTER FIFTY-SEVEN

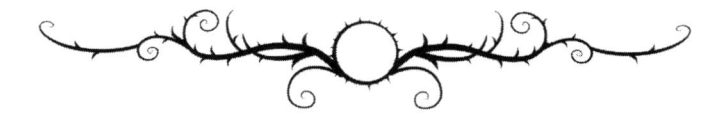

I woke twice, briefly, in the night, aware of being watched. Vespasian had pulled the truckle bed out into the room and was sleeping at some distance from me, lost in the far shadows away from the guttering fire. But though the shape of him beneath the covers was immovable, I was sure I saw the black glitter of his eyes under half closed lids, and believed he was awake and aware.

When I stirred in the morning, he had gone. I had a hangover.

My head thumped with a malicious regularity, but the rest of my body breathed easy, blissfully relaxed. There was no deep pain. The assault which had previously so ravaged my body, was just a memory.

Tired muscles ached from hours in the saddle, I was weak and light headed from days of nausea, very little food and a surfeit of wine the previous evening. The tracery of bruises, cuts and healing scars stung and any sudden movement still made me wince. Where Vespasian had specifically probed the wound over the dragon brand, the skin was inflamed and the whole area sore. Even my unpractised wrist was swollen, throbbing from the weight of the sword. But none of it compared to the pain of before. No agony remained of Lilith's claw in my breast. Even the brand seemed to have shrunk. I stretched my legs, curled my toes and exhaled very deeply. It was delicious.

Then I remembered what Vespasian said before I fell asleep, and my contentment faded.

I tried to get up and open the shutters. The sunshine was buzzing outside, a whole golden morning waited beyond the sickroom. But staggering from the bed was not as easy as I'd expected and my legs collapsed neatly beneath me like an ironing board. I giggled, clambered to my knees and squirmed back under the coverlet. I was then surprised to discover myself, though still semi naked, wearing soft woollen hose, lacings loose, beneath which I was conscious of the remarkable and unexpected folds of a man's linen braies.

I began to hone and practise the words I intended saying to Vespasian once he reappeared, a dignified combination of intense gratitude, and denial of his unwelcome wedding plans, but found that I had a disconcerting time given me to repeat, and then forget them. Vespasian did not come.

"I might have been dead by now," I said in exasperation when he finally strode into the room many tedious hours later.

He had brought me a bowl of soup spiced with cumin and a mug of mulberry wine. "I'm delighted to find you so full of humble gratitude," he said. "You will now eat, and drink, and regain even more of your strength."

He put the bowl and spoon into my hands and the cup on the chest beside the bed. He was leaving again. I would never get to use my much practised speech. "At once?" I demanded. I relented. "I suppose you have a lot to do."

He paused at the doorway. "After being away from the estate for something in the way of twelve years, yes, I find there are one or two things I need to attend to."

"Alright. It doesn't matter," I said. "And I am grateful. Incredibly, stunningly endlessly grateful. So grateful that I can't think of the right words. But you said something else last night which has worried me ever since, and I wanted to talk about it."

"Ah," he said, coming back reluctantly into the room. "I understand. Then I shall stay just a few minutes longer, if you will eat that soup."

I ate the soup, which was thick and very good. The nausea did not return. "Though I have a headache," I said.

"A modest superfluity of wine last night," he suggested, looking down at me. The fire had dulled into a scatter of peat ash without flame but the room retained the warmth and was already daytime bright. He now lifted open the window shutters so the sun streaked in through the sheepskin parchments and haloed around the gleam of his hair. So often tangled and ignored, his hair now looked newly washed and combed, reflecting the light like black polished metal or the square jet crystals of the brooch at his shoulder.

All my studied speech was lost. I said the first thing that came into my head. "You've put me into under-pants," I said. "Women don't wear braies."

There was a slight pause before he answered, while controlling the vague twitch at the corners of his mouth. "What an unexpected child you can be, Tilda," he said. "You're wearing a gentleman's hose, my own in fact, and they come complete with braies as the laces combine. I thought you might enjoy some unexpected modesty, so both for your own sake and for mine, a little added coverage seemed – let us say – suitable. But from now on I imagine you'll be able to dress yourself and there will be fewer mistakes. It seems the skills of undressing a woman and of dressing her again, are quite diverse, and clearly I am more adept at one than the other. Soon I must even forgo the repeated pleasure of undressing you. Instead I'll order new clothes made up. You can of course choose your own fabrics."

I had finished the soup and handed back the bowl. I certainly didn't want the wine. "It wasn't clothes I wanted to talk about," I said, studiously polite. "If you have the time, that is. It was about finding me – a husband."

He sat, most reluctantly I thought, and faced me. "You've already told me several times," he said, "that you don't wish to be married. Considering the lame proposals I know you've already received from some of your young companions, I can appreciate the reasons for this. I thought I might find you someone a little older, somewhat more intelligent and considerably more wealthy."

Molly wasn't used to medieval arrangements. "That's a horrid idea," I said. "I suppose you think I've been unchaperoned in and out of your bed for so long now that you have to make me respectable." I was falling over my words in such a panic that I bit my tongue. "But no one knows me, and I'm no one anyway, so there's no one to be shocked. I don't want to be parcelled off on some stranger."

His face showed a mixture of mild surprise and stifled amusement. "Since I'm virtually your guardian," he said patiently, "this would seem a natural development. I'd try and find you someone you could approve of."

I was losing any hope of composure. "Approve of? Someone who would only beat me on Saturdays, for instance? For God's sake, Vespasian, or whatever I'm expected to damn well call you these days, am I supposed to think that conciliatory? You tease me with talk of undressing me and in the same breath you tell me to marry a man I've never met. And what should I tell this poor deluded creature about all the scars on my body, and the nightmares, and the brand of a dragon that you say will never fade? If I ever let him undress me at all, that is, which I doubt. He'll think I'm a witch."

I thought of adding, and I suppose in a way, I am, but thought better of it. "It was easier when you were sick," sighed Vespasian. "You were less argumentative."

"And you're quite monstrously unfeeling," I said, with a great deal of feeling myself. "I suppose you don't know what else to do with me, and you don't want to have me just wandering around the kitchens and getting in your steward's way. But after everything that's happened, I think it exceptionally nasty of you to talk about palming me off on some unknown man."

"I accept your apology," said Vespasian, straight backed, a threatening glitter in the black eyes.

"Yes, I know," I said, deep breaths again and taking a gulp of wine after all. "I do apologise. You've been wonderful of course and I owe you my life. Many times over and much more than just my life. But –"

He was standing again, and was ready to leave the room. "If you wish to continue this quarrel later," he said, "I shall come back prepared. In the mean time I have a lot to do and you are making your headache a great deal worse."

Which was true. But how did he know I had a headache anyway? "I just wanted to say," I added quickly as he opened the door, "that if you want me to get respectably married and consider it so important to my non-existent reputation, then you should marry me yourself."

There was complete silence. He stood at the doorway, the door half open. After a moment he closed it again and strode back over to me. He was frowning so deeply that his eyelids were almost closed and the soft curl of black lashes almost masked the glint of annoyance. He was not in the slightest amused. At first I thought he would come and sit beside me on the bed again, but after a moment he walked off to the window and stood with his back to me, gazing out over his own courtyard. He spoke slowly and with some care, his voice so soft that, as usual, I had to strain for every word.

"My dear child," he said, "as you are aware, I have been Arthur, I have knelt at Lilith's altar and I delighted in her foul breath for some years when I was young. My alchemy was pitch as night until I learned better, when it was almost too late. In all other senses," he turned then and looked at me steadily across the room, "both before I knew Ingrid and again after her departure, I have been as profligate and corrupt in dissipation as whim and desire led me. The circumstances of Ingrid's death made me angry, perhaps, at the world, and it seemed that very little mattered. I explored most aspects of lust and indulgence, and my imagination in those areas was extensive and diverse. You do not want me either as lover or husband, Tilda, and I will not listen to arguments. You know what I did to you."

He turned back to the window, but he did not again go to the door. He was silent, perhaps lost in thought. I tried to answer softly as he did, controlling my voice so that it would have more substance. "Then all that rich experience could be mighty useful," I said, "since I have none."

He answered at once, his back to me, "It is out of the question. We will not talk of this again."

It was insultingly dismissive and I was increasingly angry. "It's impossible to understand you," I said, aware I was now shouting. "Sometimes I trust you completely. You're the only person I trust. You've saved my life so often and nursed me and protected me. All right, so you don't want me and I'm a peasant brat who can't marry a baron and I'm not attractive to you. But why be all snarls and malice and treat me as though I was your enemy?"

He came then, and sat on the bed as I'd hoped he would. "You must not trust me," he said, quite gently. "I am not your friend, Tilda, and you shouldn't think of me that way. If I treat you harshly, it is to warn you away, because I'm no fit companion for you at all."

I stopped shouting and lapsed into a momentary acceptance of rejection. "I'm not a child to be patronised," I said, ashamed. "Remember, somewhere, somehow, I have my own dark side. I am the gatekeeper to Hell."

He smiled then, for which I was deeply grateful. "Not anymore I think. Unless the veleda returns to claim you, there's no need to think anymore on that."

"I'm sorry," said Tilda. "I suppose you think I'm terribly precocious. I shouldn't have said what I did." I was shivering. The coverlet was pulled up to my chin and I knew I was blushing. "I am grateful for everything. Besides, I certainly don't want to antagonise you."

"Perhaps a little late," he murmured.

"Yes, how unwise of me," I muttered into the bedcover, "since I know very well what a foul temper you have." Looking up, I saw the corners of his mouth twitch with what I recognised as sudden amusement. "Well, you do," I said. "You know very well that you do. Anyway, you don't have to worry that I'll go chasing after you or jumping into your bed. I won't marry anyone." I wished he would go.

But since I now wanted him to go, he did not. "I am not some naïve village boy," he said, "or one of your youthful admirers such as Walter or Richard." He smiled more gently and leaning forwards, he took my hand in his, which startled me. His hand was warm and I knew mine was icy cold and trembling. "I've always been aware of your infatuation, Tilda. It was why I treated you with as much respect and whatever kindness I was capable of. Not much perhaps, but at least I did not bed you, when you tried to make me do so. I would not then, and I will not now."

Tilda hadn't realised she'd been so obvious, or her attempts at attracting him so inept. She was blushing furiously and on the point of tears. "You can rape me, then?" she shouted at him. "But you can't be tender?"

His eyes went black and he released my hand quite suddenly. He stood, frowning for a moment. "You know my reasons for that," he said.

"For that, yes," I said. "But not for this."

His eyes remained on me for one moment. Then he turned abruptly and left the room, closing the door quietly behind him. I curled back onto the pillows and cried through a churning nausea and the raging acceleration of my headache.

The day seemed long and doubly tedious and there was nothing to do except contemplate a cold, lonely future.

It was evening again before he returned. I had cried, slept and woken. The headache still pounded at my temples but I was stronger, and I was hungry. He came over directly as he entered the room and stood over me again. I was immediately aware of a change in his face. The bruises of exhaustion around his eyes were emphasised and beneath the prominent cheekbones, his face seemed drawn and shadowed. I knew how badly wounded he had been and a moment's guilt made me regret my overflowing emotions, having made everything harder, for both of us. Again he sat beside me. "Rejection is a hard teacher, Tilda," he said. "You've already been so badly hurt and I shouldn't have hurt you more. But it's better if you accept the inevitable."

The sun had gone from the room and I thought I could hear a steady drizzle outside the newly raised shutters. It was early evening, wintry dark, and becoming cold again. He saw me shiver. "I'll send a boy to rekindle the fire. Are you hungry?"

I nodded. I hoped my tears had dried. "I'm feeling much better," I said, as evenly as I could. "But I'm tired. So are you. You look terrible."

He smiled. "I imagine I do." He suddenly swung both legs up on the bed, one knee bent, leaning back against the foot board, facing me. He was appraising me so intently from beneath lowered lids that I felt Tilda's blush renewed. The candles had not been lit and we sat in deepening shadows. Knowing myself examined, I pulled the blanket up to my chin again.

"That's surely a little pointless now," he pointed out. "But I confess I find your easy blushes endearing."

His sensuality was mesmerising. Deeply aware of sensations Tilda had no idea how to control, nor even barely recognise, she was uncomfortable with the hard lurch in my groin and its steady pounding rhythm. I wondered how in God's name I'd been married for seven years and enjoyed two other lovers previously without ever having experienced anything quite like this.

Tilda was still blushing. "You can't help being nasty, can you?" she sniffed. "Shall I throw all my covers off then? Or should I just wait until you go to your own bed, since you seem unlikely to come to this one, and crawl into the straw with you?"

This time he grinned. "Do you hope to seduce me, Tilda? You are delightfully unpractised. But remember, I'm old enough to be your father."

I watched him watch me. I hadn't seen him blink. His head back against the foot board was unmoving. "A great exaggeration," said Tilda. "I'm eighteen and in my nineteenth year. I'm not only of marriageable age but almost beyond it. The queen wasn't quite fourteen when she married."

Vespasian continued to grin. "For all my vices, child, I am not the king."

"And I'm not a virgin," said Tilda, with some courage.

This time he did not seem angry. "Perhaps I am not quite old enough to be your father," he said. "But I repeat, I do not intend to make love to you, and nor will I allow you to seduce me. I believe I have rather more control than you seem to give me credit for."

"I give you credit for plenty," said Tilda crossly. "As you keep saying, you've undressed me many times, you've nursed me and washed me and you know every part of me. And," it was impossible to hide the blushing but I continued anyway, "it seems you never found me remotely attractive."

Through the growing shadows I was aware that Vespasian's mouth had begun to twitch alarmingly. "Have I hurt your pride? I think I told you once that the ravages of pain and torture have never appealed to me. However," he continued, "if you want me to tell you that I find you beautiful, I can tell you that you are. It doesn't make me change my mind."

It was not an argument I would ever have chosen. Tilda was feeling wretched. My headache returned. Vespasian continued watching my reactions and the only concession to his tiredness was the casual hand raised, long fingers smoothing the hair from his eyes.

"All right," I said, "since you seem happy to sit there and grin while you humiliate me, I shall ask the obvious question. So, you don't love me. I understand that. I don't have a dowry, or a title, no powerful father or property to offer. But does what I suggest seem so disgusting to you? Aren't you even a little bit fond of me?" His eyes were soft, the corners of his mouth curled. He said nothing but Tilda was encouraged, and hurried on. "You know me – better than anyone ought – to know anyone," I said. "So there wouldn't be any nasty surprises. Either – physical – or otherwise. I mean, you probably recognise me more easily naked than clothed. You've touched – well, never mind about that. At least you'd know what you're getting. You're not in love with anyone else. And I suppose, if you ever did suddenly fall in love with another woman, well, I'd understand and say nothing. I'd expect you to be unfaithful anyway. And I'd try to be good, really I would, and not be demanding and not be jealous. You obviously believe in arranged marriages. So am I that bad? I've made my own feelings pathetically clear. And you've very studiously rejected them. Why?"

I did not expect the answer he gave me. "If I told you honour," he said after a pause, "I suppose you would laugh."

I was aware that my mouth was hanging open, and had to close it.

"No," I said, "I would spit. You've no right to speak to me of honour. I do not accept it."

"I should have beaten you, as a child," he said, still smiling. "You've become quite insufferably disrespectful and it's undoubtedly my fault."

"I've spent most of my life being ridiculously dutiful," I pointed out. "All it seems to have gained me this past year is a great deal of pain and misery. And, my lord, Vespasian, or whatever I'm supposed to call you, you know this honour you have the gall to speak about now, is nothing more than moralistic hypocrisy. You may have thought yourself honourable not to have taken me to your bed when I was a hero worshipping child, but it did me no service in the end. And anyway," I ended in a flurry of frustration, "what the devil am I supposed to call you now? Baron de Vrais?"

His eyes beneath the heavy lids danced with malefic amusement. "Call me whatever you like, madam," he answered me. "I should hate to limit your resourcefulness. No doubt the back streets of London have taught you many more interesting names to bless me with over the years."

"There you are," I said, my voice rising, even more irritated by his benign disguise. "You can't even help being nasty. It's your nature. It's pointless trying to talk to you."

"Then I suggest," he said sweetly, "since I'm a rapist and a lout, unpleasant of character and insensitive from birth, you make the simple decision to stop these most improper advances and accept my offer of a respectable husband and future, which I can arrange over the next few weeks. I will even throw in my own friendship, if that's of any use to you."

I heard myself gulp. "It isn't," I said. "It isn't enough."

His eyes narrowed though the smile remained bland. "Then I'm sorry. It is all I can offer you," he said. He stayed, still watching me from the other end of the bed, his outstretched foot beside me and the long muscled line of his calf. "Have you always considered me impossibly unprincipled? I suppose you have," he went on. "Strange as it may seem, however, I have my own standards, which I believe and uphold implicitly, and will not prostitute. Remember, my card is judgement and it is myself I judge." I stared back and said nothing. "Now, once I can be sure of your reaction," he said, "I'll check your bandages. Then I'll send for food and have the fire made up."

I thought I'd made sufficient fool of myself. I nodded, modestly lowering my eyes, and found I was examining his foot. There was a small hole in the heel of his tights, which I ought to darn. "Whatever you say, my lord baron," said Tilda.

Vespasian snorted. He remained where he was for a moment, then swung his legs back over the side of the bed and stood, looking down at me again. "Very well," he said, and briskly pulled the coverlet down from my chin. The bandages were stained where blood had seeped and spoiled their crisp whiteness. He sat and began to unwind them. He had another folded roll on the bed beside me. Again half naked under his hands, I shivered. He washed away the blood, examined the wound, and began to spread a second layer of the sweet blue unguent. This time his fingers were very gentle. He did not look up at me but concentrated on his work. His eyes and hands were on my breast when I said what I had no intention of saying.

I said, "Did you find me attractive when you raped me?"

I thought he would strike me. His hands froze instantaneously and, heavy with shock, his eyes flew to my face. "Don't be a fool," he said, the threat unsuppressed in his voice. "I did not make love to you, Tilda. I have never pretended anything but the truth. I was violent and I hurt you. It was a terrible abuse, but to subjugate the Gate Keeper, it was imperative. My – actions – saved us both. Because of that we vanquished Arthur and his cult. It helped us overcome Lilith. But it is not something I care to remember nor am proud of."

"I understand," I said, refusing to acknowledge the pounding fear in my heart and stomach, "but I also suffered the pain and the degradation. So don't you owe me the love you denied me then?"

He sat quite still, looking back at me. I realised, with total surprise, that he was not breathing quite normally. I knew then that I'd stung him deeply, and was pleased. After a moment he looked down, releasing me from the intensity of his gaze, and returned to the bandages. He controlled his breathing, and his hands, and carefully did not touch me as he unwound the folded linen beside him. I had now forgotten to breathe myself. This time, so rare for a man who usually kept his emotions utterly hidden and expressionless, I now felt I could watch his thoughts struggle with each other, one decision fighting against another.

Finally, after what seemed an intolerable pause, Vespasian looked up again and the anger had quite faded from his eyes. He looked desperately tired. "It is in trying to repay you what I know I owe you," he said, "that I have been refusing you my more – intimate – companionship."

So I tried to control my own voice, as he did. "But, since I am not young enough to be your daughter," I said, "why can't I have what I want, instead of what you judge to be proper for me?" In silence, he returned my gaze with a look of unusual and disconcerting intensity. Tilda was, as usual, deflated. In abject apology, she mumbled, "My lord baron?"

The silence seemed to hang in the warm air, floating sweet and heady with the perfumes of the herbs and ointments. I had the strangest sensation, as if an eternity was suspended there, waiting for the answer. Vespasian had not taken his eyes from mine. Then I heard him sigh, very softly, an extended exhalation of breath.

"If," said Vespasian at last, his eyes black and unwavering, "you promise never to call me that again, even in public, I shall do what you ask."

Then the words echoed and made no sense. He might as well have been speaking Latin. I wasn't even sure anymore, what exactly it was I'd asked him. "Tell me," I demanded.

He blinked, and breathed deep, as though I'd broken a spell. He looked down at the bandaging that he hadn't completed. The tiny hole in the centre of the dragon had begun to bleed slightly and the thin scarlet trail slid across the crease between my breasts and down onto my ribs. It felt hot. Vespasian leaned over to the bowl of herb scented water, rinsed his hands and washed away the blood with one wet finger. His hand was still cool on my breast when he said, "Very well, little one. I pray you'll never regret this, but, if you'll have me, my Tilda, I'll take you to wife." He looked back up into my eyes, and the wandering smile flicked at the corners of his mouth. "If that sounds ungracious, and certainly less than chivalrous, I am sorry. I am very tired and I believe this to be a mistake, not for me, but for you. But I swear, once committed, I will try to make you happy." Then he leaned over, with one elbow close to my ear and his face just inches from my own, one hand remaining soft across my breast, and spoke in Latin after all. "Tentigo absolutus," he said in little more than a whisper, just before he kissed me, "I have, of course anima mia, been quite foolishly in love with you for a very, very long time. Stifling it, and treating you so carefully with the respect you deserve, has been a sad habit and one I've long yearned to abandon," and his voice drifted through my head like soft murmurs, a breeze over water just ruffling the tips of the ripples along a dancing surf.

CHAPTER FIFTY-EIGHT

We exchanged oaths two days later, standing together in front of the fire in the bedchamber. I wondered if I'd have to wear Vespasian's hose and cotte for the occasion, an idea I found deliciously incongruous, but instead I wore rich velvet and embroidered satins, clothes borrowed from the local dressmaker. The chief steward and Vespasian's secretary were discreetly present, unessential but useful witnesses.

Then Vespasian kissed me lightly on the forehead, and carried me back to bed before I collapsed.

We sent word the following day to the Baron of Tennaton that his small and scruffy friend Matilda nobody, had become the Baroness de Vrais, which made Tilda giggle, a habit she was trying to grow out of.

It was shortly after the exchange of vows and sitting up in bed, that I told him reluctantly, "I shall try to be a good wife, though I'm not exactly sure what that entails. You may have to explain it to me." He had brought me hot hypocras and was once again checking my bandages. I felt excitement rather than guilt, but having pushed him into a marriage he considered unsuitable, there was one thing I felt I had to know. "But will you," I asked, looking carefully and demurely down at my lap, "– not that I should complain, and I won't complain, and I know your habits after all – but will you, inevitably, be unfaithful? All the time?"

He had laughed out loud, pulled me to him and kissed my cheek, almost roughly. "Absurd child," he'd said. "Do you expect so little of me?" The amusement in his eyes now seemed a permanent condition.

"You may always have thought me naïve," Tilda said, "but I could hardly help noticing – before I mean – your behaviour that is, and I suppose you'll have even more opportunity now."

He was still laughing. "Inamorata mia, you are incorrigible." He lifted my chin and smiled into my eyes. "No, I give you my word, which is worth considerably more than you undoubtedly realise, that I will never take any other lover. No such wish nor any such desire will exist. I swear it. Nor will I indulge in any behaviour, improper or otherwise, which may cause you further unhappiness."

"That," I said, now smiling myself, "sounds far too good to be true."

Through the long years of her adolescent passion, she had thought she knew Vespasian well. She had always recognised instantaneously the signs when he was intoxicated, the points of colour high on the cheekbones and the unnatural glitter deep in the black eyes. She knew when he was tired, with the soft bruising around the lower lids, and his hand easing back the strain from the brow. She recognised the first signs of anger when his eyes narrowed and the hint of malice touched the corners of his mouth into the semblance of a smile – and the rare good humour when the genuine smile was echoed in the depths of his pupils, the jaw relaxed. She had always known why he bedded pretty, undemanding Isabel, who would be satisfied with gifts to her vanity and ask for neither fidelity nor consistency.

Now Tilda discovered that she had never known him at all.

The first night my medieval husband came to me, I was still weak and still in bed. I wore only a chemise. The chamber was low lit but the fire high, and when he undressed, the flames gilded him in black and gold and scarlet. Never having seen him naked before, I found him unutterably beautiful. His body was long and lean, tinged by candlelight, creating a perfection I could never have imagined. He appeared unaware of his beauty, and even of his nakedness, though I know I stared.

He sat on the edge of the bed facing me, put his hands on me and drew me into his arms. There was something thrillingly different about his embrace. He had held me before, but simply as protection. This time I felt his undisguised desire. I felt the smooth and sinuous muscle of his arms, the sleek sheen of body hair across his lower arms and chest, black though barely noticeable, and the inner strength of his whole body. Where he'd touched Tilda often but only as her doctor, strictly disciplined neither to arouse nor to wound, now his fingers danced in wonder, all magic unleashed. What he'd done that once when he was neither doctor nor friend, she did not ask and did not want to know. But Vespasian discovered all those secret responses of her body, and I felt him use his knowledge. As he removed my chemise, his hands wandered at once, practised and passionate and exploring.

He clearly knew Tilda was nervous, but asked nothing and instead breathed, "Mona mia, trust me," and for the first time kissed me hard on the mouth. Where his passions had been tamed for so long, he now allowed himself free licence, taking what he wanted but sweeping me always with him. Eyes heavy lidded, his watchfulness intensely intimate, every glance and every brush of his fingertips was whispered alchemy.

He made love to her for a very long time, building her very, very slowly to full knowledge. His ultimate climax was immense and prolonged but he raised me even further before he drank deeply himself.

Each night after that I lay in bed, my cheek on the hard dark rise of his breast and his hand gently on mine, I could taste his desire and the sweat of him. I adored his nakedness though Tilda was slow to the pleasure of exploration and he was gentle with her, conscious of her wounds and careful of her inexperience. Kissing the ear he whispered to, so that it tickled and reminded me of sunshine on the cornflowered fields, he said, "Now you have me, you seem remarkably timid in discovering what you have." He took my hand. "Look – touch here – like this –"

I loved the hair on his body, a fine dark silk, almost invisible in its drift across his chest, curling around the dark nipples, concentrating in a narrow flat line down the stomach like an arrow to the groin. I loved to kiss his nipples so they hardened and rose like small obedient buttons. I loved the strength of every part of him, supple contours and elegant muscle. And most of all, I loved what he did to me.

When he kissed me, as he did constantly, sometimes with tenderness and sometimes in passion, I felt his breath like fire on my skin. Once I said, "I adore it. You kiss with such hunger. I often wondered why you never kissed Isabel."

He seemed bemused. "I do not forget, amorcito, that I've known you as a starving street chit, huge eyes and breastless. What were you? Ten years old I think? You used to watch me with an adoration I found disconcerting." His wandering hand between my legs did not pause as he smiled at long lost innocence. "No, I doubt I ever kissed poor Isabel, for after all, a kiss, wherever it is planted, is the more intimate of all intimacies."

"But you sacrificed Isabel," I murmured. Muffled within the crook of his arm, it was not an accusation. "You never intended her death, but I think, through neglect, you allowed it."

"Are you trying to discover," he smiled into my navel, "whether I'm still capable of the foul temper you once accused me of?" His fingers searched deeper. "Maybe you're right. Perhaps I was more insensitive even than I realised. So much suffering because of me, and for you most of all. But Isabel was never meant to be a sacrifice. The sacrifice was supposed to be myself."

"I know," I said, but then, because his touch was such exquisite artistry, I said nothing else. I gave myself to his travelling fingers.

I knew he loved me now because I contained the gentle sweetness Tilda wove through my nature and loved Tilda because of the knowledge and determination I brought her. But we didn't talk about the duplicity of my character. Vespasian called me Tilda, but he knew we were both. Only once, one night, late after love making, he lay with one arm around me, the other playing in my hair, long fingers tangling and then unknotting the curls. "I wonder if I might find it dull now," he murmured, words lazily slurred, "keeping just one woman at a time in my bed." And I did not answer because I had no idea what to say.

Vespasian continued to nurse me until all the wounds on my body were thread scars and silver memories, and only the dragon remained clear and dark as it coiled around my breast. He touched it often while caressing me, his fingers tracing its curves. I knew he found it beautiful, which I considered strange. I believed it grotesque.

His own wounds healed quickly. I took over his nursing from the estate's physician, who doubled as barber and apothecary. His sewing was better than my own but his touch was less gentle and less patient. There were three serious injuries to Vespasian's head, a deep cut to one cheek, a gouge to the upper forehead and a graze to the jaw which had removed nearly all the flesh in one long strip. These were all healing under a series of tiny black stitches. I made him sit quietly on the bed, back against the pillows and eyes closed, while I treated the wounds with the herbs he prescribed himself, with old wine thick and red as blood, and with dressings of egg white. The stripe around his neck from Lilith's claws remained like a ragged collar but it was not deep. The more serious injury to the left arm had already been sewn in a beautiful straight row of little black butterflies by the doctor, but it bled for many days and I changed the bandages many times, washing and disinfecting. "If it's bleeding," I said, "I think it's a good sign. It keeps it clean."

"No doubt a good sign if I faint in your arms from lack of blood," suggested Vespasian. "Does this coincide with the four fluids, the humours? I've no idea what I am. Red cholic, I presume."

"I was never educated in that sort of thing," Tilda said, rebandaging his arm. "In fact, I was never educated in anything at all, though my mother taught me my letters. What little I know about anything, I learned from you."

"Which means that all you know is either improper, or irrelevant," smiled Vespasian. "But this estate will soon run itself, once I've finished putting things in order. There'll be no necessity for you to become mistress of the house in anything but name."

More than a week passed before I knew the house which had become my own. From the great hall through archways and cloistered window recesses with their thick cushioned seats, a passage led to the kitchens, the buttery, the pantries, the brewery and the bakery. Out through the kitchen doors the vegetable garden ran between the outhouses and chicken runs, swinging back around to the long thatched stables, barns and paved courtyard, then again to the front of the house. From the small corridor between kitchen and buttery, steps led down to the wine cellar with its huge wooden barrels, a cooper's delight of well tapped and aromatic wealth.

The main hall was high beamed and lit by hundreds of beeswax candles in sconces and along the vast oak table. The carved chair at its head was cushioned in velvet. Tapestries and embroidered arras lined all the walls except at the high end, which was painted with a mural of water falling from rocks into a sunlit pool and a spreading yew tree, whose branches dipped down to the water, creating a cave within its shadow. There was a door in the wide girth of the tree's trunk and Vespasian did not open it for me.

Instead he showed me the chambers and parlours, rooms on the second floor connected by passages with deep alcoves containing the privies. The master bedroom had its own private nook, a garderobe incorporating a separate latrine which I found marvellously modern. There was also some piped water, brought up from two deep wells at the back of the house, supplying not only the kitchens and bakery, but also a sluice on tap within the main corridor between rooms which could fill buckets to be heated over the fire, and from there to a standing barrel bath.

Eventually I said, "There's a doorway in the painting of the yew tree, which you keep locked. Is it a secret?"

"Everything here is open to you," said Vespasian. "Everything is yours."

It was a small chapel and a place he would have preferred not to show me, although he did, with grace and explanations, without prevarication or defence. Once it had been beautiful, in the time of his father perhaps. Now, although sunlit, it was dark.

A rare glass window astounded me, thick coloured squares caught in black lead and fashioned into a blaze of beauty, mullioned chips in a mosaic of swirling pattern which trapped and refracted the light, distorting it into a thousand colours beyond the five shades the glass had been stained. The rainbows spun their beams amongst the drifting dust and spangled along the rows of a thousand strange objects. The high table might once have been a pulpit. Now it was hung with a tiara of cobwebs and beetle tracks, dead flies, lost brown leaves and a shallow pewter bowl, once baptismal, now stained black and crusted with the disintegrated memory of some viscous substance. Beside it stood a tall bottle, carved in silver, and marked Red Mercury.

There was no cross, no image of the Christ or the blessed Mother Mary. The walls were lined with shelves and the shelves were filled with rows of jars and leather bottles, carved wood and fragile bone objects buried under their years of dust, skulls both human and animal, a number of pestles and mortars in various sizes, bowls and gourds of dried herbs now long shorn of perfume, platters holding crystals and small rocks, the sudden glitter of jewels and gold. There was a time-piece, its complicated function in pieces spread over a low table, a mass of various mathematical instruments for measuring, for weighing and for calculating, an astrolabe and several globes marked with patterns of stars and meteors. One shelf held an assortment of equipment for distillation, some in etched glass, still catching the light beneath their grey powder cloaks. There were alembics, fine tubes of bone and several small sculptures and figurines, divinities perhaps. Most numerous of all, there were huge dust trailed piles of papers, charts, maps and scribed books bound in softest leather and marked in gold.

I recognised the vellum charts of astrology, similar to those Sarah Ableside had once shown Molly. "I know that's part of alchemy," I said, very quietly because the room troubled and awed me. "You once told me your birthday coincides with Candlemas. Do you know your horoscope?"

"I have the Sun in Sagittarius," he said. "Scorpio is in Ascendance and the Moon in Pisces. I imagine this means little to you. But I also know your chart."

"My birthday's in August," I said, wondering if I should tell him Molly's.

"Sun in Leo, the golden lion, symbol of instinct," he answered softly. "You don't know the hour of your birth, but I know you have Pisces Ascending with your Moon in Sagittarius. We're both a combination of fire and water."

I nodded. "Yes, she is too," I murmured.

"Your other spirit?" he smiled. "It would have to be. In alchemy acqua nostra represents fire and in turn, its partnership with water is represented by the perfect star." He held his hand outstretched to me, the heavy ring he had always worn suddenly illuminated with coloured brilliance from the window. Around the central ruby, the gold was deep etched with the six pointed star. "It is perfect balance, power and spirit."

"Then, if you know the zodiac so well," I said, "you know all our futures."

"Would you have me tell you?" The glitter in his eyes seemed to recede and he looked away. "Not yet," he said. "I think not. Perhaps – one day – I shall see. I will keep no secrets from you, but some knowledge does not bring the satisfaction you expect. Now, when you have finished with curiosity, let us leave this room, and I shall lock it up again."

Earthenware plates held the last traces of soot from long cold fires, jars of liquids were dried into smears and the marble tiled floor was dust deep, though marked with a light pattern of recent footprints.

Instead of the crucifix, on one wall hung a mighty ouroboros, ten times the size of the one I had once been given. The serpent's eyes were emerald and his tongue was pure gold. The opposite wall was a great map of the heavens, each star stamped in silver and above, the moon, full golden behind its veneer of flaking age, marked at the side with a long scrolling calendar in a thousand tiny numbers.

On a stool before the pulpit, was the pack of tarot cards that Vespasian had presented to Lilith in the grove when he had repudiated her own. The tarocchi of Hermes. Vespasian stood behind me, waiting for me to see all I wished, and then to leave. "You put the cards back?" I asked.

"No," he said. "They never left this room. That is not the way alchemy works. Symbolism is always the key."

"But they're the same cards," I said, though I was careful not to touch them. "You called them the cards of Hermes, instead of the others, which were the pack of Thoth."

"You do not understand," he said, his voice soft in my ear. He had put his hand on my shoulder, and turned me gently, to look into his eyes. "Hermes and Thoth are the same being. It is all the same, and as it is above, so it is below. Reality is ultimately the most unreal, for the physical is only a living symbol of spirit. Do not look for easy explanation, my love, for the truth is far too simple to understand." He leaned over and kissed the tip of my nose. "We are all confused, Tilda," he said, half smiling. "Would you believe in a God small enough for you to comprehend?"

"This place," I said, sweeping my arm around the lost murmuring of old worship, "could be beautiful. I should like to try and understand."

"What? More questions?" Vespasian smiled but I thought his eyes suddenly sad. "No, it will be dismantled," he said. "Amongst the beauty of alchemy which you see, are the traces of black prayer, which must be destroyed. If you like, I will restore it to the Christian legends."

I pointed. "I know that," I said, "without having to ask." Above the glittering silvered stars on the wall beside us, flying over the moon and spread in scarlet dark clawed wings and flashing eyes, was the pattern of the dragon, symbol of the fifth essence and the inner sacred fire.

Vespasian nodded. "It has protected this house for many years," he said.

"Then you shouldn't destroy it," I whispered. "It saved my life."

"It is over," said Vespasian. "I will not hide behind the memory of old beliefs."

He was leading me from the room, a gentle pull away from the past. Behind me he locked the door. "But the dragon brand you gave me," I said. "You told me it wouldn't fade." I looked up at him suddenly. "I know why – but how? How so indelible? So eternal?"

"With fire," he answered, his voice reluctant. "With fire and magic. I made sure you were in a trance, piccina, and felt nothing, but I'm sorry for the pain it's caused you since. It was the greatest protection I could give you. I couldn't know whether I'd always be around to keep you safe. Indeed, I expected to be killed. The fifth essence is a far greater guarantee, as you saw, in the end."

He told me the truth, as he always did, but I knew there was something more than that. "You were worried, weren't you," I said to my toes, "even though you – claimed the rights of the gatekeeper – someone could come later, and take the power away from us both?"

"More with Molly than with Tilda," he said softly, "where my influence was weak." He led me out into the courtyard and under the sun where the breeze blew away the smoky sadness and the scent of incense and witchery. "Enough now," he smiled and the sun reflected in his eyes, "I've promised I'll no longer deny you the answers you require of me, but think first, vita mia, before you ask. You should limit your questions, for sometimes the truth can hurt us both. Now, let us return to present pleasures and lock the Wiccan memories behind their crumbling doors."

But sometimes, in the sweet soft blue shadows of our bed and in the warmth of his arms after love making, I still asked Vespasian about the puzzles that slipped between my thoughts. "Do you have children?" I asked him one evening. The bedroom fire was spitting low but it was peaty and aromatic with branches of laurel and herb. "Do you even know? You've admitted your past, and in any case, I always knew what you did, as well as Isabel. You could have sired children, even without knowing."

I kept my face buried in the curve of his shoulder but I knew he was laughing at me. "You forget," he said, "I've my own magical guarantees against unwanted pregnancies. Are there any other equally immodest questions you've saved up for me, to accuse me while I'm vulnerable?"

"I don't believe you're ever vulnerable," I sniffed. "But there is something else. It's about Uta." I had some difficulty saying her name. "She said you promised yourself to her. Did you? I know in the end you were foresworn, and I know I shouldn't ask. But did you make love to her? Did you ever touch her at all? She's the only one I worry about. I'm not jealous of anyone else."

I knew he'd stopped smiling when I felt the line of his jaw harden against my cheek. "May I remind you," he said, very soft voiced, "that in this honeyed and unenlightened age, wife flogging is perfectly legal."

But I knew he would never strike me. "I still have nightmares, you see," I murmured, "especially about Uta, because I know I killed her. I didn't mean to but I did. Sometimes the last sight of her comes back and haunts me. You told me once you could cure my night terrors. So, will you answer me, even if you're angry I asked?"

He had made love to me for an hour or more, there on the wide velvet bed in the flickering firelight and the drifting perfumes. I was sorry to spoil our echoes with the vision of Uta's death, but Vespasian relented then, and spoke softly into the top of my sweat damp hair, his careless hands closing a little tighter and more consciously around my breasts.

"It is true," he said, "that I promised her my body and my service. I was Arthur's prisoner in my own home and I knew they held Richard and by then, also Gerald, whom I was pledged to keep safe. Then I discovered they had taken you." He shifted and, leaning down, kissed my eyes. "Arthur did not trust any promise I could give him for I'd already killed several of their brood on my previous visit. You may remember the occasion, since you insisted on embroidering my shoulder." The badly stitched wound still ran haphazard in a thick white scar beneath his collar bone. "Lying chained in a reeking dungeon seemed an inordinate waste of time. I took the easiest form of quick release, which was to lie. Uta, in spite of her disdain, was gullible." He had caressed my nipples into pronounced arousal, but his mind was elsewhere. "It's a great arrogance, but I confess I always knew the affect I could have on women, if I wished it. This was the quickest way to obtain my freedom."

"I'm not blaming you for anything," I said. "I just wanted to know. My dreams trouble me."

"Then know this," said Vespasian, words lost in the shadows, so I could barely hear. "I never touched her, nor ever desired her. Do you imagine I'd fuck a woman who had lain with Lilith, or swive with a mouth that licked Lilith's feet? I promised what I had no intention of fulfilling. It was a risk I believed to be worth the result. I remained foresworn until you took the card from the tarocchi pack in my name."

"Or Lilith would have claimed your soul?"

"Hush child," he said, bending to kiss my mouth closed and smother the words I might still have said. "All this is passed. I have left it all behind, the bright passion of alchemy as well as the dark night of necromancy and lost religions. I will cleanse the last room in this house that carries the memory." He ran his fingers absently across my nipples. "Your own magic is, I believe, also passed. I see no sign in you of the power of Janus, Cernunnus or Thoth, who all hold the keys you used to open the doorways. With the banishment of the veleda, when Lilith pierced the dragon – here – and was broken, she no longer orders you and I do not think you are any longer the gatekeeper."

"It's true," I confessed, reaching up my hand to his cheek, "that I seem to have reverted to myself. I'm one person again, though a combined nature, with memories of places I have never been. It's like being twins in one body."

"It is a remarkably beautiful body," he breathed, kissing my palm, and moving his own hand down to the soft skin of my inner thighs. "Here you are silk." He sighed. "Do you regret, Tilda, the strange experiences you and I have shared? They have brought you more pain than is just in a God-fearing world, but whatever happens to us, makes us what we are."

"You say I'm fire and water in astrology," I said, "Fire and water have no regrets. They're both moving, insubstantial elements that see, learn, absorb and move on."

"Acqua nostra," murmured Vespasian, as though it was an incantation. "The water which in alchemy becomes the inner sacred fire, and the fifth essence which you will always carry, the dragon flying across your breast and guarding your heart."

I smiled into his shoulder. "You say you'll never return to magic and alchemy," I said, "but you can't disguise your beliefs. You quote without thinking."

"Perhaps," he said. "But alchemy aspires to perfection and that is the most dangerous thing of all. I shall try to forget the things that bring shadows. I shall teach you to ride, Tilda, and we'll go hunting in the forests here behind the house. Not for deer and boar, but for sunlight and silver pools, and squirrels and otters playing in the moonshine. I shall show you a deeper magic, of sensual beauty and of love. I will teach you the magic of happiness."

CHAPTER FIFTY-NINE

All through the long winter Vespasian kept his promise. I learned happiness as a poet discovers the perfect melody he has searched for all his life. When spring ruffled the land and the blossoms brought out the bees and the first bud and leaf was shy lemon green under the timid sun and the rain was a scattering of dancing gold and the wind gusted down our valley, I was as happy as I had ever thought to be in my life and happier than Tilda had ever imagined was possible. It was Jasper, not Vespasian Fairweather, who made love to me with all the languid sensuality that I had never before discovered, and it was Jasper who began to educate me to the life of a lady, Baroness de Vrais of Stourbury and Gloucester, and (officially though no longer practically) of Demis-Bayeux. We visited Gerald and stayed many days but it was being alone together that we cherished too much, and so avoided company.

We made some concession to other nobility who rode over, curious about the baron returned, and once Jasper made his representation to the king for the claim of his title and estates, John acquiesced and proposed that he would come to stay with us in autumn, for the hunt. In the meantime, we had time to ourselves.

And then, after five soaring months of everything Tilda had ever hoped for, it was Beltane. The cattle were taken from their stuffy barns and put out to pasture and the house martins moved in, nesting all along the eaves under the thatch. I had walked down to the stream with Jasper in the morning to watch the fish jumping. He had pointed out the great dark shadow of the pike on the pebbled bed and the slide of the ripples as it darted from ambush. He had showed me the wedge of pearly spotted frog spawn caught against the water weed and the splayed footprints of the heron along the soft muddy bank. We sat under the willows and I took off my shoes and wriggled my toes in the cold water and he had reminded me of the forest pool beside the other house, and how I had often gone there to swim, and how he had followed me. "You were beautiful then," he said, "but you're more beautiful now."

"You told me then," I reminded him, "that you thought of me as a daughter."

"I lied," he said.

As the long afternoon shimmered under its high sun, the field workers began their Mayday celebrations. With a great deal of raucous music and singing, dancing and drinking, work stopped and the children ran between the cottages with streamers of vine. One old man had a lute, which he played badly, another a fiddle, which he played well. Two children had drums but no sense of rhythm and the local priest who had arrived on his mule up from the village, was trailed by his wife and six sons, none of whom he was supposed to have.

Afternoon slipped into a merry twilight and then a tipsy sunset. The soaring coloured kites and swirling flags of the shrinking sun paled suddenly into cloudless ivory and Beltaine was nearly over. I went back inside where the long shadows drifted across the tiles. Jasper lit the candles and ordered the fire in the hall to be set ready against the evening chill. He poured me a cup of our own wine, last year's laying and a little raw but strong with a perfume of apples and raspberry and we sat close on the window seat, watching as the last of the peasants trooped back to their cottages, tripping over their feet, the final vestiges of song like a rustle among the trees. The barn owl woke, silently swooped and was off to hunt mouse and shrew in the gathering darkness.

"Soon it will be summer," said Jasper. "Will you come with me up to Stourbury, when the wheat is high, and help me put the other estate in order? It has been left longer to ruin and the work will be harder."

I knew he'd avoided returning to the other estate, for it was there he'd found his wife hacked in blood on the bed of their love making and all his life and happiness spread in wretched ruin. I was therefore deeply content, flattered perhaps as few other things flattered me, that now, with me, he felt strong enough to face that place again. "I'll come wherever you go," I said. "Did you think I wouldn't?"

"I knew you would," he said. "It is still polite to ask."

I managed to hide my approval. "Polite?" I grinned. "Too unexpected for comfort."

He leaned forward and kissed me, a little harder and a little longer than daytime kisses were apt to be. "Then come with me now," he said, very softly, "and I'll remind you what comfort really means. For you are, anima mia, utterly irresistible."

With his fingers tight on my wrist, he led me across the hall and up the steps to the bedchamber, so that I spilled my wine as I followed him, and lost one of my shoes on the stairs. He lit no more candles and the hearth was empty, but the unshuttered windows still allowed a pale light, the last azure tinge before the Earth spun away from the sun and dropped hard into night. I thought I saw the evening star, a sudden glitter just above the horizon, the star I now called my own. I turned back to Jasper. He'd quickly pulled open his own cotte and shirt, and now undressed me slowly, touching and caressing and moving the warmth of his breath through parted lips down my breasts and across my stomach. I arched my back and felt the heat pulse from toes to finger tips. When I was unclothed, he removed his own, and lay beside me, the smile fully lit in his eyes and the curve of his mouth extended into soft delight. "You have no idea, bien-aimé, my Tilda," he whispered before making love to me, "the joy you bring me, every day."

The moon was huge and full and right outside our window when he lay back, arms spread wide, gazing at me as I curled beside him, holding to the warmth of his neck. I leaned forwards then, and kissed his eyes closed, the long black lashes soft silk on the tip of my tongue. "Sleep, beloved," I said. "I'll go and tell Edmund to lock up, and hold supper for tonight. Some of the men are still drunk under the pigeon coop, but I'll tell Edmund to move them on before settling the horses. I won't be long. When I come back, I shall slip into your dreams, and kiss you there."

He sighed, and held my hand for a moment before I pulled the eiderdown over his nakedness and slipped from the bed, dressed hurriedly in a quickly belted robe, and tiptoed down again into the hall. It was very quiet and the great moon shone in silver pools across the marble. The fire had been only half set and remained unlit. I snuffed the candles, all except one.

It was not long before I returned to the house, hurrying to be all the quicker into the warmth of my lover's arms. Outside a sharp little wind had turned bitter and the warm day had become a cold night. All the servants had been at the celebrations and the kitchens were empty. I carried my candle into the hall where its small flicker danced up amongst the beams, all red and black like London's scurrying rats. It was coming from the door in the yew tree that I saw the figure.

I had dismissed the cook and already said goodnight to our steward Edmund so no one else should have been in the front of the house except Jasper, half asleep upstairs. I called out and the figure stood in the far darkness, waiting for me. I walked over, and at once felt ice trickle across the back of my neck.

"Had you forgotten me?" said Malcolm.

I had. I had forgotten all of them, all the vile nightmare. I couldn't speak. Someone behind me said, girlish English and a cherubic sweetness, "Well dear, what a delightful place you have here. Perhaps we should have come before. But of course, you didn't invite us." I couldn't breathe.

There were three, the two women and the man. In the women's presence, Malcolm swaggered. I turned and stared in disgust at the squat Ableside sisters, Ruth and Sarah, who had no right at all to be in my bright new world. "I have opened no doorways," I shuddered. "How have you come?"

"Why, dear," smiled Sarah, "you never did understand the way it really works, did you? Even though you were such a part of it yourself."

"The veleda is dying," said Ruth. "Cernunnus has taken back the keys," and she stretched out her hand to me so that I froze and stood immobile before her, as if spell bound by the point of her finger. "You have no power of any kind, and revert to who you should always have been, a shred of useless humanity without knowledge."

"But Jasper has knowledge," I whispered. "He beat you all once and he can do it again. He will hear you and come down."

Malcolm laughed, a snivelling sour giggle that came more from his nose than this throat. "He won't hear us," he said. "Now we have Lilith and you no longer have the seal of Thoth or the ouroboros and nothing to help you at all."

"I can scream," I said, "and he will hear. He said you whipped me once. You've never paid for that. But you'll never touch me again and you'll feel a hundred times more agony than you ever inflicted on me. I still have the dragon brand and in that room –" but I was pointing to the yew tree on the wall where the door led to the chapel. It was from there that Malcolm had come and now the door was fading out and the painted tree was turning to barren winter with all its rich coloured leaves disappearing under a white crystal spatter of snow.

"But he cleared the room," sniggered Malcolm. "Did you make him do that? Were you a good little housewife and scrubbed away all the power? It's clean washed and everything destroyed."

"You see," smiled Ruth, "it is we who have the ouroboros now," and she opened her palm. The little curved serpent lay tucked snugly into the fleshy swell of her plump hand, its sad blue eyes glimmered dim, its tail forced between its blunt teeth. It was the modern copy I had seen in the other world, the thing that had once given me faith that she, and her sister, and Thomas Cambio, were all friends and would help me.

"It isn't real," I said and heard my voice shaking. "You got it from the antique shop in my village. It's a copy."

Sarah shook her head, a sorrowful aunt. She was still wearing the clothes from my world, the modest flowered cottons and fluffy cardigan. "Dear, dear, what ignorance my dear. A copy? No, this is more genuine than anything you have ever had from your treacherous lover."

Ruth still held me quite still. My voice barely formed, my hands could not move. It was not the power of total paralysis that the veleda had once exercised over me, nor the sweet trances and escape from pain that Vespasian had given me, but I could neither run nor shout. I tried to cough, spitting for freedom, but couldn't unravel invisible bonds. "Vespasian's was real. It protected me and saved my life." I glared at Malcolm. "When you came to the convent, you drugged me so I wouldn't see you, but you didn't expect to find the ouroboros on my wall. You had to leave, and I woke and saw you. What had you come to do? Kill me?"

Malcolm spat on the floor at my feet. His spittle defiled the smooth marble. "No, bitch," he said. "I came to demand the power of the gatekeeper from the filth that stole it before."

"Rape me?" I raised my chin. "But Jasper already protected me from that, something even stronger than the ouroboros. You can't know. You ran away before the end of the battle."

Malcolm slapped me. I wasn't surprised it was a slap instead of a punch. I tried to smile although I thought my lip was bleeding. Ruth stepped between us, reinforcing the spell that kept me almost immobile. "But you see, dear," she said sweetly, "we have a greater strength, for Lilith is with us." I looked back into her eyes and I saw Lilith's eyes. I looked across at Sarah and again I saw Lilith's eyes. "Poor Molly," Ruth continued, "and dear little Tilda, the ignorant child you dragged into all this with you, what a sad waste. Such a shame, my dear, but I'm afraid, it's quite over for you now."

"We are one," I said, remembering and reciting. "Tilda and I. Molly and I, we are one. Purity and love unite, so we became fused. Evil destroys and detaches, so although Lilith lives in each of you, you're separate entities. If you're in danger, you'll turn on each other and rip each other apart. Then Lilith will dissolve back into the air. The ouroboros is the symbol of eternal and infinite purity, and that's something you're frightened to touch. What you hold is a copy."

"Well, bitch, your master's taught you a few things over your few months swiving together," said Malcolm. "But you'll never understand Lilith's power."

Everything was ice. I myself was turning to ice. "Jasper will come," I said. "He knows Lilith's power. He repudiates it. He's beaten her before. He knows when I need him, and he'll come."

Sarah had taken the ouroboros and was holding it high in front of my face, just centimetres from my nose. "A copy?" she sniggered, "you think this is a copy? It was once perhaps, a pathetic piece of wood chip, whittled by some peasant in your dull little village. But Thomas took it from the shop and changed it, transforming it into something far more exciting. Didn't you hear of the explosion?"

"In the antique shop. Yes."

"Look at the eyes," giggled Sarah, so intense that her voice became a small frenzy, a high pitched squeal. "It sees you. It's alive. It holds the soul of your cousin. Speak to it. Greet your long dead relative. She can hear every word you say."

I was utterly silent. I stared. I dared not believe it. Ruth said, "Lilith within Thomas entered the shop where the copied ouroboros was for sale, and she took it. The explosion was the transference of your cousin's essence into the serpent. What a delightful trick, don't you think? And because we sisters owned what you thought was a sign of the bright magic and puerile purity, you trusted us. Yet all the time, your little cousin was sitting on our shelf, watching us worship Lilith."

"Who had killed her in the first place," smiled Sarah. "Don't you think it's a sweet story? All the signs of a charming fairy tale, surely?"

I still hadn't spoken. I was bursting with unfulfilled urgency, the desperate hope that Vespasian would hear our voices and come down. And I sobbed for my dearest Sammie, whom I had almost forgotten. I looked at her pretty eyes, sublimated into the carving and drained of emotion. I recognised their flicker of understanding. I knew her. But she was a moth within the flame, and Jasper was deep sleeping after our loving. So I called on the only other relation I knew and the one who could help me most, if she wished to do so.

Beyond the long windows, still unshuttered for the night, the moon swam through her gossamer cloud cover and rose higher amongst the stars, full round silver in Scorpio and exactly six months since Samhain's victory. I looked straight into her mesmerising magnificence and I called my mother. Then I turned back to Malcolm, Ruth and Sarah, and the growing force of Lilith's shadow within the hall. "You mistake me," I said, loud and very clear, until quite quickly I knew neither my own voice nor the inspiration for the words. "If Cernunnus opened the path between our worlds for you to pass, then he has usurped my place. I demand he renounce the gateway. I call on the veleda, who designated me alone. I command Janus and Thoth to recognise my prerogative and relinquish their keys. I call on Hermes, who witnessed the tarot and knows my claim is just. Only Vespasian may speak in my stead, and I no longer delegate. I hereby reclaim my position and impose my right. I will close the gates and with the power given to me, I shutter and lock all paths. Now no glimmer passes and Hades itself shivers behind its stream."

They laughed at me at first. Sarah was still holding Sammie's false ouroboros in my face, but my reaffirmation of my own power had snapped the spell that held me and I reached out, jerkily as my muscles responded again, and took it from her fingers. She seemed unable to stop me. I put it to my mouth, and kissed it. Someone screamed and I clutched the carving, afraid it was Sammie. But it was Lilith. No one laughed again.

The little coiled snake had begun to stretch and open. The explosion that had trapped my cousin now imploded, and the wood shattered and fell to ashes. For one brief moment I saw her. Sammie stood at my side like a white light, shimmering in the shadows and brighter than the moon glow. She smiled at me and put out her hand. I felt the dizzy pleasure of her warm fingers on my shoulder, the pressure of reassurance. She breathed, "Thank you," and diminished into the pools of moon halo before me.

With the thin frightened figure of Malcolm now cowering between them, Lilith was two, one crouching small as if to spring, the other soaring and baleful as the demon within. Then I realised, with a pride bordering arrogance, that I had grown myself. I looked behind me. The painted yew tree was shedding its leaf-bound snow cover. The drooping branches with their huge spread stroking the ground beneath, now lifted in a sparkle of deep green, feathered in the moonlight. The hall of the beautiful house I could now call my own, was turning into the nemeton, Vespasian's sacred grove. The soft silver water of the mural called in gentle song. Other trees crowded round, pushing in through the walls, leaning down on us from the beamed ceiling. A massive oak seeped its gall. I saw my chestnut tree with the hammock swinging a little in the summer breeze. I saw the willows from the woods of the estate, where Vespasian had taken me to look for robin's nests and the scurry of the weasel. The marble tiles had become grass under my feet and the herbs spread upon the grave mounds by the cold pool. I looked at Lilith, still split between the sisters she had chosen to inhabit. "The gates are almost shut," I said again. "You are out of time and out of place. Leave now, or you will suffocate."

She was snarling, one toad, one skull faced wolf. "You've no power to hurt me," she said, one voice from two gaping mouths.

"That's a lie," I said quietly. "You know it is. I've hurt you before. I don't have the strength to kill you but I can banish you into the air and it will be centuries before you can reassemble. You've chosen to bring two bodies from another time and if I close the gates, those bodies die and you'll suffocate unless you fly out. If you try to touch me and keep the gates open, I'll flay you with the dragon brand, the fifth essence and purity of the inner sacred fire."

I was holding a sword. It had come into my fist like the trees had come into the hall. At first I thought it was my own, that I'd lost in the grove at Samhain, but then I saw it was Vespasian's. It was too heavy for my wrist, its hilt carved with the design of the caduceus of Hermes in solid gold, the two entwined serpents, crowned and twisted around a central pillar that ran down into the blade. I grasped it with both hands and raised it before my face.

"Fool," spat Lilith. "You dare make such an enemy? Do you know what I can do to you over a lifetime of torture? You'll not always have the protection of the veleda."

Sarah was the toad, Ruth the wolf. They circled me, crocodile skins, snarling and spitting, wide lipless mouths into bottomless throats, humanity dissolving in demonic transposition. As I faced one, so the other came behind me, iced breath on my neck. Unwilling to touch the dragon brand, they attacked not with the claws and teeth they both exposed, but with the venom of their breath and the threat of death from terror.

I felt fear eat me from the inside like acid. I struck out a hundred times, and though I missed a hundred times, I swung again, heaving the weight of the blade I could now barely support. The sword tip was increasingly unsteady and unpractised, but this time, its own skill and not mine, the steel pierced Sarah's leg. I lunged and sliced downwards to the ankle and Lilith spat slime. "With the doorway closed, you cannot sustain breath for two," I gasped, hardly breathing myself. "One will have to kill the other." She knew. Ruth had already turned on the weakened Sarah.

While the wolf ripped apart the toad, I killed Malcolm with two strokes of the sword as Vespasian had taught me, many, many months ago in the old forest outside the house he'd built for Ingrid. I cut first across the pelvis as he stood, cringing beside me, snivelling and trembling. The blood spurted onto the trunk of the yew tree. Then I cut down, two handed, and his head fell from his neck. I hoped there had been time for him to feel the pain.

I turned back to Lilith. The toad was dead, crumpled in puddles of bloody venom and popping eyes. I looked at the wolf. Ruth was gasping, holding her furred muzzle, clawing at her throat. "It's too late," I said. "I've closed the way. All the doors are shut."

She was shrinking, rejecting the useless body of the woman, and stretching out all her fury to take her up into freedom, away from the power of the grove. I watched her for a moment. If I tried to kill

Lilith, I would shatter like glass. Reluctantly I waited until she was quite gone, wisps of steam in a current of parting smoke, then a lost wail which disappeared and became the screech of an eagle, or a whistle of the wind across the waves. Then I killed Ruth.

She had no defence, just a cherubic maiden aunt, soft lilac and glasses on her nose, but I ran her through with the bloody sword and watched her fall beside Malcolm's decapitated body. Then I stood panting for breath and was myself again.

Before, I'd felt terrible guilt, knowing I'd killed Uta and the others. Now I adored it. I could kill and kill again for what I killed had no right to life.

Panting, I looked around. Behind me the mural of the yew became paint, the little locked door reappeared and the great trees above and around me began to whisper and rustle, moving back into their huge shadows. There was neither music nor breeze and the moon seemed to shrink as her silver puddles fell on the marble floor tiles like little apple blossoms in the night. I dropped the bloody sword where Ruth, Sarah and Malcolm lay dead and empty.

The silence was complete, a huge silence that shouted at me over my heart beat. I walked to the small staircase across the hall which led to the master bedroom. I already knew what I would find.

CHAPTER SIXTY

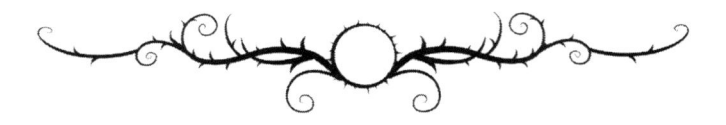

He was on my bed. They had taken him in the slumber of his only vulnerability, the deep contentment after love making, during the seduction of all his senses.

As they had to his first wife and to his young mistress, they had split his sternum and his belly to the groin. His arms were flung out to his sides as I had left him, waiting for my return. Instead, he had embraced death. The blood was so thick across the fur and velvet coverings, it was black rivers in the shimmering moonlight.

I had expected it, in the end. There had been too much noise for my beloved to be sleeping still, and too much living magic for him to drift on through his dreams, had he been free to come. He would not have slept through the entrance of Lilith herself into his home. I had known, before I saw him. But I had not expected the butchery.

They had put out his eyes. All his life had been in his eyes, rich black caverns and a tunnel into every emotion, secret and passion, power and sensuality and love, liquid shadow, beautiful eyes that spoke without words, a vocabulary more intense than all the other languages he spoke. I had loved his eyes so very much.

At least, even with magic, there had been no time to flay his wrist and ankle as they had done to Ingrid and Isabel. I sat on the edge of the bed and took his hand in mine and stroked the long sensitive fingers and kissed his palm and told him how much I loved him. His face streamed with the sticky, drying blood from his eye sockets, but the little curl at the corners of his mouth retained the sweetness of dreaming smiles. I could not believe he had suffered. All the terrible savagery of his torture had been done to an empty body, after the departure of the soul. They would not have dared kill him slowly. His power was too great.

I sat there beside him for a very long time in the dark, listening to my own stifled breathing as the moon slid past the window and the clouds covered the stars and total blackness shifted in around me. I kissed my lover's mouth, though it was becoming tight and hard and cold, and where I held his hand, the fingers soon gripped me so tightly that I thought he spoke. I stroked his ruined face and carefully combed his hair with my fingers, smoothing it back from the savagery of his destruction. I put my other hand slowly across his opened breast, absorbing the last liquidity of his life's blood, the beauty of the skin as it became alabaster and the elegance of curve where the muscles still rose beside the great wound.

It was an hour perhaps that I sat, lost in love for him, whispering promises. Finally, I unclasped his fingers from mine, apologising softly for my brief abandonment.

"I will not be gone long," I murmured, "for I will not ever leave you now." I kissed him again on the mouth, and then slowly left the room. Downstairs the three bodies sprawled in their dark corner, sinking within a low hanging fog of menace and the stench of remaining evil. I passed them by, opened the big door of the hall and stepped out into the courtyard. Above the high tiled roof of my house, the moon swung up across the jutting turrets and blazed full again, shedding her cloudy aura. I walked down past the stables and across the lane into the rise of the first trees, ghost trunks looming over me. I knew what I was looking for.

Vespasian had taught me herb lore. I knew hemlock and scarlet yew berries. I knew the soft white fungi and the creeping nightshade, toadstools and roots of monkshood. I collected what I needed, kneeling there in the moon spangled dew.

I made up the drink back in the kitchens, very carefully filtering, stirring and pounding. I lit a tall candle and stood it beside the mortar. The flickering shadows danced over my hands like sunlight on a stream, but the drink I mixed was dark brown and rank. The remaining leaf and stringy tubers I destroyed with the candle flame, leaving no poison for the servants to find in the morning.

Then I took the opiates from where Vespasian stored them, locked safe, the strongest redress and the greatest scourge, which he had always forbidden me. The two little cakes were wrapped in leaves, then in a sealed jar, and kept in a cool cupboard. I unwrapped one and took it to my bowl. The opium shone like polished marble. I crumbled a little into my drink and then heated the cup over the flame, sitting patiently though my blood stained fingers scorched. It was my left, the hand that Arthur had forced through fire and it still hooked a little unnaturally, hard to straighten, with puckered flesh on a raised palm. There was less feeling there now and I could hold the cup with very little discomfort, but in truth, there was little feeling in any part of my body for I was numb.

I took my cocktail upstairs and sat beside Vespasian on the drenched bed. The great fur counterpane which had been so smooth and rich beneath our naked bodies, now was hard and blood crusted in a welter of carnage. But it was my lover's blood and nothing of his could feel obscene to me. His blood was already on me, on my hands and my mouth where I had kissed and caressed him. The black gape of his empty eyes stared up at our bedroom shadows, no lids left for me to gently close. This was the bed that had known all the passion of his loving and now it sheltered only bitter misery. I kissed him again before I drank from the cup. The poison tasted foul but I finished everything there was, through to the dregs which I left because they were gritty.

Then I lay down, curled very close to my husband's side, and put my arm tight around him. He was still beautiful, but so cold. I knew I would die slowly but I hoped the opium would bring some narcotic relief and the assurance that I would not vomit away all the lethal dose I was determined to endure. I did not want to writhe, and disturb Vespasian. I shut my eyes, squeezed tight, and breathed away my life.

CHAPTER SIXTY-ONE

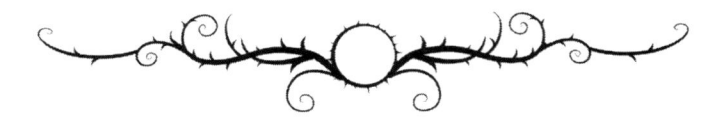

I woke. I should not have woken.

I lay still, my eyes closed, terrified that it had all failed and that I was still alive and all the horror would begin again. Then I opened my eyes. Above me was the frilly lampshade and the electric light and the white plaster ceiling with its cheap cornice and the stain where the rain had leaked through the roof three years ago. I was Molly and I was back.

I curled tight, hugging my knees around the terrible nausea of disgust, and sobbed in desperation until fatigue eventually stifled me into silence, which was four hours later perhaps, and a pearlised dawn was fading into the night sky outside my attic window.

I stretched out a little, every muscle stiff, and put my hands over my tear streamed face. Something caught the corner of my eye. I raised my hand and looked.

On the third finger of my left hand, too heavy but not too large, I was wearing Vespasian's ring. For as long as I had known him, he had worn it. It was solid gold, stamped with the six pointed star of fire and water, within which nested a ruby, size of a pearl. It should have been too big for my finger but it was not. It should still be on Vespasian's hand, but it was not. It should have perished eight hundred years ago, but it had not. I held it against my cheek where it felt cold, as his body had, and cried and cried and cried again.

I could not rise from the bed for many hours and I recognised neither hunger nor curiosity at my return. I slept a little, from exhaustion and misery, but woke again to the same desolation. The day had turned dull with a dreary cloud cover but I felt none of it. Eventually, when the long afternoon had dragged into a slow twilight, I sat, drawing my legs up to my belly, and leaned back against the pillows.

Then finally I saw the other messages in my room. Beside my bed and scattered wildly across the carpet, were the tarot cards of Thoth, my own pack, randomly thrown as I had left them myself. But in a neat row on my little dressing table and in front of the mirror, were three cards, face up. They were The Moon, The Fool, and The Star. Then, on the soft velvet padded stool in front was another card, this time face down. I got up slowly and went to look. I turned the card over. It was The Aeon, Judgement, and it was the card I had taken for Vespasian. I clutched it until I had almost folded it into creases, wet with tears. I sat with it on the carpet and stared at it as if I could not let it go. Then gradually it started to fade and a pool of liquid colour trickled through my fingers and stained the carpet red until finally the card was quite blank, damp cardboard with nothing on it at all. "The Aeons have passed. He has been judged," said the whisper in my head. "It is done," and I howled until I was sick.

I dreamed his eyes returned to me, deep in happiness, soft black memories, long lashed like a woman's, penetrating and intense, until all my dream spun around his eyes and the words they called to me: Love, purity, eternity. Do not cry for me, they said. Solve et coagula; dissolve the body and impress the spirit. It seems that death is the opus magnum after all. Do not cry for me, for I am always with you, if you look for me. And you wear my ring, which is my eternal oath.

But I cried anyway, for I couldn't help it. For three days I ate nothing and became dizzy and ill, drifting in a state of unreality. No one came to me and I did not leave my own property. I sat often in the hammock under the chestnut tree and closed my eyes against the green shadows, singing softly to myself the lilting medieval tunes Vespasian had taught me, and had sung to me sometimes, my head in his lap, beside the stream in the woods.

Once I felt Sammie was close, but she passed on then, a warm smiling rustle like breath before sleep, now beyond my grasp. But each night Vespasian filled my dreams.

On the fourth day when weakness had me verging on delirium, my front door opened and I heard it close and the footsteps go into the kitchen. I ran downstairs. Absurdly, I expected Vespasian. There was no one else in my world, and no one else who could come to me but him.

It was Bertie. He carried a small suitcase and looked thin. I stopped mid stair and tried to remember who he was.

"Good God, Mol," he said. "You look as though you've seen a ghost. I've been waiting for you. I thought you were going to come and pick me up. I had to get the train."

"I'm sorry," I mumbled. "Did I do something wrong? I don't know. I'm confused."

"Oh lord, Mol," he sighed. "Have you gone all vague again? Isn't it enough, me going crazy, without you losing your marbles too?"

I stared at the man I ought to know and searched in my head for his name. Now I had even lost my own. "Am I Molly? I thought I was Tilda." I frowned. "Have you come to stay? I'll tell the girl to light the candles and cook can get the turnspit to roast a swan."

He put me to bed. Poor Bertie had just been released from hospital, but perhaps it did him good to have to cope with a mad woman instead of being treated for madness himself. "Molly, sweetie, don't you remember a thing?" he begged me, sitting on the chair at the foot of the bed. The rest of the tarot cards, except for number twenty of the major arcana, were still scattered across the floor and he eyed them with some mistrust. He had brought me tea and a sandwich, which he made me eat. "You came to visit me plenty of times over the months, for goodness sake. You've been a real brick, stood by me and everything. Very good of you, seeing we're divorced."

"Are we?" The sandwich tasted disgusting, soggy white slices of bread substitute and tasteless slimy artificial ham. The tea was hot tannin and stuck to my tongue. I longed for the rich tang of the bacon hanging from the rafters, smoked in the rising musky blue from the fire, for the mellow glory of the wine from our own estate, for the hot baked unbleached bread, crusty from our ovens. "Did I marry you? I can't imagine why. I used to be married to someone else. Someone terribly, wonderfully special."

Bertie looked after me until I remembered who he was, and who I was, and that I loved tea, and ham sandwiches, and modern food, and could turn on electric lights and gas cookers and use a toilet that flushed. From the day Lilith had left him sprawled on my carpet reliving all the raging memories of the murders she had committed using his body, Bertie had been in a psychiatric hospital. The police had never arrested him. They did not believe he was capable of murder and torture and black magic and assumed his nightmare confessions were the result of a nervous breakdown, both understandable, and curable. No one had ever been accused of the murders, and no others had occurred. For six months Bertie had slowly recovered and Molly had visited him and taken him chocolates and promised him her spare room indefinitely once he was pronounced fit to return home. And now he was.

I cried at night and called for Jasper and woke with my pillow soaked each morning, but during the days I sank back into a reluctant reality. Bertie was a sweet nurse. He was not the healer Vespasian had been, but then, I was no longer suffering from terrible physical wounds, the scars of torture or the pain of battle. My injuries were purely emotional. A few pale scars still threaded across my body but most had faded to invisibility. Except the dragon of the sacred fire. That still stared back at me from the mirror, tucked into my cleavage, with a tiny black spot on the snout where Lilith's claw had broken off in my breast and nearly killed me. But I avoided looking in mirrors.

Although we no longer lived by the medieval calendar and it was hundreds of years since the Gregorian had replaced the Julien, I found our dates had once again coincided. I had fallen back into Molly during the terrible night of Beltain, the first day of May. It was the eighteenth of May when I remembered that I had to visit my mother. But I had no energy and my mind remained so utterly bleak; it was another five days before I did so.

"I don't know why you bother," said Bertie when I told him. "You haven't seen her for years, why go now, when you're still so bloody insecure yourself? She won't even recognise you, you know she won't."

"She might, this time," I said. "Besides, I think she's dying."

"Well, the asylum will phone up and tell you when that happens," said Bertie. "Frankly, I just don't think you're up to the journey. You're still not with it, girl. Only last night you asked if there was any spiced wine in the vat, and you'd take some up to Jasper. I mean, what the devil am I supposed to do with you Mol?"

"Just ignore me," I said. "I'll get over it I suppose. It's just – dreams. I'm depressed. Don't worry."

My mother was kept in a great white place just outside London. I travelled down by coach, which allowed me a more gentle arrival and a cosy, jogging trip with sunshine through the windows and all the pretty Cotswold countryside. Tilda enjoyed travelling in unaccustomed comfort. She was still with me. We would never be parted now.

The taxi from the coach station sped through industrial grey and introduced Tilda to more startling changes. I had phoned ahead and I was expected. The ward sister clacked through long pale corridors to the private room on the third floor, which I had been paying for out of my royalties for many years. "Oh, there's been no change," she told me, all brisk and efficient and bored. "We'd have contacted you if there'd been anything. I'm afraid she's still basically catatonic, though in excellent physical health of course."

"I had this feeling," I said, "that she was dying."

"Oh dear, how wretched for you," said the nurse without the slightest sympathy. "But I really don't think that's likely. Like I said, there's been no change."

The room was deeply shrouded, a haven of silent shade. The curtains were pulled across the window and the lump in the bed under the white covers was completely immovable. I bent over her. My mother's face stared back at me. Large boned, heavy features, slack mouth, no expression, it was the veleda, but empty of soul. "Hello mother," I said. "You ordered me to come. So I'm here."

There was no response. The eyes were open, as they had always been, but they were glazed, milky lidless stare. The drops the nurses used to keep her eyes moist still glistened in the corners and stuck like little grains of sand along the sparse white lashes. I could hear her breathing and see the slight flaring of the nostrils as they absorbed air, and then exhaled. I pulled up a chair and sat beside her and waited.

It was some time before I realised her breathing was grating in her chest and becoming laboured. "Will you speak to me?" I asked. "You told me to come. Do you know that I've lost him?"

I saw her blink. It was the first voluntary movement I had seen her make in years. I continued to wait. A young nurse came past the corridor with a trolley and I went out and took a cup of tea. Then I returned inside and waited some more. I had my nose in the cup and was thinking not of my mother but of Vespasian, when the voice came and startled me so much, I choked. The veleda said, "It's interesting, this business of humanity."

I put the cup down and stared at her. Her gaze had become focused and she was looking at me, her body all long and thin and stretched out under the covers, but her face was faintly animated and she had spoken quite clearly. "Who are you?" I whispered.

"If you don't know, why have you come?" said the woman. "I am the veleda. I am not your mother. I owe you nothing."

I nodded. "I only came because you told me to and because you said you had a gift for me." I paused, then muttered, "I also came because I love you."

"I suppose," she said, "you think it unjust, losing everyone you love."

"Justice?" I wondered. "No, I don't think of it that way. But I wanted very much to die and now I find it difficult to accept life alone."

"Life and death are less separate than you think," she said. "You are still ignorant, in spite of what you've learned."

I would have liked to hold her hand, but I didn't dare. "Are you dying then?" I asked her.

Only her eyes and her mouth moved. They were three sparks of animation in a face that already looked long dead. "Your lover Vespasian originally summoned me from the other world," said the veleda. "Now that he is gone, I am free to release myself."

I felt my eyes fill with inevitable tears. "He died eight hundred years ago," I said softly.

"Fool," she said. "Life is an eternal instant. Have you learned nothing of alchemy?" She glared, then blinked back the pale sparkle of irritation. "But this business of love interests me. Not your feelings for him, but that endless circle of reproduction and lust and avarice that spins around humanity like an ouroboros. It's your feelings for me that I find interesting."

I lowered my eyes and watched my fingers fidget in my lap. "I still think of you as my mother," I said.

"Absurd," little more than a grunt but for one amazing second, I thought she smiled. "Yet you respond to cruelty with love. I believe it to be more of a strength than a weakness. I have found it worthy. The gift? It is not in exchange for the love, which is irrelevant, but for the interest which I have enjoyed from knowing you."

"You're paying me for being interesting by loving you when you hated me?"

"As usual," said my mother, "you have misunderstood. I never hated you. I do not have such ridiculous emotions. But I have no wish to talk about myself. First I have some advice. Be prepared next Samhain."

I stuttered, knowing I was foolish and afraid I might cry. "Do you mean –?" I said. "I hoped just perhaps, being Hallowe'en and knowing what happened before – I thought it possible, if the doors opened between the worlds, then he might come back. Vespasian. I've been hoping so much. Just for the one night of course. I thought he might come back to me."

My mother's eyes narrowed but the tiny black specks of her pupils widened. "It is not your Vespasian who will return," she said. "It is Arthur. When the witching hour seeps through and unites all worlds, then Arthur will be searching, not for lost love, but for you. Be well prepared."

I shivered. I wiped my nose. "What can I do in this modern world with a ghost such as that?"

"You need not face him alone," said the veleda.

I waited. The silence seemed to spread into me and I was suddenly afraid that she'd died, with her eyes open and the words of my gift lost on dead lips. Then I saw she was still breathing. "Please tell me," I said. "Tell me what to do."

"You are still the gatekeeper," she answered at last. Her voice was fading. "You took back your power when you banished Lilith. You still hold those keys. It is how you returned here, once the other child in you tried to die. The keys are my gift. Even once I'm gone, you will still hold the keys. They are utterly yours."

"Without you?" I whispered.

"Call on Janus," she said. "Call on Hermes, on Cernunnus and on Thoth. Use the alchemy you learned before. Your world is modern but magic is old. Remember the unchanging power you still have. If you want him, you can bring him back. Discover the courage to open the gates and call him through."

My voice echoed in my head as if it came from far away. "In truth? Not just in dreams?"

"Fool," she said again. "I've already told you that dreams are more real than the dull substance of reality. But if you want him solid, in the physical forms of this dreary place, then take him. Do you think I've given you a power so pathetic, so feeble, that you cannot summon one miserable soul from the other side? If you want him, you can have him. It was he who brought me to this incarnation, and therefore it was he who personally caused your birth, not by seed but by spirit. You are bound to him, and he to you."

I was nursing my hand as I often did, gently cradling the finger that supported Vespasian's ring. The gold felt always cold, the ruby warm. "I have his ring," I said, nodding. "It came to me. I hope that somehow, it was he who sent it. In exchange, I have lost my heart." I was staring at the ring, then looked up at my mother. "But I cannot resurrect the dead," I shivered. "That is a blasphemy. I do not believe I can ever do such a thing."

She did not answer me. When they found me still sitting there beside her in floods of tears, they thought it was because she had died, all white in her white bed, as I bent over with my tears on her blank face, holding her hand for the first time in twenty nine years.

I do not remember the journey home. Bertie was waiting for me with tea and dinner and gentle sympathy. I found it very hard to talk. He thought it was because my mother was finally dead. I let him think so. Perhaps, a little bit, it was.

For the rest, I was completely confused.

CHAPTER SIXTY-TWO

It was a warm June, with magpies on the wing, iridescent over the fields, and a kestrel nesting at the top of the church spire. A cricket sat persistent in my garden on warm afternoons, reminding me of lost contentment.

I had buried my mother but I spoke to her often in my dreams, asking her to explain what I was supposed to do and how to bring him back. I could find no hint of power within myself. I gathered herbs at night. I made elixirs in the moonlight. I went to bed early and curled myself into a ball and sobbed. I cut the tarot pack, and always came up with the card of The Moon, or of The Star, or The Fool. I could not find Judgement, because it was no longer there.

I walked up on the hills in the sunshine and trudged through the sheep droppings and picked buttercups and Old Man's Beard and sat on the mossy stone overlooking the village and called on Janus and Hermes, on Cernunnus and Thoth, and prayed to God, and half expected to see my lover come striding over the rise, with his fur lined cloak blowing in the breeze and his black hair flying loose all about his beautiful face. And when he did not, I cried and went home with red rimmed eyes and told Bertie it was the wind, whether there had been any or not.

I walked through the woods and sat for hours under the yew tree beside the pool. Sometimes I slept there. I dreamed, as I always did, of Vespasian, but when I woke, he was never there. At home I curled in the big chair and read, and burst into tears at regular intervals.

"Good God, Mol," said Bertie. "I should read a different book if I were you. That one is just turning you into a dish cloth. No point reading sad books when you're not feeling all that bright yourself."

But it was a different book each time and they were all happy stories and that was the trouble.

Then I started vomiting, lurching in and out of nausea, and being suddenly sick in the loo after a mad dash. I wondered if one of my silly elixirs had poisoned me, though it had been days since I had bothered making one. Bertie neither held my fevered brow nor wiped my face. In fact, he kept his distance and complained about the smell. What he did do, was call the doctor.

I wasn't interested in what a doctor could tell me and I wasn't impressed by the new local man who had recently replaced the other. This one was tall and young and full of himself and looked down his nose as he prodded me a bit, took my blood pressure, stuck a needle in my arm and gave me a plastic bottle to pee into. He took it back gingerly from me with his rubber gloved finger tips and muttered a few things I didn't listen to before he left.

Three days later he phoned me up. I was in the kitchen scrambling eggs but since I'd forgotten to light the gas, the eggs weren't cooking very quickly. The sudden squeal of the telephone still startled me. I picked it up and held it at a tentative distance from my ear. "Mrs. Walding?"

"Miss Susans." I suppose most people thought it odd that I seemed to be living with my ex-husband. They would have thought it a dammed sight more odd had they known even more about me.

"Ah, yes, Miss Susans. Well, the results of your tests have come back. I thought you'd like to know."

"What tests?"

"The blood tests and the urine sample I took the other day, Miss

Susans." He probably thought I was a little backward. "Well, I'm delighted to give you the news."

"What news?"

"You're pregnant, Miss Susans," he said. "Probably two months along. If you'd like to make an appointment to come in and see me next week –"

I had dropped the uncooked eggs and the slippery yellow liquid was all over my fluffy pink slippers. I left the mess where it was and kicked off the slippers and went upstairs to my attic and lay on the bed and closed my eyes and told Vespasian he was going to be a father.

For several glorious long days I nursed my stomach, and although it gave me nothing but bilious attacks, I cuddled it as a precious and miraculous event in waiting. I traced the gentle hillock that would swell and bloom and give me back some of the joy I so longed for. I wondered, quite desperately, whether my baby would look like its long gone sire. I dreamed of a daughter, a little girl who might never know her father, but who would be as beautiful and as beloved. Then I dreamed of a son, who would be dark and charismatic, and who would by right be the Baron de Vrais, which made me laugh. It was a long time since I had been able to laugh.

I thought I understood then what my mother had meant, and how I would get him back as she told me I could. Not in person, but in kind. So I acknowledged and accepted the pleasure this would bring me, in spite of the terrible bleaching pain of the loss. I opened myself to a new happiness and disciplined myself to think less of the father and more of his child. I did not tell Bertie.

It was the eighteenth of June when Bertie came to tell me he was leaving. I had still not told him about the pregnancy and now I knew why instinct had kept me quiet. If he'd known, he might have felt he couldn't abandon me. He wouldn't have left. "You look so much happier these days," he said, "In fact, you're blooming, so I thought it might be safe to tell you, sweetie. The thing is, well, you know me, I've met this girl. She's really nice. You'll like her."

"Bring her over one evening," I said. "I'll make dinner." I knew that I glowed. I could feel it inside.

"Well, it's a trifle more than that," said Bertie. "Of course, we have to take it slow but I'm fine now. And she came out yesterday."

"You met her in hospital?"

"Yes, but she's not crazy or anything, just depressed. It can happen to anyone. Well, you ought to know."

"I do know."

"She lives with her parents, but they're old and need looking after." Bertie wore a hopeful smile. "We're engaged."

I was very pleased for him. It didn't matter if it worked really, since, knowing Bertie, it might not. There was the eternal instant, and happiness in the hand was what mattered, and never mind about the bush until you fell into it and discovered the thorns. "I'm delighted," I said.

"So I'm going to live with her," said Bertie. "You'll be alright now, won't you? You can always phone if things go wrong, and I'll drive up. You know I'd do anything for you."

"I'll be fine, honestly I will," I told him. "I'm very fond of you Bertie, but it will be nice to have the house to myself."

"I thought you'd say that," he grinned. "So, I'm off tomorrow."

"I hope you'll be very happy," I assured him. "Invite me to the wedding."

"Mind you, once I'm gone you'd better employ a cleaning woman," he nodded. "Honestly, Mol, you've become a real slut. I had a shocking mess to clear up the other day when I got home from the pub. Sloppy egg stuff all over the kitchen floor and your silly slippers all covered in gunge. I threw them out."

"I'm much, much happier now," I said. "I promise I'll be alright."

Then he pulled a small pewter jar from his trouser pocket and popped it on the kitchen table in front of me. "One more thing, sweetie, before I forget again. This is yours, I think." It seemed as though, for reasons he did not understand himself, he did not like touching it, and he went and wiped his hands on a tea towel. "I found it in my pocket all those months ago, when they took me off to hospital. I woke up with it and they took it off me, along with everything else I had. They gave it back when I left of course, and by then, I couldn't remember where I got it. It's got some sort of gravely stuff inside. Weird if you ask me. It's not mine so it has to be yours."

I had stopped breathing. "Yes," I whispered. "It's mine."

"Well then," said Bertie. "Now we're all clear. I'll be off in the morning, pet. Just don't forget, phone if you want me. I'll come back and visit of course. I'll bring Philippa with me. You'll like her."

"I shall," I said. "I like most of your girlfriends. Including me."

It was Thomas Cambio's jar and it contained the pellets which had previously taken me from this world, back to Tilda and to Vespasian. I took it with me the next day. I'd already collected the dew that night, there in the garden under the soft haloed moonlight. I'd mixed it with coarse salt, rosemary needles pounded into powder and added to the other herbs I'd collected. I'd sealed the mixture in a plastic container with a tablespoon of hot water and both it and the pewter jar were in my jacket pocket. I said goodbye to Bertie and I locked my cottage door in case something happened and I never returned. I didn't know, really, what might happen. But I knew something would.

I walked through the woods, enjoying the sun on my face, the dazzle between the trees and the rich scent of loam. I walked until I came to the hollow yew tree and then I sat there for a while under the spread of its boughs. I called on the old divinities, very softly, for I knew they were not far away. Then I took the two containers from my pocket and added one of the small grains from the pewter jar to the herbal mixture. It sank, smoked a little, and dissolved.

I did not drink it as I had before. I had no wish to return alone into the misery of a medieval life without Vespasian. Instead I waited until the mixture was misty with steam and then I hurled it against the trunk of the yew. It splattered up the bark in smoky streaks.

"Open," I commanded. "I have claimed back my keys. Janus and Thoth, Cernunnus and Hermes shall relinquish to me. I demand my rights. I choose to unlock the doorway of sequence and duration once again, and I call forth the man who was stolen from me. If he will come to me of his own free will and if he does not wish to go on the other pathway alone into the future, then I command time and space to bow before him. As it is above, so it is below and the power is mine to unbar the way. Open for him now, and for me."

I stood there with the empty pot in my hand, staring at the great bulbous trunk of the tree and the shadows of its own warts and cracks. Nothing happened and the song of the wood lark was the only sound in a surreal hush. I have no idea how long I stood. Time did not exist. The planet stopped. No leaf fluttered and the trill of the water had faded. I neither moved nor breathed.

Then a voice, very, very soft behind me, said, "You called, beloved, and I have come."

I spun around. He was not quite real, still a gleam in the spangle of light and shade, and through him I could see the rushing of the stream. I reached out both hands, and they passed through him. I was trembling and crying and laughing.

"You must give me Time," he murmured. "But see, I am here."

I couldn't blink, I couldn't look away. He was golden and beautiful and true and I drank in his face and his reality. "Can you really stay?" I whispered, although afraid to ask. "Do you – want to?"

"It is why I am here," he said. "Though there will be a great deal to learn and this time, you will have to teach me."

There was no bloody wound, no blind eye sockets and no pallor of death. He was alight, the shimmer of his smile tilted soft. He wore the clothes I had always known him in when he was the Vespasian of the early days, rough linen shirt and worn leather belt, threadbare woollen hose and his black hair dishevelled. "I'll have to get you some modern clothes," I said, the words tumbling out though it was perhaps the most irrelevant of all things to say and my voice was unsteady, struggling through the tears.

"Your own," he eyed my short skirt and bare tanned legs, smile tucking deep, "are certainly interesting."

I was bubbling, simmering with excitement, not quite believing. "Not just an hour, like Samhain? Not just a day? You can really stay – and come to live? You won't like all the changes," I babbled, yearning to touch him and wind myself around him. "But there are things like electricity and cinemas and planes and plumbing to make up for it. Somehow I can't imagine you wearing jeans and driving a car."

He was growing in solidity. His eyes were vivid with intrigue and delight, his smile now secure. His hands had become hard and brown and strong, and he had taken one of mine in his. "If I knew what either of those things were," he said, "perhaps I might be able to put your doubts to rest. Do you imagine me so shockingly inept? I believe I can grasp most skills, if given time."

I laughed, clutching the hand that held mine. "I don't suppose there'll ever be anything you can't do, if you want to."

"What benign faith," he said, the sparkle of irony and the wandering twitch back at the corners of his mouth. "I am flattered." I could no longer see the water through his body. He drew me closer, then pulled me down on the grass beside him and sat with me under the yew, stretching out his legs, his back to the trunk. The warmth of his thigh muscle was hard against my skin, his hand was alive, his pulse strong. He turned my palm over, lifting it to his mouth. "A small hand," he said. "I see you carry Tilda's injury. But of course you are still her, and whichever face you wear, anima mia, it is the woman who combines you both that I love."

"And look, I have your ring," I said, drunk with delight. "It came to me. I woke with it on my wedding finger though I don't understand how. Did you send it, as you did the ouroboros? Must I give it back?"

"Did I send it?" His voice drifted on sunbeams, and he frowned, as if still unsure of where he was. "Perhaps. I don't remember. Some memories are vague. But now it is yours, and symbolic, as all things are. Perhaps I shall find another, since new life brings new symbols."

"I'll have to write more books," I said, "and make enough money for us to buy everything we want and do wonderful things together. Modern life's rather expensive. It's not just silver pennies anymore. But there's a whole world for us to explore."

He raised an eyebrow. "Have you forgotten me so quickly?" He pulled me back against his shoulder where I nestled, his fingers crawling into my hair and smoothing my cheek. "Don't you remember that I make my own gold, when I wish?"

My arm crept happily around his waist." Now, that should prove interesting," I said. "I wonder how we'll explain it to the taxman." Through the stuff of his shirt I could feel his heartbeat and the smooth, muscled strength of his breast. His shirt was partially open and I kissed the little warm hollow between his collarbones.

It was becoming believable, all the glory and the magic of it. I couldn't stop touching him, smoothing my skin against his, searching for the expression in his eyes. "Will I wake up?" I said. "Will all this light go out? I don't think so, not anymore. I think you're truly real, truly returned. But you were dead, Vespasian. How did I bring you back from the dead?"

His hand in my hair, he lifted my face up to kiss. "No, bien-aimé, I was not dead." He smoothed the ball of his thumb under my eyes, gently wiping away the smear of spent tears. "The gatekeeper can open the paths for the dead on Samhain, but has no power to resurrect ghosts permanently from their Hades on the other side. None of us have that power. Did I die afterwards? Yes, perhaps, but I had already left my body as I have done before, coming into this future world of yours many times. I saw Lilith howling down upon me, but I was already leaving. I had neither strength nor magic sufficient to overcome Lilith's fury in that moment, so before she could touch me I was on my way here, where I believed I would find you. She slaughtered an empty carcass, while I was already spinning through time." He smiled wide, eyes alight. "But then, amorcito, I had to wait for you to find the keys and let me in. You were slow and I remained in limbo, slipping between your dreams. No matter, I've learned patience. Now Vespasian is gone into history, but you have your Jasper."

His kiss was as intense and as hard as love and desire had ever made it. I felt his breath hot in my throat and the pressure of his hand behind my head. "I just pray you won't hate it here, in this modern world," I said, catching my breath. "It's so different. People are different. It's a plastic world, my love. You might find it boring."

He laughed. "Must I learn then," he said, "to be tolerant and not autocratic? To adopt diplomacy instead of arrogance? Accepting the jargon of equality and forget impropriety?"

"Good gracious," I said. "I doubt you'll ever be capable of all that."

His eyes narrowed and the sparkle deepened. "Oh my beloved," he said, as if reciting poetry. "When my strength returns, I'll show you how to find true delight in this or any world. Without fear or boundaries, I'll show you more pleasure and glory, across continents and oceans, than you have ever imagined. I will show you the inner meaning of true mysticism and the great wheel of alchemy. I will lead you into paths unknown, rich in all the perfumes of natural beauty and the secrets of the eternal soul." He paused, and leaning down, lifted my chin, kissing me again, quick and hard, his tongue against mine. "Love is a pathway more exciting than any you have opened as the wife of Janus," he said, his voice becoming husky in my ear. "As the wife of Jasper de Vrais, speranza mia, I believe you will discover a deeper and a greater magic."

"Even in this bland modern world?" I clung to him, gasping with all the exhilaration of his words and the belief I had in him.

"As you adapted to your past in my world, so I shall enjoy new opportunities in yours. I'm well aware that fashions change." He laughed, a gentle chuckle as he traced one finger up the length of my thigh where my short cotton skirt had crumpled. "As long as fornication has not yet gone out of style?"

"Are we still married?" I asked, holding up my finger with his ring bright in the sunlight. "Even after eight hundred years?"

"Tonight we build a fresh union," he whispered to my eyes. "And I shall show you what a new born is capable of." He slipped his hand down past the buttons of my shirt onto my breast. "Do you still carry the dragon of the fifth essence?" He smiled at the curve of my body where his fingers slipped deep into my cleavage, gently exploring. "I see that you do. And this body is a little more charmingly – developed – than Tilda's," he said. "It will be the start of a whole new adventure."

I took a deep breath and looked up rather shyly. "There's another reason for that," I mumbled, "and I have something rather unexpected to tell you."

His eyes were black sunshine. His breath was sunbeams. He seemed unable to wait and as I yearned to touch him, so he reached to hold me. His long fingers had begun to undo the buttons of my shirt. Now he paused, smiling, waiting for me to continue.

"You might be even more surprised than I was," I gasped, "though I think, I hope, I truly believe, you will be just as pleased."

His breath was in my eyes and his fingers cradled my breasts. "Come closer, mona mia," he whispered to me, though indeed, we were already tightly entwined, "and tell me – everything."

Dear Reader,

Did you have a tear at the end? I know I did while writing it. I have been asked so many times, to write a sequel, and I am pleased to announce that now there is one! It's a much shorter novella, but the plan is to carry on with the series and release a new novella twice a year.

Get Dark Weather on Amazon

ABOUT THE AUTHOR

My passion is for late English medieval history and this forms the background for my historical fiction. I also have a love of fantasy and the wild freedom of the imagination, with its haunting threads of sadness and the exploration of evil. Although all my books have romantic undertones, I would not class them purely as romances. We all wish to enjoy some romance in our lives, there is also a yearning for adventure, mystery, suspense, friendship and spontaneous experience. My books include all of this and more, but my greatest loves are the beauty of the written word, and the utter fascination of good characterisation. Bringing my characters to life is my principal aim.

For more information on this and other books, or to subscribe for updates, new releases and free downloads, please visit barbaragaskelldenvil.com

Printed in Great Britain
by Amazon